DISTANT DREAMS

JUDITH PELLA
AND
TRACIE PETERSON

DISTANT DREAMS

BETHANY HOUSE PUBLISHERS
MINNEAPOLIS, MINNESOTA 55438

Distant Dreams
Copyright © 1997
Judith Pella and Tracie Peterson

Cover by Dan Thornberg,
Bethany House Publishers staff artist.

The song opening Part One is anonymous and was taken from *Long Steel Rail: The Railroad in American Folksong* by Norm Cohen, University of Illinois Press.

Published by Bethany House Publishers
A Ministry of Bethany Fellowship, Inc.
11300 Hampshire Avenue South
Minneapolis, Minnesota 55438

Printed in the United States of America.

Library of Congress Cataloging-in-Publication Data

Pella, Judith.
    Distant dreams / Judith Pella and Tracie Peterson.
        p. m. — (Ribbons of steel ; #1)
     I. Peterson, Tracie. II. Title. III. Series: Pella, Judith.
Ribbons of steel ; #1.
PS3566.E415D57   1996
813'.54—dc21   96–45906
ISBN 1–55661–862–X   CIP

Dedicated to my husband, Jim, with
love and thanks for the help you gave
me on this project.

—Tracie

With special thanks to:

Anne Calhoun
Assistant Archivist, Baltimore and Ohio Railroad Library,
and the Museum staff of the Baltimore and Ohio Railroad

Herbert Harwood, Jr.
Author of Impossible Challenge II

Mike Hawkins
Topeka Railroad Days

John Goodnough
Susquehanna Valley Railroad Historical Society

Susan Tolbert and Roger White
Smithsonian Institute, Railroad Transportation

And the Iron Horse, the earth-shaker,
the fire-breather . . . shall build an empire
and an epic.

Ralph Waldo Emerson

JUDITH PELLA began her writing career in collaboration with Michael Phillips, a partnership that led to five major fiction series. She has also written the LONE STAR LEGACY series and *Blind Faith*, a contemporary romance story in the PORTRAITS series with Bethany House Publishers. These extraordinary novels showcase her creativity and skill as a historian as well as a fiction writer. With a bachelor's degree in social sciences and a nursing degree, her storytelling abilities provide readers with memorable novels in a variety of genres. She and her family make their home in northern California.

TRACIE PETERSON is a full-time writer who has authored over nineteen books, both historical and contemporary fiction. She authored *Entangled*, a contemporary love story in the PORTRAITS series. She spent three years as a columnist for *The Kansas Christian* newspaper and is also a speaker/teacher for writer's conferences. She and her family make their home in Kansas.

Contents

PART THREE
Spring 1836

PART FOUR
Late Spring 1836

PART FIVE
Summer-Fall 1836

PART I

Summer 1835

Away, away, o'er valley plain
I sweep you with a voice of wrath;
In a fleecy cloud I wrap my train,
As I tread my iron path.

My bowels are fire and my arm is steel,
My breath is a rolling cloud:
And my voice peels out as I onward wheel,
Like the thunder rolling loud.

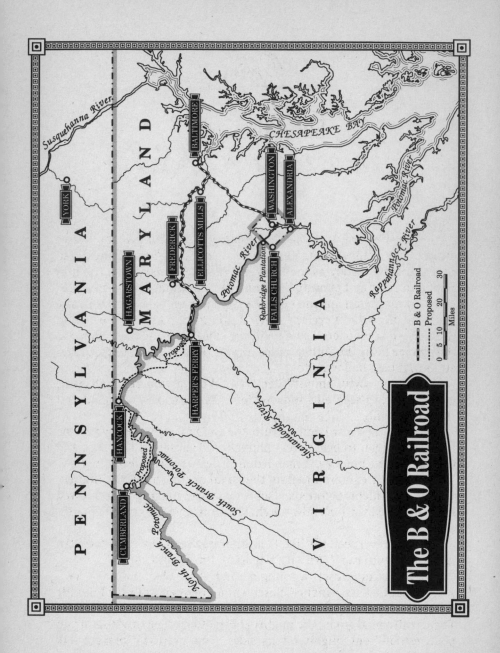

PENNSYLVANIA

MARYLAND

VIRGINIA

Susquehanna River

CHESAPEAKE BAY

Potomac River

Rappahannock River

Potomac River

Shenandoah River

South Branch Potomac

North Branch Potomac

YORK

HAGERSTOWN

FREDERICK

ELLICOTT'S MILLS

BALTIMORE

WASHINGTON

ALEXANDRIA

Oakbridge Plantation

FALLS CHURCH

HARPER'S FERRY

HANCOCK

CUMBERLAND

Proposed

Proposed

----- B & O Railroad
· · · · · Proposed

0 5 10 20 30
Miles

The B & O Railroad

One

Enter the Beast

The whistle blast, shrill and frightening, broke through the festive atmosphere of the crowd. Heads turned and a momentary hush fell over the noisy throng as the black monster lumbered down the iron ribbon, hissing and panting like some ancient mythological creature.

Every man, woman, and child watched in awe, held captive by the fearsome mechanical cyclops. Then murmurs of fascination began to rise from the onlookers, some pointing, some daring to press closer to the strange beast. But others shied away, horrified at the hideous creation that man had wrought.

"What an awful smell!" declared a young woman in disgust, quickly lifting a scented handkerchief to her nose. She appeared as if she might faint.

Many in the crowd agreed with the woman, especially when the iron beast began to belch great plumes of black smoke that rose and tainted the fine blue sky. A man led his wife away, fearful that her delicacy might be compromised by the strain of such a sight. Children, who only moments before had danced in circles begging to be allowed to see the beast's arrival, now sought the protective arms of their mothers.

"Have ya ever seen the likes!" murmured a man in a coarse woolen jacket and worn cap. "Why it's a-sparkin' the ground afire."

"Don't get too close!" a young mother warned her child.

The giant colossus inched closer while workmen waiting alongside cleared back the undaunted curious ones and put out the patchy fires. Then, with a final groan, the mighty contraption rolled to a stop, steam pouring out from spigots on its sides. Now even the bravest folk jumped back several paces.

One wide-eyed girl, however, did not move. Mesmerized by what she saw, Carolina Adams did not retreat but rather pressed forward. Her brown eyes never leaving the machine, her petite form straining on tiptoe to see through the crowd, Carolina was drawn closer. Caught in the spell of wheels and gears and sounds and smells, she hardly felt the gloved hand on her arm, restraining her curiosity.

"Carolina! You are a proper young lady and such a ghastly exhibition is quite beneath you. Besides," Margaret Adams said with a glance around the crowd, "there are many fine young gentlemen here today. If you are to secure a good marriage, you should at least pretend to be refined."

Carolina looked up at her mother with a frown. She had no desire to secure a good marriage, at least not yet. But despite her feelings, Carolina held her tongue, knowing Margaret Adams, the epitome of genteel womanhood, would brook no disobedience from her children—especially not in public.

"That pout is most unbecoming," said Margaret, "and tells me your heart is not in obedience." Her narrow gray eyes made it clear the matter was not open to discussion.

"She's just a child, Mrs. Adams." Joseph Adams, Carolina's father, was the only one who dared debate the woman. "And this is a celebration."

Margaret turned a frosty glare on her husband. "She is fifteen years old, Mr. Adams. She is hardly a child."

"I simply meant . . ."

The conversation between Joseph and Margaret competed with the rising din of the crowd, and Carolina found it impossible to concentrate on what was being said. Besides, in spite of the fact that the discussion was on her behalf, she was far more interested in the activity around the machine. Trusting that her parents were preoccupied for the time being, she attempted to get closer to the track. With little thought to appearance, she elbowed her way through the crowd. Her heart was pounding. Through her mind raced a million thoughts and questions about the strange machine. Even her mother's certain reprimand couldn't dissuade her from drawing as near it as possible.

I must get a better look, she thought, forcing her small frame through the sea of bodies.

"Ladies and gentlemen!" A man dressed in a natty tweed suit and bowler hat had hopped up on a wooden crate. He lifted his hand with an exaggerated flourish. "I give you the future of transportation! Nay, the very future of America! The Locomotive!"

The crowd cheered.

"We are here this twenty-eighth day of August, in the year of Our

Lord 1835, to celebrate the grand opening of the Washington Branch of the Baltimore and Ohio Railroad!"

Carolina felt her heart beat faster. The machine was nearly close enough to reach out and touch. What must it be like to ride on such a contraption? Were the railed tracks smooth or bumpy? Did the world just whip by you as you rode along, or did it seem to stand still in awe of man's newest invention?

"Here at the foot of Capitol Hill, under the watchful eyes of thousands, we are honored to have Philip E. Thomas, President of the B&O Railroad, with us today."

Just then one of the two train-bound bands struck up a chorus of "For He's a Jolly Good Fellow," to which a hardy cheer followed.

Philip Thomas, gray-haired but lively, took his place beside the man. "I am pleased to announce the trip from Baltimore to this, our nation's capital, was accomplished without incident, and, furthermore, we covered the distance of thirty-some miles in less than two hours and ten minutes."

The crowd responded with oohs and aahs. Several men began to inspect the wheel mechanisms while Thomas continued. "I am pleased also to announce that this is but the first of many roundtrips to come between our fair cities. A regular schedule of two trips per day is planned, and should this prove inadequate, we are prepared to add additional trips to accommodate those who wish to ride."

He spoke next of the future of the B&O Railroad, but Carolina heard little of what he said. Forgetting her mother's warning, she ventured ever closer to the locomotive. It still hissed, with billowing puffs of steam erupting from safety valves on the side. Two men peered down from the engine's standing platform, thoroughly enjoying the crowd's reaction. However, for the ceremony they had been required to wear their best black frock suits, and they looked most uncomfortable. The younger of the two tugged at his starched white collar, while the older man mopped sweat from his brow.

Carolina smiled up at them sheepishly, knowing she was being quite brazen in her approach. The men could hardly fail to notice the pretty girl in her fashionable afternoon dress of powder blue linen, trimmed in navy, with a matching bonnet tied smartly at her chin. The men gave her friendly grins.

Mother will skin me alive, Carolina thought, brown curls bobbing as she cast a quick glance over her shoulder.

But she couldn't stop herself. The black giant enticed her forward. What was it that drew her? The other women in the crowd were not so fascinated; in fact, many were absolutely terrified. Carolina was a bit scared herself, but more so at her own inexplicable reaction. But she'd always had a curious nature.

"Too curious for your own good," her mother would often say.

Something inside her wanted to know the how and why about everything. She was constantly plying her father with questions. Poor, dear Papa! But he always answered patiently, even if her questions were sometimes not appropriate from the lips of a young lady.

Thomas's words momentarily intruded into Carolina's thoughts: "The development of our great nation will depend upon machines such as these. Today, we celebrate the innovation of man's mind, but tomorrow we seek the dream of our future. And this, ladies and gentlemen, will be the key to all our dreams."

It was as if the man were speaking directly to Carolina. How many times had her mother scolded her for her frequent daydreams? But she couldn't help it. She knew she had too many lofty notions. She dreamed of far more than a proper young lady should. Of things fit only for a man. Or were they?

Was this train, then, the key only to male dreams? Or would it somehow involve her? *Could* it? In her mind it seemed as if its powerful bulk could do anything, even satisfy the nameless longing that had always haunted Carolina.

Suddenly Carolina reached out her hand toward the smooth black iron of the engine, but just as quickly, she pulled her hand back. Glancing warily around, she wondered if anyone had noticed what she had been about to do. Completely wedged in by the crowd, her parents were still talking, apparently unaware of her absence. The rest of the crowd was riveted either to the man on the platform or the commotion behind the tender where several workmen were busy detaching the other three engines and their accompanying passenger cars.

Thomas had finished his speech and the announcer was once again at the podium. "Who from our fair city will take the first ride?" asked the man. Then he looked directly at Carolina and shouted, "You, young woman! You may have the first ride!"

Carolina gasped. Was he actually speaking to her? Realizing she was suddenly the center of attention, her mouth dropped open and her eyes widened in horror. If her mother had previously been ignorant of her actions, she would definitely know now. But before Carolina could protest—not that she *wanted* to—she was being handed up to a small platform attached behind the engine. The back of the platform held a tenderbox of coal, but space had been cleared in order to allow several people at a time to enjoy a standing ride.

"This is usually filled full," said the engineer. He was the older of

16

the two men who had noticed her before. "But I reckon your company is better than coal any day!" He winked at her from behind a dimpled smile.

"'Fraid we wouldn't get very far without fuel," said the younger man over his shoulder. As the locomotive's fireman, he was already adding a heaping shovelful of coal to the firebox.

"But why am I up here and not in one of the covered cars?" she asked hesitantly.

"Mr. Thomas thought this to be a bit more exciting," the older man told her. "You get a real feel for the machine this way."

"It's more dangerous," the fireman told her with a jaunty grin, "but more fun, too."

Carolina nodded with rapt attention. She wished they'd tell her more, but both men had seemingly forgotten her as they went about their tasks. Her heart pounded so hard that Carolina feared she actually might swoon. This is dangerous, she told herself, but her mind refused to equate the relevance of such a thought.

If Carolina had previously known excitement, then this was pure bliss. She stared past the engineer in his frock coat to the wide mouth of the firebox. The younger man was tossing in coal, almost as if he were feeding a ravenous animal.

Four more people were selected from the clamoring crowd to accompany Carolina before the engineer gave the signal and the track was cleared to allow the locomotive to move forward. Carolina looked down upon the crowd, feeling lucky indeed that she was one of the fortunate ones. Her mother would never understand, and Carolina made a pointed effort to avoid those eyes she knew would be filled with disapproval.

With a lurch and a scraping of metal against metal, the machine strained to move. Bit by bit it inched its way forward. Carolina held her breath and gripped the platform railing. Her pulse raced. A young boy at her side puckered his face and looked as if he might cry, but the man beside him lifted him up and hushed his fears. The other two passengers were white-faced and spellbound while the train groaned forward another twenty feet, then stopped once again.

"Well, what did you think, young lady?" the announcer asked Carolina as he helped her down from the engine.

Carolina's only response was a speechless stare. Then someone else shouted from the crowd, "What was it like?"

This broke her spell. "It was wondrous!" Carolina declared. Even her mother's inevitable ire couldn't spoil the moment. "Absolutely wondrous!"

Carolina watched as if in a daze as new passengers were loaded aboard and the train moved again. Swallowed up in the sea of moving people, Carolina felt the impact of the moment. She had actually ridden the beast with its churning, hissing, groaning voice. She had touched the future. Her future?

Looking down at her hands, she noticed for the first time black smudges on the white kid gloves from where she'd held on to the rail. In complete amazement she traced the outline of the stains, then smiled as if discovering a wonderful secret.

Two

Repercussions

"Carolina!"

The harsh voice of Margaret Adams instantly jarred Carolina from her awed musings. She glanced up to see her family approach.

"How could you?" Margaret was pale in spite of the strength of her voice and appeared almost as if she might well faint. "Putting yourself on display for all the capital to see. When I think of what Washington society will say about my daughter in their homes tonight . . ." She ended with a shudder. Then, reaching out to take her daughter in hand, she noticed the soiled gloves. "They are ruined, of course." With an indignant huff she dropped Carolina's hand and continued. "Well, we've no choice now but to return to the hotel so that you can repair the damage to your appearance. I hope you realize just how you have disgraced our family today."

"Nonsense, Mrs. Adams," said Joseph. "Be reasonable. The child merely rode the locomotive. It isn't like she robbed a bank." Mutton-chop whiskers and bushy dark eyebrows made his face seem stern and unyielding, but there was a hint of amusement in his eyes, and the corners of his lips twitched as though he might break into a smile any moment.

A giggle escaped Carolina's lips at her father's words, further alienating her mother.

"You both find this so amusing. . . ." Margaret's voice dropped to a whisper. "We will discuss this back at the hotel. I, for one, desire no further public display." With a snap of her parasol, she turned on her heel and strode away.

Joseph winked at his daughter before hurrying forward to take up his wife's arm. Carolina's older sister, Virginia, fell into step beside her.

19

Virginia's face was so grim Carolina wished she could be swallowed up by the earth.

"I think it's positively horrid what you did to Mother," hissed Virginia.

"I did nothing wrong."

Virginia snorted. "You embarrassed our whole family and have the nerve to say you did nothing wrong! Why, Mother might not even be able to attend the social coming up next week at the Baldwins' all because of how you behaved today." Then her glare turned especially rabid. "There's a good chance she won't even allow *me* to attend. If that happens, Carolina, I will never forgive you."

Before Carolina could respond, her sister stormed off to join her parents.

"Looks like you've ruffled Virginia's feathers again."

Carolina turned to see her oldest brother. "Oh, York, I never meant to put everyone into a stir. But did you see it?" She quickly forgot her sister's anger as she noted how her brother's eyes lit up.

"Yes, I did!" He squeezed her arm affectionately. "And I might add that I am pea green with envy. I had planned to take the locomotive to Baltimore on my way back to the university. But you've beaten me to the chance of being the first in our family to ride the Washington rail." He spoke with more pride, however, than envy. "What was it like?"

Carolina smiled like a child. "Terrifying and wonderful all at the same time."

York laughed out loud, bringing a glare from Virginia, who turned, unable not to notice the happy duo. Attempting to be more decorous as they walked on the street, York quieted, smoothing back an unruly lock of dark brown hair from his forehead. "They'll come around," he said softly.

"Joseph Adams!" a voice called.

Leland Baldwin, one of Washington's private bank owners, had spotted the family and spoiled Margaret Adams' hopes for a hasty retreat back to Gadsby's Hotel.

"Good morning, Baldwin," said Adams, tipping his hat in greeting.

The rotund Baldwin panted to a stop as the family paused for him. "Good morning!" he said, out of breath. "Ladies." He lifted his top hat with an embellished sweep toward Margaret and the girls.

"Good to see you, Baldwin. How are you?" asked Joseph.

"Splendid! And you?"

"We are well. I must say this new rail line is quite the ticket for our city. And what a celebration! I heard you personally had a hand in arranging the fine feast of French cuisine Gadsby's is supplying at the party afterward."

Baldwin seemed pleased that Joseph would credit him with the accomplishment. "A well-deserved celebration. I wanted to show those Baltimorians that we here in Washington City know quite well how to entertain. Maybe even persuade a few of them to invest their money right here in the capital."

"Seems it will be a likely possibility, thanks to inventions like that grand locomotive."

"A mere flash in the pan."

"You weren't impressed?"

"From a purely business standpoint," answered Baldwin, "I don't believe it has proven itself enough to merit all the attention. It's a novelty, a toy so to speak."

"So, you don't consider it a sound investment opportunity?"

"I could name ten better." Baldwin became animated as he launched into a speech on money and investment, obviously his favorite topics.

Carolina listened to the interchange for a moment, hoping to hear more about the train. But when it quickly turned to other topics, she grew bored and let her mind wander. She glanced over her shoulder as the steam whistle of the locomotive blasted a mournful call. What was it about that monstrous machine that so consumed her? Staring down at her soiled gloves, she lifted them to her nose and inhaled the scent of oil and smoke.

What have I done? she wondered. What have I done?

———

Inside the stately elegance of their hotel suite, Carolina awaited her mother's further reprimand. Virginia had taken a seat beside her mother, as if hoping to bear witness to the punishment of her sibling. Joseph and York uncomfortably wandered to the window and gazed at the street below as if they hoped that might fend off what was surely coming.

Carolina stood by the mantel twisting the ruined gloves in her hands. Silently she wished she could get the matter over with. Taking up her handbag, she crammed the incriminating gloves inside, hoping that with them out of sight things might go better for her.

Just as her mother opened her mouth to speak, a child's excited voice called out. "Father! Father!" Georgia Adams burst into her parents' hotel sitting room without warning. Behind her huffed and puffed a portly black woman, holding the hand of another younger girl.

"You should have seen it!" Georgia exclaimed.

"Georgia Elizabeth! Remember you're a young lady," Margaret admonished her daughter.

Joseph grinned. It was well known that his wife's scolding was doomed to defeat when it came to Georgia. Caught between her desire to be a refined southern belle and her love of tomboyish activities, at thirteen, Georgia struggled to find her proper place.

"Now, what's this all about?" asked Joseph.

"You should have seen it, Father!" Georgia barely remembered to restrain her unladylike excitement. "It was loud and smelly and hissing and evil. It frightened me to the bottom of my boots!"

"Ah, you must have seen the locomotive."

"We did, Papa." This came from ten-year-old Pennsylvania, who wrenched away from her mammy's hold. "I wanted to ride on it."

"Not me!" Georgia said, pulling off her gloves and bonnet. "I thought it perfectly awful."

"You are such a baby, Georgy," said Carolina with just a touch of arrogance in her tone. "It wasn't evil at all. It was just a machine, albeit a very complicated one." For a moment, as she recalled her wonderful experience, she forgot the impending trouble with her mother.

Virginia wasn't to be left out of the conversation. "Mrs. Handerberry said that a woman in the family way shouldn't be allowed anywhere near it."

Margaret gasped. "See what vulgarity this horrid machine has wrought with our children, Mr. Adams?" She fixed a stern gaze on her husband as if he were one of her offspring.

"The Washington Branch of the Baltimore and Ohio Railroad can hardly be blamed for childish outbursts," Joseph replied with an undaunted chuckle. "The railroad is a vital link for the city," he added with more earnestness. "I have no doubt it will change the course of this country's history. That's why I wanted you all to see it today and why I'm prepared to give the railroad all the support it needs. Think of it! The possibilities! It will only be a matter of time before we can travel all the way to the Mississippi in a few days instead of weeks or months."

"Ta, ta, Mr. Adams," chided Margaret. "There you go with your wanderlust dreams. If I would allow it, you would no doubt have us dragging about the country on the back of that ghastly machine. I declare there is no reasoning with you. Go ahead and spend your money investing in the thing, but do not encourage us to believe it important to our way of life. We do have a plantation and responsibilities to our community. I hate to think this railroad would become an additional child in our house."

Joseph laughed heartily, surprising not only his children but his wife as well. "I'd then have to find another state's name with which to name it. We'll have to add more states to the Union before we can have another child, Mrs. Adams!"

"Not so, Papa," Georgia chimed in, "there are still plenty more states."

Margaret blushed crimson. "I am appalled at such talk!" But her stern visage betrayed a hint of amusement as she and her husband exchanged a private look.

For several moments all was quiet, then Pennsylvania, whom all affectionately called Penny, came and laid her head on her mother's lap. "I thought it was exciting," she murmured sleepily.

Margaret softened noticeably. In front of the rest of the world, she had her reputation and social bearing to consider. But here, with the cherublike visage of her child's face beckoning her touch, Margaret had no further consideration of public humility and breached etiquette. "Little one, I think the activity of the day has overtaxed you. You are flushed and warm. Hannah"—she turned to the slave—"draw this child a bath." The black woman trundled off to see to it.

"We will discuss this again another time," Margaret said with her still-softened expression fixed pointedly on Carolina. "Carolina, would you please help Hannah with Penny?"

"Yes, Mother." Carolina took her little sister's hand. "Come on, Penny. If you are good, I'll tell you a story when you are finished."

"What kind of story?"

Carolina waited until they had passed into one of the bedrooms of the suite. "I'll tell you a wonderful story about railroads." Carolina kissed Penny's pale forehead, then helped her undress.

With Penny off to her bath, Carolina rejoined her family in the sitting room.

Virginia was whining. ". . . not to mention we have to ride all the way back to Oakbridge tomorrow." Carolina could only imagine what her sister was complaining about now.

"Is Penny cared for?" Margaret asked Carolina. She seemed to have forgotten the earlier tensions.

"Hannah has her in the tub."

"I'm hungry," Georgia suddenly interrupted.

"Supper is at seven." Joseph took out his pocket watch. "Your mother and I will be dining at the White House with President Jackson."

"I don't understand why I can't go along, too," said Virginia. "I am eighteen."

"That will be enough, Virginia." Joseph's tone was such that it instantly hushed his eldest daughter. Even patient Joseph could only take so much of Virginia's grumbling. "Mr. Jackson did not extend an invitation to include my children, not even my *almost* grown-up daughter. Therefore, I would appreciate it if you would accompany York and Georgia to the dining room. Carolina, your mother has reminded me that we gave the servants the evening off, so would you mind sitting with Penny and Maryland?" Maryland was the youngest of the Adams brood.

"Not at all, Father." Carolina was pleased that her father recognized that she was better at caring for the little ones than Virginia. Perhaps he also understood that she'd prefer the solitude of the suite to the bustling dining room.

"I've arranged for supper to be brought up for you and your little sisters," said Margaret, rising. "Now it's time for us who are going out to dress for supper."

Three

Kindred Spirits

The ladies exited the room, but Carolina lingered at the door, the events of the day still stirring her thoughts.

"Father," she began, "may I ask you a question?"

Joseph's gaze met his daughter's inquisitive eyes. "I have never refused you yet, child. What is it?"

"I wanted to ask you something about the locomotive." She hesitated. Even though only her father and brother were present, she knew she was crossing the boundaries of propriety to speak of things normally reserved only for men.

"What was it you wanted to know?"

She forged ahead. Papa would understand. "I heard a man say that the engine gets its power from the water which is heated into steam."

"That's right," Joseph replied, proud of his daughter's ability to grasp such things. "What don't you understand?"

"How does the steam move the wheels? I saw the place where the water is put in and the firebox where the coal is burned, but how does it transfer to the wheels?"

Joseph looked in amazement at his daughter. He cast a glance at York, who also seemed surprised at his sister's unusual interest.

Carolina mistook her father's look for tolerance. "Forgive me for not acting like a lady today, but it was all so wondrous that I just wanted to know more."

"There is nothing to forgive. I'm simply astonished at the way your mind works. God forgive me for saying this, for I do not wish it so, but you should have been born a son."

Carolina smiled, knowing her father had bestowed a compliment upon her.

Joseph continued, stretching out his hands to illustrate his words.

25

"The boiler is filled with water, which in turn is heated by the fire. The steam then enters a cylinder where there is a piston. This piston is connected to a driving rod. This is the rod connected to the large drive wheels. When the rod pushes forward, the wheels turn and the train moves. The rod them circles to push the piston back. This allows the exhaust to exit through a valve and the whole process begins again."

Carolina took it all in. "It's much simpler than I thought."

"Of course there's more to running a locomotive than this, but that at least is how the steam is transferred to power the wheels." He smiled, not indulgently, but as if he shared a great secret with his daughter.

"Thank you, Father." She kissed his cheek, then left the room.

Alone in her room, while Virginia sought their mother's opinion on her selection of a dress for dinner, Carolina sat on her bed, took her handbag, and pulled out the blackened kid gloves. She had already decided to keep them to dream on, as a young girl might dream on a piece of wedding cake under her pillow.

Hearing Virginia's approach, Carolina quickly hid the gloves inside her blue satin slippers, which she then tucked into the bottom of her carpetbag. She couldn't bear more railing from her sister.

By even the most stringent standards, Joseph Adams was a successful man. From an old family distantly related to the Adamses of presidential fame, he was an established member of the American gentry. As master of the large and prosperous Virginia plantation called Oakbridge, he could have wielded influence enough. But several astute business investments had also placed him in a position closer to the nation's central political realm. And it had made him wealthy beyond the family inheritance.

Joseph loved the serene beauty of Oakbridge, and his family brought him great joy. He knew that others of his peers envied him. Yet none of them would ever guess at the discontent that dwelt deep inside a secret part of his being. His wife might glibly comment about it, but even she didn't know just how deeply it affected him. No one knew.

At forty, he had only just begun to let go of it, to resign himself to the hard fact that his dreams would never be realized. But as a child he had done nothing but dream. He had been an impressionable boy of eleven when Lewis and Clark returned from their fantastic journey, and from that moment, Joseph had begun to harbor a longing after similar adventures. Exploring the wild lands of the West filled his thoughts. He began early to prepare his parents for the inevitable fact that he would leave them as soon as he was of age. They, of course, weren't thrilled at the idea, but he was the younger of two sons, and so, with the elder boy to carry on the family estate, they could afford to indulge Joseph. Thus, he studied everything he could about the western lands and even met Lewis and Clark and was given the opportunity to study their maps.

By the time he was fifteen, Joseph was well prepared for a life of adventure. Then a tragic accident changed the course of his life forever. While fishing in their boat, his father and brother collided with a large riverboat and both drowned. Aside from the horrible grief of sudden death, young Joseph was thrust suddenly into the position of head of the family. His mother, never a strong woman, and his sisters now looked to him for care and leadership. And Joseph's sense of duty turned out to be stronger, or at least more compelling, than his sense of adventure.

All the dreams were laid aside. Fifteen-year-old Joseph took up his duties as a plantation master. He married a week before his eighteenth birthday and had his first child by the age of nineteen. Realizing the futility of continued longings after adventure, he squelched them quite successfully except for occasional moments of weakness, such as when he named each of his children for states, several of which he might never hope to see himself. The greatest irony was that now he was wealthy enough to finance any journey he wished. He talked often about going to Europe with his family. But he never did. What was the use? Adventures simply were not for a forty-year-old man with a demanding wife and seven children.

But lately some of those old longings had begun to haunt him. The advent of the railroad had tugged at that deep, almost hidden, hunger within. Three years ago Joseph had read an article in the *New York Courier and Enquirer* by a Dr. Carver that proposed a transcontinental rail line. The idea of a railroad traversing thousands of miles from sea to sea was outlandish at best, but it had sparked that old, as Margaret called it, "wanderlust" in Joseph. Even on a smaller scale, the imagination could soar on what the railroads might do. In 1833, when South Carolina built a one hundred thirty-six mile line—touted as the longest in the world—Joseph had almost cheered.

It was a mere coincidence that this line had been built in Carolina, the state after which his fourth child was named. His daughter had already been born. But Joseph sensed it was not at all by chance that Carolina seemed to possess many of her father's qualities. It was bound to happen that one of his children would be filled with a thirst for reaching out beyond herself and given a soul for dreaming. What a shame that child had to be a female! Joseph had been compelled to relinquish his dreams to the demands of family responsibility. Would his daughter be forced to do the same because of her gender?

Joseph smiled.

Being a man hadn't *helped* him much; perhaps being a woman wouldn't *hurt* his daughter.

"Father? Did I miss something?"

Joseph had almost forgotten his son's presence. "Forgive me, York. I'm afraid I got carried away with my thoughts. What were we talking about?"

"Carolina."

"Yes, of course . . . and she was the cause of my wandering mind." He paused and glanced at his son. At twenty-one, York was a level-headed, mature young man, and with his younger son, Maine, having already returned to his seminary studies in England, Joseph found himself grateful for a few lingering moments of father-son companionship. "You know, York, I see no reason why your sister's obvious intelligence shouldn't be indulged a bit."

"Mother would say you already do that, Father."

"Ah yes, Mother . . ." What would Mrs. Adams think of the idea that was this minute taking root in her husband's mind? Well, he was the man of the house, wasn't he? And Carolina was his daughter, too. "I've been thinking of hiring a tutor for Carolina."

York cocked an eyebrow at the unconventional idea. "Many people we know would think you are wasting time and money doing such a thing. What of feminine delicacy and all that?"

"I've never thought much of such notions. Didn't God create all men equal?"

"And women?"

"Come now, York, I've taught you better than that. Just as there are strong men and weak men, there are strong women along with the weaker. I believe your sister is one of the strong ones. Nevertheless, if she has a desire to broaden her mind, why should her gender stop her? I doubt it will cause insanity as some might claim."

"Do you think you could find a tutor? It would have to be a man."

"It won't be easy. Pity you and Maine chose schools so far from home. Still, there must be a man around who would overlook gender for the weight of coins in his hand—a man of honor and a gentleman, of course. Is there anyone you can think of?"

"Not readily, Father, but I will put my mind to it. Carolina is bright, and it would be a shame to waste her abilities."

"It would be different if she didn't want to improve her mind, but

I know she does. Do you know the other day I found her actually reading over some papers left me by the President's cabinet?"

"She is amazing," York agreed. "Perhaps it wouldn't be impossible to find a teacher. But are you going to tell Mother of your plans?"

"I wouldn't dream of disturbing her delicate sensibilities over such a trivial matter." Joseph ended his statement with a sly grin.

Mrs. Adams would oppose him mightily over this. There was probably no lady in all the Americas more caught up in social etiquette than she, and probably no one more ambitious of social position. To her, propriety was practically a religion in itself. Yet Margaret Adams was no cold, insensitive fish, either. Joseph could not love her as he did if that were so. Yes, she was demanding and a bit overbearing at times, and she believed it her God-given duty to present a stern front to her children. And Joseph probably only made matters worse in his tendency to overindulge his children. Yet beneath her very proper nature, Margaret was a woman who, above all else, loved her family. Showing tenderness wasn't easy for her, but when alone with her husband she often expressed her tender maternal love. And for this reason, Joseph knew that when she was made aware of Carolina's deepest wishes, she would capitulate in even her social awareness.

Four

At the White House

*T*houghts of Carolina followed Joseph throughout the evening. Even at the White House, his mind kept drifting to his daughter and her love of learning.

When the dozen men who were dining with the President retired to a sitting room, apart from the ladies, for brandy and cigars, Joseph took a moment to study them with a new perspective, wondering what they would say to tutoring his daughter. Of course, these were powerful politicians who would hardly have the time or inclination for such a task. But did they have eligible sons?

He almost chuckled out loud. While most fathers were looking for husbands for their daughters, he was looking for a teacher. It felt rather good to be a bit unconventional.

"And what is your take on the matter, Mr. Adams?"

Joseph looked up. He hadn't realized how far his thoughts had traveled. "I'm afraid I missed the question."

The man, obviously irritated at Joseph's lack of interest, drew up haughtily and repeated the question. "I asked of your opinion on the issue of our country's great expansion."

"Well, Mr. Cooper, I think we are witnessing a great manifestation of our dreams. With the West opening up to settlement and trade, it won't be long before we add many more new states to the Union. As we add states, we strengthen our Union."

"Well said, Mr. Adams!" said Andrew Jackson, exhaling a smoky puff of his cigar. "And I suppose we'll need plenty more if your sons carry on your tradition of naming children after states."

The President let out a loud guffaw to accompany his jest, and Joseph laughed easily with him. Whatever else might be said of Jackson, he was an enjoyable character, and for all his sometimes coarse mannerisms, he was a gentleman at heart.

In spite of Joseph's familial ties to the Adams dynasty, Joseph had never been a strong supporter of John Quincy Adams, Jackson's predecessor. The man was unquestionably brilliant, having proven himself invaluable in the foreign ministry. But he was a hard man, a terror to his enemies, and demanding and critical of his friends. Joseph had fallen under Adams' criticism when he had declined a seat in Congress a few years back. But at the time Joseph's children were young, and his wife was expecting their sixth child. He simply felt the demands of political office would have taken him from where he was needed most. Adams never forgave him.

When Adams won the presidency in 1824, he had done so without Joseph's vote. At that time Joseph had begun to be drawn to the man who had gained a reputation as "the hero of New Orleans," the westerner, Andrew Jackson. Not many of the plantation gentry supported the candidate who was quickly becoming known as a man of the people—the common people, that is. The flamboyant, quick-tempered military hero hardly exuded a gentlemanly refinement. But he epitomized the kind of ideals that were truly American—an independent spirit, a drive for honest hard work, tough aggressiveness, ingenuity, and, most of all, character and honor.

Joseph had to admit that Jackson's western ties had also made the President appealing to one whose gaze was often focused in the direction of that compass point. And Jackson was magnanimous enough not to hold Joseph's surname and distant family ties against him. John Quincy Adams might be one of Jackson's most hated political adversaries, but he detected in Joseph loyalty and vision, and that was almost everything to him. Thus, Joseph was often called upon to advise the President and was even considered a part of that informal, and to some, infamous body known as the "kitchen cabinet."

But now the conversation was continuing, and Joseph, freshly aware of his esteemed position, brought his mind back to the matters at hand.

The fellow named Cooper was saying, "I couldn't agree more—with the importance of new states, that is. Land sales have surpassed expectations. We believe sales this year will exceed the record of 1819's five million acres."

"We can credit the President with this rush," said Joseph. "I personally must thank him, as my coffers are much fuller due to some wisely made land purchases."

"And no doubt sales of the same. I heard there was good money to be made in land speculation."

"It had to happen," said Jackson. "If I had not freed up the economy by putting an end to the tyrannical hold of the Bank of the United States, thus encouraging the development of private banking institutes, many of those good men and women would be forever trapped in the cities of the East. Not that I favor everyone going west. The West is a harsh taskmaster and not for the weak of heart. But now, with loans more readily available, a poor man who is willing to work hard can purchase his own tract of land. Bank credit is definitely an American heritage."

"Not only that, Mr. President," a new speaker chimed into the conversation, "but without the new lines of credit, the growing prosperity of the railroad would never have been realized."

Jackson grinned. "Gentlemen, some of you may not yet have met Mr. Philip Thomas, but I expect you will hear much of him in the future. He's the president of the Baltimore and Ohio Railroad."

Joseph was the first to shake Thomas's hand. "I, for one, am fascinated with the railroad's development."

"The railroad is the key to our future," said Thomas.

"I recall hearing those very words from a fellow at the fair today. Seems to me he looked a great deal like you."

"Indeed, I take the credit. I believe the truth of those words to go beyond mere jingoism, Mr.—"

"Joseph Adams."

"Well, sir, I am convinced America must have the railroad if it seriously intends to open up the West to true settlement. With the growing number of people moving west, there has to be a means by which they can support themselves. Agricultural and livestock interests are promoted with the promise of cheap, and in some cases, free land. But there must be an adequate and profitable way to move those crops and animals."

"And you believe the railroad will resolve this issue?" Joseph already knew what he felt the answer to his question was; however, he wished to see if this man, who was obviously "in the know," supported his beliefs.

"I know it will." Thomas spoke with an easy confidence, which Joseph took to be as much a confidence in his so-called product as in himself. "Canals certainly can't be expected to meet the need. Digging them is ten times the work, and the water sources have to be consistent. Where will they find enough water in the 'Great American Desert'? The railroad, on the other hand, can meet the needs of the settler and come nearly to his front door. Why, there may well come the time,

Mr. Adams, when you could expect track to be laid right up to your plantation."

Joseph replied with an ironic smile. If only there had been such a thing when he was fifteen. He said more practically, "Though I heartily support the railroad, I don't know if I'd like the tranquility of Oakbridge so compromised. Nevertheless, I understand what you're saying. You truly think such accessibility possible?"

"Possible and reasonable."

Joseph wanted to hear more, but it was time to rejoin the ladies. As the men filed from the sitting room, he sidled up to Thomas and said, "Perhaps we can discuss this at a later date?"

"It would truly be my honor," said Thomas. "I would very much like to show you our plans. Might I call upon you at your hotel?"

"We are leaving in the morning," Joseph replied. "But I would welcome you anytime to my home. Are you familiar with Oakbridge?"

"I am, sir."

"Then I shall look forward to a visit from you soon."

On the drive back to the hotel Margaret wore a curious expression, one filled with wonder mixed with a bit of perplexity.

"I trust you had an enjoyable evening, Mrs. Adams?" he asked, hoping to learn the cause of her unusual look.

"I did indeed." She paused and shook her head. "Do you know, Mr. Adams, that these women actually thought it wonderful that our Carolina was chosen to ride the train?"

"Do say!"

"It's true enough," Margaret said with such a look of astonishment that Joseph nearly burst out laughing. "I can hardly believe it. I fretted that I would never be able to hold my head up in society again, that I'd be censured, even ridiculed by my friends. Instead I find that they are quite—how shall I say it?—quite delighted by the circumstance."

"You didn't tell them about her ruined gloves, did you?" Joseph asked with good-natured mockery.

Margaret couldn't restrain her smile. "I suppose I owe Carolina an apology for reacting so harshly."

"I suppose you might be right, Mrs. Adams."

Margaret glanced up and said with affection, "She is your daughter, through and through."

"Ah, the wanderlust. . . ?"

"That and more. I would swear there runs gypsy in the blood of both of you."

33

"Mrs. Adams!" Joseph exclaimed with a laugh. "Please do not seek to ruin our good name even in the privacy of a hired coach."

They chuckled together and Margaret snuggled closer to her husband, saying no more. She didn't need to. Joseph easily realized how very accurate her observations were. Too often he'd seen that same distant look in his daughter's eyes that reflected his own desires, that same eagerness to learn and the drive to be constantly at one new thing or another.

"She should have been a son," he muttered.

"What did you say, dear?" Margaret asked.

"Nothing," Joseph replied. "Nothing at all."

Five

Granny

*C*arolina tiptoed into the darkened room and held her breath at the smell. The slave quarters of Oakbridge were hardly different than slave quarters anywhere else—thin plank-board structures with a single room to house several people. They were whitewashed once a year, which was probably the only thing that kept some of them standing. Carolina tried not to notice the contrast between the grand white Georgian mansion and the shanty-style huts, but it was like trying to ignore the difference between night and day. She could not understand how it could be this way. Her papa was a kindhearted man who treated his "people" with respect. She supposed it was just so much the way things were that it was easy for them to go ignored.

And Carolina now ignored the squalor for entirely different reasons. Since returning from the capital yesterday, she had been anxious to share her experiences with one she knew would truly understand.

"Granny, are you here?" It took a moment for Carolina's eyes to adjust to the dark, but she heard a soft rustling in a corner of the room.

Buried beneath the covers of a handmade rope bed, an ancient black face peered up at her. "That be yo lil' missy?" the old woman asked.

"It's me, Granny," Carolina replied with a loud exhale. "Granny, wouldn't you like me to open the window a bit and maybe leave the door open for some fresh air?" The smell of unwashed bodies, urine, and smudge pots assailed Carolina's more delicate constitution.

"Sakes no, child!" Granny croaked in a rough old voice. She then pulled her withered arm from under the patchwork quilt and motioned Carolina forward. "Ain't takin' no chances on catchin' de fever. Come sit and tell Granny what yo saw in de big city." The woman's West In-

35

dies accent mingled a combination of British reserve and island warmth.

"It was truly wonderful," Carolina said as she sat on a three-legged stool that had been left at the bedside for just such talks. "I wish you could have seen it."

As Carolina's eyes adjusted to the dim light, she saw the old woman smile broadly, revealing a set of crooked yellow teeth with a couple of gaps where teeth should have been. As nearly as anyone could calculate or remember, Granny was at least one hundred years old, though some claimed her to be more. Time had taken its toll in those years, and the old woman, once a hard worker and faithful slave, was confined to her bed, nearly blind, but fully conscious of the world around her.

Carolina took her hand and rubbed it gently. "You aren't going to believe me," she said with a lilting voice, "but I did something quite daring. Quite risqué!"

"Yor right, child," Granny chuckled with a deep chesty laugh. "I don' believe it. Yo never done nuthin' darin' in yor life."

Carolina laughed. "Well, I did just that. Remember I told you about the new locomotive coming to Washington City? Well, I rode on it!"

"No!" Granny said in complete amazement.

"It's true. You must let me tell you about it." Carolina closed her eyes so she could conjure up every detail from that momentous day. "The engine was a huge black machine," she began. "Bigger than the old work wagon that used to take the men to the far fields. In the center was a huge caldron—they called it a boiler. It was full of water and pipes, and when the fire was lit underneath it, steam would build up inside." If Granny couldn't see Carolina's eyes glint with excitement, she surely must have heard it in her voice. "Two men, an engineer and a fireman, rode on the engine, and they kept the fire going and guided the engine down the tracks. Behind this was a place called the tender. This is where I rode. Usually passengers ride in cars that look rather like the stagecoach, only the engine pulls it instead of horses. It made a noise like thunder, Granny, and spit fire like a dragon in fairy tales!"

"My, my," Granny breathed, shaking her head from side to side. "The man what has to drive dat beast must surely be brave."

"Oh, he would have to be," Carolina replied, giving the old woman's hand a tiny, careful squeeze. Carolina feared the paperlike skin would tear under any undue pressure. "The men there told me it was very dangerous to ride on the tender, but that the man who owned the locomotive wanted to let just a few people see what it felt like to be right there in the middle of everything."

"How come dey put a child like yo on de thing?"

"I was just standing there," Carolina replied and leaned down to whisper, "right where I wasn't supposed to be, of course." Granny laughed and so did Carolina. "Mama had already scolded me for having an unnatural interest in the locomotive." The heavy stale air was beginning to get to Carolina, and she got up to open the door.

"Granny, there isn't a single case of fever in the whole of Oakbridge. I'm going to open this door just a bit or else I might pass out from the heat." Better the old woman think her hot than offended by the smell of the room.

"Suit yo'self, but when old Granny catches de fever—"

Carolina interrupted. "You won't catch the fever." Taking her seat again, Carolina continued. "I didn't tell you about the tracks. These are long metal strips—rails, in fact—that's why they call it a *rail* road. They run in twos, side by side, about as wide as you can stretch your arms out from tip to tip, maybe wider. The locomotive and the rest of the cars ride on top of these rails."

"What keeps dem from fallin' off?" Granny asked.

Carolina puzzled over that one for a moment. "I suppose I really don't know. Oh, but, Granny, I wish I did. I loved the locomotive, and I wanted so much to ask a hundred questions. But they were very unladylike questions and ones which I'm sure my mother would have found most appalling."

Granny nodded. "When I was a girl in de islands, I saw such ships as I thought never to be possible. Dey held the wind in their sails and by this, dey went across de world. I wanted very much to go on one of those ships. It was my dream. I wanted to know how dey worked and where dey could go. When I was twelve, de man put me on one of them and never again was I to return home."

Carolina wondered what it would be like to be taken away from her home and all that she knew. Even if given the chance to ride the locomotive far and wide, she would still want to return home to share the experience with those she loved.

Granny stared up with unseeing eyes. Thick white membrane nearly blotted out the color that once had shone cocoa brown. "I thought for a long time how de thing I loved had done took me away from de people I loved. My mama and papa and all my brothers and sisters stayed on de island, while I came here to America."

"How sad," Carolina said, patting the old slave's hand.

"No, not so much," Granny replied. "I had a good life in de islands, but I found a good life here, as well. A fine man, yor grandpappy, done bought me from my master and brought me here. He treated me good."

"But you never saw your family again?"

"No, and I never saw me another sailin' ship again, either." Granny closed her eyes. "I still remember de snap of the sail in de wind. I can still smell de sweetness of de island air and de salt of the sea. I still see my mama washin' clothes and tendin' my papa when he nearly done cut off his foot choppin' cane in de fields. Dey be here now," Granny said, thumping her hollow chest. "Dey be here."

Carolina felt a lump in her throat. "But your dream took you away from the life you knew. From the people you loved and cared for."

Granny smiled and this time it was the old woman whose weary hand offered the comfort. "Sometime yo trade one for de other. I loved dat old sailin' ship, and I loved my mama and papa. Can't keep things from happenin', child. Life goes on without much recollectin' as to whether yo want to go with it. Yo make good out of what yo get, and God, He do the rest."

"I'd like to travel on the train," Carolina whispered, as though by doing so, she was breathing life into the dream. "I have never before in all my life seen anything like it. I heard a man say that one day the train will be able to go from one ocean to the other. I'd like to see all of the land in between, Granny. I'd like to see the mountains in the West and the great Mississippi River. I'd like to know what other people are like and even meet up with Indians."

The old woman chuckled. "Yo got a big dream, but yo got a big heart and a strong mind. I figure yo know the truth about life, and yo know a truth about yo dat no other men know."

"What truth is that, Granny?"

"Can't say. Only yo know for sure. Think on it and it come to yo. Just be rememberin', ain't nobody to blame but yo for de choices yo make—" The old woman paused and looked straight at Carolina, as though she could see her clearly, and added, "—or don' make."

———

Margaret Adams had paused outside the slave quarters upon hearing her daughter's voice. Coming back from the sewing house, she'd not given much consideration to the old woman, but now, recognizing the voice of her daughter in conversation with the ancient slave, Margaret thought to check in on her.

She'd really had no intention of eavesdropping, an act she surely would have scolded her own children for doing. But the words passing between Carolina and Granny were so tender and intimate that Margaret shrank from intruding. However, she could not make herself move on, either. Carolina was talking of things and feelings she had never expressed to her mother. That fact made Margaret more sad than hurt or upset. How she wished she could understand and accept her daughter like the old slave woman could.

How like her father she was! Margaret had never really understood him and his talk of travel and such dreams, but she couldn't help smile a little at hearing almost identical words of adventure from her daughter's lips. It was as endearing to the mistress of Oakbridge Plantation as it was frustrating. Still, it was that same wanderlust desire that she'd seen quelled in her husband, and with its demise went a special part of what had attracted her to Joseph Adams in the first place. Not that she'd ever tell him that. No, the dreams had to be put aside, for there were far too many practical matters to be dealt with that would not allow for such a disease to supersede the importance of home. However, listening to her daughter's words brought it all back—the nights they'd lain awake talking, just she and Joseph. He'd told her of distant lands where no white man had ever been, and he shared his desire to explore those places.

Life had imprisoned him in an honorable way, Margaret thought, but it did nothing to take away his heartfelt desire, even *need*, to go west into the unknown. Now her fifteen-year-old daughter was expressing the same desire she'd heard in her husband's voice so long ago. When had he stopped talking about journeying west? Was it after Carolina had been born and he suddenly found himself father to four children? Perhaps it was when his sisters married and moved away, one to England and one to Georgia. Maybe it was after his mother died and he had felt more strongly than ever the responsibility to carry on the family heritage at Oakbridge. Or had it been after Margaret had given birth to a baby named Hampshire and the next year to another called Tennessee? Their deaths from fever had profoundly affected the family. Margaret had fallen into a deep depression after that, and only the birth of Virginia a year later had brought back her sanity.

She frowned, fearing that life had taken from Joseph the very precious spark that had once ignited a passionate love between them. She'd not been overly attentive to him of late. With a plantation to run and seven children demanding her attention, she had rather forgotten about his dreams. This business of the railroad, she feared, would bring it all back. But was it really something to fear? Certainly Joseph would never go traipsing off after his dreams this late in life. She must make a concerted effort to be more sympathetic about these things in the future.

Then a notion came to Margaret that rather stunned her. She'd never given serious heed to Carolina's prattle about dreams. Yet, for the first time, Margaret sensed that it might not be wise to discount

Carolina's talk as mere whim. Perhaps it was in the excitement she now detected in her daughter's voice as she poured out her heart to the slave, but there was an earnestness in the girl's voice that was disturbing. Yet it also touched Margaret, causing her to regard Carolina in a whole new light.

A bit embarrassed at these uncharacteristic emotions, Margaret turned quickly and started to hurry away.

––––––––

"I'll come by again tomorrow, Granny," Carolina told the old woman, backing out the door. "I'll close this tight, so don't you worry about catching the fever."

Carolina had no sooner secured the latch than she caught sight of her mother. "Mama! What brings you this way? Is something wrong?"

Margaret smiled in a way that Carolina couldn't understand. It was as though her mother saw her there, and yet she didn't.

"Mama?"

The momentary cloudiness left Margaret's eyes, and she reached out and tenderly stroked Carolina's cheek with her hand. "You remind me so much of your father."

Carolina grinned. "So you have said on occasion."

Margaret took Carolina's arm and looped it through her own. They walked very slowly toward the house. Her mama had seemed in a hurry a moment ago, but now she kept to a leisurely pace. Carolina didn't mind at all, for she was in no hurry for this tender moment with her mother to end.

"Carolina, I heard you talking to Granny. I hope you'll forgive me for listening," Margaret admitted. "It took me aback."

Carolina said nothing, hoping she'd not offended her mother with talk of her dreams. Yet she could think of no way of asking her mother about this.

Yet as Margaret continued, she didn't sound offended. "Your father used to share his dreams of vagabonding about the countryside. I suppose I could see very little prospect in such an affair, and I did much to take his mind from such things." Margaret stared at the huge three-story white house they now were approaching. "Your father had to acquire a great deal of responsibility at an early age."

"I know," Carolina replied softly. "He reminded me just the other day that he was no more than my age when he became the man of the plantation."

"Yes, and so much more. He had to care for his mother and take on the full responsibility of a task he had not been trained to do. You see, his older brother had been given the lessons in land management and dealing with the slaves. Until the accident occurred, your father was pretty much free to seek his own way. He wanted to go west and see the rest of the world, just like you. Listening to you just now brought back the memory of him as a young man."

Carolina looked up at her mother. She seldom looked upon her in any other way than as "Mother." But now she suddenly saw her as a person apart from that. Did her mother have dreams and hopes? Maybe even a few silly notions? She was hardly an old woman like Granny, whose life was all but used up. Margaret Adams was still a lovely woman with hardly a wrinkle marring her alabaster skin. There were hints of gray in her hair, but they were only noticeable because of the dark coffee brown color that the rest of her coiffure boasted. Carolina was usually only aware of her mother's stern demeanor, enhanced even more by her tall stately figure. But now it occurred to her that some of that might well have been sadness, not sternness. At thirty-eight, Margaret Adams had known much of life—its tragedies, its joys, its disappointments. But once, not so very long ago, she had been a southern girl of ease just as Carolina was now.

Growing quite serious in her expression, Margaret stared down to meet her daughter's gaze. "I was harsh with you at the celebration. Much too harsh and I apologize, Carolina dear. I worried overmuch that I would face the retribution of my peers and did not give enough consideration to the revelry of the day."

Carolina could only remember a handful of times when her mother had ever made such a grand gesture. She opened her mouth to reply, but Margaret raised her hand.

"Hear me out, Carolina. A mother has the best of intentions toward her children. She takes them from the cradle to the world outside, and somewhere in between she must instill godly values and sensibilities to civic duties and personal ambitions. In teaching young girls to become young women, a mother must guide them carefully to take on the tasks of life that will one day bring them to motherhood as well." Margaret stopped and smoothed back an errant strand of Carolina's unbonneted hair. "I mourned the dreams your father gave up when he assumed the responsibilities of this plantation and a growing family," she said soberly. "But it had to be done, and oftentimes I've had to be the bearer of the harsh realities that killed off those dreams."

Even more, Carolina began to see a side of her mother that she had never suspected existed. Always before it seemed that her mother simply detested travel and the idea of seeing anything outside of the plantation boundaries.

"I had little choice in the matter," Margaret continued. "I found myself with child almost immediately after our marriage, and from that point on, there was little consideration for travel and nonsense. Your father couldn't even join the army because his responsibilities to the plantation were so great. Too many people demanded he grow up and deal as an honorable man with the needs at hand. His own dreams seemed a small price to pay, at least to everyone else."

"But not to you?" Carolina asked with more wonder than she had intended to show.

Margaret smiled sadly. "No, not to me. You see, I knew what it cost him." She lifted her eyes to the house once again. "Only I realized what it took for him to turn his back on the life he'd plotted out for himself, to accept the yoke of a life that should never have been his to bear."

"But he knew," Carolina thought aloud. "Papa knew you understood. That's why he doesn't get mad when you speak of the wanderlust. It has always seemed a private joke between you both. Now I think I understand."

Margaret started walking toward the house again, and Carolina kept pace, hoping she would say more. For several minutes, only the noises of the life around them filled the vacant silence. Singing came from the wash house, and they could hear Naomi, Oakbridge's mistress of the summer kitchen, instructing three small children on how to peel potatoes.

"Granny was right, you know," Margaret finally said, pausing again and taking hold of Carolina's hands. "There is a truth inside you that only you can know. You must be true to that or else you lose a very special part of yourself. I cannot say that I will always approve of where that truth might direct you, but it is the very core of what makes you the person you are. Seek God's guidance on it, pray much, and remember that going your own way is more than *having* your own way. You might have to conform your dreams to meet social, physical, and spiritual limitations, but God will teach you best."

Carolina nodded and felt as though her mother had bestowed a most wondrous gift upon her. The demands of society would cause her mother to once again become the prim and proper mistress of Oakbridge, but Carolina would forever have this small sliver of her mother that would always be hers alone.

"Never," her mother said in parting, "never let fear keep you from living life. I fell victim to that as a young woman, and I have paid the price ever since." Without warning, Margaret pulled Carolina into her arms and held her close.

Carolina thought she might cry. It had been ages since her mother had shown her any real affection. Perhaps somewhere in her concerns for Oakbridge and the appearance she had to maintain, her mother felt that such displays were unnecessary, but to Carolina they were sorely missed. She wrapped her arms around her mother and hugged her tightly. No matter what happened from this point on, she would always remember the tender love of this moment.

Six

The Banker and His Son

Leland Baldwin squeezed his body into a stout leather chair behind his massive mahogany desk and considered the ledger before him. The opening of the Washington line was nearly a week past, and the glory he'd relished for his part in organizing it was fading. He had to return to the mundane demands of business. But he didn't expect to enjoy his work; it was simply a fact of life, a man's duty.

There were, however, enough aspects of his work to keep him duly challenged and interested. The banking business was a complex one and often irrational. There were too many variables to count at once, and frequently something remained overlooked until it was too late and the damage was done. Wasn't Nicholas Biddle a good example of this? Biddle had run the Bank of the United States as though it had been his own private game. Of course, given the background of Biddle's power, for all intents and purposes, it *was* his game.

Nicholas Biddle and banking were one and the same. Having been drawn into the system as savior to the country after the final war with England earlier in the century, Biddle had been almost single-handedly responsible for keeping the government functioning financially. Called upon by then Secretary of War James Monroe, Biddle was advised of the gravity of the situation and enticed to offer his help.

Leland still found it hard to believe that a mere twenty-one years ago, Washington City had been sacked by British Admiral Cockburn. This struck a tremendous blow to the spirit of the American people. And though America rallied and soundly defeated her enemy, the War of 1812 had emptied the Treasury and paralyzed the government. Someone had to do something, and that someone became Nicholas Biddle.

Biddle went among his rich friends and found funds for the government to borrow. He fought, even against his father wishes, to re-establish the Bank of the United States as a means of bringing the country out of financial ruin. The central bank would stabilize the country's economy, but it would also place a tremendous amount of power in the hands of one man, namely Nicholas Biddle, who would come to be known as "Tsar Nicholas."

With the war over and the bank reestablished, Biddle at first declined the position to become director to the major stockholders. He had done what was necessary out of loyalty to his country. But Monroe wouldn't hear of it and insisted that Biddle accept one of the five government directorships. Again feeling a patriotic sense of duty, Biddle accepted.

What came next, however, was not all that unusual. Biddle, tasting fame, power, and fortune, was very soon corrupted by the same. He became more powerful than anyone could have foreseen, and soon he was the president of the Bank of the United States. But for all those who hailed and loved him, there stood an opposing force who despised him. Tsar Nicholas soon made enemies, and among them was Andrew Jackson.

It was said of Biddle that he alone destroyed the bank when he deliberately chose to unite with Senator Henry Clay, Jackson's sworn enemy. When Jackson sought to bring Biddle down once and for all, private banking was issued a tremendous boost. The government discontinued making deposits to the corrupt and hopelessly misguided Bank of the United States. Instead, Jackson saw to it that banks more friendly to his own political goals were given these deposits. Leland Baldwin was in the right place at the right time and stood with the right side.

Baldwin often wondered if it had been entirely prudent to tear apart the Bank of the United States. Not that he wasn't honored when Amos Kendall, fiscal agent for the President, approached him to include his bank in the historic transfer of public monies to private banks. But the entire matter was far from over.

Biddle's Portsmouth bank had shown undue favoritism to anti-Jackson men, and the President saw clear lines being drawn. Leland could still recall Jackson voicing doubts regarding the need for a national bank in his annual presidential messages. Thus, the fight was on. Now there were rumors that Biddle's bank would be refused a renewed charter next year. If that happened, it was anyone's guess as to where things would go from there.

Leland had tried to make the most of the new banking freedom. With taxation funds, custom house collections, and land office deposits being shared among a variety of private banks, Leland's Democratic standing had caused him to prosper. But perhaps he had gone too far. In studying Biddle's methods and mistakes, Baldwin had been lured by the possibilities of personal gain.

He had offered easy credit at low interest to his closest and most beneficial friends. He extended loan notes in return for favors, and he hoarded with a passion as many of Jackson's "yellow-boys"—newly minted gold pieces—as he could. Gold could be spent any day, but the value of paper bank notes was questionable. Maybe he had already put too many bank notes into circulation.

By the look of the accounts Leland now studied, he immediately realized a major problem. Too many assets were frozen in long-term loans. The preferred loan form was short term at high interest. Thirty or sixty days at most and certainly no longer than ninety. But here, in the black and red of his ledgers, Leland saw how many low-interest notes he had issued to friends and business interests that would not pay back for one or more years. And though the notes were payable upon demand, Baldwin knew he would forever ruin his social standing to force money from his friends.

"Pure stupidity on my part," he mumbled in disgust. He was simply too generous for a banker. However, generosity was probably not his major motive. He had an aversion against turning away business—any business—when it came his way.

He hated to think what might happen if a run on the bank occurred in the near future. Clearly he had more bank notes on the street than solid reserves to back them. It would take only one person issuing a panic, and the entire bank would collapse. There was also the fear that once Jackson's administration came to an end, the Bank of the United States might once again find favor in the eyes of the government. If that happened, Leland's bank might be required to turn over the government deposits in full, and that clearly wasn't possible.

Taking out a handkerchief, Leland mopped great drops of sweat from his forehead. It wouldn't happen. It couldn't. Jackson wanted the common man to have available cash and the benefits of bank loans. Westward expansion depended on it, and even Henry Clay wanted to see the West settled. Only people with money could accomplish such a feat, and Leland knew that land speculation demanded a ready supply of cash. He drew a deep breath. By the time Jackson was gone, it would be too late to change things. The banks would be committed to the brave souls who went west. The West would collapse without the common man's bank, and the bank would collapse only if the government cashed in on their deposits.

"I simply mustn't worry so," Baldwin chided himself.

But he did worry.

The country was in the middle of questionable, but very enjoyable, prosperity. Still, Baldwin was no fool. There was bound to come a reckoning, and he was certain it would have Jackson's name on it.

A knock at the door came as a welcome relief from his troubles.

"Come in," he said, quickly closing the ledger.

"Hello, Father!"

A young man strode into the office. His long legs carried his lanky well-built frame with an easy confidence. At twenty-two, Leland Baldwin's son appeared to have inherited none of his father's portly expanse, nor the elder's homely, nondescript features. Young James Baldwin's thick wavy dark hair, bushy eyebrows, tanned ruddy complexion, and strong facial lines must surely have derived from his mother's side. He was dressed in the highest fashion, gray frock coat, silk waistcoat and ascot, and in his hand he carried an elegant beaver top hat.

"This is a surprise," said Leland without further greeting. "Didn't expect you until tomorrow."

"I took the locomotive. Very impressive, by the way. This is for you." In his other hand James had been holding a leather satchel, which he now laid on his father's desk. Then he dropped his lanky frame into one of the leather chairs facing the desk, and like an ill-bred ruffian, he threw a leg casually over the arm of the chair, absently toying with his hat.

With a disapproving shake of his head, Leland momentarily gave his attention to the satchel, opening it and looking inside without removing the contents. A smile broke the tension of his heavily jowled face, but it faded as he glanced up again at his son. "Did your uncle Samuel tell you anything about this?"

"Nothing, except that it was urgent bank business. And I certainly didn't presume to open it myself." James' tone betrayed his defensiveness.

Leland carried the satchel to his private safe, opened the lock, and placed it inside, firmly closing the door afterward.

"I was about to have lunch," said Leland. "You are welcome to join me."

"I wouldn't be an imposition?"

"Of course not. You've been away for weeks." Leland studied his son again, trying not to be disturbed by the tension in the young man's voice. He hardly realized his own tone equally mirrored his son's. "Besides, your mother will be joining us, and she'll be inconsolable if you decline."

"Then, by all means, I will come." James paused, as if searching for something more to say. "How is Mother?"

"You know your mother." Leland relaxed a bit with this topic he knew would be safe from conflict with his son. "She is constantly involved in one good cause or another. Last week she was gathering up food items for the orphan home. This week I believe she is raising funds to decorate the graves of Revolutionary War heroes. At the pace she goes, no doubt she will have all Washington fed, clothed, or put to rest before the end of the week."

James chuckled, relaxing too. "Then perhaps my absence wasn't even noticed."

"Oh, it was noticed. You *are* her only child." Leland said nothing about whether *he* had noticed. He was not a man to express his feelings; in fact, he hardly even acknowledged them himself. He felt it was the man's proper role to treat all aspects of his life in a businesslike manner.

Just then another knock signaled the arrival of Leland's wife. Richly adorned in a green organdy summer dress, heavily beruffled, with a matching feathered bonnet and parasol, Edith Baldwin entered the room with all the grace and elegance of a practiced lady.

"I do declare! James!" She started toward her son.

James, already on his feet, flowed easily into her motherly embrace. She held nothing back in showing her delight at her son's presence.

"How I have missed you, James! And I do believe you have grown."

"I think I'm past all that, Mother."

"He's too tall already," put in Leland.

"You are still a sight for a mother's eyes," Edith said, ignoring her husband's critical comment and turning to James. "When did you get back?"

"Only a few minutes ago."

"I do wish I would have known about the change in your plans," she said with a petulant, almost childish pout. "I have next to nothing planned for dinner."

"I will be happy with anything you have."

"It's all for the best, I suppose." Edith took a seat in the chair adjacent to her son's, and both men also resumed their seats as Edith arranged the flounces of her dress. "Now that you're here, James, there is a matter—"

"Mrs. Baldwin," put in Leland impatiently, "can't this wait? I was expecting to be at the restaurant. I do have to get back to work today."

"What about your fitting at the tailor's, dear?" she asked, absently smoothing out her voluminous gigot sleeves.

"Oh yes, that. I think I'll cancel it. I'm perfectly content with my old formal suit."

"But, dear," cooed Edith in a sweet diminutive tone that nonetheless hinted at inflexibility, "you did promise you would get a new suit. And it is a special occasion."

"What occasion is this?" asked James. "I don't believe there are any birthdays or anniversaries coming up."

"I wrote you about it. Don't you remember?" She looked positively deflated, almost as if she would cry. "The dinner party we are giving in honor of your return. Goodness! If it's not important to anyone but me—"

"No, Mother, I remember," said James quickly.

Edith brightened. "I do so want this to be special for you, dear. I've put a lot of thought into the guest list."

"I'm sure the company will be delightful."

"I hope it will be more than that."

"What do you mean?" James cocked a perplexed brow.

"Can't we discuss this over lunch?" asked Leland.

"It will only take a minute, Mr. Baldwin," said Edith. "And it is perhaps too delicate a subject to be discussed in public."

Leland gave a noisy sigh, clearly registering his disapproval. Nevertheless, as hard a man as he might be, he did know when to appease his delicate wife. "Well, then, let's get it over with."

"I wanted to discuss the guest list. There are several young ladies—"

"Mother . . ."

"James, your father and I feel it is high time you settled down and stopped flitting about the country. Now that your education is complete, it is time you start a family and take up the banking business."

James rolled his eyes.

"Don't be disrespectful of your mother, boy!" growled Leland.

"I'm sorry." James seemed contrite enough. "But I've hardly been 'flitting around the country.' A few trips—"

"Every holiday from school you are off somewhere," countered Edith. "Your father has had precious little time to teach you the business. And as far as courtship goes—well, many of the families in the area hardly even know we have an eligible son. Sometimes I think there ought to be coming-out parties for young men as well as girls."

"How positively ridiculous," said Leland.

"Well . . . what else can we do?"

"And that's what this dinner party is all about?" James asked warily.

"I have invited a handful of the best families, all of whom have perfectly delightful daughters of the marrying age. You may have your pick. See, I am willing to be flexible in this matter."

"Do we need to discuss this now?" asked James. "The dust is still clinging to my traveling cloak."

"No time like the present," said Leland, moderating his impatience. He was no less anxious than his wife to have James settled and married, preferably to a wealthy debutante. It was a closely guarded secret—even James was unaware of it—but the Baldwin personal financial situation was even more precarious than the bank's. For years Leland had been living way beyond his means, and it was now beginning to catch up to him. "Tell James about these families, wife."

"There is the Milford girl, Kate," said Edith, a hint of triumph in her eyes. "She's seventeen and quite accomplished. True, her waist is a bit thick, but that could be remedied with a better corset. The family's fortune easily makes one forget her minor imperfections. Next is Sarah Armstrong. She lacks a bit in refinement because the family money is rather new, but again there is enough of it so as to cause other considerations to dim." Edith counted the young women off on her hand as she spoke. She was clearly in her element. "The secretary of the treasury has a charming ward, his niece, or is it cousin? I forget and it doesn't matter. The girl is absolutely lovely and has the social standing and financial security to make a good wife. And lastly, but certainly far from being least worthy, is Virginia Adams of Oakbridge. Her credentials are impeccable, and though I mention her last, she is my first choice. As you well know, the family is old and well established, the fortune is old and sizable, and in spite of the distant ties to the presidential Adams, they are in quite tight with the present administration. The fact that they were close friends and neighbors before we moved to the capital makes them that much more appealing."

"My, my, Mother," James said in sarcastic wonder. His father threw him a cautionary glance, but James continued anyway. "Have you picked us a house, as well, and named our children?"

Leland wasn't surprised when his wife went on, undaunted. "Dear James, do be sensible. A good wife is an important asset."

"You've been around banking too much," said James.

"Would you rather make a poor choice you would regret the rest of your days?"

"I'm not looking for a wife at all right now," said James. "And I have no desire to settle down."

"You will have to settle down in order to properly run the bank," said Edith.

"I don't plan on running the bank," James said in an even, barely controlled tone.

Leland scowled. This wasn't the first time he'd heard this. James had been scoffing at the banking business for years. Yet it was the first time Leland heard it declared with such assertive resolve.

"Don't talk nonsense, young man," said Leland. "What other means of support do you have? You wasted your college on ridiculous courses in science and history."

"Because I have no interest in business and banking."

"Pray tell, what *do* you have an interest in?" asked Edith, horrified at the turn of the conversation.

"Railroads," said James flatly, but with assurance.

"Railroads!" mother and father exclaimed in unison.

"Yes." James smiled almost defiantly. "I had the opportunity to spend time with the president of the B&O—that's Baltimore and Ohio Railroad. I learned a great deal about their operations and found it quite fascinating. Mr. Thomas is looking for good engineers to help design the rail line. And he believes my science courses, far from being frivolous, are perfectly tailored for his needs."

"Oh, James . . ." Edith laid a hand weakly across her forehead. "We had such high hopes for you. I do believe I'm feeling faint."

"Mother, the railroad business is quite respectable."

"Bah!" spat Leland. "It's filled with risks and pitfalls. And I have no doubt half those railroad people are criminals to boot. They've approached me for loans—which I've refused handily. I've read their financial reports and can only say the entire venture is pure madness."

"Perhaps it is risky, but only those willing to risk greatly will reap in kind," James countered with a determined set to his jaw. His blue eyes burned with conviction. "You took a few risks yourself, Father, when you opened this bank."

"Banking is a reputable business."

James chuckled. "Half the people in this country won't put their money in a bank. I believe even the President keeps his personal income tucked under his mattress."

"But, son," said Edith, "the railroad is so dirty and noisy."

"Mother, can't you see all the promise it holds? I have seen the plans for a rail line from Baltimore to Ohio. Imagine that!" His excitement grew, oblivious of his parents' clear disapproval. "And from Ohio it could well stretch the distance to Chicago."

"Chicago?" smirked Leland. "Who cares about that mudhole except the three thousand people who live there?"

"Why don't you just open your mind for a minute, Father?"

"So you can drive a locomotive through it?" Leland's jowls shook in his fury as he continued. "My mind is open, James, and I'm tired of your insolence. I've paid for your education, and I will dictate how it is used. You are going into the banking business, and you are going to marry well. I'll hear no more of it. It is about time you acted like a man instead of an irresponsible boy."

Leland pushed back his chair and lurched angrily to his feet. Lunch, of course, was ruined now, but for Edith's sake they would have to muddle through.

Seven

Railroad Man

*J*ames walked along the banks of the Potomac. It was enough away from the hubbub of the capital to allow him a small respite. The waters were sluggish now as summer drew to a close. He paused, stooped down, and picked up a small flat rock, which he flung mightily into the water. The rock skimmed the surface. But it hardly reached the other side as George Washington's famed toss was reputed to have done.

James stripped off his jacket and slung it over his shoulder. His mother would chide him for looking like a vagabond, but he didn't care. The afternoon was stifling. The thought of his mother made him recall the events earlier in the day—not that they had been very far from him since leaving his parents after lunch. The meal had been terribly stilted and awkward. His father was unbending in his demands on James. His mother, in her sweet delicate way, was also quite inflexible.

Sometimes James wanted desperately to throw aside all the family constraints. They weighed him down like chains. He longed to break free, perhaps be a real vagabond, or a mountain man, or an explorer. But duty and responsibility held him back. His father called him irresponsible, and maybe he was to some extent, but where his family was concerned, he felt the weight of his sense of duty could almost break him. Perhaps if he were truly a man he'd throw aside those bonds entirely. Maybe it would have been different if his parents had had other children, other sons. But he was alone, and all the family hopes were pinned on him. His father was overbearing, his mother overprotective, yet they had only him to carry on the name and all the things his father had worked so hard to build.

But what of his own dreams? It was hardly fair that he should be expected to sacrifice those for a life he disdained. But his mother would weep and his father would bellow. James didn't want to hurt his mother or disappoint his father.

His father . . .

It seemed James had already spent two lifetimes trying to please the man and make him proud. However, he had started to give up on that nearly futile task even before he'd finished college. His growing unrest and sense of rebellion began to rear up with his very choice of colleges. Instead of attending his father's alma mater, Franklin and Marshall, James had chosen another Pennsylvania college, Moravian, in Bethlehem. The innovative liberal college, founded in the middle half of the previous century, had opened James' eyes to much. The college supported not only education for all—poor as well as rich—but the administration and faculty followed the philosophy of John Amos Comenius. This seventeenth-century bishop of the Moravian Church was often frowned upon for his spirited ideas in regard to education. Not only were men encouraged to study a variety of subjects, but there was a firm belief in education through experience. Comenius even went so far as to advocate the education of women.

James enjoyed the approach and found the proposal of women students to be questionable in worth, but not totally out of consideration. It would never have met with his parents' ideas for genteel society, but he could see the possibilities.

At first, to appease his parents' disappointment, James had taken the courses prescribed by his father, all geared toward business and banking. But such courses proved boring to James' active and creative mind. Thus, encouraged by the college's philosophy of broad course study, he had added science and history. But unable to completely defy his father, he ended up with a double load. Luckily he was intelligent enough and hardworking enough to successfully master it all.

But how far would he go trying to live a double life to please his father? And would it ever please the man? When James graduated fifth in his class with two degrees, one in business and one in engineering, Leland had only commented that James could have been *first* if he had stuck with business alone. James rebelled further against his parents' wishes when he decided to stay a few weeks longer in Bethlehem to meet Philip E. Thomas, the president of the B&O Railroad. Thomas, there to meet with an ironworks owner, had cordially received James and encouraged him to come to Baltimore. Given the chance to observe the workings of the railroad, James had followed eagerly. It had proved to be the most exciting three weeks of his life, but had also thrown his life into a spin.

Though he'd always known he didn't want to be a banker, it had seemed a more reasonable prospect at one time. It had even seemed acceptable for his parents to arrange a suitable match for him in marriage. All that had changed after he went north to school. He had seen too much and learned that beyond the political scraping and social frivolity of Washington there lay an entirely new world—a world James wanted to be a part of.

Now the very thought of sitting behind his father's desk shuffling papers and hefting ledgers horrified him. In the past he'd never had any clear focus about what he did want, thus he had easily placated his father these last few years. But that, too, was changed now. The railroad had at last lent focus to his life.

He recalled how that passion had begun to take root in him when he had stood in the railroad office looking over plans for a new engine. The plans were intricate, almost artistic in his perception. They had placed one fundamental piece upon another. A spring here, a metal bar there, a cylinder, an axle—it had all pulled at James as nothing ever had before. And his engineering training and his natural aptitude combined so that he actually understood many of the fine nuances of the detailed blueprints. Closing his eyes now, he could still picture the sketch before him. Two sets of lead wheels, two large sets of drive wheels, and no trail wheels. A 4–4–0, he remembered, each number representing the wheels on the engine. The most powerful locomotive yet to be made.

And somehow James knew he must be part of it!

The only question now was if he was strong enough to stand up to his father and devastate his mother. He just wasn't sure.

James picked up another rock but gave it only a halfhearted toss into the water. He really wasn't in the mood for this solitary walk, nor for the miserable process of self-debate. He was a man of action, not one of great introspection. He headed back to town seeking some diversion.

He wasn't surprised when his footsteps led him to the rail yard. The big locomotive he had come into town on was there, and men were busily working around it. He ambled into the yard, watching the men's labors.

A big fellow with red hair and a freckled ruddy face was railing at the men. "This ain't never gonna get done for the early morning run. Edwards, Collins, can't you two move a little faster?"

"You want speed or precision, boss?"

"Don't get smart with me, Edwards. I expect the job to get done, that's all!" The red-haired boss stalked away.

The four workers shook their heads and raised their eyebrows, grumbling under their breath. James moved closer.

"What's the problem?" he asked.

"Bad iron," answered Edwards, not bothering to question this stranger's presence. Maybe he thought that James, with his fine clothes, was one of the big bosses. "Driving rod is in bad shape. Looks like it was made out of cast iron instead of wrought."

"Cast iron would never stand up to the pressure," James said, looking over the man's shoulder.

"True enough and the proof is right here," Edwards agreed. "Who knows what else we'll find."

"That ain't all," put in the fellow named Collins. "We'll have to figure a way to fabricate our own parts 'cause they don't have what we need here."

"Mind if I have a look?"

"Be our guest—say, are you one of the owners or something?"

"No, just an interested bystander. But I've got some engineering knowledge, and I've been told I have a way with machines."

"Well, I don't reckon you can do any harm."

James tossed his jacket and beaver hat carelessly on a pile of crates. He was just rolling up his sleeves when a voice called out.

"James Baldwin, is that you?"

Turning, James spied Phineas Davis, a well-muscled man in his forties and chief mechanic for the B&O Railroad. Why, the very engine before them had been created by none other than Davis.

"Phineas!" James said, thrusting forward his hand for a hardy shake. "I thought I'd left you to better times in Baltimore."

"I came down to accompany Mr. Thomas on a fund raiser. What's the problem here?"

"Well, in spite of your wonderful design, some fool has put cast iron in the place of wrought iron."

Davis stepped forward to view the problem for himself, muttered a low growl of inaudible words and threw off his coat. "We might as well get at it or we'll pay the price come morning."

Within a half hour the men were deeply into the task. Lengthy discourse and tedious inspection proved their worst fears. Not only was the driving rod in bad shape, but the link rod was nearly broken in two at the return crank.

"Cast iron," James muttered.

"Somebody's going to hear about this," Davis bellowed.

"Thought the B&O had more sense than that," Edwards retorted. "Weren't they the very ones to demand American production rather than British, on account the Brits roll in cinders to make cheap iron?"

James straightened and wearily nodded. "Cheap iron has no place in a locomotive. This ought to be constructed from wrought iron. The best we can do is find a blacksmith and see if he can duplicate this piece enough to get it back to the B&O shops in Mt. Clare. It's either that or send for the piece."

"Glad you two came along," said Edwards. "This thing could have broke clear through while it was moving, and heaven knows what damage it would have done."

They worked for another two hours before the redheaded boss returned.

"Who are you?" he asked James, after nodding cordially to Davis.

James straightened up from where he had been bending over some machinery. "James Baldwin." He extended his hand, then realizing it was covered with grease as was most of his clothing, he withdrew it and smiled sheepishly.

"I don't recall hiring you," said the boss.

"No, you didn't."

"What're you doing?"

"Just helping out. I'm an engineer."

"You don't look like an engineer."

"I'm not a locomotive driver, if that's what you mean. I'm trained to build things—bridges, dams, railroads, whatever."

"Just be glad that 'whatever' took the form of locomotive engines," Phineas threw in. He was attempting unsuccessfully to clean the grease from his hands.

The boss scowled. "I can't afford to hire no one else."

"I'm not looking for work. I just wanted to help."

Edwards added, "Hey, boss, you should see what he's done." He proceeded to show the boss James' contributions.

The boss let James stay. Why not? It wasn't costing him anything.

And James felt in his element, up to his elbows in pipes and gears and wheels. He loved it. The greasy smell, the complicated mechanisms, the challenge of troubleshooting a problem.

When the job was completed around ten that night, he felt truly accomplished. The men let him know they would never have finished so far ahead of schedule without his help. They invited him to the tavern to celebrate. Only then did James remember that his mother had been expecting him for dinner. Thus, he was even more eager to join the railroad men in order to postpone another confrontation with his parents, this time over his tardiness.

The ale flowed freely, and although he looked far more able to pay than his new friends, none would let him pay a single coin. He felt as if he had made friends for life. When Eddie Edwards lifted his voice in an off-key but loud song, James chimed in merrily.

"From whence have ye come and where are ye bound? From Baltimore way to Ohio ground. How will ye pass the mountainous load? We've engaged a passage by railroad."

They all burst out laughing. A barmaid poured more ale. The song had originated from a celebration in 1828 when the B&O had laid its first cornerstone. Old Carroll Carrollton, the only surviving signer of the Declaration of Independence, had bantered the staged words back and forth with a Baltimore shipmaster during the parade. It was just the encouragement the railroad workers needed, and it was only moments before someone picked up the chorus again. But just as they started, from the opposite end of the tavern, a new song was raised.

"I got a mule, her name is Sal, fifteen years on the Erie Canal! Low Bridge, everybod-y down, low bridge, 'cause we're coming to a town . . ."

The railroad men stopped singing, twisting around to see from whom this intrusion was coming. A group of four or five men reclined at a nearby table. There were no smiles on their faces. They glared at the railroad men.

Undaunted, Eddie, who was six feet tall and two hundred fifty pounds, said, "Hey, do you mind waiting 'til we're finished with our song?"

The other group glanced around at one another as if silently debating the question, then a fellow who was nearly as big as Eddie folded his arms across his broad chest and said in a defiant voice, "This is a free country; we can sing when we want."

"Come on," said Eddie, warning not pleading, "don't make trouble."

"You railroad people are the only ones making trouble!"

"We're just having a peaceable drink," put in James, thinking he could reason with the thugs.

"We were here first."

The men in the corner rose as a body and all but faced off with the railroaders.

"That's the silliest thing I ever heard," said James.

"Look who the dandy is calling silly."

Eddie had been studying their new adversaries. "I've seen a couple of you blokes before. You're canal people, ain't you?"

"Maybe railroad people ain't as stupid as I thought!"

"Why you—!" Eddie lunged forward.

The tavern keeper tried to intercede. "I don't want no trouble in my place."

"Then you shouldn't 'ave let in these dirty railroad scum—" slurred the canal man.

Eddie didn't let the man finish. He flew at him with all his weight. Phineas rolled his eyes as if used to the conflict, while James, without hesitation, leapt at another of the canal men. In another two seconds the entire tavern had erupted into a brawl. Anyone not involved in the battle made hasty exits or hid with the tavern keeper behind his bar.

James was a novice at barroom brawls or fisticuffs of any sort. But he threw himself into the melee with the delighted relish of a young man who knew he'd have to pay dearly for his actions later and thus wanted to make the most of them while he could. However, after his initial attack, he found himself hopelessly outclassed by the seasoned and rough canal men. He landed but one more punch—a quite ineffectual one—and then spent the next two minutes on the defensive, until a fist aimed at him hit its mark and he was sent sprawling on the floorboards.

Slightly stunned, it took him a moment before he could lift his head and shake away his double vision. But when he was seeing clearly again, the first thing he beheld was one of the canal men lifting a chair over Eddie, who was unaware of his impending danger because he had his back to the man while busily fighting another. James struggled to his feet and, swaying and dizzy, lunged at the fellow with the chair. His effort spared Eddie by forcing the attacker to retreat, but the canal man was still on his feet and still holding the chair. James stumbled, still off balance from his previous blow. Before he could recover, the chair came crashing down on James' head. Everything went black.

When he woke, he saw a couple policemen out of the corner of his fuzzy vision. The fighters were being quickly dispersed.

"Next time you're all heading for the tollbooth," warned one of the police. "Now clear out."

Eddie staggered over to James and put an arm under his shoulders. "Can you get up, Jimmy, my boy?"

"Oh, sure . . ." But the minute James tried to stand, his knees buckled under him.

"I'll help him," Davis muttered, staggering to where they stood. He wasn't in much better shape than James, but at least he could walk on his own.

"Tommy," Eddie called to one of his comrades, "give us a hand."

Propped between his two friends, James was propelled from the tavern. The fresh air did wonders for his cloudy brain. But it also made him painfully aware of several open cuts on his lip and cheek. He raised a hand to them, then grinned.

"I'll bet you never been in a fight before, have you, lad?" said Eddie.

James shook his head, the lopsided grin still plastered across his battered face.

"Well, you acquitted yourself fine. The boys told me what you did for me. I'm beholden to you."

"My pleasure," said James.

"Here's your jacket and hat," said Tommy, handing James the items. The jacket was dusty and rumpled, the hat crushed pathetically. "'Fraid they're plenty worse for the wear."

James looked at his things, which only a few hours ago had been fine and practically new. "They're beautiful!"

Eight

Lace and Locomotives

*B*ut I simply can't wear this ghastly thing to the Baldwin party,"
Virginia cried, throwing the powdery pink satin to the bed. "It makes
me look like a child. Give it to Carolina to wear!" Virginia's voice betrayed her desperation. At eighteen, she was no longer considered the
belle of Falls Church and Washington City. In fact, she was desperately
close to being an old maid in the minds of many of her peers.

"We can't possibly arrange for another gown by Friday," Margaret
said, thoughtfully considering the discarded dress.

"But I want to look like a woman, not a child," Virginia whined.
Upon receiving her mother's reproachful glance, however, she softened her tone. "Whatever do you suggest, Mother?"

"There is a dress in my wardrobe that's never been worn. It's a lovely
shade of rose that I believe would complement your complexion. I can
have one of the girls in the sewing house take a look at it and remake
it for you. A few tucks in the waist and a few more frills and it will be
perfect."

Virginia's face broke into a satisfied smile. "I knew you would rescue
me from this. Just don't let that sassy Hester have any chance to get
her hands on it. She hates me and always makes my gowns to hang
oddly."

"Now, now. Don't worry," Margaret clucked. "Hester has her hands
full with other tasks. I'll personally see to the adjustments if you see to
putting a little lemon juice on those freckled shoulders of yours." Virginia nodded and hurried to the kitchen for lemons, nearly knocking
Carolina and Penny over in her wake as they approached Virginia's
bedroom.

"Whatever is her hurry?" Carolina asked, to which her little sister
only gave a perplexed shrug.

Penny scampered to her mother's side and lifted up a small treasure. "See what I found in the garden?" It was a tiny perfect rosebud.

"How lovely," Margaret replied. She gave Penny a distracted kiss on the forehead, then turned her attention to her older daughter. "Carolina, have you given thought to what you will wear to the Baldwin party?"

"Do I really have to go?" Carolina hoped that she could somehow avoid the ordeal. No doubt her mother would put her and Virginia on display. "I haven't even 'come out' yet, Mother. I'm still in short dresses!"

"Most girls your age would be thrilled to be allowed such a grownup opportunity. And there will be several eligible young men there. Though, of course, you will only participate in dinner and perhaps just a bit of the dancing," Margaret said, picking up the pink satin. "This would look lovely on you, and your sister has made it quite clear it isn't in her taste to keep it."

Carolina sighed in complete exasperation. "I'm not even sixteen yet. No one would seriously expect me to have a husband lined up just yet."

Margaret smiled, surprising Carolina with her tolerance of the situation. "This is only a dinner dance, not a formal ball. It can't hurt to show the prospective suitors what they can expect in the future. Marrying well is everything, Carolina."

"What about love?" Carolina knew the question was overstepping her bounds, but she truly hoped to be excused from the party and saw no other way but by complete honesty. Her talk with her mother outside Granny's was still lingering pleasantly in her mind. Perhaps that's what gave her such boldness now.

"Love follows," Margaret assured her. "Now slip into this and let me see if it needs to be adjusted. Miriam! Come help this child change her gown."

A mulatto woman appeared at the door. Her starched white apron made a stark contrast to the dark cream color of her skin. "Yes'am," she replied and instantly went to unhook Carolina's dress.

"Mother, truly," Carolina protested as Miriam worked. "By your own rule you know Virginia must marry first. Since she's still available, why muddy the waters, so to speak?"

"I want to make sure, Carolina, that you don't find yourself in the same desperate predicament as your sister. Eighteen and no husband, not even a prospect."

Her day dress was lifted over her head, and Miriam quickly had the pink satin in place before Carolina could utter another word. The cold material caused Carolina to shiver, but it was a good feeling neverthe-less. Satin always had a way of making Carolina feel truly lovely. Miriam finished with the back hooks and, after adjusting the sleeves to expose Carolina's milky white shoulders, stepped back to await her mistress's bidding.

"Why, it looks as though it had been made for you," Margaret said, taking in the vision of her daughter.

Carolina caught sight of herself in the mirror. She had developed quite young, and the dress was designed to show off just the right amount of figure without leaning into a dangerously overexposed area. The satin hung off her shoulders in sleeves of demi-gigot fashion. Fit-ted from the elbow down, Carolina couldn't resist the urge to puff out the tops as she took in her reflection. She wished it had the newest style of sleeves that she had seen in *Godey's Lady's Book*, instead of the old muttonchop style. But at least it had a fashionable fitted waist. The form-fitting bodice showed off her womanly shape, rounding softly just above her breast with elaborate handmade lace. The snug waist blossomed out in three tiers of flouncing to the floor.

Yes, Hester and the girls in the sewing house had done a fine job of duplicating the latest fashion. Carolina could not imagine what had prompted Virginia to reject it. But she could be exceedingly choosy at times. No wonder she still had not found a husband!

"I think this will do just fine," Margaret stated as Carolina turned slowly before her mother. As much as Carolina had thought the party of little interest, she found herself growing excited as she considered the gown. She might have an unwomanly fascination with science, but that in no way superseded her feminine interest in clothes and looking good.

Margaret seemed to sense the change in her and offered an approv-ing nod. "You'll turn heads, no doubt. And you'll do yourself proud and maybe even find a young suitor who will come to call."

Carolina had no chance to respond, for Hannah appeared in the doorway to announce tea. Margaret motioned for Penny to accompany her downstairs while Miriam helped Carolina change.

Once she was properly attired in her cotton day dress, Carolina took the gown to her own room. But as she laid it over the back of a chair, she caught her reflection in the dressing table mirror. Where was the grown woman that had seemingly stared back at her only minutes ago? Carolina reached a hand up to her carefully secured bun and pulled it loose. Rich brown hair tumbled down and fell about her shoulders like a cape. Taking the pink satin gown in hand, she held it up against her body and shook her hair loose to fall across the material. She thought herself very much to resemble a child playing dress-up, and the thought seemed to haunt her. Why had she allowed herself to get caught up in the party?

"I have no desire to attract anyone's attention," she said and tossed the dress aside as unmercifully as her sister had done earlier.

Plopping down in the window seat of her bedroom, Carolina stared wistfully beyond the panes of glass, remembering the hissing steam engine that had captured her fancy. She could close her eyes and almost see it.

Reaching beneath the cushion of the seat, Carolina pulled out the kid gloves she'd hidden there. Lifting them to her nose, the sharp smell of oil mingled with smoke lured her like Ulysses' sirens back to that wonderful experience. Her heart raced with excitement as she recalled the sensation of the locomotive's first lurch forward. Then it was gone, and Carolina opened her eyes only to be confronted with her stationary position in her own bedroom.

At least her mother was no longer angry with her. Her mother's change of heart had amazed Carolina. And it had eased the tension that seemed to be perpetually between them. Margaret Adams' brief and somewhat humble moments outside Granny's shack had given Carolina new feelings for her mother. Still, Carolina had no doubt that had it been Maine or York who had taken that first ride on the locomotive, the question of propriety would never have arisen.

"If I were a man . . ." Carolina muttered, unaware that her mammy, Hannah, had come into the room and was once again rescuing the poor gown from the floor.

"What you say, chil'?" the portly slave questioned.

"Oh . . . nothing," said Carolina, stretching out her legs with a heavy sigh. Her pantalettes peeked out from beneath her hem, reminding Carolina of her hopeless plight. "If these were men's trousers instead of pantalettes, I wouldn't have any trouble getting an education or knowing more about railroads."

"What you talking 'bout, missy?" Hannah placed her hands on her thick waist. "You is a lady, Miz Carolina."

"I know. And that's the problem. Sometimes I think I should have been born otherwise. As a man, I could go to school and study. As a man, I could board a locomotive, maybe even drive it, and no one would give it a second thought." She added with another sharp sigh, "I should never have been given a brain!"

Hannah shook her head. "You is gwanna have a hurting head for all dat worryin'."

Carolina hadn't expected Hannah to understand. If her own mother and father didn't, how could she expect an uneducated slave to see the logic in her statement? But even Carolina had to admit it wasn't really very logical—just emotional, just like a silly female!

Nine

Reaching an Understanding

*F*or several days after James' altercation in the tavern, life in the Baldwin home was rather tense. There was the inevitable confrontation the morning after when he came down for breakfast with his obvious cuts and bruises. His mother nearly fainted, and he was taken soundly to task for his scandalous behavior.

After that he tried to be away as much as possible, and, in fact, quite successfully avoided his father altogether. The two or three occasions he encountered his mother were too brief for any in-depth conversation—he saw to that by making excuses for a prompt departure. His mother finally cornered him one evening while he was in the process of slipping out of the house. This time his mother was quite firm, and he would have had to be outrageously rude to avoid her. Something, of course, he could not do.

And his mother, perhaps fearing he would make another of his flimsy excuses, came quickly to the point after directing him to the parlor. "James, we must discuss the matter of your party tomorrow evening."

"Surely my presence is all you will need, Mother."

"I would also like assurance that you will be taking the evening seriously. That you will make an earnest attempt to consider the young ladies I have previously mentioned."

"Be reasonable, Mother," James said, refusing to be seated. Instead, he stood by the fireplace mantel and looked down at his mother, purposely not removing the coat he had donned in order to leave. "I cannot simply choose a wife as though picking a winner at the tracks."

Edith was undaunted as she looked up at her son's face with the bruises still visible. "If I thought it would lead you to matrimony any quicker, I'd line them all up at the track gate and fire the start of the race myself."

James grinned, causing pain to shoot across his face. Sobering considerably, he continued. "Well, it won't, so don't try." He'd always enjoyed his mother's sense of humor, but her pushiness was another matter altogether. He tried another tactic, hoping that somewhere along the way he would find one that would work. "I simply have no desire to marry at this point in my life. Why is that so difficult for you and Father to understand?"

Edith Baldwin put down the cross-stitching she had almost automatically taken up upon sitting. She'd devoted her attention to it throughout her son's tirade but now gave him a pained expression.

"You have no desire to marry? What have you a desire for? Scandalous tavern brawling?" She laid a hand across her forehead, then motioned a servant to pour her a cup of tea from the silver teapot she had called for, no doubt in hopes of having a prolonged and pleasant interlude with her son.

James rubbed his cheek. "It was a matter of honor."

"Still, the party is tomorrow. How can you expect any respectable young woman, much less her father, to look at you with serious intentions toward marriage?"

James emitted a heavy sigh and threw up his hands. "I don't care to attract any woman toward marriage."

"But what of a family, a wife, children? You must realize the importance of those things."

"Of course," James said with complete exasperation. "I simply have no desire for them in my life at this time."

"Oh, James, you are twenty-two years old, yet at times you seem more like a boy of twelve."

"Maybe that is because you and Father persist in treating me like a child," he said, barely able to hide the bitterness he felt. More lightly, he added, "Even if it is so, what is wrong with that? Why shouldn't I be able to have fun and do the things I enjoy?"

Before his mother could respond, Leland Baldwin huffed his way through the double oak doors and grunted. "Mrs. Cooper is in the front room. She begs a moment of your time, Edith dear."

Laying her cross-stitch aside and forgetting her tea, Edith made her exit, leaving the men alone.

Dismissing the servant, Leland closed the double doors behind her and grimaced. He seemed to James to bear the weight of not only his broad frame, but of the very world itself.

"Mother was just trying to convince me of the benefits of marriage," James said, trying to sound lighthearted. "I think she truly just longs for grandchildren to show off to the likes of Mrs. Cooper and the rest of Washington."

Leland's expression grew even more serious. He looked long and hard at his son's face, opened his mouth as if to comment, then closed it again. After several more moments of silence he did speak. "I must confide something to you, James. Something that comes as no easy revelation. Something that gives me great displeasure." He took a seat and motioned his son to do the same.

Giving up on his hopes of a fast escape, James shrugged out of his brown double-breasted redingote and tossed it to one side of the sofa before taking a seat. Besides, the day had become unbearably hot, and his father would no doubt make it hotter still. Undoing the buttons of his waistcoat, he waited for whatever secrets were to be shared.

Leland frowned disapprovingly at James' display of undressing but said nothing on the matter. "I'm afraid there is much in the world that is not as it should be," he began. "The banking world is unstable, and while there is a great land boom going on in this country, there are also problems that can barely be imagined, much less dealt with. I'm afraid I've made some bad choices."

James took note of his father's worried expression. Gone was the pretense and confident face that Leland Baldwin wore for the rest of the world. In its place, James found an aging expression that gave him much cause to worry. However, James felt an odd sense of pleasure at his father's uncharacteristic letting down of his careful guard before his son. It was almost as if his father was accepting him as a mature man, even an equal.

"Father—?"

Leland waved off the comment he would have made. "No questions, just hear me out."

James nodded, feeling a strange tension twist his stomach into knots.

"We are fast running out of money, son. That is the simple vulgar fact. There is no way to reconstitute our financial affairs without a new infusion of money. I realize that sounds as though we are selling you off to the highest bidder, but nothing could be further from the truth. The fact of the matter is that unless you marry before our financial collapse is made public, you will be unable to marry well. If you do not marry a woman of means, it will be ruin for our name and all that I have tried to accomplish."

"Why was I not told sooner?" James questioned with a deliberate slowness.

"I had hoped to avoid this discussion altogether. Your mother, even now, has no idea that such problems exist, and I would very much like for you to keep the matter in the utmost confidence." He looked up and grimaced. "She hasn't the mind for such problems and feels that all about her is loveliness and grace. She cannot possibly comprehend the dealings that go on in the back alleys and barrooms. She cannot understand with her woman's mind what costs there are to bear and how poor choices can destroy the wealth of generations gone. I would keep her innocent of this, but without explaining it to you, how else can I convince you to marry?"

James said nothing for several moments. He glanced around the room, noting for the first time that many items of great value were no longer in their proper places. "Have you sold off very much?"

Leland shook his head. "No, not so very much. I can't without giving your mother cause for worry. But we are in trouble, James." He paused, as though unable to speak the next words without tremendous effort. "We are deep in debt."

"I see." James suddenly realized his fate was sealed.

"It started off harmlessly enough," Leland said. He took a cigar from a silver case on the table and held it for a moment. "Jackson encouraged the masses to go west and opened banking to the point where people of all walks expect ready cash. This coupled with Nicholas Biddle's demands that loans issued smaller banks be paid in full to the Bank of the United States, and . . . well . . . I'm afraid I've overextended myself."

"I see . . ." Still, James could find no other words. He suddenly saw his future and all the plans he'd made twisting in the wind as though on a gallows. Any pleasure he had felt on being considered an equal by his father quickly diminished. Now he was equal in ruin as well as plenty.

"I've tried to approach the President on the matter," Leland continued. "I informed him of how this banking fiasco is affecting the common man and such, but his answer to everything is, 'Go see Biddle!' "

"Is all lost, then?"

"There is hope for recovery in time. I've managed to put aside a small amount of gold, but it won't go far. A few minor issues can be dealt with immediately. Others can wait for a short-term extension, but ultimately all will need to be dealt with. It's simply a matter of stabilizing our financial affairs."

"And who do you have in mind to stabilize our financial affairs?"

"The Adamses are quite wealthy. Joseph has made a killing in land speculation. I heard only last week he sold off a tract of land in Maine for over three hundred percent profit. It was said that the entire deal netted him over two hundred thousand dollars on land that cost him only a fraction of that amount. He's also well invested in a hundred other areas. Iron, coal, shipping. You name it and Joseph Adams has managed to make money from it." Leland seemed to become excited at the very idea of getting his hands on such a fortune. "Virginia Adams is most eligible, and your mother believes her to be quite accomplished. There are also younger daughters, but of them only Carolina is old enough to consider for immediate use."

James raised a brow at his father's choice of words. After a moment of reflection he spoke. "I've not seen either of them since they were in short dresses and we were neighbors in Falls Church." James thought back to those days when the Adams children had been his playmates—the boys had been close friends, especially he and York. But he remembered Virginia and Carolina. Virginia had been pretty and quite a flirt even then, but rather frivolous, if he recalled. Carolina had enjoyed riding and chasing about in the woods far more than her sister, and she had been far more quiet and thoughtful. "How old are they now?" But after a moment's calculation, he answered his own question. "Virginia would be eighteen and Carolina fifteen."

"Yes, but give no serious thought to the younger one," said Leland. "The eldest daughter is usually married off first. And I understand Margaret Adams is especially mindful of that tradition."

"Well," James said carelessly, "I've heard it said Virginia Adams has matured into a very attractive young woman. I suppose a man could do much worse." Seeing his father's expression light up considerably, he raised a hand. "However, I draw the line at banking. I will not be a banker under any circumstance. I love the railroad, and I intend to continue working on some design ideas I have for a new engine."

"But can that ever pay you enough to support a family? It will do precious little good if you marry a woman of means, only to have to live on it as your only support."

"Philip Thomas of the Baltimore and Ohio Railroad seems to think I might very well make a long and healthy career with the railroad. He's offered to look over my designs with his chief mechanic and engine designer, Phineas Davis. Not so long ago, Mr. Davis was awarded four thousand dollars for his locomotive design."

Leland gasped. "Four thousand dollars?"

James knew he had his father's attention now. "That's right. Four thousand, and that was for only one of many engines he was to develop. He's a genius, and I would love nothing better than to study under his tutelage. He and I have become well acquainted and quite companionable."

"But surely you cannot expect to be paid that kind of money," Leland said in a voice that defied James to prove him wrong.

"Well, maybe not to start with," James replied. "Unless, of course, one of my designs strikes the fancy of Thomas, as it did Davis's grasshopper design."

Leland shook his head. "Please don't get technical with me. I have no mind for such things. What I do have a mind for is saving this family's name. Do I have your word that you will seek a bride with haste?"

James drew in a deep breath. The moment had come to lay all of his cards on the table. "Do I have *your* word, Father, that I may continue to pursue the railroad instead of banking as a career?"

Leland hesitated only a moment. "Prove two things to me first, and then I shall agree to it."

"What two things would that be?"

"First produce for my eyes some form of cash support from your railroad work. Secondly, agree to take a wife within a year."

"A year? No respectable young woman is going to break with tradition and marry that soon."

"Oh, I think she will"—Leland smiled thoughtfully, as if he had someone in mind—"if she's desperate enough to avoid being labeled a spinster."

"I hardly consider marriage to me an act of desperation." James smiled roguishly and winced at the soreness which remained in his bruised cheek.

"It will take a desperate woman to marry you if you cannot refrain from barroom fights," Leland replied, noting James' untimely wince. "Now, do we have an understanding?"

James nodded and the feeling of tightness in his stomach matched that in his jaw. "I will do as you ask."

Ten

Evening at the Baldwins'

The Baldwin home in the Washington suburb of Georgetown had been built in 1815, a sturdy brick structure, box-shaped and plain except for its Palladian-style arched windows and doors. Joseph recalled Leland's bragging about the "pretty penny" he'd forked out for the structure and large grounds when he purchased the place some ten years ago. Such things were important to Leland; not that Joseph thought less of the man for that. Oakbridge was worth two or three times as much as the Baldwin home, but it meant less to Joseph because it had never been the thing he desired.

A servant led Joseph and his family to an anteroom where the Baldwins were greeting their guests. At least Leland was there. His wife and son must have been called away for the moment to attend other duties.

"Adams, good to see you again," Leland said with a nod. "Glad you could come to the party."

A small string orchestra was playing softly in the next room, and the hum of voices rose up as accompaniment in conversation. Leland bowed his rotund frame to greet Margaret Adams, who had just turned from offering final instructions to her daughters.

"My dear Mrs. Adams, you are a vision," Leland remarked, taking her gloved hand. "I know Mrs. Baldwin will be delighted that you could make it on such short notice."

"We are quite happy to have been included, Mr. Baldwin," Margaret replied. "Virginia and Carolina could scarcely speak of anything else. And how kind of you to include Carolina, though she has not yet come out."

"Ah, but such a grown-up young lady," Baldwin said with a wink toward Carolina. Then he nodded at Virginia and flashed her an especially broad smile. "And you, Miss Adams, are a shining example to your little sisters of lovely southern womanhood."

"You are too kind, sir," Virginia replied with a demure smile.

"Now come, you must join the festivities. There is quite a joyous group of young merrymakers here already enjoying a few refreshments before dinner is served." At this he ushered the family into the adjoining room.

The girls were quickly swept away into groups of their friends. Laughter and animated voices greeted their entrance, while Leland quickly offered the elder Adams some refreshment.

"I don't believe we care for anything just yet," Joseph said. "Where is that son of yours? I do believe Mrs. Adams told me this party was in celebration of his college graduation and return to Washington."

"Indeed, indeed. No doubt some admiring young woman has him dutifully entertained," Leland said with an awkward laugh. "He is a handsome boy, if I do say so myself, and the young ladies hardly give him a moment's rest."

"Margaret!" Edith Baldwin exclaimed, coming forward to embrace her dear friend. "It has been ages since we've been together. How very uncharitable of you to keep yourself away from the city. I have simply died of boredom without your company."

Margaret smiled. "You have no idea how very busy seven children can keep you. Why we only just sent Maine and York back to classes, and the girls are . . . well . . ." She paused. "The girls are simply girls and require their own style of sorting out from time to time." The foursome laughed and all eyes searched the room to where Virginia stood talking to several other young ladies. Joseph did not immediately see Carolina, but she was no doubt obscured by the crowd of about fifty guests.

"Your Virginia is quite beautiful," Edith noted. "That gown is perfectly suited to her color. Wherever did you find the material?"

"Here in the city," Margaret replied. "I believe Goody's Dressmaking could arrange a bolt for you."

"How positively charming. And your gown is quite appealing. Is that a creation of Goody's, as well?"

Edith and Margaret were lost in rapid conversation regarding the most current fashion. Completely forgotten, the men found their own topics to cover.

"She and James would make a handsome couple," Leland spoke up, causing Joseph to raise his eyebrows.

"She? Oh, you mean, my Virginia? Yes . . . the prospect of seeing them together would not be at all displeasing to me," Joseph offered, still watching his oldest daughter conduct her greetings. "When does

James plan to join you at the bank?"

Leland frowned briefly, then quickly tried to repair the obviously unintended gesture with a nervous laugh. "It seems my son has other ideas. They may not pan out, however, in which case he will come on board within the month."

"What interest can it be that would draw him away from the lucrative position of banking?" Joseph asked.

Leland looked uncomfortable. "He has found the new railroad to offer a wealth of attraction. I've given him a short time to prove it capable of supporting a man and . . ." he paused to offer an uneasy smile, "a family."

Joseph nodded. "I believe the railroad to be a valuable asset to our country. James is coming into the thing at just the right time. The railroad will only grow in popularity and profit."

Leland showed noticeable relief at Joseph's words. "Perhaps you weren't aware, but he has a degree in engineering as well as business. No doubt both could be of value to a man with his interest."

"But of course," Joseph replied eagerly. "A young man with James' obvious talents and schooling could only benefit a new and upcoming business like the railroad. I heartily approve of his interest and hope it works well for him."

Leland took out a handkerchief and mopped his perspiring brow. The room was rather warm, but it almost seemed as if Leland had been not so much affected by the heat as by his concern over Joseph's reaction to the discussion about his son. Joseph was more flattered by the idea than concerned.

———

Without hearing the conversation, James took in the scene from behind curtained double glass doors. This entryway had been sufficiently cordoned off by a rather large buffet covered with flower arrangements and candles. It would not allow anyone to come through and disturb his vigil, yet afforded him a chance to observe the merrymakers without being seen.

Remembering his comment about picking a race horse, James felt very nearly akin to that as he studied the young women his mother had invited. Each was certainly not without merit. As his mother had noted, Kate Milford stood a little more robust than the others, but her smile was genuine and her eyes were wide and alluring. Sarah Armstrong, overdressed in a French concoction of blue watered-silk and feathers, had a loud distinguishable laugh that she'd not yet learned to contain. His gaze passed over several other young women before coming to the shapely form of Virginia Adams.

So this was Virginia all grown up, he thought, and smiled at the way time had arranged his old playmate. She was a delicate thing with a tiny waist that he could no doubt easily span with his hands. Her skin was milky white, with the slightest flush in her cheeks. Her gloved hand gracefully produced a fan, which she used to cover her perfectly shaped mouth whenever she laughed. Something inside his chest tightened at the thought of actually marrying the girl. Perhaps his parents had presented a tolerable idea after all.

Realizing he had put off his entrance to the party as long as his parents would tolerate, James straightened his back and gave the velvet collar of his black frock coat a fastidious final dusting. To enter the room where the party was already promising a delightful celebration, James had two choices, since the flower-covered buffet blocked the usual route. He could either pass through the library or make his way around the house by way of the kitchen. Choosing the shorter path through the library, James burst into the room and collided straightway into a young woman.

Reflexively his arms reached out to steady her as the impact sent her spinning. When he had righted her on her feet, James immediately unhanded her and gave a brief bow.

"Forgive me," he stated formally, then raised up to meet the warmest and widest brown eyes he'd ever seen.

"I must say, you gave me quite a start!" she said with a nervous little laugh.

James was momentarily lost in the alluring smile of full cherry red lips. Her rich brown hair had been drawn up high atop her head with long curls trailing down the back. A delicate pink ribbon, matching the color of her gown, was tied as a band across her head and woven into the hair in the latest fashion. For several moments he scarcely knew what to say, feeling quite the fool for his flustered reaction. Seemingly unaware of his discomfiture, the girl turned away, apparently to leave. He quickly straightened and drew a long deep breath, wondering how to detain her without appearing even more the fool. Then he noticed a book lying on the floor, apparently having fallen from her hand.

"I do believe you have dropped something," he said quickly as he scooped up the volume. He glanced briefly at the book as he held it out to her. *The Principles of Science.* An interesting choice of reading material for a girl, he thought.

"Thank you, sir." She reached out a dainty gloved hand.

James held the book tightly, momentarily forgetting it as he studied her again. Then her disturbingly puzzled gaze caught his, and with a sheepish chuckle, he handed it over.

"Again . . . thank you," she said and turned once more to leave.

"May I ask why are you in here, instead of out there enjoying yourself with the others?" he asked.

She shrugged and her gaze dropped to the book. "This looked more enjoyable by far." She glanced up at the rows of books with an appreciative smile.

He thought her response rather odd, but he was of a progressive enough mind to pursue it. "Perhaps you would like some direction in finding something more to your taste—in a book, that is."

"If you know the library, then you must be James Baldwin."

"Yes, I am. Now, how about some Shakespeare?"

"Shakespeare has his merits, and I do enjoy him, but that's not what I was seeking just now."

"What exactly were you seeking?"

"A book on locomotives. Have you any?" Her compelling brown eyes danced with hopefulness.

"Locomotives?" James questioned. "Why in the world . . ."

"Because I find them of great interest!"

Did he detect a hint of defensiveness in her tone? "But you're a woman," James protested, unable to imagine the delicate flower before him having any such true desire to immerse herself in the properties and workings of mechanical things.

She rolled her eyes in a most fetching way, though he was certain she had meant it to be derisive. Why had his mother failed to include this young woman in her list of prospective brides? Perhaps she was new to the area. Just as he was about to inquire of her name, however, she spoke.

"Surely you can't believe, Mr. Baldwin, that a female has no capacity for anything more complex than cooking and sewing. Why, look at this—" She excitedly thumbed through a few pages. "The Second Law of Thermodynamics. My brother told me about this the other day, and I was wondering if these principles could be applied to the transference of heat in the steam engine of a locomotive. There seems to be a relation to me, and that's why I was looking for something about railroads that could verify my thoughts. Do you know anything about this subject?"

The bright eagerness she exuded made him forget the notion that such talk from women was decidedly unfeminine.

"As it happens, miss—forgive me, but I don't know your name."

She frowned. "Of course you do. I am Carolina Adams."

76

"You?" He didn't hide his surprise. "But she—that is, you are only a child."

"I am fifteen!" she said defensively.

"I know, but here you are dressed like a lady in a gown and all."

"Not by choice."

"Oh? You mean you didn't want to attend my party?"

"Well . . . I didn't . . . that is, it is nothing personal, you see. It's just that . . . I don't know . . . I guess it is as you said, I am too young."

"And is that why you sought out the library, because you felt intimidated by all the elders?"

"Not really. I just suppose I prefer the company of a good book."

"To a party?"

"It's hard to explain. But I want so much to know things—things I'll never learn at a party. I have so many—"

But at that moment the chime for dinner sounded.

"You were saying?" James asked. She was a child, of course, but a very intriguing one.

"That was the call for dinner, wasn't it?" she said. "I should be going."

"Let me accompany you."

"I can find my way, really." And before he could say another word, she spun around, her silky curls dancing around her pale smooth neck, and walked quickly away.

Impulsively, he almost hurried after her, but then thought better of it. Why bother pursuing a child? True, at fifteen, she could become betrothed to a man, but a marriage would not be quickly forthcoming. Nevertheless, James was seven years her senior, and there were plenty of lovely, more suitable women at his disposal.

At my disposal, he thought ruefully. I'm starting to think like my parents.

Still, he was in no position for whimsy. He had to be practical. What was more important to him than anything else was his career with the railroad, which could only be achieved precisely by thinking more like his father. In this vein, it was not Carolina but rather her sister Virginia who would best further his ambitions. It was certainly no great sacrifice. He'd already seen and approved of Virginia. It would not be hard to shake the little sister from his mind.

Eleven

Two Sisters

*C*arolina had no idea why she'd hurried so from the library. And why she still had the science book in her hand as she entered the dining room! She quickly stowed it behind a large vase of flowers on a windowsill before finding her place at the long dinner table.

The encounter with James Baldwin had been odd at best, downright disturbing at worst. She mused over it during dinner as she studiously avoided even looking in James' direction. It was a wonder to her that he had failed to recognize her at first. He'd thought she was one of the eligible young ladies, not a child who had not even yet come of age. Imagine! It was rather thrilling to have a man of his stature think of her as a grown-up lady. But appalling, too.

It made her more aware than ever of her fast-approaching maturity. In a few months she would be sixteen and would be officially presented to society; then no doubt other men would look upon her in the same way. She wasn't ready for such things. Yet she did not want to remain a child either. It was terribly confusing.

But no more so than the interchange in the library with James. Oddly, the moment she'd told him who she was, a subtle change had come over him, and he began treating her like a child. He wanted to know if the "elders" frightened her, obviously considering himself to be one of those elders, as he most certainly was. Even worse, she had fumbled for words to explain things that proper young ladies shouldn't even think about. It must have seemed quite silly to a man like James, even if she *had* been able to explain them.

Then she had rudely insulted him by implying she had no desire to be at his party in the first place. How could she have done such a thing? And to the very person in whose honor the party was given! For that she deserved the harshest reprimand her mother could think up. Instead, her mother, unaware of her rude behavior, let her attend the ball after dinner. It was the last place Carolina wanted to be, but she felt so guilty she didn't have the nerve to impose her desires upon her mother's generosity. Nor did she have the heart to return to the library. Someone else might catch her there, and she might make an even worse fool of herself.

She followed the other guests from the dining room and up the sweeping staircase to the ballroom, where she quickly made her way to the farthest corner and prayed to fade into the artfully carved woodwork. James entered the room acting for all the world as though nothing were wrong, and Carolina could only conclude that he had not suffered the same effects of their meeting as she had.

She studied him for a long moment. My, but he is dashing, she thought, noting the wavy darkness of his hair. The snug fit of his coat showed off a wealth of masculine lines, and the set of his jaw was lean and hard. He had grown into a handsome man—much too handsome, Carolina thought, for his own good. He was a far cry from the Jimmy Baldwin who had tormented her as a child. He and York had been great friends, and they had found much amusement in unmercifully teasing her and her sisters. Even back then Carolina had suffered a wide gamut of emotions in regard to Jimmy Baldwin, from anger at his boyish cruelty to starry-eyed admiration of her brother's best friend.

She watched now with no less confusion as a bevy of young women suddenly began swimming around him in adoration. She mentally calculated that he must be twenty-two, knowing him to be seven years her senior. Still studying him, she caught her breath when he flashed her a smile. How utterly awful to be caught watching him! Now he not only knew she was watching him, but by the way she felt her face flush, he would know how embarrassed she was at being found out.

Fully expecting him to torment her further, Carolina made her way to where her father spoke with Leland Baldwin. Surely James wouldn't attempt to disgrace her in front of his father.

"Are you having fun, my dear?" her father asked with a wide smile.

Carolina knew he understood her misgivings about being forced to come to the affair. If they wanted to marry off Virginia, it was all well and fine, but there seemed to be little or no reason to drag her along behind. Seeing Leland Baldwin's anxious expression, Carolina nodded. "It's a lovely party."

"Now don't feel shy about dancing, Miss Adams," Baldwin said. "Even if you are the youngest girl here."

Margaret and Edith appeared, and Carolina was forced to endure their scrutiny and suggestions for male companionship that evening.

"Sarah Armstrong's brother, Daniel, has been asking after you,

Carolina," her mother said softly. "I believe he would very much enjoy a dance."

"He's a splendid young man," Edith offered supportively. "He recently graduated from the military academy, and he looks positively handsome in his uniform."

Carolina prayed for patience and the ability to endure the driving force of not one mother, but two. Her decision was made for her, however, when she spotted James making his way toward them.

"If you would introduce us, Mrs. Baldwin, I would be happy to share a dance with him." Carolina knew she sounded rather flustered, but she had no desire to face James Baldwin again.

———

James watched his mother leading Carolina across the ballroom. They had their heads together as if planning a very important strategy, which as far as James could tell from his dealings with women, they probably were. He smiled to himself and was pleasantly interrupted by a feminine voice.

"Hello, Mr. Baldwin," Virginia Adams purred.

James turned and gave a bow. "Another Miss Adams, I see. Good evening."

Virginia smiled demurely and used the fan to her advantage to gaze at him coquettishly from over the rim. "I was hoping to congratulate you on your recent graduation."

"That's very kind of you." James studied Virginia for a moment and found himself comparing her to her sister. He was, in fact, so lost in this comparison that he didn't hear what Virginia said next.

"I'm sorry"—he smiled in a way that endeared him to young women—"I'm afraid my mind was rather preoccupied. I didn't hear what you said." He spoke the words in a manner he knew would be flattering to Virginia's sense of pride.

"I merely said it was a lovely night for a party," Virginia replied.

"Perhaps you would enjoy a dance?" he asked. "I would be honored if you would allow me to escort you to the floor."

Virginia smiled again and snapped the fan shut. "I would be simply delighted, Mr. Baldwin."

They joined in a lively reel, and James thought himself quite fortunate to have attained the company of Virginia with no more trouble than a few well-placed words. He reminded himself of his duty to the family and reveled privately on how easily entertained Virginia seemed to be. But disturbingly enough, it was Carolina Adams who imposed on his thoughts even as he danced with her sister. She was nowhere to be seen, and he wondered where she had disappeared to with his mother.

"Oh, look!" tittered Virginia. "There's Sarah Armstrong and Boyd Harris together. I heard they might become engaged soon." She waved to the couple. "Isn't Mary Lindsay's gown divine? It was shipped here all the way from Paris."

Virginia went on and on, filling him in on gossip about everyone on the dance floor. James' mind wandered in his complete indifference to Virginia's prattle. He thought about what Carolina had said concerning thermodynamics. He was still stupefied that a female even knew of such things, much less took an active interest in them. He would have liked to talk to her more about her ideas. Incredible! But now that he thought of it, Carolina had always had a unique turn of mind. As a child of five, she had forever barraged him with questions. Jimmy, why do the clouds move when there is no wind? Jimmy, what makes the ground steam after the rain? Why are butterflies different colors?

She had really wanted to know the answers, too, and would give him no rest until he'd come up with something. No wonder he tried to pay her back with incessant teasing. Back then he had dismissed it as childish curiosity. But now . . . he wasn't so certain. It seemed to him just from that brief encounter in the library that Carolina Adams was hardly a child any longer. And thus, her curiosity must be something else. Intelligence, wit, and mental acuity seemed rare in a woman, and yet here was a woman with a brain—or more accurately, a woman with the desire to use her brain. It was an intriguing notion. And Carolina Adams was an intriguing woman—or rather, *girl*.

But again, James had to force his thoughts back to the present moment and to the *woman* in whose company he now was. Intriguing fifteen-year-old girls with older unmarried sisters could have no place in his life. He would—and could—find contentment with Virginia. It was only his rebellious nature that was making his thoughts stray toward anyone else. Thus he threw himself with great zeal into the dance.

When a waltz—that most scandalous of dances—began, Virginia looked up at him hesitantly, then put her hand in his and waited for his lead. James put a gloved hand lightly to her back and guided her in a rotating whirl around the room. Virginia stepped lightly, with grace. Her smile was bewitching. Any man would be crazy not to feel blessed to have the attentions of one such as she.

"I suppose I should have allowed another to take this number," James said with a roguish glint in his eyes. "Have I threatened your reputation?"

Virginia laughed softly. "I suppose one waltz will not ruin me this night."

James offered her a warm smile and led her gracefully through the room of twirling couples. He liked the waltz for a variety of reasons. One, it put the couple very close—face to face—and it was much easier to talk if one desired to do so. Then, too, for all its movement and constant flow in and out of other whirling partners, it was a dance that seemed to exclude the others in the room.

Virginia's cheeks were pink from exertion, and her eyes were glowing bright in anticipation of what was next to come. James found her by far the most beautiful woman in the room. Clearly more womanly and exquisite in appearance than her sister. He tried to find some flaw in her face, some single thing on which to fault her, but he could not. Her complexion was smooth in an alabaster radiance, her nose delicately upturned, and her brows naturally arched above smoky blue eyes. Weren't Carolina's brown?

He pushed back the reminder of warm dark eyes and resumed the silent scrutiny of his dance partner. Pulling her a little closer, he was rewarded with her look of astonished pleasure. Yes, this was how it should be. He need desire nothing else.

"I do declare, Mr. Baldwin, we are very nearly close enough to share secrets."

James' lopsided boyish smile invaded his serious expression. "Do tell, Miss Adams. Is there a secret you wish to share?"

Virginia lowered her face slightly and raised her eyes in a manner she must have known to have a devastating effect on suitors. "Perhaps," she said rather breathlessly, "if we knew each other better."

"Then we must make it so," James replied. "I think I might enjoy hearing secrets from one as lovely as you."

When the music ended, Virginia excused herself. James watched her sweep from the room, captivated by her elegance and grace. She had proved delightful company. No talk of locomotives or mathematics here, he thought, with a curious glance to see where Carolina might have taken herself.

As the music once again played a popular tune, James spotted Carolina on the arm of Riegel Worth, an old school chum. She seemed bored with his oafish attempt at sociable dancing; nevertheless she remained perfectly companionable and attentive. James thought to rescue her when the music ended, but she looked up and met his gaze; then, as if reading his intentions, she latched quickly on to the arm of Riegel and pointed him in the direction of the refreshment table. Laughing to himself, James dismissed thoughts of interrupting her respite and made his way toward the veranda for a breath of fresh air.

"James! I thought I'd lost you to this houseful of beauties," Leland joked with a hearty laugh. "Have you made your greetings to the Adamses?" he asked, nodding toward that very pair who were with him on the veranda.

"Good evening, Mrs. Adams," James said, giving a formal bow. "Mr. Adams."

"James, your father tells me you are leaning toward a career in the railroad," Joseph said enthusiastically. James felt a flood of relief as the man continued. "I have great interest in the locomotive myself."

"It's a booming business," James related. "I feel confident this is just the beginning of something truly great."

"I couldn't agree with you more," Joseph confided.

"James, I saw you dancing with Virginia Adams," his mother said as she joined the group. "You make a handsome couple."

"She is quite a beauty!" Leland exclaimed. "You'd have to go far to find another as lovely and well suited to becoming a wife."

James looked up to catch a glimpse of pink satin as Carolina Adams passed the entrance to the ballroom on the arm of a uniformed young man.

"Quite so," he said enthusiastically. "Why, it is uncanny how one family could have produced such a brood of lovely sisters. A man would be fortunate to marry any one of them."

Margaret seemed pleased at this but quickly added, "You are too kind, but, of course, our Virginia must marry first since she is the eldest, and then we will consider suitors for Carolina. It would hardly be fair to allow the younger ones to outwit their siblings for proper marriages."

It seemed a silly and antiquated tradition to James. But he had no inclination to argue the point. Besides, Virginia was the one he'd been instructed to consider. There was little sense in giving further attention where . . . anyone else was concerned. Virginia was clearly a beauty not to be ignored, and her head wasn't bulging with unfeminine notions about science and railroads.

Leland, seeming to rescue James from making further comment, said, "I know we'd be quite happy if our James and your Virginia should find each other to be of interest."

"As would Mrs. Adams and myself," said Joseph.

James knew with those words, however subtle, a bargain had been all but struck. He made no protest. He and Virginia Adams would indeed make a fine couple. They would raise their own brood of beautiful children. And he could still happily pursue his love of the railroad.

Twelve

York Adams

*Y*ork Adams reached a hand up to his cheek and pulled it away crimson with blood. His blood. He stared evenly at the man who'd just now inflicted the wound.

"So you're no longer a pretty rich boy," the man chuckled.

"Your guard must have fallen off your rapier, Bedford," York panted. They had already been hard at this twenty minutes. It had been a brutal match, but York had never expected to see blood drawn.

"Did it now?" sneered York's opponent.

"I would give you the benefit of the doubt, at least, considering that this was intended as a gentlemen's exercise."

"That's the trouble with you plantation gentry," the man countered. "You believe the entire world runs on gentlemen's rules of order. Well, I've news for you, Adams. The world is neither interested in nor concerned overmuch with your rules." Bedford smiled, but not in a friendly manner. "I would make this *exercise* a bit more sporting."

"You must be crazy."

York looked at the man, clearly seeing the hatred in his eyes. Hatred that York felt was undeserved and unearned. Bedford was new to the university, but since his arrival he had been hostile toward York and several of his friends. It had been subtle at first, and York had sought to befriend the man. But finding no success in that, he had deemed it best to ignore him. York had never been able to figure out the cause of the man's animosity beyond vague regional differences, for Bedford was from New York. But when Bedford had suggested the fencing match, York, viewing it as an overture of friendship, had accepted. Now he saw that friendship was the farthest thing from the man's mind.

"Well," taunted Bedford, "are you going to fight like a man, or would you hide behind your mother's skirts, you southern dandy?" As if to punctuate his words, Bedford lunged again with his unshielded rapier.

York sidestepped, avoiding the thrust, but now he was angry. York lifted his rapier and prepared to continue the fight. "I see now you had no intention of this being a friendly bout. No doubt you have no idea at all what it means to be a gentleman." Popping the guard from his rapier, York lunged forward, catching the man's shirtsleeve. It tore the material in a quick sweep but drew no blood.

The man stepped back and stared hard at York for a moment. "Your quaint little world leaves no room for growth. Things are very seldom what they appear, Adams. You can never trust appearance in any form."

"You talk too much, Bedford," York decreed, making a wide sweep with the rapier.

"I couldn't agree more," a voice said, coming from behind York. At this, both York and Bedford came to attention. It was their fencing instructor.

"Sir," they responded in unison.

"Fencing has never been dependent upon the tongue, gentlemen." The man stepped up to York and noted the cut. "Mr. Bedford, that will be twenty demerits for wounding a fellow student. I believe that brings you to a total of one hundred. Will you pay a fine or do the time?"

"I protest, sir!"

"Indeed?" The instructor did not seem surprised. "Did you or did you not intentionally mark this man's face?"

Richard Bedford glanced at York with a smirking air. "Is it my fault he is a poor swordsman? He did not protect himself, and I was unable to stop the assault."

"And whose idea was it to remove the shields from the rapiers?" demanded the instructor.

"We both agreed," said York quickly. He'd show that northern scalawag how a true gentleman—a southern gentleman!—behaved.

Bedford glowered at York but said nothing.

"It is understood when you enter this classroom that the utmost care is to be given the opponent. I see no reason to be lenient to either of you. You both knew the rules. Your demerits will stand, Bedford, and I will see you at the end of the day. Mr. Adams, you too shall have twenty demerits. Now, I suggest you take care of that cut."

"Yes, sir." York watched the instructor walk away, then turned to Richard Bedford. "I demand to know what your grievance is against me!"

Bedford shrugged, as though his earlier hatred meant nothing. "I forgot myself. I simply got caught up in the heat of the moment." He brushed back sweat-soaked blond hair and noted the cut in his sleeve. "This shirt cost a pretty penny. I suppose it matters little to one of your status. No doubt you'd simply order another one made by your slave labor."

"Is that what this was about? Shirts? If that is so, take your choice from among my own. A simple shirt is not worth a fight."

Bedford laughed. "You take everything far too personally, Adams."

York narrowed his eyes. "Wasn't this personal?"

Bedford's face grew menacingly dark. "No," he stated in a voice of icy calm. "If this had been personal, you would have known it."

————

York's confusion over Bedford's actions followed him into his lecture on "Political Debate and the U.S. Government." He always looked forward to this class because it provided a forum for discussion on some of the many political views of the day. In his last two years at the university, York had discovered within himself a passion for politics, and now in his last year, he had settled upon politics to be his future direction. The fencing session, however, took away some of his zest about the class. York had always managed to steer clear of trouble in school. He was generally well liked by his peers and his professors. Thus, Bedford's unwarranted antagonism was disturbing indeed.

"Gentlemen, we will come to order," a stately older man said, taking the podium.

York quickly found an empty seat and tried to focus on the professor's introduction of the subject. Professor Samuel Bainbridge was the best in his field, and York felt honored to have a place in his class.

"We find ourselves as subject to no man, save that one man whom we elect," began Bainbridge in a practiced orator's tone. "The monarchy is dead in this country, although some might debate that fact given our current President, King Andrew the First." Laughter followed this, though York could not truly agree.

York liked Andrew Jackson, a longtime friend of his father. Jackson understood the needs of the plantation owner, and York admired the way he'd handled foreign affairs. Joseph Adams had told his son that Jackson was often more bluff than gruff, and never was it so true as when dealing with opposing nations and international breeches of agreement. One of York's favorite stories, in fact, centered around the 1832 affair of Naples, in which King Bomba had issued multiple excuses for not paying the United States due monies. Jackson had taken the affair in stride and sent his commissioner to Naples to personally receive the payment. It was in true Jacksonian style that he also sent Master Commandant Daniel T. Patterson and five men-of-war ships. The ships sailed boldly into the Bay of Naples, firing their cannons, but only as an honorary salute due the king,

Jackson had stated. The apparent bluff worked, as the commissioner sailed home with the money due the U.S., and Jackson established himself as a man to be reckoned with.

The professor was continuing. "Today we find ourselves faced with an ever growing country and the problems that accompany such a state of affairs. As with any growing family, there needs to be addressed the issues of housing, clothing, feeding, and the general well-being of those involved. Jackson wears his grudges against Henry Clay as a cape of indifference towards his American System. The views of strengthening the West—albeit Jackson hails from Tennessee—appear to wane in the White House for fear of giving credit to his adversary."

"I hardly think that the reason, sir," York protested without thought.

The old man, with his thick mop of gray hair and matching gray muttonchop whiskers and bushy eyebrows, was of strict and severe temperament. He permitted debate in his class, even demanded it, but only at his bidding and never in the midst of his lectures, which he considered akin to the prophecies of God. He halted his lecture and stared long and hard at the source of interruption.

"You have something to add to this lecture, Mr. Adams?"

York glanced around him at the now silenced room. His classmates stared at him as though he'd gone mad. Richard Bedford was throwing York another smirking glare, which only had the effect of riling York further.

"I . . . I simply feel if we are to address this particular subject fairly and impartially," York began in a halting voice, "we should eliminate supposition and speak only on the facts at hand."

The professor's eyes narrowed. "And you suppose I have not done this?" His tone was indignant.

"When you make a statement such as you did, suggesting the President is opposed to Clay's proposals because of purely personal conflict, I believe you are interjecting supposition for fact."

"And what might those facts be, Mr. Adams?"

There was a steadily rising murmur from among the students, and York realized he'd opened his mouth in a way that would not allow him to simply bow out gracefully in apologetic retreat. Not that he desired to do so. Still, he'd not set out to disrupt the lecture, either.

"Henry Clay's proposed American System virtually ignores the southern states," York stated, drawing a deep calming breath. "To pay homage to the plight of the western territories and their need to sell surplus crops and livestock to the eastern coastal states, while turning a deaf ear to the equally important needs of the southern states, is signing a death warrant to that population. Clay's approach does not allow for the development of the South either through industrial incentive or through internal improvements such as railroads and highways. To ignore those states jeopardizes the very structure of southern living."

"You mean it threatens your peculiar little institution, don't you?" Richard Bedford called out.

"Slavery is not the only issue related to the South," York said with a sigh. "Not every southerner, in fact, very few southerners actually own slaves, so even if you are in opposition to that institution, you can hardly condemn an entire population."

"I condemn anyone who stands by and allows for one man to own another. Henry Clay may not come out straightforth and speak it in his proposed plans for the development of this great nation, but I believe the underlying fact remains that perhaps the South, or at least its peculiarities, should die out."

"And what would you replace it with?" York questioned angrily. "Immigrant labor of the type found in northern factories? Are those people treated any better than slaves? Nay, I for one say they are treated worse. They live in squalor, bedding down in tiny dormitories owned by the factory. They are paid a wage and then that wage is stripped from them for their room and board, leaving little with which to do otherwise. They work sometimes as much as seven days a week in twelve- to sixteen-hour shifts. Is that northern freedom and compassion?"

Richard was on his feet, as were several other students.

"They come and go at will," Richard protested, coming to stand directly before York. "They are not the property of another, and they are not bound to stay where they are oppressed!"

"Oh?" York's brows raised in question over steely blue eyes. He had inherited his father's looks and temperament as well. His cool, calm disdain for the man he would have rather considered a friend was evident only in the undercurrent of his voice. "They are free to come and go, eh? They come to America with little or nothing. They are put to work in hideous conditions for long laborious hours with few or no breaks, often under the lock and key of the owner with guards standing watch to ensure production, and you call this freedom?"

"They can leave anytime they choose." Richard's voice took on a menacing tone.

"And how would they do this?" York questioned sharply.

"Yes!" Another man, several seats away exclaimed. "How can the immigrant factory worker simply pick up and walk away? He has no hope of survival if he is blacklisted from one factory for walking out. News travels quickly, and among industry owners it travels faster still.

If a man protests his surroundings at a textile mill in Boston and leaves in hopes of finding a better position in another factory, the owners of the mill will see to it that no one else will have him. He'll be forced to come back to the first party and accept lower wages and longer hours as punishment for his actions. That is, *if* he is even accepted back. And this is freedom?"

Richard was livid. "He can always move on. Take himself west or elsewhere. There is no man holding him on a leash, forbidding him to leave. There is no threat of the whip when he refuses his lot in life."

"We do not whip our slaves!" York interrupted in rage. "My father nor his father ever had cause to whip a slave. We treat our people well. They have good housing, clothes, food. They never need worry for fear of starving or that in illness they will not have the money to obtain help. In turn, we ask for their labor in the fields and the house. Our people are treated with dignity and concern."

"Our people! Our people!" Richard mocked. "They should be no man's but their own."

"Hear! Hear!" A cheer went up from several men who'd come to take up Richard's cause.

"Gentlemen," the professor interrupted as though he'd suddenly come into the room. "Enough. Take your seats." For a moment no one moved. York was nose to nose with the red-faced Richard, his determination matching that of his classmate's in unwavering resolve.

"Another time," Richard finally murmured.

"Happily," York answered the unspoken challenge.

Hours later York was still uncertain what had sparked his anger and why he'd disrupted the entire lecture in his support of Jackson and plantation lifestyles. He'd never been called upon to truly defend his way of life before, and it bothered him greatly that those he'd thought to call friends were now indifferent to him.

He made his way across the campus, sorting through the matter in his head, when Richard Bedford's now familiar voice called out. "My father worked his own land. He cleared the ground tree by tree, and he plowed and planted without the assistance of slaves."

York looked up to find Richard directly in front of him. From the look on his face, it was clear Bedford was itching for a fight. "I refuse to apologize for a way of life that is perfectly acceptable and in no way is any of your affair," York replied.

"Are you telling me to mind my own business? Is that it?" Richard took another step forward.

"I simply remain baffled that a virtual stranger could turn so quickly into an enemy."

Richard gave his trademark smirk. "Enmity is the only course I could choose with the likes of you. I wonder," he said, sarcasm dripping from his voice, "do you defend your peculiar institution for the labor it provides you in the fields or in the bed?"

York felt his face grow hot. He'd never once been accused of the hideous thing Richard was now suggesting. "Take it back, Bedford," he stated between clenched teeth. His hands were already balled into fists.

"Why? It's no secret what's imposed upon slave women by heartless slave masters. Did you suppose we northerners couldn't figure out where mulatto children originated?"

York stared at Richard with a hard fixed look of disdain. He could form no ready words for those horrible remarks, and even if he could, Richard's question did not merit an answer.

Richard laughed at York's struggle to maintain his composure. "Perhaps you handle it as a rite of passage. Father teaches son how to carry the tradition forward. Is that how it was, Adams? Did your father take you out back and teach you to—"

Richard's words fell silent as York's fist made contact with his mouth. It was the fight York felt Bedford had desired since their fencing match. It was unfinished business as far as he was concerned. Bringing his fist back for another hit, York was blindsided by a fierce uppercut to his face. Bedford, it seemed, was blessed with the ability to project a solid left.

Reeling from the blow, York staggered several paces and shook his head to clear away the clouded image of Bedford's advancing form. Striking out with his right, York found his blow easily glanced off of Richard's brown frock coat. Without waiting for another blow from his adversary, York gave a surprising followup blow with his left and then brought the right up again and took heavy toll on Richard's midsection.

Bedford gasped for air, and York paused to give his opponent a moment to recover—that was the gentlemanly way. But Bedford had not been as incapacitated as it had appeared, or he had recovered with amazing speed. For no sooner had York stepped back than Bedford charged. Like a battering ram, he knocked York to the ground, and before York could regain his wits from this unexpected attack, Bedford began raining down brutal blows from which York could find no cover. In another moment, dizziness marred York's vision with images of two Richards, and then one of those two images made final contact with York's temple, and after that, blackness was all he saw.

Thirteen

Business Proposition

*O*n Wednesday, following the Baldwin soiree, Joseph Adams hosted a group of investors from Baltimore and Washington. Meetings of this type weren't all that unusual at Oakbridge because Joseph Adams had gained a reputation as a man who was more apt than many to lend an open-minded ear to a person's dreams. This time was different, however. This time the discussion was about a rail line, and it involved Joseph's dreams as much as those of the men he was entertaining.

Carolina had been dying to observe the meeting, but even Joseph dared not offend his guests by having a female present for business discussions. Nevertheless, Carolina contrived that the door to the study be left open a crack. Josie, a male slave who was Carolina's age, had agreed to do the deed for an extra piece of pie, which Carolina promised to bring him after supper.

Carolina perched herself in front of the door, thankful not only that the study was out of the way from the more frequented parts of the house but also that her mother was busy supervising the midday meal for all the guests.

"The problem we face on a daily basis is the ever increasing cost of laying track," a man spoke authoritatively. Carolina recognized the voice as belonging to her father's old friend Malcolm Norris.

"Yes, Norris, I can certainly appreciate the indisputable truth of ledger sheets," Joseph replied. "I see from the meticulous records your company keeps that the price of track is running roughly twenty thousand dollars per mile on the straightaways, and upwards of sixty thousand on the more difficult stretches. Does this take into account rises in cost for future track?"

A new voice replied which Carolina didn't recognize. "This is our most reasonable calculation. We've based it on the rising cost of sup-

91

plies and labor, but we feel confident it's a fair estimation."

"You have done your homework, Mr. Thomas," said Joseph. "I see you've brought something along to show me."

"This is a rough design of the track we propose to lay in the spring," said Thomas. "We'd like to seek your immediate help in this area. As you can see, the original track laid in this area will make the job of placing the second line much easier. The second, however, is quite urgent for a number of reasons. One is that the iron strap rail is grossly inefficient. There are 'snakeheads' all along the western route."

"Snakeheads?" Joseph questioned.

"Our term for protruding pieces of strap that have pulled away from the track," offered Thomas. "These are the cause of many derailments. The early sections of the line were laid using this method. Now, however, we find that the T-rail is much more efficient. This is a solid rail of iron, shaped in a 'T.' It's used all along the Washington Branch of the B&O."

"I see," Joseph replied, "and this prevents the derailment problem?"

"Well, it certainly reduces the risk. The rail can still pull away, but it is much more efficient."

Carolina heard things being moved about, the crackle of paper, and the shuffle of feet as the men no doubt gathered about the plans. How Carolina wished she could look at them, too.

"What are you doing?"

Carolina started at the intrusive voice over her shoulder. It was Georgia.

"Shhh!" Carolina hissed with her finger to her lips. "Don't want them to hear."

"Mother will skin your hide for eavesdropping."

"Don't you dare say anything!"

Georgia shrugged and moved closer to the door, her curiosity aroused, too. "What are they talking about?"

"They're asking Father to invest in the railroad," Carolina whispered. "I hope he says yes."

"What do you care?"

Afraid they would surely be discovered with Georgia's undaunted questions, Carolina tugged her sister down the hall. The rustling of their petticoats was disturbingly loud.

"Georgy, don't you see what opportunities for excitement and adventure the railroad holds? Just think if our family could be part of it. If Father invests, I want to know everything about it."

Georgia sighed. "Virginia says a proper gentlewoman shouldn't trouble herself with such things. She says it puts an undue burden on our delicate constitutions."

Carolina almost laughed that someone as spunky and irrepressible as Georgia should listen to such rubbish.

"I'm sure Virginia would say tree climbing puts an undue burden on our delicate constitutions as well," said Carolina, "but I don't see you eliminating it from your life. If she wants to choose that way, fine, but she doesn't have to choose your way and mine as well."

Georgia frowned as if her older sister had lost her senses.

"Georgy," said Carolina earnestly, "don't you have any dreams?"

"I just want to be married before I'm an old maid like Virginia. If I'm not married at sixteen, I will positively die."

With as much dignity as a thirteen-year-old could muster, Georgia flounced out of the room, leaving Carolina to dream alone.

———

Joseph's hand trembled with rising excitement as he studied the drawings spread out before him. Here it is, he thought to himself. A way to touch those distant lands I've only dared to dream of.

"Gentlemen, I am most intrigued and quite willing to consider your proposal. I would, however, appreciate a period of time in which to pray and seek other counsel."

"When can we expect your answer?" asked Philip Thomas.

At the White House he had impressed Joseph as a visionary who also had the drive to see his visions to their conclusions. Joseph found him compelling without being pushy.

Joseph peered thoughtfully into the faces of the half dozen other men. They were all board members of the Baltimore and Ohio Railroad. Some were longtime friends of his, such as Malcolm Norris; others were well-known and respected businessmen. They all impressed him as worthy of his support.

"I will have an answer for you before the month is out," he said.

"Good enough," Malcolm Norris replied. "You've been most gracious to entertain us this morning, Joseph."

"Yes, indeed," Philip Thomas said, extending his hand. "I'll look forward to hearing from you."

As the men exited the room, making their way to the dining room where luncheon was waiting, Joseph drew Norris aside. He put aside the more formal restrictions of their earlier meeting

"Malcolm?"

"What is it, Joseph?"

"Might I speak with you of a personal matter?"

"Of course. There's nothing wrong—?"

"Oh no, nothing like that," said Joseph, only imagining what his friend might be thinking. "I was wondering if you had any suggestions regarding a suitable tutor I could hire? I'm interested in someone with a broad knowledge, but specifically strong in mathematics and the sciences. And it would be an added boon if he were knowledgeable of railroads."

"Is this for your son Maine? Does he desire to become involved in the railroad?"

"No, in fact he's already off to seminary in England. It seems his thoughts lead him toward the study of theology. This is rather for . . . ah . . . well, for my daughter Carolina."

"You don't say?"

"I'm hoping the right tutor could be persuaded to overlook her youthfulness and her gender."

"You actually want your daughter to tax her mind with such things? I mean, how could it possibly benefit her?" Norris looked genuinely concerned. "She certainly wouldn't be able to use it for any purpose."

"No doubt that's true, but she has a love of things scientific and a keen, intelligent mind. And I must admit, I have a soft father's heart toward her. It surely couldn't hurt to give her a simple education." He paused, wondering if even to his friend he appeared to have lost his senses. Maybe he was crazy. But he was determined to pursue his designs. "Carolina isn't like her sisters," Joseph went on in his most convincing tone. "Don't get me wrong—she's a polished young woman, accomplished in French, sewing, elocution, and the Bible—but she has a mind that seeks out for more, a mind she wants to *use*. How can I ignore that?"

"As a father myself, I suppose I can understand," Malcolm admitted. "But can it lead to anything but heartache for her? And what if it actually did her harm?"

Joseph had always thought the notion ridiculous that an education beyond finishing school might be responsible for insanity in women. Yet it was a commonly held belief. Often higher education for women was not only frowned upon but forbidden as well.

"I would sooner cut off my right arm than see my daughter hurt," Joseph said hastily. "However, until I am convinced it truly would be harmful, I want to see this through."

"I am a forward-thinking enough man not to stand in your way."

"Then you will keep it in mind, Malcolm? And if you hear of anyone—"

"You can count on me, my friend. And perhaps my cooperation in this matter will help you keep your mind on our business proposition."

"It certainly couldn't hurt," chuckled Joseph.

PART II

Fall 1835

If railroads are not built, how shall we get to heaven in season? But if we stay at home and mind our business, who will want railroads? We do not ride on the railroad; it rides upon us.

—Thoreau

Fourteen

The Hour of Reckoning

*J*ames left the house feeling that for once, in a very long while, he had managed to make his parents happy. He had agreed during breakfast that courtship with Virginia Adams was not at all disagreeable to him, and neither did it seem to be objectionable to her. He further informed them that Saturday afternoon he would be escorting the lovely Miss Adams to the birthday party celebration of her dearest friend, Kate Milford, and that there was some talk of a harvest party to be held by the church for the young people. James was pledged to accompany Miss Adams to that affair as well, should it actually develop into more than talk.

With his mother's approving smile and his father's heartfelt "Praise be," James left for the rail yards. With any luck at all, Phineas Davis would already be there with his Baltimore entourage. They were testing a new engine today, something Davis had posted him on nearly two weeks ago. It was hard to believe a month had gone by since the Washington Branch had been opened to the public.

Whistling to himself and feeling rather happy to be alive, James enjoyed the colorful autumn day. Indian summer, he thought, and lifted his face to catch the waning warmth. Soon rain and snow would fly, and the streets would turn to complete muck, but for now, Washington City was actually a lovely sight.

His objective was the depot, which was housed in a three-story brick building just west of the Capitol, at the intersection of Pennsylvania Avenue and Second Street. The ticket office and a small car house were located here as well, and additional acreage had been purchased to expand the rail yards and build an engine house.

Narrowly missing an oncoming freight wagon and two careening carriages, James thought perhaps he should have taken a mount to the

97

station. Washington streets were not safe for pedestrian traffic. The city's geometrical streets had been laid out by L'Enfant in the fashion of spokes to a wheel. This was to provide better defense to the city, yet it had mattered little to the British when they'd advanced and burned much of Washington, including a portion of the presidential home, during the War of 1812.

Still, the nation's capital had risen like a phoenix out of the ashes and been rebuilt. Even the presidential house had been reconstructed and whitewashed, giving it the commonly used title of White House. Approaching this area, James marveled at the paved section of Pennsylvania Avenue that served as entryway to the White House grounds. This forty-five-foot-wide strip had dressed up the grounds considerably and led to landscaping, regrading of walkways, and construction of gardens. It showed a pride in the President's home that James felt was long overdue. Now the stretch between the Capitol and White House was a more picturesque walk, even if the bustling of political affairs kept many from enjoying that view.

"James Baldwin!" a voice called out from nowhere. Glancing around for the source, James smiled broadly when he found Phineas Davis striding toward him.

"You're just in time to ride back with us to Baltimore," Davis said excitedly. "You're going to be quite impressed with our speed. We coaxed her up to twenty miles per hour on the last run."

"Impressive, to say the least," James offered and clapped Davis on the back. "Congratulations."

"We had a good team," he said, falling in step with James. "No chance of cast iron where wrought iron should be. In fact, we're trying to work toward using more steel. It's expensive, though."

"But if the steel lasts longer in the life of the engine, the cost would be offset in the long run."

"That's exactly what I've proposed. We're still building them cheaper than the English and better suited for our needs."

They were at the rail yard by now, and James was eager for a look at Davis's latest design.

James waved a greeting to Eddie. The sooty-faced man hailed him exuberantly. "Ain't she a beaut?" he beamed, motioning James to the locomotive.

"I heard she did twenty miles an hour. Not bad at all," James replied. He considered the engine for a moment, noting the continued use of the vertical boilers. Many people faulted Davis's little four-wheeled engines with their vertical boilers. The new rage in train engines was for larger horizontal boilers and multiple drive wheels.

"Everything I've read seems to indicate that the real source of power and speed will be in larger boilers," James said. "But if the vertical ones were built taller, they'd never clear the tunnels and overhead bridges. Horizontal boilers seem to make a world of sense. They can be built to whatever length you choose, as well as widened somewhat. So why keep using this design?"

Davis was not offended by the question as some designers might have been, for he knew James' query sprang from his eagerness to learn rather than criticism. "The horizontal boiler does indeed mean those things you suggest. But this design works best for our line, which is mostly crooked and winding. The longer the boiler and engine, the more likely it will derail. I do have several designs for horizontals—in fact we're building a prototype—but we're just not ready to use them on the B&O because of the risk."

"Can't the line be straightened?" James asked. "I read only yesterday in the *American Railroad Journal* that most railroads are choosing to make the switch. Surely the B&O doesn't want to be left behind." Davis frowned, and James, worried that he'd insulted his friend's design, added, "But don't get me wrong, this a great engine."

"You haven't told me anything the folks back at Mt. Clare haven't. There are changes in the works. We've considered a short horizontal, but it'd mean losing out on speed and power. Most lines now boast a regular rate of fifteen miles per hour and the capability of hauling larger loads because of their more powerful engines. It really leaves the B&O no other choice. They'll have to straighten the lines."

"All of them?"

"Not so much on the Washington run, but west to Harper's Ferry is nothing but twists and turns. They'll have the trains spending more time in the ditch than on the rail if they don't straighten them out."

"Will they spend the money to do that?" James asked earnestly.

Davis shrugged. "Who knows? I've heard there are fund-raising campaigns already afoot. I know, too, there are sections of track in such bad shape they'll have to be redone in order to put any style engine on them. They followed the river too closely, so the track curves and bends along every inch of the Patapsco and Monocacy Rivers."

"You about ready, boss?" Eddie interrupted. "You're loaded with coal and water and the steam's up for the trip."

"Come with us, James," Phineas said. "In fact, ride up here with me," he added, motioning to the tender car. "I want to watch them work her over."

"I don't know," James said hesitantly. "My folks will be alarmed if I don't turn up for supper."

"We'll send someone over to let them know you'll be back late tonight. There's a shipment of flour coming down and you can hitch a ride on it. Besides"—Davis smiled down from the iron step—"I want to discuss your employment."

James brightened at this. "Employment? With you? With the B&O?"

Davis laughed and jumped onto the tender. "Yes to all three. Now, are you coming?"

"I'd be a fool not to," James declared. "Eddie, can you get one of the boys to take word to my folks?"

"You bet. In fact, I'll do it myself. I still remember the way after dragging your pathetic frame home last month." The men laughed at the memory, and James bounded up the steps to join Phineas behind the engine. This was turning out to be the best day of his life.

––––––––

James watched the hypnotic pumping of the drive rods. This design of Phineas Davis was referred to in the industry as a "grasshopper engine," due to the way the drivers stuck up like the back legs of the insect.

"We're going to push her for all she's worth," Davis yelled over the noise of the engine. The engineer nodded approvingly and passed the word to his fireman, who seemed not to have heard. The fireman mopped his brow and squared his shoulders. He'd get more of a workout than either of the other three men.

"You'll never have another ride like this," Phineas said in clear animated excitement.

He loves this engine, James thought, grinning at his friend. His own passion for the railroad was rapidly equaling that of Davis.

"Our biggest worry will be to stay out of the fireman's way!" Phineas laughed at this as though it were some kind of private joke, and James pressed closer to the tender car railing.

They passed quickly from city to countryside and were well away from Washington in a matter of minutes. The ride continued through the noisy clatter of metal on metal, hissing steam spigots, and a belching smokestack. James watched the men at work while he leisurely leaned against the railing of the car. He could never imagine working at anything else. It felt so absolutely *right*—the wind in his face, the clatter, even the jaunty sound of the whistle. The idea of a stuffy office without the sting of coal smoke and axle grease in his nose was absolutely appalling to him. As if reading his mind, Davis turned to meet his gaze.

"So, you want to work for me?" he called out without warning. James was quick to reply. "Most assuredly."

"Wait!" Davis laughed. "You haven't heard the terms. You don't know what I'm offering you yet."

"I don't care!" James yelled. "The answer is yes!"

Davis was still laughing when there was the sound of a sharp thud. James heard it but had no time to puzzle over its cause, for in the next instant the car lurched. James jerked his head around to view the locomotive, which in that very moment seemed to leap from the track. It all happened too quickly for more response than a shocked gasp. As the mighty locomotive was colliding with the earth, it pulled the tender car with it. James merely gaped in stunned silence. Then he seemed to snap back to life and instinctively reached out to Phineas even as the world began to go topsy-turvy. He caught hold of his friend's shirtsleeve, but before he could get a firm grip, Phineas was thrown forward into the engine.

James cried out, but he was too late. Phineas was tumbling headfirst into the careening engine, while another lurch sent James backward in the opposite direction. His body slammed into the railing with such force he was sure he must have bent the metal before plunging over the top of it.

The whole affair lasted only moments, though to James it seemed to go on and on. First, the sound of the engine groaning, hissing, and shuddering into silence. Then the look of shocked wonder on Phineas's face as he must surely have realized his peril. Finally, the terror in James' heart as he felt his own body hurled against the thick trunk of a towering oak. And then—silence.

It seemed as though the world fell silent at once. James thought for a moment he'd gone deaf it was so complete. A rhythmic beat was born out of the silence. Pulsating and growing louder, James reached his hands to his ears. It was a heartbeat. His heartbeat. At least he must still be alive. But for what seemed an eternity, all James could do was concentrate on breathing. In . . . out . . . in . . . out. Each pain-filled breath made him certain he'd sustained some broken ribs. But soon it wasn't good enough to just lie there breathing. He had to do something. Struggling to move—in fact, willing his body to obey his mind—James tried to rise. But he collapsed into the dirt as pain shot through him. Lifting his head, he saw Phineas lying facedown not far from the derailed engine. He didn't seem to be moving. James clawed at the dirt and tried once again to rise so he could get to Phineas and help him. But his pain was too great, and in despair James fell back once more.

All at once other sounds erupted, and James was nearly overwhelmed with the noise. Men yelling, nearly screaming, some shouting out orders and running pell-mell around him.

"Get that fire out!"

"Someone go get help!"

"The city is only a few miles back, I'll go!"

"I thought I saw a farmhouse over there."

"Where's Davis?"

The confusion assailed James from every side, and superimposed over it all was an incessant moan permeating everything. It confused James, for he could not understand where it was coming from. Searching around him it appeared no one but Phineas and himself were injured, but Phineas still had not moved. Then James realized with a start that the cries were coming from his own mouth. With each move he tried to make, his body protested in the only way it could.

Sharp pain coursed down his right side. It began like red-hot fire, branding, mutilating, destroying. He strained against it, crying out. Biting his lip and tasting blood, James tried to crawl forward.

He screamed out and his head began to swim in darkness. "No!" He fought the blackness that tried to claim him. "Phineas!"

"Easy son," a man in a black coat said, taking hold of James. "Just rest and we'll tend to you."

"No, take care of Phineas," James moaned, trying in vain to motion toward his friend.

The man glanced up, then lowered his face in a grave expression. "He's beyond caring for."

"No! No!" James twisted violently. The last thing he saw before succumbing to the pain was one of the other men placing his frock coat over the head and shoulders of the silent man. Phineas Davis was dead.

Fifteen

York's Return

*O*ctober eased in with an early winter chill to the air, a somber reminder of the days to come. Almost gone was the fragrant aroma of summer flowers, although the haunting smells of honeysuckle and gardenia still lingered in the air. The fields, once richly alive with cotton and corn, now lay fallow. The plant stubble had been plowed under as if to hide the evidence of its earlier existence.

Oakbridge bustled with activities to ready the plantation for winter. A portion of the livestock was sold off in order to keep down the cost of providing winter feed. The slave quarters were spruced up and mended as needed, and great stacks of firewood and kindling mounted up outside the barn through the arduous labor of the slaves. Elsewhere, Margaret Adams had already taken an account of the soap, candles, and food items they'd managed to produce during spring and summer. The plantation was responsible for the lives of over one hundred people, including slaves, and the obligation was taken quite seriously.

Carolina, however, spent a great deal of time stretched out on her window seat, where she watched the sad transformation of autumn to winter. The trees soon would be all bare and everything brown and dying. The house seemed too empty and quiet lately. Penny and Georgia had gone off to school; Maine and York were packed off to universities that she could only dare to dream of. Mary was napping in the nursery. Virginia was the only company Carolina had during the long hours of the grammar school. But she desired to converse only on the subject of James Baldwin, that "menace to womanhood," as Carolina was wont to call him.

How unfair life is, Carolina sighed. If not for the conventions thrust upon me, I too might be off to a university.

Her mother had desired to send her to Miss Damper's Finishing

School. This fine institute, her mother had assured her, had done wonders to transform Virginia into quality wife material. But Carolina didn't wish to become quality wife material. Marriage to any man was the furthest thing from her mind. It didn't matter that many of her friends were engaged and that some were already married. It didn't matter that her own mother had married at the age of sixteen. What mattered most to Carolina was found between the pages of books. Any book.

When I read, she thought, I am able to move beyond the four walls of my room. When I study some new subject, something that forces me to focus my attention and give my all, I can very nearly feel the blood course through my brain. When I touch the works of Shakespeare or Plutarch, I feel an understanding into the hearts and souls of mankind. How can I cast that aside in order to learn how to serve dainty teas and paint with watercolors?

There is a restlessness inside me, she thought, lifting the edge of the lacy curtain, that refuses to find peace.

Carolina stared out across the withered yard and sighed. What's wrong with me? Why can't I be content with what I've been blessed with? I've never been a greedy person or one to ask for more than what was offered, so why am I acting so contrary to the person I've always been before?

The book she'd been reading clattered to the floor, but still she could not take her eyes from the outstretched land. There is a world out there, she reasoned, that I know nothing about, except through the books I've read. A vast and wondrous place with people and sights that I might one day know. Visions of the locomotive engine loomed before her eyes. I might actually one day board the train in Washington and ride it all the way to the Mississippi. From there I could float downriver and see New Orleans, then travel west and see what all the fuss is about in that place they call Texas.

Texas . . . what am I thinking? If I could just ride the B&O to Baltimore, I'd consider it the adventure of a lifetime.

Carolina mused on these thoughts for some time when a ruckus arose downstairs that made it difficult for her to continue to concentrate on her morose reflections. Hurrying to the stairs, she was stunned to find her brother York standing in the foyer, involved in a rather heated argument with their father.

"I didn't ask to be expelled," York retorted. "I simply defended our lifestyle and your good name."

Joseph caught sight of Carolina's surprised expression and called an end to the discussion. "We'll deal with this later."

"What has happened?" Carolina asked. "York, what are you doing home from school?" Neither man seemed inclined to answer, and so she asked the question again.

"Your brother got into a bit of a confrontation," Joseph finally said.

"You mean he was in a fight?" Carolina asked, unable to hide her shock. In all her years she'd never known York to resort to fisticuffs under any circumstance. Turning to her brother, she noted the cut on his cheek and frowned. "I can't imagine you putting a hand to any man."

York seemed to calm at his sister's words. He reached out a hand and patted her soundly on the head. "It's a long story and not one fit for feminine ears."

"Carolina, leave us to talk," her father ordered. "York, we'll take this up in the study."

Carolina watched them walk down the hall. York's shoulders were hitched back, stiff in a defensive nature. Joseph's frame was just as rigid, but only in an attempt to quiet the fury that lay just within his means to control. Father and son, so much alike, she thought, that their very natures and temperaments were generally equally matched. But not this time, she had a feeling. This time was different.

———

"Father, hear me out. You have no idea what it's like up north. There is no understanding or sympathy for the plight of the South. They don't understand how the same tariff laws passed to aid them in stirring up factory productivity and industrial manufacturing could also be harmful to the South in keeping us from trading abroad. I tried to explain our circumstance, but all I got was a fistful of slavery issues and lewd innuendoes."

"People have questioned slavery since the institution was brought to this nation. Before that even," Joseph countered. "It still doesn't justify your actions in getting yourself removed from school. You were nearly ready to graduate. Couldn't you just have apologized?"

York drew a deep breath. "I refused to apologize for one very good reason. Richard Bedford not only insulted my way of life, he insulted me and impugned our good name."

Joseph sighed and threw himself into a stout leather chair. "And pray tell, how did he do this? He doesn't even know us."

York came to where his father sat. "He sees all southerners as whip-bearing plantation owners who carry on illicit affairs with their female slaves."

Joseph's eyes widened. "He said that?"

"Exactly that, though he didn't express it in such kind words," York replied, shrugging out of his hopelessly wrinkled petersham coat. He tossed it to an empty chair before continuing. "He suggested it was a rite of passage taught from father to son. I simply lost my ability to reason and could take no more. I didn't apologize because his behavior wasn't warranted. Nevertheless, no one gave me the option to apologize as a means to remain in school."

"I see." Joseph had calmed considerably under his son's explanation.

York saw that his father was past the initial shock and dismay of finding his elder son suddenly sent home in disgrace. He knew once he'd been allowed to explain the circumstances, even Joseph Adams would see the intolerable situation for what it was.

"So now what will you do?" Joseph questioned, eyeing York sternly.

"I honestly don't know." York plopped down on the chair opposite his father and folded his hands together in a pensive pose. "I know I have little desire to return to college. Especially in the North."

"But you have less than a year left to complete your degree."

"I'd have been finished now if not for that bout of measles two years ago. Besides, why should I waste my life at something I find essentially pointless?"

"If you don't desire to continue with your education," Joseph said seriously, "there is always the plantation. You are, after all, the elder son and the plantation will fall to your shoulders eventually."

York shook his head. "I've no desire to run a plantation," he stated simply.

Joseph started at the words. "No desire! Desire doesn't figure into obligation and responsibility. You have a duty to your family, and upon my death they will look to you for their well-being."

"I thought you above all other people would understand. I thought you'd remember what it was like to be forced into something you didn't want." York didn't like to cause his father pain, and from the shadow that seemed to cross Joseph's face, he knew he'd done just that. "I'm not saying that I'll never want the responsibility of Oakbridge. I'm just saying it isn't what I want at this time."

Joseph fell silent for a long time, and York knew he was probably remembering the hopeless feeling of giving up on his dreams of westward exploration. Refusing to be the one to break the silence, York studied the rows of books and waited for his father to speak.

"I suppose," Joseph finally said, his voice sounding tired and old, "I can well understand your reluctance to run Oakbridge. I do, indeed, remember the apprehension and anguish I felt upon becoming master of this plantation."

"It isn't a lack of love for my home, nor is it a lack of respect and love for you," York said, suddenly desperate that his father not see this as a personal rejection. "I truly love Oakbridge, and the life I've known here has been perfect. I fought once for this world of ours here, and I would do it again. And . . ." He let his words trail off as he considered just the right way to voice his thoughts. "I wouldn't trade my life for all the gold in the world. I love you, Father. I admire no man as much as I do you."

Joseph smiled at his son with weary resolution. It appeared to York he had battled with himself and come to at least some form of conclusion.

"If not the plantation, perhaps there is a job in Washington that would suit your interests," Joseph offered.

York perked up at this. "I would like to consider the possibility."

Joseph nodded. "On my next trip to the city, I will take you with me. We can approach some of my friends there and see what types of positions are available. In the meantime, there is always the newspaper to consider. I seem to remember advertisements for a variety of positions. Perhaps one of those would be acceptable to you."

"Thank you for your understanding, Father," York said with a genuine affection. "You won't be sorry."

———

Carolina had returned to her room and had tried to concentrate once more on *A Midsummer Night's Dream.* Then hearing footsteps pass by her door that she could identify as only York's, Carolina slammed the book closed. She knew she had to talk to him. She and her brother were close, though nearly six years separated them in age. Still, he was the brother she had always sought out for advice or consolation. She supposed she revered him a bit, as only a sister could revere her big brother.

She went to his room and knocked. "York, may I come in?" Carolina said.

"Come ahead," he answered, but in a tone that did not at once set her at ease.

Opening the door and peering in hesitantly, Carolina smiled. "If this is a bad time, I can come back."

"Nonsense." York stood over a large trunk with several items in his hands. "I was just unpacking."

"You aren't going back to school?"

York shook his head. "No. I'm done with college."

"What happened?" she asked. "How can you possibly say that you're done with college? Why, an education is practically everything."

York laughed. "And why do you say that, Carolina?"

"Because it is. There is so much to learn, York, and where else, if not the university, will you learn it?"

York put his boot brush and polish on the dresser before taking a seat on the edge of his bed. Carolina waited for him to speak and wondered if he'd consider her question too childish.

"There is always the school of life," he finally said. "I don't relish hours poring over books and the written philosophies of men I've never heard of. I'd rather hear the teachings of men who will change the future, men who might very well walk across my threshold tomorrow and say, 'You there, come along with us. We have a plan.' "

"But so much of the future has come from thoughts of the past," Carolina said. "How can you deny the importance of learning from what has gone before?"

"I don't deny it. I simply don't wish to steep myself in classes of it. I'm not unread—I enjoy a good book or newspaper now and again. But I have no real desire to waste any more of my life listening to old men prattle about the past."

"Then what will you do?"

"Father's already asked me that. I can only say again what I told him—I don't know." Carolina thought it odd that there was no real discouragement in his tone. He seemed almost invigorated by the prospect of uncertainty before him. "Father and I agreed that I would go into Washington when he next travels there, and that we would approach some of his friends with regard to employment."

"I can't believe you'd rather work at some old job than go to school," Carolina replied with a wistfulness to her tone. "I would so love to go to a university and learn all there is to know."

"Perhaps you think too highly of the university, Carolina. You can't possibly learn all there is to know in four years—perhaps not even in forty!"

"I'd like the chance to try, though!"

"Bah! What good would that do you, a woman?" York leaned back on his elbows and grinned. "You'd never get anyone to seriously consider that proposition."

"There are schools, I've heard it said, that take on women for the purpose of a college education."

"Sure, women's colleges. You could get a degree in crocheting or quilting. No wait—maybe you could graduate top in your class of china-cup painting." He laughed merrily.

Carolina felt hot tears sting her eyes. How could he be so callous? How could he be so harsh with her dreams? At one time he'd cared more about her desires than anyone else. What had happened to the brother she'd once known so well?

"School obviously has its flaws if it's made you like this!" she retorted in a huff and turned to leave.

"Carolina, wait!" York came to her and quickly turned her to face him. Seeing her tears, his expression softened. "I didn't mean to hurt you. I'm sorry for being so ill-tempered. The university has left a sour taste in my mouth—that much is true—but I didn't say those things to wound you so deeply."

"Then why?" She wiped at her eyes, wishing desperately to not appear as a sniveling female in her brother's presence.

"Because even if there were a college of credibility which would allow for your admission, what would it profit you?"

"What do you mean?"

"What could you possibly hope to gain by getting an education? You wouldn't be allowed to use it in a place of employment. No man in his right senses is going to hire a woman to work when there are fifty unemployed men standing at his door."

"What if that woman is smarter?"

"What if she is? Can she hoist a load of cotton? Can she keep banking ledgers and understand the needs of fellow businessmen? Can she run a shop based on anything of masculine interest and hope to be well thought of by her peers or even taken seriously by those who would criticize her nature?"

"Is it fair to penalize a woman for her gender? Can she not be allowed to expand her mind without facing public ridicule?" In her anger, the tears were resurfacing.

"Be reasonable, Carolina. What man would want a woman the entire world knew could outthink him? Even though I will concede there are women who are more intelligent than their husbands."

"Husbands! Who said anything about husbands?"

York laughed. "I wish you could have seen your face just now. I might as well have suggested you take a dose of castor oil."

At this Carolina couldn't help but smile. She was a bit ashamed of her outburst. "I'm just tired of everyone trying to marry me off. I have other desires right now. It isn't that I never want to marry—I just don't want it right now."

For a moment, all York could do was stare. Carolina wondered if she'd somehow managed to alienate him further.

Finally York cleared his throat. "I suppose I should tell you that I had similar words with Father in regard to my future. I told him I had no interest in running the plantation."

Surprised by this declaration, Carolina held back her questions regarding her father's reaction and said instead, "Then you should understand what it is to be expected to be one person, when inside, you're someone else entirely."

"I suppose I do."

Carolina sighed. "I'm sure if anyone can understand me, you can. You've always understood me in the past, York." She walked to the window and pulled back the curtain as she'd done earlier in her own room. "There is a whole world out there, denied to me because I am a woman." She dropped the drapery and turned. "People cover it up, put a veil over it, and expect you to forget that it's there. But I can't, York. I know it's there. Even with the drapes drawn tight and my face buried in my pillow, I know it's there. And I know it's calling me to be there, too. I want to learn mathematics and science. I want to study the stars in the sky and understand about the universe. I want to read about the countries of the world and the people who live there. Who they are, what they do, why they do it." She felt her face flush. "I want to know about locomotives and the railroad. Oh, York, don't you see? Husbands and babies will always be there for me, but an education can never be had once I'm tied to those responsibilities."

York stared blankly at her for a moment; then his eyes seemed to brighten in understanding, and he went to Carolina and embraced her warmly. "I understand. I do understand. And, Carolina, while I'm still here at home, I'll do whatever I can to help you. I'll try to teach you some of the things I've learned, although science is not one of my strong suits."

Carolina laughed and stepped away from him. "Neither would it seem that fighting is a subject to which you've taken well. Your face bears evidence of that." Then she grinned. "Oh, York, thank you so much." She reached a hand up to touch a bruised place above his eye. "I just needed someone to understand," she said softly. "I just needed to know that I wasn't alone and that somehow my dreams were attainable."

"Well, I can't get you into a university," he said in voice clearly filled with emotion, "nor can I make those around you accepting of your love for the unusual. But I will do what I can, even if it is merely listening to you."

Carolina nodded and leaned on tiptoes to kiss his cheek. "Now I know why you were always my favorite."

"Because I spoil you?" York teased.

"No," she stated quite seriously. "Because you don't run away when I show you the innermost reaches of my soul."

Sixteen

Shattered Dream

*J*ames Baldwin refused the meal set before him in spite of the look of concern that crossed his mother's face. "I'm not hungry," he stated firmly. "Please just go away and let me sleep."

"But James," Edith begged, "you must regain your strength. The doctor said—"

"I don't care! Just go!" He immediately regretted his sharp words when his mother's face fell in complete dejection. "I'm just tired, Mother," he said softly, adding a weary sigh as if to further convince his mother of his lie. "Please . . ." But he let the word fade away without stating what it was he desired. He couldn't very well speak words he didn't know, and right now he had no idea what it was he wanted.

Edith took the tray and turned at the door. "If you need something for the pain . . ."

"No, nothing. I just need to rest," James replied. In truth, the pain was nearly driving him mad, but the ghoulish dreams induced by the doctor's potions were worse by far. It wasn't until his mother had closed the door behind her that James allowed himself to grimace.

His right leg, splinted and swathed in bandages, was still swollen and the source of much of his discomfort. The doctor had commented on the nasty break, at first even voicing the possibility that James would lose the leg altogether. Pounding his fist against the mattress, James tried desperately to ignore the throbbing which radiated upward from the leg into his groin.

"Better to have let me die than live as a one-legged man," he muttered. He could only wait and watch in complete helplessness while time decided his fate, as it had that of Phineas Davis.

Phineas. The very thought of his friend seemed to block out the other harsh realities around him. James could still see the look of surprise on his friend's face when the engine had derailed. Eddie had later come to tell him that a portion of the iron rail had broken away just enough to cause the track to shift. When the engine's wheels had struck this portion of track, the thing just naturally derailed. Given their speed and Phineas's precarious perch, the fatal action had resulted in his being thrust headfirst into the iron engine. His neck had snapped and death was instantaneous. The engineer and fireman had been thrown clear, and besides James' injuries, no one else had been hurt.

"Why?" James murmured to the empty room. "Why did he have to die? Why not me also? How can I face life like this?" The very real possibility that he might never walk again, at least not without a peg or a crutch, was nearly more than James could take.

Closing his eyes, James could see it all again—it haunted him day and night. His nightmares were full of the images of crashing engines and shattered bodies. Over and over again that locomotive would be cruising down the track with laughing men aboard—oh, how that laughter pricked at him! Then, in a mere heartbeat, the laughter turned to screams and agony and the grinding of metal upon metal. James grew terrified of sleep, but waking brought little improvement. As bad as the horrible dreams were, nothing could possibly hurt more than reliving the moment when he'd known for certain that Phineas was dead.

It should have been me, he thought, and not for the first time. Life had seemed so perfect. He was going to work for Phineas and the B&O Railroad. He would have designed great engines with his mentor. Now he wondered if he could even look at another locomotive without the image of death and destruction preying upon his mind.

Looking around him, James saw the trappings of a lifetime of ease. Everything in this room was a part of him, and yet he had never felt as alienated from all that he'd once known as he did now. Dark burgundy wallpaper with tiny gold stripes and gold fleur-de-lis designs were joined midway by walnut wainscoting. James had always remembered it a warm and inviting place, but now it seemed to be a dark and brooding room.

Lead toy soldiers still stood on the fireplace mantel, symbols of happy carefree days when James had been a boy. On one side of the hearth shelves of books lined the wall, and he could see several of his childhood favorites still there. In the opposite corner a small writing desk, long outgrown by the occupant, looked as though it were simply awaiting the child who'd left it so many years ago.

Had he really been gone from home so very long? There had been visits during the five years of school up north; why, then, had he not noticed how very juvenile this room had remained? Suddenly he felt out of place. How many times had his father told him to behave like a man instead of a child? Yet now he felt like a man—an old world-weary man.

At his own request, the heavy burgundy draperies had been pulled tightly shut to keep out the sunlight, and even the flames in the hearth had died out for need of attention. Still, he could see well enough from the bedside lamp that this room belonged to a boy with dreams and hopes for adulthood. The man he now was did not belong here. In fact, he was imposing upon the fond memories once witnessed in this room.

The heavy knock on the door snapped James' thoughts back to the dreary present. "Come in," he called resolutely.

Leland Baldwin entered the room with an expression of sheer determination. "James, your mother said you weren't eating. You can't hope to recover if you don't care for your needs." He held the same tray Edith had offered only moments ago.

"I have no appetite," he replied, hoping the words would send his father away.

"Nonsense," Leland said, placing the tray on his son's lap. "You have to eat."

James barely held his temper in check. His eyes narrowed and his voice dropped to a low gravelly tone. "I am not hungry."

Leland stared at his son for a moment before replying. "Eat. That is an order."

With lightning reflexes that James had not even known he possessed, he thrust the tray from his lap, spilling it with a loud clatter and crash onto the floor. "Order all you want!" he yelled. "You've ordered my way in most every detail of life. Will you order me to live as well? Will you order the pain to cease? While you're at it, order the dead back to life, and I will honor you all of my days!"

Leland paled a bit and his jowls trembled when he spoke. "It is understandable that you mourn the loss of your friend. Your mother and I have experienced our own sorrows in wondering what it might have been like had that person laid to rest been you instead."

"I wish it had been." Even as he spat the words, James knew his father didn't deserve them. But he had so much anger inside him, it had to be released somehow.

"You don't mean that," Leland replied.

James thought he detected anger in his father's tone. "I do mean it. I have no desire to live as a cripple."

"Then you might as well wish your mother dead as well!" Leland bellowed. "Is that what you want? Do you want us dead from grief too painful to bear? Think on this, James Edward Baldwin. Would you have your mother endure the sorrow you now know? You think it bad, and granted it is a hard thing to bear, losing a friend, but you scarcely knew the man. Imagine a mother losing her child—her only child. It would kill her."

James was taken aback by his father's harsh tone. He'd received nothing but compassion and concern from both parents since the accident two weeks past. The thought of anyone, much less his mother, bearing up under the anguish which flooded his soul and the phantoms which haunted his nightmares caused James to reconsider his behavior.

He stared up at the ceiling in an unsuccessful attempt to hide his emotions. There was such a thin line between his anger and his despair. "I did not expect life to be so . . . fragile." His voice caught on the words, but he continued. "I thought youth to be excluded from this very private club of sorrows." James gave up trying to hide the tears that came to his eyes. "He was there with me alive and well, laughing and offering me the job of my dreams, and in the next moment he was gone. That's all. Nothing more remains of Phineas Davis except the locomotive engines that claimed his very life. And nothing more remains of my dream." Much to his consternation, it was this thought that grieved him as much, if not even more, than the loss of his friend.

Leland nodded sympathetically, and James thought the man looked rather awkward. His father knew well how to deal out anger and rebukes, but sympathy and tenderness were subjects of which he knew little. Still, he was showing an effort, and James thought him kind to do so.

"Railroading is a dangerous business," Leland said, clearly uncertain how to deal with his son's introspection. "I've always said it was a great risk. Maybe now you'll consider coming to work for me."

James looked at his father for a moment, then turned his eyes to the fireplace. The coals barely hinted a glow of life. "That's me," he said, motioning toward the hearth. "I'm dying out inside. Losing heat, the very thing that keeps me alive. It would be a simple thing to rekindle the flame. A little puff of air here, a bit of fuel there, and maybe with just the right amount of care, the warmth would return to burn again."

Leland's puzzled expression told James he hadn't a clue of the matter on which his son spoke. "I can have Nellie stoke up the fire," Leland told James, going to the door to call the servant girl.

James shook his head. "Do as you like, but that's not the kind of fire I'm speaking of. I'm talking about me. About my passions and dreams. I've desired to be a part of the railroad for so long now that I've had no other focus or goal within me. I burned for that goal, and the fire of desire drove me forward. Don't you see, Father? Is it really so hard to understand? Yes, Phineas is dead and that grieves me, but without my dream, what am I? Who am I? I lie in this bed and stare up at the ceiling, wondering what's to become of me. Phineas's future is decided for him, but what of me? What of my future? Does that sound selfish? Am I a horrible person for grieving more for my lost life than for Phineas's?"

Leland grimaced. "I fear your medication has caused you confusion. I'll get Nellie in here, and she can clean up this mess and build you a cozy fire. Would you like something to read?"

James sighed. His father had no mind for dealing with another person's anxieties and fears. Especially when they were those of his son. "I don't need anything"—he paused and looked away—"or anyone."

If only that were true! He had never felt more needy in his life, not only in his body, but in his heart as well. And the worst of it was that he could not make himself believe there was hope for anything better. He feared he'd always be as he now was. Lost, impotent, angry, heartbroken. A skeleton of a man held together only by despair.

Seventeen

The Cost of Fear

*T*hree days later the doctor visited and, for once, left the sickroom without that grim look in his eyes.

"Ah, Leland!" he said as he met the elder Baldwin downstairs in the parlor. "To be young! It never ceases to amaze me what the miracle of youth does for the healing process."

"Are you saying James will be all right?" Leland chose his words cautiously, afraid to get his hopes up.

"The boy's leg is mending nicely. We will have to keep it splinted and immobile for some time yet, but he is well past the worst of it."

"He won't lose the leg?"

"I believe I can safely say he won't. Beyond that, of course, we must wait and see. But with proper care, I do believe he can expect full, or practically full, use of his leg."

"Thank God!"

"I am, however, concerned with his mental healing. He seemed not nearly as elated over my news as one might expect."

"He took the death of his friend quite hard."

"Well, we must work on lifting his spirits."

"What do you suggest?"

"I'm going to send over some crutches this afternoon. Getting out of that bed will work wonders, I am certain. He mustn't put any weight on the leg, and make sure he only gradually extends his activities."

But when the crutches arrived, James greeted them and what they represented with little enthusiasm. He did make use of them, yet he smiled little and continued to be quiet and withdrawn. Leland had no idea what else to do for his son. Finally desperate, he procured several old issues of railroad periodicals. Leland was willing to concede to James' previous interest if it would do the boy some good. But James politely thanked his father and laid aside the material unread.

Then one day, after a week, Leland had an inspiration. He went to the rail yards and spoke to the manager who knew James. Leland was also introduced to several of James' other friends—common sorts mostly, but if they were able to help his son, he'd be more than willing to rub shoulders with them.

———

James was sitting in a chair in his dark room trying unsuccessfully to focus his attention on a newspaper when the visitors arrived. He couldn't very well refuse them, so he told Nellie to send them up. But the last thing he wanted was to entertain railroad people.

Eddie, Tommy, and Dale Collins came into his room with friendly cheerful greetings. James tried to respond in kind, but the smile he wore felt like a paper mask.

They filled him in on all the latest happenings and gossip at the rail yard. James politely nodded, pretending he was interested. He didn't know why he wasn't. It made him extremely uncomfortable to hear about the railroad, or even think about it. He knew there was more to it than simply his grief over Phineas, but he could not identify what was bothering him—in truth, he was afraid to identify it. Yet even before his friends had arrived, James had been experiencing an odd discomfiture whenever he thought about the railroad.

"Your father tells us you are getting up and around now," said Eddie. " 'Tis wonderful news!"

"We'll have you down at the yards and back to work before you know it," said Tommy.

"I don't know . . ." James squirmed uncomfortably in his chair.

"Why wait? That is, if you're up to it, Jimmy me boy," said Eddie enthusiastically. "We got a new engine in a couple days ago. It's only a prototype, but it was one of Phineas's last designs."

"Phineas. . . ?"

"It's his design for a horizontal boiler," Dale explained.

"They finished it?"

"Sure. In his honor, you might say."

"Why don't you come down and see it?" asked Tommy. "Your pa said you can get up."

"That's true, but . . ." James could not think of an excuse. So Phineas's prototype was finished. James thought of Phineas's excitement for the project and how, before the accident, he himself had longed to see it. Now . . . it just didn't seem right when the designer himself would never see the finished result of his labors. Yet by refusing to go,

James felt a bit as though he were turning his back on his friend. He was torn, wanting to go, longing to once again be among the things he so loved; yet he was oddly reluctant.

"Don't you worry. We'll give you a hand," said Eddie, misinterpreting James' hesitation.

In the end James couldn't say no. He was growing weary of his self-pity. Getting out might be just the remedy he needed to rise from the awful slump he had been in lately. Maybe it would even help him get over his friend's death.

He couldn't deny the surge of excitement he felt when he and his friends arrived at the rail yard. The smells of metal and grease and the burning of the forge; the sounds of machines, men yelling, hammers clanking; the sights . . .

Yes, it was good to be back. He was almost overcome with how much he felt he belonged here. At first it was easy to ignore that gnawing disquiet he also felt.

Phineas's engine was a beauty, a fine tribute to the man's talent. James recognized the 4–2–0 design immediately. John Jervis had created the design in 1831, but as was often the case, he hadn't patented the engine and freely gave it as his contribution to the industry. Now it was one of the most popular designs. Jervis, knowing that the curving uneven American tracks were a problem for many lines, had lengthened the wheel base and added swiveling lead wheels. This was a masterful stroke of genius, and while swiveling wheels had been used in England to follow the large drive wheels, no one had yet put them on the front to help guide the train on the tracks. Phineas had obviously studied this design and converted it for use with the B&O's twisted tracks.

Awkwardly maneuvering the crutches, James approached it with a kind of reverence. His friends, flanking him, understood and beheld it in the same manner. The horizontal boiler engine seemed almost foreign in a place where only vertical grasshopper engines had traveled before. James studied the wood lagging surrounding the boiler's waist. These narrow wooden strips were designed to hold in precious heat and conserve fuel. Even a stationary boiler could show a heat loss varying from twelve to twenty-five percent. A moving engine was a greater liability still. As air passed over the boiler's surface the effect was heightened, and in cold weather it became a very disagreeable situation.

"Lagging, eh?" James murmured, continuing to note the differences. Glancing up he saw the large black smokestack. A steady stream of smoke oozed from the opening. She was fired up and ready for action. The very thought caused James to involuntarily shudder.

" 'Tis too bad he never got to ride it," Eddie said in a hushed tone.

James only nodded, a lump in his throat preventing speech.

"Come aboard, Jimmy. See her up close," Tommy encouraged. "Duke won't mind."

"Duke?" James questioned in a hesitant voice.

"He's my fireman. Hey, Duke, this here is a friend of Phineas Davis. James Baldwin's his name."

Duke, a coal-smeared youngster, barely old enough to be called a man, looked down from the platform and gave a nod.

"Come on, Jimmy," Eddie encouraged, "you might as well have a look around."

"I don't think I could with these—" He gave one of his crutches a shake.

"We'll help you."

"Well—" But before he could finish, several hands were hoisting him onto the engine. He was set on the locomotive platform as smoothly as if his friends were experts at handling cripples. James' sudden light-headedness seemed to have nothing to do with the procedure. He gripped the rail, fearing he might lose his balance. His hand shook.

At that moment the station manager ambled by. "Are you fellows going to take James for a ride?"

"There's an excellent idea!" exclaimed Eddie. "How about it, Jimmy?"

James' mouth was dry. He wanted to tell them no, but, again, he couldn't. He felt himself nod.

"Get her steam up, Tommy!" called Eddie.

Tommy nodded to Duke, who began dumping even greater quantities of coal into the firebox. Swinging the coal shovel to and fro, he narrowly missed James' crutch.

"It ain't no race," Eddie growled. "Watch out for his leg."

The fireman grunted in reply, lost in the rhythmic loading of the coal. When Tommy was satisfied, he began cranking the bell back and forth.

Clang. Clang. Clang. It was a warning to those who waited below to clear the track.

"They didn't put a whistle on," Eddie said, as if James had asked a question. "What with her being a prototype and all, they figured they'd save money."

Clang. Clang. Clang.

The sound set James' nerves on fire. With every sound of the bell and hissing groan of the engine, he felt an odd sensation grip him. What should have been a wonderful moment was rapidly spiraling into a nightmare.

Tommy eased the lever forward and grinned. "Here we go!"

The moment the locomotive lurched, James knew it was a mistake. His stomach knotted and an awful cold chill washed over him, accompanied by rising nausea. His hands grasped the rail so tightly his arms began to ache, but that was the least of the awful physical afflictions assailing him.

Stop! James wanted to yell, but his lips were frozen; he couldn't speak. The machine rolled forward while his chest constricted. What was happening?

In a few minutes they were away from the yard and moving into the countryside. James had not yet moved a muscle. Duke and Tommy were busy tending the engine, and even Eddie, caught up in the moment, didn't seem to notice his distress. He tried to shake it off but with no success. It only became worse. He broke into a cold sweat, still shaking—all over now, not just his hands. He closed his eyes hoping to steady himself but was rewarded only with a horrifying image—an engine heaving up upon its rail and tumbling over and over in a deadly somersault. He opened his eyes with a strangled cry that thankfully was swallowed by the roar of the engine.

He was going to die!

His body was going to be crushed and mangled by the gears and metal of this monstrous machine. It was going to take his life as it had Phineas's. It had already smashed his dreams, but it would not be satisfied until it had obliterated all remaining life from him.

Stop!

But only his trembling lips formed the words. He had to get off. He had to save himself. He didn't want to die.

"Stop! Stop! Stop!"

He only realized that sound had escaped his tortured lips when Eddie appeared at his side.

"Something wrong, Jimmy lad?"

James turned his head slowly, stiffly, as if he himself were a machine. He was panting hard as if he had just run a race. But seeing Eddie's solid friendly countenance helped snap James' mind back to a semblance of sanity.

Still he couldn't speak.

"Is it your leg, lad?" asked Eddie.

James grasped desperately at the excuse. He nodded, then forced out the words, "The pain . . ."

"Ah, was foolish of us to take you out. The jostling is too much," said Eddie. "We'll get you back right away, lad."

The few minutes it took to return to the yard were torture, not, of course, to James' leg, but to his mind. His distress did not cease until several minutes after he stepped off the locomotive. Eddie and Tommy felt terrible, too, thinking they might have brought on a relapse. And though James knew it was cruel of him, he said nothing to dispel their fears. How could he admit to them that his leg was not the problem? He could barely admit it to himself. The truth was too awful to face, much less speak of. Yet James knew enough to identify the cold nausea and other symptoms he had experienced as only one thing: fear.

And he realized, if vaguely, that this was the nebulous emotion that had been troubling him all along. The accident had made him deathly afraid of riding the locomotive.

Back home in the safe loneliness of his room he berated himself for his weakness. He had become as fainthearted as a woman. What kind of man was he that he couldn't rise above a mere accident? He'd fallen from a tree once when he was a child and battered himself pretty badly, but that hadn't stopped him from climbing other trees. Had he been braver as a twelve-year-old than he was now?

But it had been different then. He'd had no concept of death as a child. Now he *knew*. Death might be waiting around any corner to reach out and grab him, as it had Phineas. And the locomotive, as nothing else, stood in his mind as the embodiment of death. With its flaws and its belching fire and its hard crushing iron, it seemed more a weapon than a vehicle.

Yet fear of death could not be the only reason for his violent reaction to riding the locomotive. He'd had no problem riding the carriage to the yard—and heaven knew the Washington City roadways could be deadly at times!

James shook his head. He could sit for the rest of his miserable life trying to figure out what had happened, but he didn't want to. He did not want to think of it at all. The very *thought* of the locomotive made him tremble like a silly girl. His only hope seemed to be in simply staying away from the railroad.

Simply!

He might as well have been made a cripple by the wreck. But what else could he do? Maybe it would get better with time. Maybe someday . . . but if that never happened, would it be so bad? He always had the bank. But that thought made him nearly as sick as that of the railroad.

"You are a pitiful creature," he mumbled to himself as he went to his bed, stretched out, and tried to sleep. Could his life be over before it had even had a chance to begin?

He fell into a fitful sleep, filled with broken dreams and belching iron monsters.

Eighteen

Joseph and Margaret

The late afternoon was chilly and clouds were rolling in. A typical autumn afternoon, but the clouds had dark edges as if building up for a good drenching. Joseph walked with Margaret in the garden as she inspected the few remaining flowers. He didn't mind the chill, and Margaret was always quite relaxed when in her garden, her special place in which she took great pride. This would be the best time he'd ever find to discuss with her the matter of York's troubles at school.

In the time since his and York's talk, Joseph had not had a chance to speak to his wife about the situation beyond a few vague comments. And Margaret—God bless her!—understood his moods well enough to wait until he was ready to talk. He supposed he had needed time to adjust to this abrupt change in his son's direction in life . . . time, too, in order to accept the fact that his firstborn son had no interest in his beloved plantation. He still hadn't fully adjusted, but he knew it was time to draw his wife into the situation.

"Margaret—"

But just as he spoke she lifted a leaf of a dahlia and grimaced. "Oh, look at this—more snails. I thought I had them under control." She turned to the slave who was making the rounds of the garden with her. "Andy, run into the kitchen and fetch a box of salt. I don't want these snails to get out of hand again."

"Yes, ma'am!" said the old man whose main job it was to make sure Margaret's garden remained the talk of Falls Church. He was too old to work at any other task on the plantation, but Margaret never failed to make him feel the most important man on the estate. He hobbled back toward the house.

"Now, what was it you were saying, Mr. Adams? Forgive me for interrupting you."

122

"Not to worry, my dear. I enjoy the garden almost as much as you and want to see it thrive. But do you think you should be outdoors after being under the weather last week?"

"I am in perfect health now," she said. "And the garden has been so lovely this year, I want to ensure the last blooms are not neglected."

"Well, I must say, the dahlias are a fine grand finale to the season."

"The roses, too, have been remarkable. And still blooming this late. Andy has worked wonders keeping away the aphids."

Her eyes danced as she inclined her head toward the section of roses. Joseph hated to disturb the moment with an unpleasant discussion. But he and Margaret had always dealt with the children together, both equally involved with decisions and discipline. They might not always agree, but they usually supported each other. It hadn't been fair of him to keep quiet this long about York.

"Margaret, can we discuss York?"

"I thought that's why you came out, Mr. Adams."

"Did you, now?" His eyes danced with amusement and wonder at his wife's perception.

"You had such a serious look on your face, and the matter of York's expulsion from school is the most serious matter confronting us at the moment."

"I appreciate your patience with me regarding my silence," Joseph said. "I did not want to leave you out, but—"

"Say no more, Mr. Adams. I perfectly understand your reticence. But now that you do want to talk, I am listening." She smiled warmly.

He related the details of his conversation with his son. "I don't feel inclined to block his desires," he said with a weary sigh, indicating it wasn't something he did with ease. "And it may be that if we let him get a taste of the real world, so to speak, he may see for himself the need to finish his college education."

"Yes, that sounds wise, but what if he lands on his feet and finds he doesn't need to finish his final year of college?"

"I see nothing wrong with that. If he is happy and content, then what else matters?"

"Yes . . ."

They had come to the end of the garden nearest the house, and Margaret had completed her daily tour. They started walking toward the house.

"Mr. Adams, I have to admit that I had hoped he would finish. So many of our friends' sons have graduated college. James Baldwin has received two degrees. I . . . suppose I don't want anyone to think less of York."

"York is a fine young man, every bit as intelligent as the Baldwin boy," said Joseph with conviction. "Our York will go far in life, with or without that final year of college. Mark my words!"

Leaving the garden path, they walked around to the back of the house and to the entrance, via a long porch that led into the kitchen. They met Andy as he was coming down the porch steps, carrying a large box in both hands.

"Very good, Andy," Margaret said. "Now, dose those snails good. I can't stand the thought of them harming my dahlias!"

On entering the kitchen, they found the place a bustle of activity with preparations in progress for supper. But adding even more energy to the scene was the presence of little three-year-old Maryland, who had come to the kitchen on some errand with Hannah, though it appeared to Joseph as he stepped into the room that the mammy's errand was merely gossiping with the kitchen women.

Maryland ran up to her parents with exuberant greetings. It was difficult to continue the previous conversation, and Joseph wished he had suggested they take another stroll through the garden. There was one other thing he wanted to speak to his wife about, and he doubted she would now have time to return to the garden. He did manage to get her away from the distracting kitchen. In the foyer, they paused at the door to the small family parlor.

"Mrs. Adams, there is another matter I wish to mention. I plan to go to Washington City within the next few days."

"You intend to make the trip with rain threatening as it is?" Margaret asked her husband in surprise.

Maryland, the youngest of the Adams clan, had followed them from the kitchen and now ran circles around her parents as they spoke. Joseph opened the door to the parlor and they went in.

"We'll be well ahead of any rain. Besides, York and I will hardly melt."

"So you're taking York as well?"

"Taking York where?" asked Virginia as she swept into the room.

"Your father is going to the capital."

Virginia's face puckered into an instant pout. "And I suppose I cannot go along?"

"Sorry, Virginia," said Joseph. "As your mother just mentioned, it's threatening rain any minute. Besides, the trip will be a brief one. I have papers that must be delivered and several people I must meet with. All business, you see."

"It would have been a good time for me to pay my respects to James Baldwin. I haven't seen him at all since his accident." She seemed to

Joseph to be less concerned about the man's well-being than she was about being deprived.

"Why don't you send a letter with your father?" offered Margaret. "I'm sure Mr. Baldwin would appreciate it."

"And," said Joseph, "if you tell me of some trinket you have your heart set on, I might be able to include a bit of time for shopping."

Virginia's face lit up at this. "Papa, I would very much like a new gown. Could you bring home some material? Several bolts of silk, perhaps, so that I can choose?"

Somehow this request didn't surprise Joseph. His pretty dark-haired daughter loved little else as much as she adored clothes and all the accessories that accompanied them. This was far more in character than her sitting by the bedside of an injured suitor.

"What is all the commotion?" asked Carolina, who was passing by, an open book in her hands.

Margaret sighed and gave her eyes a roll. "I feel like the Pied Piper—attracting children wherever I go!"

Joseph laughed. He knew his wife loved nothing more than to be surrounded by her children.

"And what about you, Carolina?" Joseph asked, his spirits rising.

"I beg your pardon, Father. I didn't hear what you asked."

"I'm going into Washington City and thought perhaps you might like me to bring you back some trinket," said Joseph.

Carolina's eyes widened and delightful anticipation clearly shone on her face. "Papa, do they have books on locomotives?"

"Carolina, whyever would you wish to read such a thing even if there were?" her mother questioned; then, not waiting for an answer, she cornered Maryland and retied her hair ribbon for the third time that morning.

"I'm very interested in the railroad," Carolina explained, and Joseph thought she was making a great effort to be patient. "Do they have such books, Papa?"

How very typical that he should buy Virginia a dress and Carolina a book. "I would imagine there might be a few. It is a relatively new subject in this country. I'll do what I can."

"Oh, thank you!" Carolina exclaimed. Her eyes sparkled with a fire that reminded Joseph of his own passions for the new railroad.

"And, Virginia," he said, turning to his eldest daughter, "I will bring back the best material money can buy."

"I'm going to start planning the dress right now!" Virginia's eyes matched her sister's in anticipated delight. Then she added almost as an afterthought, "After I write that letter, of course!"

Joseph chuckled at Virginia's childlike glee; it was far less typical than her request for a dress. True, she was eighteen and a woman, but he thought she had always tried too hard to be grown up. Even when she was ten she had been far more concerned with proper decorum than with usual childhood pursuits. Thus, it pleased Joseph to see her practiced ladylike facade slip, even if only momentarily.

Joseph turned to Margaret. "And what about you, Mrs. Adams? A new gown for you as well?"

Margaret smiled, seeming to forget her concerns about Carolina's request. "I've clothes enough for now. However, perhaps you could bring me some new embroidery thread. I find my supply is dwindling. And, of course, you won't forget the other children."

"Certainly not. I'll go now to take their orders."

"Me, Papa, me!" Maryland stopped her cavorting and looked up at her father. "Me go, too." She held up her arms to her father.

Joseph leaned down and picked her up. Her dark brown curls framed a dainty, almost cherubic face. "I cannot take you this time, Mary, but Papa will bring you back some rock candy."

"Yes, yes! Candy!" Maryland clapped her hands, then reached them up to caress her father's face. "I wuv you, Papa." She placed a wet kiss on his cheek, then squirmed to be put down.

The minute her feet touched the floor, Maryland went running out of the room chanting, "Candy, candy. Papa get me candy!"

Joseph exchanged a look with his wife. Margaret seemed displeased with his promise to Maryland. "A very little bit of candy will not hurt," he said. "Now, I must make some preparations for the trip."

"How long do you plan on being away?" asked Margaret.

"I should be home within the week."

Margaret looped her arm through her husband's. "I will miss you, Mr. Adams." Her displeasure was forgotten as they moved toward the stairs.

"And I will miss you, my dear—"

"Mr. Adams, careful how you speak in front of the children," she scolded, but not harshly.

"They should know you are dear to me, wife. An occasional term of endearment can do no harm." He looked down at her. After twenty-two years of marriage and nine children, Margaret Adams was still as lovely as she had been on their wedding day. And he well knew there was far more to her than the reserved and proper shell she revealed to the world. "Now, perhaps you can help me pack, my d—ah, that is, Mrs. Adams," he said tenderly.

126

As they began their ascent up the stairs, Maryland raced past them still singing, "Candy! Candy!"

"Mary!" Margaret called. The child ignored her mother and jumped down the last two steps before turning to race back to the top. "Maryland Adams!" Margaret scolded. The precocious child turned with a grin. "Stop running on the stairs. Young ladies do not run."

Maryland's only response was a giggle before she took off in another streak.

Margaret sighed and looked at her husband. "Where does she find the energy?"

"I remember when the other children were small and there were four running the stairs at once." Joseph laughed at the pleasant memory.

"Maryland makes up for four," said Margaret wearily.

Nineteen

Oakbridge Tutor

*B*aldwin!"

Leland Baldwin glanced toward the street and saw Joseph Adams alighting from a cab. He quickly pocketed his timepiece and straightened his coat. He had been on his way to a meeting with a local merchant regarding a sizable loan and was running late. But Leland stopped and gave his full attention to Adams. After all, the prospect of receiving some of the Adams fortune was far more important than his shelling out money for a loan.

"I had no idea I might run into you today, but it was just in my mind to look you up," said Joseph, extending his hand as soon as his feet touched the street.

"Adams, it's good to see you. I'm on my way to the bank. Why don't you come over and sit a spell with me?"

"I'm sorry, but I can't just now. My son York is meeting with Mr. Brubaker about a job."

"I didn't realize York was finished with school. Is he out on winter interim?"

Joseph pulled his heavy outer coat closer and his brow creased. "Ah, no . . . that is to say . . ." He shifted uncomfortably. "York has decided to take a break from college and formal education. He desires to go to work right away. You know, see if he can make it without the tedium of finishing an education."

"Not everyone is cut out for the scholarly life. I know I wasn't," said Leland.

"Nor was I. But a college education is becoming more and more important to success."

"We didn't do too badly, now did we?" Leland chuckled, then added more earnestly, "I wish I could offer him a position at the bank, but I'd like to believe James might be taking on those duties as soon as he's fully recovered from the accident."

"Ah yes. How's he doing?"

Leland shrugged, wishing he knew the answer. "It's been almost four weeks. The leg seems to be mending just fine, something the doctor wasn't even sure was possible. He's up a bit, on crutches, but has no real interest in much of anything. I suggested he come down to the bank, but he's stuck his nose into a few of his old books and nothing else seems to attract his attention."

Joseph was quiet for a moment, then said, "You know, James might be able to help me out. In fact, the more I think of it, the more ideal I think he might be. Do you think he'd be interested in doing some tutoring?"

"I thought you said York had given up on school."

"He has, but this would not be for him. You see, I've wanted to hire someone to privately tutor Carolina," Joseph replied, then held up his hand as if to ward off the expected assault. "I know how inappropriate extensive schooling is for a woman, but Carolina, like your James, has an interest in the railroad and the book learning that goes along with it."

"James doesn't hold much interest in the railroad now," Leland stated honestly. "The accident took the life of a man he greatly admired."

"Yes, I read that Phineas Davis was killed. Strange how no one else but James was injured. Hand of God watching over them, if you ask me."

"I tried to tell James that, but he's angry at the loss. Thinks God has set out to personally offend him, or some such nonsense. Who can tell? I can scarcely get two coherent words out of him at a time. He's always talking nonsense about life and death and the inner fires of his soul."

Joseph nodded indulgently. "I think I can understand. Perhaps a change of scenery would do him good. What with his injuries, I think it would be most appropriate that he come live at Oakbridge. He could tutor Carolina in return for room and board, in addition to a generous salary." Joseph nudged Leland with his elbow. "There would even be the added advantage to him of spending more time with Virginia."

"Is she still interested in him, even now after the accident?" Leland immediately began to think of the possibilities.

"I am fairly certain she is. She's wanted to visit him but felt it out of line to come alone. She's tried to get her mother and me to come pay our respects, but this is the first time I've come anywhere near Washington since the accident, and Margaret has been under the weather with a spell of catarrh. Nothing serious, just a great deal of unladylike nose blowing, and you know how our very proper ladies can be about public displays of illness. Virginia's nursed her mother faithfully, but I tease her that it's more for the purpose of getting her on her feet and to Washington than for making her mother feel better. She would have come with me now except for the inclement weather."

Leland felt a flicker of hope. Virginia Adams was still interested in courtship with his son! Good thing, too. Things were getting no better financially. Deals he'd made in good faith only weeks ago were already showing problems. Then, too, he needed desperately to travel north to see his brother Samuel regarding their private ventures, but James' accident had forced him to remain close to home.

"I'd like to present the idea to James," Leland finally answered. "I think it's a good one, but it is hard to tell these days how my son will respond to anything."

"I am certain he would be welcomed with open arms—by everyone!" Joseph added that last with a wink.

"Joseph, are you saying that an engagement could be expected soon?"

"I'm sure with James staying at Oakbridge, the course of—how shall I put it?—true love would be greatly expedited."

"Perhaps," said Leland with cocky confidence, "even by Christmas."

Joseph laughed. "Well, maybe not that soon, but certainly by spring, eh?"

Leland forced a laugh and thought to himself that spring might well be too late. "Do you see him tutoring at Oakbridge all that long?"

"Certainly as long as it takes for him to fully recover and desire to move on," Joseph replied. "I've heard tell his full recovery will be slowed by the extensive damage done his leg. If that's true, I can certainly extend my home to him for however long he might need. We can arrange rooms on the first floor for his own use, and, of course, I would personally see to the arrangements and the actual move to Oakbridge."

"I'll speak to him later today. How long will you be in town?"

"Two or three more days. We have a room at the Brown Hotel. Send word there and I'll be happy to personally present the idea, in full, to James."

"I'll do that. You'll hear from me by nightfall."

Leland walked away with a new air of confidence and hope. If he could put James under the roof of Joseph Adams, then courtship with Virginia Adams would be assured. What sensitive young woman could resist nursing and pampering the man of her desires? Given Miss Adam's obvious concerns and interest in James, Leland felt certain she would manage him quite well.

————

"The answer is no!"

"James, you need to listen to reason," Leland said in complete and utter calm as he sat in the darkened bedroom in a chair adjacent to where James sat with his leg propped up on a footstool. "I've invited Joseph Adams to come to tea this afternoon and discuss the matter in full. You will listen and you will be interested."

"Don't tell me what to do!" James snapped, then grabbed his crutches and struggled to his feet, as if he could easily escape his father's will. He hobbled across the room to the door. The right leg dragged considerably, and pain shot through his body like a white-hot fire. Grimacing, James gave up and returned to his chair.

"Why are you forcing this upon me?" James said, panting from the exertion of his effort. "Haven't I endured enough?"

Leland seemed to recant his former firmness. "I'm sorry, son. You know the reasons why I need you to marry. Miss Adams is a marvelous girl, and she holds great concern for you and your condition."

"She has no qualms about marrying a cripple?"

"The doctor now assures us you will recover fully—"

"Three weeks ago he thought I'd lose my leg! He knows nothing."

"I wish to hope for the best, and it appears Virginia Adams does the same."

"But tutoring her sister? What can be more demeaning?"

"Any port in a storm, son."

"You are not the ship being forced to go where you do not wish to go. But then . . ." James paused and sighed heavily. "Who says I am fit for anything else, or that I care for anything else? I haven't the courage to end my misery, so it makes perfect sense for me to spend my days in the company of girls." He laughed dryly. "And now it seems that particular girl has far more gumption than I possess. She'll get her education one way or another."

"Stop that kind of talk!" exploded Leland. "You have only yourself to blame if you have no ambition. The accident was a terrible thing, but it wasn't the end of the world. But for now others will have to have gumption for you. We will have to force you to do what is right."

"And I suppose I must go along like a lamb led to the slaughter—"

His father's face grew taut and crimson with his angry retort. "If you care about this family you will do as I request. If not, I'll cut you off without further consideration."

James laughed. "You wouldn't do that to Mother."

"No, I wouldn't. It would be *your* doing entirely!"

Leland's words stung as James knew they had been intended to do.

James realized the battle was lost. To turn his back on his mother's needs was something he could not bring himself to do. He had already put her through too much anguish. His father had made it very clear that without his cooperation and marriage to a rich young woman, there was only doom and destruction in the family's future. James' original purpose in agreeing to his father's proposition—that he would marry Virginia in return for being allowed to pursue his railroad career—had now diminished. He no longer cared about the railroad. He couldn't even think about the cursed business without breaking into a cold sweat! Yet he was not so selfish that he could turn his back completely on the needs of his family.

At the sound of the front door bell, James looked up. "I suppose that is him now?"

Leland nodded. "Will you help me or not?"

"What choice do I have?"

———

The mulatto, Nellie, finished serving beverages to Leland, James, and their guest, then offered tea cakes and tarts filled with all types of jellies and fruit. It was an effort for James to be sociable. He'd seen no one besides his family and the doctor since that fateful visit from Eddie and the others. He wondered if he could have so soon forgotten the social graces. Glancing toward the French doors he noted the steadily falling rain. A perfect accompaniment to sealing what he viewed as his dreary future.

"That'll be all, girl," Leland barked. "Just leave the tray there on the table. We'll serve ourselves." She nodded and hurried from the room, sliding the double doors together to afford the men privacy.

"I'm delighted to hear your recovery is progressing so well," Joseph told James as he lifted his cup of black coffee.

"James is frustrated that he must crawl before he can walk," Leland remarked, watching James for some reaction.

"Father forgets I already knew how to walk. It's the relearning that causes me grief," said James, purposely averting his eyes, pretending to concentrate on adding cream and sugar to his tea.

"And I can well imagine the pain is such that you struggle to keep your focus elsewhere," said Joseph.

James sensed the compassion in Joseph's words. But his response was dry, perhaps even harsh. "I get by."

"Certainly. The fact that you're sitting here receiving me is proof of that. I can't tell you how happy I am that you've agreed to hear my proposal. I've been laboring over this for some time, in fact, since the opening of the Washington Branch of the B&O." Joseph's face registered instant regret for having made mention of the railroad, the cause of James' accident.

"Please go on," James said kindly, taking pity on the older man.

"It's just that since then, Carolina has had her eyes opened to the railroad and locomotives. Though I must say she has always had a mind for things scientific."

"I remember," said James, and his expression momentarily softened as he recalled happier days.

"The railroad has only been a recent catalyst to open my eyes to the strength of her desire to learn. She desires to be educated beyond her grammar school. To her way of thinking, finishing school is out of the question because she has little interest in learning how to properly entertain, when she's watched her mother do it all of her life. Carolina is well finished enough, but her mind seeks out things like science and mathematics."

"Can she ever hope to utilize those things, even if she has the ability to grasp them?" James questioned.

"If anyone can find a way to do so, it will be Carolina. She has a quick mind and a stubborn nature. That nature serves her well when it comes to learning a new subject. It caused more grief when it came to doing things she had little desire for," Joseph said with a smile. "She's a good girl and I feel it can't possibly hurt her to learn these things. So what if she later puts them aside to marry and bear children? She will at least have touched a bit of her dreams."

"Better some small portion than none at all, is that it?" James' gruff tone momentarily returned.

Joseph eyed James with perplexity for a moment. James wondered if he'd gone too far. He knew from his father's worried expression that he was deathly afraid James would botch up the entire matter.

After several uncomfortable moments of silence, Joseph finally spoke. "I put aside certain dreams when I took on the responsibility of becoming a plantation owner. Dreams that were important to me." He breathed deeply and continued. "Carolina is special to me—I suppose, in part, because she is very much like me. I'd like to see her obtain her dream, but it seems unadvised to attempt a university education at this point. If you can find it in your heart to overlook her gender . . . forget that she's a young woman . . ."

James heard little past that point. Forget she was a woman, indeed! He'd thought several times of the dark-haired woman-child, with her eyes all afire. Carolina had spirit and a streak of tenacity that said to everyone around her, "I am capable of daring great things!" Her sister might be the beauty of the family, but Carolina was unique in her own way, and while he had never seen the sense in giving a woman too much education, he admired Carolina's perseverance.

Joseph was saying, ". . . and so, you see, I believe it will be beneficial to both of us."

James stared blankly at Joseph Adams, realizing he'd missed part of his statement. But even without having heard the man's words, he could well imagine what had transpired in the speech. No doubt, between his father and Adams, plans were already being laid for the joining of the two families.

James acted as though he'd not missed a single word, and at the same time steered the conversation from where he knew it would eventually lead. "Do you have in mind the subjects that you'd like taught to your daughter?"

"Besides her interest in locomotives, I would say that might be best left up to you and Carolina to decide. She's mentioned the desire to learn Latin and Greek, mathematics, and astronomy. Are you comfortable with those subjects?"

James nodded. "Very much so. However, I must say I am not qualified to teach about the railroad and would prefer to forego that subject."

"That might disappoint Carolina, but I am certain she would be grateful for whatever you feel qualified to offer her."

"What have you in mind with regard to arrangements?" James sounded very much like his banker father, ironing out the issue of contractual terms. James knew what was expected of him, and the more they discussed, the more acceptable the idea became.

"Since you are unable to get about easily," Joseph offered, "I thought it only fitting to have you stay with us. Your room and board would be provided, with a salary in addition. However much time you feel you could give us, you would be welcome to stay on at Oakbridge. Whether that lasts out the year or until you make a decision about your future, it would be most acceptable to me, so long as Carolina is satisfied with the arrangement."

"What does she say on the matter?" James questioned.

"Yes, Joseph, have you told her or the elder Miss Adams of this plan?" Leland asked.

"No, certainly not. I wouldn't want to get their hopes up. I know my daughters well enough to know they would both be pleased for entirely different reasons."

James smiled to himself, remembering his encounter with Carolina the night of his mother's party. He wondered if she would find it all that amusing or appealing to have him as her tutor. At first consideration, he had thought the idea of tutoring a girl rather demeaning. Yet, thinking of Carolina and the feisty ambition her father alluded to, James began to be intrigued at having a part in something so radical. The rebel in him rather liked the idea.

"I suppose we could give it a try," James said, amazed that he was actually feeling an interest in something for the first time since the accident. "When would you like to get started?"

Joseph's face fairly radiated his delight. "Immediately! The sooner the better! I have an appointment this evening for dinner and several appointments tomorrow, but I'll be returning to Oakbridge the following day. I'll make arrangements then and inform the family of my delightful news. I believe I could return to Washington City in a week to escort you to Oakbridge."

"You need not make another trip here," Leland jumped in. "I can have the boy brought out to you."

James said nothing of the fact that his father hadn't offered to see to the chore himself. Perhaps he would be glad to have him gone from the house. James hadn't considered this before. He knew his mother was severely depressed, and perhaps his father saw this as the perfect opportunity to remove part of her despair.

"I'll send you word then as soon as all preparations are made," Joseph replied. He drained his cup and stood to leave. Extending his hand, he offered James a smile. "I think you'll find Oakbridge and the quiet of the countryside very conducive to healing."

"I suppose I just might, at that," James answered, shaking the older man's hand.

Twenty

York's Good Fortune

At exactly half past six that evening, dinner was served in the White House dining room. York stared in complete amazement, feeling rather like a country bumpkin in contrast to the French diplomat at his right. The man appeared in a heavily embellished frock coat of purple velvet and gold trim and stared at York's plain black coat as though he thought the young man had somehow wandered to the table by mistake.

Joseph Adams sat several chairs closer to the head of the table, where Andrew Jackson was offering a choice of drinks to be served with the huge tureen of turtle soup. Dinner at the White House was not what he had expected when his father announced they were to dine out this evening.

An elderly Negro man poured York's drink and moved on to the next patron without so much as a word. Behind him came another servant who ladled soup into a fine china bowl. No sooner was one course finished than another appeared at the table—wild turkey, fish, and other dishes York wasn't in the least bit familiar with. Each dish was presented and placed upon the table for all to see, and after the oohs and aahs went up in chorus, the servant would remove it to the sideboard for carving. The process went on and on, and when finally dessert was offered upon a tray, York couldn't believe himself capable of taking even one more bite.

York took in the brilliantly lighted room and counted over thirty candles burning in the chandelier overhead, with even more in candlestick holders and candelabrums on the sideboards and table. Gilt-rimmed paintings, accompanied by gold and silver bric-a-brac, reflected what seemed to be a thousand dancing flames in their luxurious wares. York had grown up knowing wealth and finery, but this was by far and away the most impressive setting he'd been privileged to experience.

Jackson's loud boisterous laugh sounded from the far end of the table, causing all heads to turn in hopes of hearing the cause. At this encouragement, the President easily broke into one of his stories.

"Mr. Adams just reminded me of a fine day we enjoyed together back in thirty-four. It seems we both had chanced to be present at the National Jockey Club to watch the trial races of the White House horses. These were some of the very best examples of horseflesh I have yet to this day seen." Murmurs arose around York to acknowledge the President's expertise in the area of horses.

"Mr. Van Buren had come along," the President continued, "as well as my nephew Jack and several others. York, you'll be interested to know that fine stallion your father purchased a short time back was none other than the horse I put up that day." York nodded acknowledgment and waited for Jackson to continue. "Bolivia was a fine animal, but better still was Busirus, a stallion owned by a friend of mine." Everyone at the table was captive to his story, and Jackson reveled in the attention. "Well, it seems old Busirus was too much horse for the White House jockey. Who was riding that day, Mr. Van Buren?"

"I believe it was Jesse." Martin Van Buren spoke up from where he sat beside his son, Major Abraham Van Buren.

"That's right, it was. Well, Jesse was put atop Busirus, and before any of us knew it, the horse was stompin' and snortin' like he intended to breathe fire and brimstone down upon us. I yelled up to him to hold the animal, but that horse had a mind of its own. Then I spotted Mr. Van Buren dead center in the middle of that ordeal. I yelled, 'Get behind me, Mr. Van Buren! They will run over you, sir!'" He paused, giving Van Buren a wink. "Seems I've been telling old Van the same thing ever since." Laughter erupted, both genuine and staged. None was louder than Jackson's own guffaws, however.

York thought it admirable that the President managed to maintain a sense of humor when so many in the country were against him. Truth be told, Jackson couldn't count many men among his close friends. He had endured a great deal of backstabbing and bickering among his ranks, and to find one as loyal as Vice President Van Buren seemed an oddity indeed.

"Ladies, you must forgive me for boring you," Jackson said, suddenly standing. "I suggest you retire to share a bit of gossip and music while we gentlemen make our way to some serious cigars and brandy."

There was no question of doing other than they were directed. York watched the elegantly dressed women make their way to one room, while still another set of doors was opened to admit the men. York had no interest in either cigars or brandy, but he found the flow of conversation around him to be a superb after-dinner delight. Joining his father, who was already in conversation with Jackson, York stood by, engrossed in the matters being discussed.

"I was just telling the President," Joseph said, turning to his son, "that you hope to obtain employment here in Washington."

"Yes, sir, I do," York said, wondering what more he could possibly add. Thus far his search had not been very encouraging. Two or three businessmen were interested in him, but York could not get excited about any of these prospects.

Jackson sucked in a deep breath on the smoking cigar clenched between his teeth and blew out again before speaking. "I could use another loyal man at my side." With a wry smile he added, "Should I acquire one, it would bring the number to three." He laughed loud and hard, and even York couldn't keep from chuckling.

Jackson leaned over to add in a hushed voice, "And I'm not too sure about that number. My mulatto, George, is quite loyal, but sometimes I believe Mr. Van Buren is just along for the ride." He laughed again, slapping York on the back. "So what do you think, Mr. Adams? Would you be interested in becoming my aide?"

York was too astonished to speak. What could he possibly say at a moment like this? The President of the United States was offering him a position. Even if it had been a job mucking out the stables, York would have been honored.

"I . . . I don't understand," York finally managed to stammer. "You're offering me a job, Mr. President? Just like that?"

Jackson sobered. "Good men are increasingly hard to find. I trust your father implicitly. With you at my side, I can keep close tabs on what he has to say. The pay is good, although not the best, but the job has its benefits beyond wage."

"I'm honored, sir," York said with a slight bow. "I would consider myself privileged to work and learn at your side."

Jackson smiled and turned a knowing look on Joseph. "Shall we place bets on how long he'll stick to those words?"

Joseph laughed. "Now, Mr. President, you know I'm not a betting man. York has a certain interest in the politics of our country. Perhaps this type of position will give birth to a new political genius."

"Better yet, maybe he'll be the death of those old ninnies who seek to be the death of me." Jackson's eyes twinkled above a mischievous smile. "Besides, you can live on here near the White House, where we have fresh milk every morning."

"I beg your pardon?" York frowned, thinking he'd missed something.

Jackson flicked ashes onto a tray held by a nearby servant. "Frank Blair, editor of the *Globe*, once heard of my dietary need for milk. So one day, he shows up bright and early, pail in one hand, pad of paper in the other. And he's continued to do so for over two years now. I think he just comes to make sure no one has killed me off in the night. Frank couldn't stand it if some other newspaper cut him out of a first run on a big event like that!"

York found it amazing Jackson could joke about such a thing, considering the attempt on his life earlier in the year. A deranged house painter had accosted him inside the Capitol rotunda, firing not one, but two pistols at point-blank range. Both weapons had misfired, an event calculated at one chance in one hundred and twenty-five thousand. Jackson escaped unharmed and had gone after the scalawag with his walking stick raised high in the air, but a young army officer reached the man first.

York admired the President's bravado and suddenly realized he was going to enjoy working with this man. He'd heard a lot of controversial things about Andrew Jackson and criticism from his classmates up north. Jackson's volatile temper was well documented. But, from his father, York also had been appraised of the man's finer qualities, such as his generosity and loyalty to his friends. And now the great man was standing right in front him, and York had the opportunity to form his own opinion completely independent of those he'd held previously.

"When would you like me to start?" York asked without reservation.

"The sooner the better. There's a great deal to be done. The next election is a year away, and we must mount our efforts now to ensure that Mr. Van Buren takes my place. And of course there's the Texas matter."

"What of the Texas matter?" eagerly asked a man unknown to York, who had just joined them.

"Ah yes," Jackson said, thoughtfully rubbing his chin. "Texas."

Everyone in the room paused in their individual conversations to openly eavesdrop on this conversation. York, himself, wondered how things stood in that strange state of affairs.

"Texas is a problem I've long ignored," Jackson replied. "I must admit, I spent so much energy trying to get back money from the French—no offense," Jackson said, nodding to the Frenchman who'd dined at York's side. "The matter took a great deal of my attention, and while I managed to recover those funds, I'm afraid Texas has had to wait."

"But what of it now?" The same man who'd first broached the subject pressed the issue forward.

"Mr. Turner, that is a good question, but one that I fear I'm not yet ready to openly discuss. Let's just say the matter is under consideration. I favor adding Texas to the United States but would prefer it be done by means of purchase and not by act of war."

"Still, sir . . ."

Jackson held up his hand. "I believe I hear the ladies serving coffee. I suggest we join them."

York watched the man effectively put in his place, but the issue was an intriguing one. Texas was an entire world away. Separated not only by the eastern mountains and hundreds of miles of open land, but by the mighty Mississippi River itself and, beyond that, yet more land. If there was war with Mexico over the issue, York might well be expected to take up arms in support of his country. He might actually find himself fighting in a battle for a place he'd never even seen before.

Thinking on this and the prospects of his new job, York was content to find the evening draw to a close. There were many questions he wanted to ask his father, and the ride back to the hotel in their hired carriage would provide a perfect opportunity.

"Mr. Adams, I'll expect you at your earliest convenience," Jackson stated in bidding farewell to York.

Joseph looked first to York and then to his friend. "We depart for Oakbridge in the morning. York can arrange his affairs and return to the city on the day after, if that meets with your approval."

"It does indeed," Jackson replied. "I'll have arrangements made here for your lodging."

It was pouring down a cold rain when they emerged from the White House. The ride back to the hotel was cold and damp, but York hardly noticed as he and his father discussed the events of the evening. The trip was far too short, and York's curiosity was not even close to being satisfied. He would have kept his father up for hours longer that night, but Joseph was tired and begged to be excused.

There would be another chance to quiz his father. In the meantime, nothing could quench his elation over his astounding good fortune. This is what he had always wanted, though he'd never dreamed he'd reach such heights so soon. And to think he had done it without a college degree!

Well, he thought wryly, as he retired to his bed, having a father in the right place had helped. But he was determined to prove his own worth, his personal merit beyond his father's influence.

Twenty-One

Touching a Dream

*N*ews of York's impending departure was hailed as blessed good fortune by all but Carolina. Watching her mother and father chatter on in rambling delight, Carolina saw her chances for furthering her education slipping right through her fingers. A sort of *coup de grace* to her dreams.

"You're awfully quiet, Carolina," her father said, putting an arm around her shoulder. "Didn't you like the book I brought you? A few more trips to town and you will be able to start your own library."

"It's perfect, Papa," she said, trying her best to sound enthusiastic. In truth she *was* excited about the book. Her father had finally managed to locate a work devoted to the railroad: *A Practical Treatise on Rail-Roads* by Nicholas Wood. It was the 1832 edition of a British work published a few years earlier, with an added special section on American railroads.

Yet she couldn't keep from thinking about York's promise to help educate her. How could she explain to her father that she had hoped he would have taken longer than this to procure employment? She knew it was selfish to be unhappy for her brother when he was obviously elated with his sudden accomplishment.

She tried to smile and enter into the family discussion over York's good fortune. "York will no doubt have President Jackson's full attention when he shares his concerns over Mr. Clay's American System."

Joseph smiled and squeezed her shoulder. "No doubt."

"Well, I for one am beside myself with joy," Margaret joined in. "When Mr. Adams told me of your expulsion from college, I couldn't help but wonder what was to become of you. It seems once again, God has controlled the situation from the start. My friends will be positively green with envy. Even the ones who despise General Jackson."

"Especially those, Mrs. Adams," Joseph interjected. "They would be even more desirous of an inside ear to the President's office."

"Well," York said with a boyish grin, "now I feel completely justified in putting a fist to old Richard Bedford's nose. Without such an inspiring act, I'd still be listening to them sing the praises of Henry Clay."

Joseph narrowed his eyes a bit. "It wouldn't be wise to consider settling further arguments in the same manner. Mr. Jackson is given to explosive shows of temper and in the past has had to back up his words with actions. I pray you will be a temperate man, son."

Carolina listened to this exchange with little interest. Her mind was mulling over her losses. She idly fingered the pleats of her plum print muslin gown, wondering how she could compensate her plans. There were always her books, and Father seemed more than happy to purchase new volumes for her whenever she requested them. Perhaps she could teach herself Latin. What if she were to get hold of a primer used in the local boy's school? She knew for a fact they had rote classes in Latin and Greek.

"And now for something that will be of particular interest to you, Carolina, as well as the rest of the family."

"What?" Carolina asked distractedly.

Joseph paused when Hannah appeared in the doorway. "Bedtime, Georgia, Penny."

"But, Papa, you were going to tell us some news," Georgia protested.

With an indulgent nod, Joseph dismissed Hannah. "I'll send them along directly, Hannah. Make their beds ready."

"Yessuh," Hannah replied and closed the door.

"Well, tell us, Papa," Georgia insisted.

Carolina felt as anxious as her younger sibling, but her mind was also racing with thoughts of York's announcement and its implications for her. Somehow this day had turned out to be most unusual.

"The news is this," Joseph began. "We're to have a houseguest."

"Who?" Virginia asked, suddenly taking her eyes from the needlework in her lap.

Joseph smiled broadly at her interest. He looked to Margaret, whose puzzled expression matched Georgia's and Penny's. Carolina couldn't imagine it being of any interest to her. Guests were not that unusual at Oakbridge. Perhaps one of her aunts would come for a visit. That could be entertaining. She'd not seen her cousins in some years.

"Well, do tell us, Mr. Adams," Margaret said anxiously.

Joseph nodded. "Our houseguest will be none other than James Baldwin."

"James!" Virginia exclaimed, then tried to recompose her voice. "Whyever would he be coming here? Isn't he still recovering from his accident?"

"Exactly so," Joseph answered. "That's partially why I invited him to stay on at Oakbridge. I have hired him to do a job for me, and it seemed best to keep him from having to travel back and forth to Washington City."

"A job, Mr. Adams? What job?" Margaret suddenly questioned.

"Yes, Father," Virginia chimed in. "What job?"

Even Georgia and Penny echoed the words, while York obviously seemed to know of his father's plans. Only Carolina remained silent. In her mind she was remembering her silly behavior on the night of James' party. Now, she thought, I'll have to live with James Baldwin's superior attitude and, no doubt, his teasing. Perhaps it would only be for a few days.

Joseph took a seat on the settee beside his wife, obviously enjoying prolonging his news and tickling everyone's curiosity. "I've hired James Baldwin to tutor Carolina and further her education."

"What!" Margaret, Virginia, and Carolina exclaimed in unison.

Laughing at the unfeminine outburst, Joseph leaned back and casually draped an arm around Margaret's shoulders. "For some time, it has been brought to my attention that Carolina wished to expand her mind with an unconventional manner of education. She desires to learn of the stars and the universe, the whys and wherefores of machines and such things, and of the many other mysteries of life."

"I cannot abide such an unladylike endeavor. What will our friends say, Mr. Adams?" Margaret had actually paled. Carolina's soaring hope began to deflate.

"Mrs. Adams, there comes a time when a person should do not what he feels will be deemed acceptable in the eyes of man, but in the eyes of God." Joseph spoke with firm conviction.

"Are you telling me that God told you to do this?" Margaret asked indignantly.

Carolina stared at her father and mother's exchange with open mouth. She noted that Virginia looked horror-struck.

"It's not that God called down to me from on high, but rather after much prayer and searching for the right answer, James Baldwin practically fell into my lap. I approached him on the subject, considered the possible benefits to all members of this family," he said, turning to wink at Virginia, "then asked him for an answer."

"And he said yes?" Margaret asked with astonishment. "He, a college-educated man, agreed to tutor our daughter in masculine subjects of study?"

"I believe, Mrs. Adams, he too could see the possibilities in living at Oakbridge."

Carolina could care less about those other so-called possibilities. She knew full well her father was implying the benefits that might bring Virginia and James closer to matrimonial bliss, but she didn't let it concern her in the least. Her father had hired a tutor to teach her! Then she stopped her excited thoughts. That tutor was Jimmy Baldwin, the same tormenting soul who'd given her such grief as a child and with whom she had a less than becoming reintroduction at the party. He'd seemed far from inclined to believe she was in need of furthering her education on that night. Perhaps this was a sham on his part. Perhaps he only planned to gain residency at Oakbridge in order to spend his days in Virginia's company.

"But it isn't proper," Margaret said sternly. "A young woman of Carolina's age and maturity can certainly not be left alone for long periods of time with a young bachelor."

"I could chaperon their sessions," Virginia suddenly offered.

Carolina could tell by the "cat-in-the-cream" look on her sister's face that she was already planning her days to be spent at James' side.

"I think that might be the very answer," remarked their father. "You could get to know each other rather well, what with seeing each other on a day-to-day basis." Joseph smiled at his wife conspiratorially.

"Would I have to be tutored, too?" Georgia questioned, obviously appalled at the idea.

"What's a tutor?" Penny asked, trying to stifle a yawn.

"Both of you need to be off to bed," Margaret said, getting to her feet. She suddenly seemed much less hostile to the idea of James' coming to Oakbridge. "I believe I see the benefits on which you were speaking, Mr. Adams." She smiled over her shoulder at her husband. "Once again, you seem to have resolved a commonplace problem with a most unusual answer. Come, Penny, Georgia."

The girls went quietly with their mother, while York yawned, stretched, and got to his feet. "I have packing to oversee. With your permission, I'll excuse myself as well."

Joseph waved him on, and Carolina reached out to touch York's arm as he passed her. "I really am happy for you, York. I know you'll enjoy Washington and your new job."

York leaned down and kissed her on the head. "I wonder if you'd still be saying that if James Baldwin wasn't coming to teach you in my place."

Carolina grinned. "I suppose I wouldn't be quite as gracious, but I'd still be pleased for you."

"As I'm pleased for you. Sleep tight on these dreams, little sister," York said and took his leave.

"What room will we put James in, Father?" Virginia asked almost shyly.

Carolina turned to her father. "Yes, where will you put him? Maine's old room? York's?"

"No," Joseph replied. "His injuries will not allow for climbing stairs at present. He's still working to get around on crutches, and the less he has to strain his leg, the quicker his recovery. I thought we might turn a couple of the downstairs drawing rooms into a bedroom and sitting room for James. He could hold his teaching sessions in the sitting room and not have far to travel should he grow tired and need to rest."

"That's wonderful!" Virginia said, and tossing her sewing aside, she got to her feet. "I'll speak to Mother right now and get things started. We can arrange very pleasant accommodations for him." She hurried from the room, obviously delighted with her new task.

"Well, what do you think?" Joseph asked when only Carolina remained.

"I don't know what to say," she answered honestly. "I'm stunned. When York announced his plans, my hopes were utterly dashed. Now you tell me I'm to have a regular tutor, not just studies fitted in here and there, but a scheduled period with lessons and such. I don't know what to say because words seem completely inadequate." Carolina felt herself close to tears.

"You are pleased, then?" Joseph asked, leaning forward.

Carolina threw herself at her father's feet and hugged her head to his knee. "I'm more than pleased. I must be dreaming—only now I'll really be a part of those dreams."

"It's no dream, Carolina. It's what I've felt called of God to do for you."

She looked up to meet her father's gaze. His compassionate blue eyes met her dark inquisitive ones. "Did God really talk to you about me?"

Joseph nodded. "In a way. In here—" He thumped his chest. "I see so much of myself in you. So many dreams, so many hopes. I think God gave me a second sight to see past the conventions of this age. I think He let me know the path for your life will be anything but *conventional*. I sincerely believe that God looks at the heart and soul of a person before their gender. So why shouldn't I?"

"Oh, Papa, thank you! Thank you for understanding. I'm glad you're close to God. Maybe one day I'll be close enough to Him, and He will talk to me as well."

"I'm certain He will if you open your heart to Him," Joseph said, giving her head a gentle pat. "Now, off to bed. Dream your dreams and know that in but a few days, they will come true."

Carolina got to her feet, still dazed by the news. "I love you, Papa."

Joseph stood and kissed her on the forehead. "And I love you," he replied.

Carolina made her way to her bedroom and undressed in the silence of her room. On her bed was the book her father had brought back from Washington. Lovingly, she ran her hand over the thick volume. *"A Practical Treatise on Rail-Roads,"* she murmured. The author had composed this discourse to teach the technical details of the railroad. "Well, Mr. Wood," Carolina whispered, "I'll bet you didn't write this with a fifteen-year-old girl in mind."

Twenty-Two

The Houseguest

Oakbridge underwent a transformation over the next few days that heralded the arrival of James Baldwin in grand style. While Virginia and Margaret had their heads together over the accommodations for the new houseguest, Carolina found herself worrying about the entire affair. James hadn't seemed the leastwise supportive of her interest in mathematics, yet here he had agreed to tutor her. To Carolina it seemed to hint of a situation not quite disclosed in full. He must want terribly to be with Virginia, she surmised while rummaging through the attic for the extra oil lamps her mother had instructed her to bring down. The thought of James and Virginia sharing stolen glances and intimate words while she was struggling to learn Latin and Greek didn't appeal in the least to Carolina.

"I'll bet she takes all of his attention, and I won't really be tutored at all," Carolina grumbled, finally managing to locate the lamps. Taking up a slender cobalt blue lamp, Carolina noted that the wick was practically new. The other one, a twin to the first, was in nearly identical condition. That was one less task to see to. Both lamps needed oil, but that would be easily remedied.

Carolina took the back stairs down from the attic, which led directly into the kitchen. Naomi was beating a mixture that looked like the batter of her famous applesauce cake. Putting the lamps down, Carolina went to the cupboard for oil.

"Is that applesauce cake you're making?" she asked over her shoulder.

Naomi grinned broadly. "Mr. Adams says we's havin' Mr. Baldwin in tonight. I figure this to be a sure winner."

"Indeed," Carolina replied. She went to the task of filling the lamps while Naomi poured the concoction into a large round pan. "Did Father tell you that Mr. Baldwin will be staying on here at Oakbridge?"

"Shor 'nuf, Miz Carolina. He says that boy is to be treated like family."

Carolina grimaced, uncertain why she felt such frustration at the thought. No doubt her father and mother had already decided his future as a potential member of the family. They certainly seemed sold on the idea of wedding James Baldwin to Virginia. That wasn't the problem, though; rather, it was the fact that she was being used to cement the match. But her father couldn't be in on such a deception. Surely he was concerned for her future as well and was not simply using her! Whatever the whole truth, there seemed too much chance for her dream to turn into a nightmare, or at least to become an awkward and unpleasant experience.

Finishing her task, Carolina put the oil back in the cupboard and took up the lamps. "I'd best take these to Mother before she begins to fret." Naomi only nodded and busied herself at the stove.

Carolina left the room and found her mother and Virginia, heads together, blissfully involved in what they did best—organizing the household.

"Here are the lamps you asked for," Carolina announced, thrusting them forward. She looked around at the room. Her mother had done wonders. The room, normally a music room, had been made over into a bedroom. It was quite unconventional, but her mother had made it very charming. Near the white marble fireplace a French-style sleigh bed had been placed. The oak bed was much lower than the normal four-poster beds that were favored in Oakbridge bedrooms. This would accommodate James' physical needs. Beside the bed was a small doily-topped table. Her mother placed one of the blue lamps here, the other on a corner desk.

The remainder of the room was rather stark. An imported Persian rug of dark blue and red graced the floor and fit in well with the dark blue brocade of the draperies, but aside from this and the few paintings on the walls, the room was void of furniture.

"I've arranged to have a large wardrobe brought in for that corner over there," Margaret said, as if reading Carolina's mind. "Why don't you check the adjoining room and see what else you think it needs."

Carolina was honored that her mother would think her capable of contributing valuable information on the matter and quickly took her leave. Stepping through large double oak doors, Carolina again was amazed at the transformation. A long table and trestle bench took up space near the floor-to-ceiling windows, receiving maximum lighting. Near this were three freestanding bookshelves. Several straight-back rococo chairs were placed around the room, while two more comfortable sofas of the same style were positioned opposite the study area.

The pale yellow draperies had been pulled back and afternoon light flooded the room. All around her, Carolina noted the muted yellow tones of the chair and sofa cushions, as well as the delicate print of the wallpaper. It was a perfect room to study in. Her mother had been quite right to pick it for just such a purpose.

"What do you think?" Margaret asked, sweeping in behind her.

"I think it's wonderful, Mother. So bright and airy."

"I thought yellow would draw in the light more naturally."

Carolina nodded. "It does. I'm so excited."

Margaret smiled and Carolina instantly felt a return of the warmth she'd shared with her mother after returning from the railroad celebration. "Mother, I am very grateful to you and Papa. Thank you so much."

"I'll still expect you to conduct yourself as a lady," Margaret admonished, then added with a wink, "and for you to make sure your sister conducts herself as one, too."

Carolina tried not to frown. She turned away quickly, hoping her mother would drop the matter. "Is this new?" she asked, crossing to a tall glass-door secretary. "I don't remember it."

"Something your father found, although I'm not sure where. He thought it would be useful. See here, the door folds down to make a writing surface."

Carolina let out her breath slowly and felt a surge of relief that her mother did not pursue the issue of Virginia and James. "It looks quite serviceable."

"Is that the carriage?" Margaret strained her ear toward the door. "I believe they've arrived."

She hurried from the room, leaving Carolina to wonder what she should do. A quick glance down at her gown reassured her she was dressed appropriately. The dark green print of the cotton day dress suited her complexion. Cream-colored piping and ruching trimmed the form-fitting bodice and came to a point at her waist. She was grateful the gown was not overly childish, as many hanging in her closet tended to be. This was one of her newer long dresses, and it made her feel pretty and grown up.

She could hear the voices of her mother and father in the vestibule and felt a sudden anxiety sweep over her. How should she act with James? When they were children she had held him in some awe, to be sure. Though at the same time he had been Jimmy Baldwin, the terror of little girls and, as such, had drawn her ire equally mixed with the awe. But during her meeting with him at the party she had realized they were so much closer, in maturity if not in age. Well, perhaps in this new circumstance things would not be much different than when they were children. The awe and the ire would still be present. But might there also be a new ingredient in the mix—that of friendship as well? Such a notion brought only more confusion to Carolina's mind.

"Oh, dear," she said aloud, not even realizing she'd done so. Catching her hand to her mouth, she struggled to shake her sudden nerves. Everything will work itself together, she thought and rechecked her hair in the mirror near the door.

"He'll never even look at me," she said softly, imagining his teasing blue eyes and dimpled grin. She tucked a curl back into place and noted with satisfaction that she was in as fine an order as she could get. "I'm here to learn," she reminded herself and opened the door. "Let Virginia concentrate on appearance and flirtations."

She came into the foyer just as they were entering. Her father and mother and Virginia were there. The other children were absent because Mother had told them not to accost their new houseguest all at once. James, on his crutches, was in the midst of the others, his head inclined toward Virginia, who was speaking to him. They didn't notice Carolina for a long moment until she daintily cleared her throat.

"Ah, Carolina," Joseph said.

At that same moment James stumbled as his crutch slipped on the highly polished oak floor. He bumped into Virginia, who instinctively reached up and caught him by the arm. There was an awkward moment before he smiled his thanks.

"I am afraid I have yet to get the hang of these things on polished surfaces," James said, referring to his crutches.

"We pray you never have to." Virginia batted her long lashes and kept her hand on his arm.

Then James turned toward Carolina and added almost as if she were an afterthought, "Miss Adams, how good to see you again. I won't shake your hand for fear of falling flat on my face."

As Carolina took a moment to study him she thought at first that he hadn't changed a bit since seeing him at his party. He'd lost weight, but that was to be expected after what he'd been through. But on closer scrutiny she noted something else about him that was different. Something in his eyes . . . it was as if the joke on his lips was out of sync with his eyes, which did not seem to respond at all to his amusement.

"That is perfectly all right, Mr. Baldwin," she said in her most poised voice. "I am glad you could come."

"Come now," Margaret said, motioning the servants to follow with

James' baggage. "We have your rooms ready. You may rest until dinner and then perhaps you will feel up to telling us of your mother and father."

James smiled. "I assure you, I will be happy to do so." He glanced from Margaret to Carolina and held his gaze on her in a way she found most disconcerting. She didn't know if it was worse to be ignored or to be so scrutinized. "So, I am to be your teacher," he said.

"Yes," she said in a breathless manner, unable to quell her anxiety. She realized she was twisting her skirt in her hand like a child.

"Perhaps later today, after I settle in a bit, we can meet and discuss the strategy for your studies?"

"There is plenty of time for that tomorrow," said Margaret. "Goodness! We don't intend to work you to death, Mr. Baldwin."

"I don't mind at all, but I certainly don't wish to push my pupil—"

"That would be fine, Mr. Baldwin!" said Carolina quickly. "I'm ready when you are."

"Excellent! Give me an hour to unwind a bit."

Carolina ignored the displeased look from her mother and the spiteful look from Virginia. She didn't want to lose a moment of her long-awaited studies. And she feared that before too long she would be vying heavily with her sister for James' attentions.

Twenty-Three

Shaky Beginnings

*A*n hour later, rested from his journey, James found Carolina reading a book in the parlor. She had seemed so at ease sitting in the rocking chair, book in hand—until she glanced up at him with anxious eyes. He wondered if he had startled her with his sudden appearance. Shrugging, he smiled as he hobbled upon his crutches into the room.

"Would this be a good time for us to discuss your studies, Miss Adams?" he asked.

She snapped her book shut and jumped up. "Why, yes—if you are up to it. Shall we do it here or in your rooms?"

"Let's go to the classroom so that we can get the feel of the place."

She walked next to him back to the classroom, where late afternoon shadows were slanting through the windows. Still it was bright in comparison to his dark brooding chamber back in Washington City. The ambiance was working well upon him, and he was, in spite of himself, already starting to feel better. Perhaps this would indeed be a good way to pass his recuperation time. With his mind stayed on the learning affairs of Carolina Adams and the courtship of Virginia, the death of Phineas and his disillusionment with his broken dreams would stop tormenting him so.

"Mother and Virginia arranged these rooms," Carolina said as they paused at the door. "They have tried to anticipate your needs, but if anything is amiss, you have but to ask and it will be seen to."

"This will be quite sufficient," James assured rather stiffly. Carolina's tension was beginning to affect him. Noting the bookshelves and attempting to make casual conversation, he added, "I have just the books for those."

"Truly?" Carolina asked without thinking.

James smiled at her uncensored wonderment. "Truly. I brought several volumes from our library that I thought would help in my teaching. Should we need additional works, I will send for them."

"If you need to purchase anything," Carolina said, the formality returning to her voice, "my father said he will make all the arrangements."

"I will keep that in mind. For now, I believe we are ready to begin."

They were barely settled at the trestle table when a tall broad-shouldered Negro appeared in the doorway, a small footstool and pillow in hand.

"Miz Adams sent me with these for Massa James," he said.

"Thank you, Jericho," said Carolina. Then turning to James she explained, "Father has instructed Jericho to assist you while you are here. He will be your personal manservant."

"That is most kind," said James.

"Where would y'all like me to put these?" asked Jericho.

"Here by the table for now."

Jericho positioned the stool and pillow, making certain James' foot was propped up comfortably. He then retreated to the bedroom to take charge of unpacking his new master's things.

The sound of Jericho's activity, accompanied by a tune the man was softly humming, drifted through the partially opened door. James hoped that the close proximity of another would help dispel Carolina's undeniable tension. But she continued to appear as uneasy as a child about to be upbraided by her father.

Unable to restrain his curiosity about the cause of this, James finally said, "You look as though you've swallowed a vial of poison. Are you nervous?"

Carolina was openly taken aback by this frontal attack. "I most certainly am not! Why in the world would I be nervous?"

James shrugged. "I haven't the slightest clue. Perhaps I misread the . . . situation."

"I'm sure that must be it." Still, her tone was taut, her protests far too ready.

"Why don't you see if there is writing material in that secretary," James said, making a concerted attempt to overlook the odd friction he was feeling between them.

Carolina hesitated, conflicting emotions flickering across her face—emotions James was at a total loss to fathom. He thought once again that he ought to be grateful for this most interesting reception he was receiving from his pupil. Yet he felt fairly certain she would be that much more infuriated if she had even the slightest inkling that she was little more than an amusement, a distraction. Not that she was, of course! James had already decided to treat this situation seriously. But there was no reason why he should be bored in the process. Nevertheless, he felt her treatment of him was unwarranted, and it was beginning to irk him.

Glancing up, James raised a brow. "You are certain nothing is amiss?"

Obviously flustered, Carolina drew a deep breath, scurried to the secretary, and withdrew the requested items. When she returned to the trestle bench, she sat down quite prim and properly, leaving a two-foot space between them.

"Now, I understand you have a desire to learn Latin," he began. "I have a good command of the language, as well as Greek. Would you care to learn Greek?" He made notes on the paper, hoping it would put her at ease.

"Well . . . yes," she answered hesitantly. "I would very much like that."

"Good." He wrote out the words Latin and Greek at the top of the page. "Next, mathematics. Your father told me that you did quite well in school. How far did you get in arithmetic?"

Carolina folded her hands. "I've been teaching myself algebra," she stated proudly.

"Oh? And how are you coming along?"

"Well enough. I can solve for 'x' in simple situations."

He noted this on the paper. "Are you familiar with the various properties? Associative? Distributive? Commutative?"

Her answer was stiff and formal. "I know them well enough in definition, but at times the application can be difficult."

James wrote several additional lines before pausing. Silence filled the room and seemed to displace his thoughts for a moment. He glanced at her and her eyes skittered away. He frowned.

"Will that be all for now?" Carolina asked. He thought he detected an air of inexplicable defiance in her tone.

And despite any previous gratitude for the distraction she was providing, he found himself perturbed. "Look . . ." he said, laying down the quill brusquely. He saw no other way to deal with it other than to simply address the matter at hand. Glancing over his shoulder at the open door, he lowered his voice. "If I have done something to offend you, *Miss Adams*"—he gave a pointed emphasis to his final words—"I believe I at least deserve the courtesy of hearing what it is so I can defend myself."

"Really, Mr. Baldwin, I don't—"

"Never mind!" he said sharply. He wanted to jump up and leave, but his confounded leg prevented any quick retreat. Thus, frustrated even more, he added, "I don't want to be here any more than you appear to want me here." It was an effort to keep his voice low. "But we both have a stake in this, and it would suit us well to work together instead of apart."

Carolina's cheeks flushed red, and she turned angry eyes upon him. "Whatever do you mean, 'We both have a stake in this'? My only desire is to further my education. I was pleased when Papa announced he had hired a tutor for me, and while I would rather it be someone else, I certainly do not intend to jeopardize this situation."

James' scowl deepened. "And what have you got against me?"

Carolina's chin jutted out, her defiance more than merely hinted at now. Her eyes glinted. "I don't believe you have my interests in mind at all. York had planned to help me"—her voice raised a bit louder than she'd intended—"but he's off to Washington. I'm forced, therefore, to utilize your services until someone else comes along."

James laughed harshly. "And you think there might be the possibility of that? Who else is going to drag himself all the way out here to tutor a starry-eyed, mean-tempered child?"

"I am not a child!" Carolina exclaimed, stamping her foot. The action seemed so preposterous and in contrast to her words that Carolina suddenly stopped her tirade, her lips quirking into an apologetic smile. "I'm not a child . . . but I will concede the mean temper. It often gets the best of me. I guess I am anxious."

"About me?" He moderated his tone also, his ire replaced by honest bemusement.

She bit her lip and jumped up. She wandered to the fireplace and fingered a vase of mums. Deciding to give her a moment to collect her thoughts, James also rose, took up his crutches and, balancing upon them, went to the sofa. "If you don't mind, my leg is killing me, and I'd like to stretch it out here for a spell."

Carolina nodded, "By all means."

He settled upon the gold-striped sofa and dropped the crutches to the floor. "Go on," he said at length.

"What do you mean?"

"I mean you were about to tell me why you're anxious."

Carolina frowned, and this time it was her own gaze that fell upon the open door. "You had asked but I didn't—" She stopped suddenly, then with resolve turned to face him. "All right, I suppose no more harm can be done, and Papa always says honesty is the best course no matter what. I know why you're here," she said, her voice low and husky. "I know my parents hope to see you married to my sister, but my goal is to receive an education, and I don't want to see that take second place to your courtship of Virginia."

James tried not to look surprised at her unexpected revelation. "I take my duties seriously, I assure you. I'm being paid to tutor you, and while I too know of the plan to see me married to your sister, I'll make sure you get your money's worth."

Carolina's eyes widened at this. "It has nothing to do with money, except maybe on your part."

James shook his head. "No amount of money would be worth putting up with this. Either you want me to teach you or you don't. Say the word and I'll leave." The color drained from her face, and Carolina went quickly to the door and closed it. She turned and leaned against it as if for support. James watched her carefully for a moment and waited for her to speak.

Carolina bit at her lower lip before approaching James. When she spoke the anger was gone from her voice. "I don't want you to leave. Virginia's happiness is important, and she seems to care quite deeply about you."

"And what about you?"

"What do you mean?" Her voice revealed her surprise.

"I know you care about your sister," he said, "but do you care enough about her to put up with me as your tutor? Can you learn from me? Will you feel comfortable enough to ask questions when you don't understand . . ." he paused and grew very serious, "or will your pride keep you from admitting your confusion?"

Carolina took a deep breath. "I want this education very much. I'm not foolish enough to sit back and allow the opportunity to slip through my fingers. I'll devote myself to prayer and study—and I will learn." She spoke her final statement as if she dared him or anyone to stand in her way.

Just then the door flew open and Virginia appeared, bestowing a beaming smile upon James and a curt little nod toward Carolina.

"Mother said you might be in here plotting out the course of Carolina's studies. I thought perhaps you would have perished from boredom by now."

"Hardly that, Virginia," Carolina retorted and made her way to the door.

James' attention was riveted on Virginia as she made her entrance, but out of the corner of his eye he spotted Carolina watching him thoughtfully. When Virginia turned to look at the notes on the table, he winked at Carolina and offered her a smile as if to reassure her that he'd not forgotten her. Embarrassed and scarlet faced, Carolina hurried from the room. James leaned back, a perplexed smile still lingering on his lips as Virginia began prattling about something he couldn't focus on. Educating Carolina Adams should prove to be more entertaining than he'd originally imagined. Then with a sobering thought James realized he had not once thought of Phineas or the railroad during his encounter with Carolina. Perhaps her education would prove to be more than entertainment. Perhaps it would actually take him away from the confines of his grief.

Twenty-Four

Misunderstood

$\mathscr{B}$ut the railroad is an important part of what I want to learn," Carolina stated with determination. "I have been interested in the locomotive since I first saw it, and there are things about it that I want included in our studies. Such as physics."

"*I'm* not interested in talking to you about the railroad," James replied firmly. His voice sounded almost angry, causing Virginia to look up from where she sat on the divan, sewing.

They had argued about this topic every single day for the last three weeks. Every time she brought up the subject, Carolina hoped that enough time would have passed for James to feel agreeable to dealing with the subject. And each time proved to be more of an argument than the day before. She couldn't understand why. James had been working on the railroad just prior to his accident. He *must* know much about it and have an interest in it.

She glanced out the window at the dreary winter day. A storm was brewing that might bring the first snow. Carolina supposed she was not being fair to James. He had been a worthy tutor these past weeks and she had few complaints. Yet she had been so hopeful that the railroad would be part of her studies. It was difficult to accept his stiff-necked attitude about the subject, considering his experience. One would think he'd be dying to get involved once again with work he had trained for.

She tried to be patient as she said, "I realize you suffered a great deal in your accident, Mr. Baldwin, but I also know you held a solid interest in the business before that. My father said—"

"The matter is not open for discussion!" James exclaimed adamantly, surprising both ladies with the force of his tone.

Carolina strode to where he leaned against a chair. A few days ago he had discarded his crutches and was now getting about with the use of a walking stick. Facing him, she stood with arms akimbo. "But why?" she insisted. She hated to be a nag, but she could not let it go. "This is so important to me."

"And my reasons are important to me."

Nose to nose they were well matched in their determination. "And if I insist?" Carolina challenged, losing her previous patience once more.

"I'd like to see you try," James retorted. "I can leave this position tomorrow and be no worse for it."

Carolina felt her resolve crumble. He was right, of course. She needed him far more than he needed her. It was important to get James to talk about the railroad, but not at the expense of losing him as a tutor. She could think of no response and for once was grateful when Virginia interrupted.

"You two have had the same conversation—or should I say argument?—every day for three weeks. It's almost Christmas; can't you put your differences aside and get along for the holiday season?"

Carolina frowned. "You're the one who wants to marry him, not me." Carolina ignored Virginia's mortified look as she continued to vent her frustration on her sister. "I don't have to get along with him; I merely want him to live up to his part of the bargain. He promised Father to teach me about the railroad."

"I did nothing of the kind!" James parried. "I told him I would overlook the fact that you're merely a girl and teach you unconventional studies of masculine interest."

"Of which the railroad is one!" Carolina raged back.

"Enough, Carolina!" Virginia was now clearly drawn into the argument. "Proper young women do not raise their voices. Why don't you go upstairs and compose yourself?"

"Yes, I would imagine you'd both like that quite well."

James smirked. "Anything would be better than this."

Carolina felt herself close to tears. Virginia was right.

Without another word, Carolina left the room. In the corridor she nearly ran straight up against her mother. Lowering her face so that Margaret wouldn't see how upset she was, Carolina hoped her mother would allow her to pass without explanation.

"Are your studies concluded for the day?"

"Yes," Carolina answered as steadily as she could. "Virginia and James are having a discussion."

"Oh, good!" Margaret exclaimed, the delight clear in her tone. Carolina felt betrayed by this, reminded again that the only reason her mother had agreed to this strange arrangement was in order to put Virginia and James together.

"Excuse me, I need something from my room," Carolina said, sweeping past without waiting for her mother to reply.

Relieved that her mother did not ask her what she needed, Carolina practically raced up the stairs. If her mother had questioned her, Carolina knew it would be difficult to explain that what she needed most was the solitude and peace of her bedroom. James Baldwin had so disrupted her life that it was impossible to let down her guard anywhere else in the house. And now with James quite capable of getting around the house with the use of a cane, this was more true than ever.

Yes, she was being taught many valuable lessons from James, but still she was not completely content. And the reason had little to do with his reticence to teach her about the railroad. It was far more than that. She'd had such high expectations when her father had first told her he was considering a tutor for her. She simply had not factored in the tension and awkwardness she was now experiencing. The whole situation with Virginia was bad enough. But she could bear that if only she didn't feel so at odds with James himself. They had reached an understanding that first day, but there was still an air of antagonism between them. It was often subtle, but it was always present. The awkwardness about Virginia and the railroad were mere symptoms of it. They had gotten off on the wrong foot from the very beginning—perhaps as far back as that awful party at the Baldwins'. It seemed they would never get right again.

It would, however, help a little if he'd at least meet her halfway by teaching her about the railroad. Why did things always have to be so hard for her? Was she asking for that much? It didn't seem so.

No one understands, she thought, not wanting to feel sorry for herself but unable to prevent it. Not one single soul in this house understands who I am and what I desire.

As she slipped into her bedroom, her gaze fell on the dressing table. There lay a copy of the *American Railroad Journal*, a recent gift from her father, which she hadn't yet had a chance to read.

"Well, perhaps there is one person who understands," she murmured with tender thoughts of her father.

She took a seat at the table and began leafing through the pages. It was an older copy, dated Saturday, October 3, 1835. The literary section of the sixteen-page periodical told of new books, including one she thought might be of interest to her mother. *The Little Scholar Learning to Talk* was the title of a book designed to assist mothers in training up their children. It might make a useful tool as her mother taught Maryland. She made a mental note to look for the book when she went Christmas shopping.

On the next page a notice that the Bank of the United States was closing up its concerns made little impact on Carolina. Where was the information about the railroad? This periodical read more like a general-interest newspaper. She found some information related to technical designs of locomotive axles, but it was dry reading and difficult for her to follow with its algebraic formulas and design terminology. Just as she thought to cast the whole thing aside, Carolina caught sight of a brief statement regarding a railroad wreck that took the life of a Phineas Davis. The name struck her as familiar. She scratched her head, then remembered that he was a designer of locomotives. But wasn't he also the man who was involved in the same train derailment as James?

"Phineas Davis was killed September 27, 1835, as the result of a derailment of one of his engines on which he was riding." It was the same man; the dates of both accidents coincided. She was just considering the implications of this fact when Hannah appeared to help her dress for dinner.

The old slave seemed to note Carolina's dour mood and said very little as she slipped the sprigged muslin over her head and went to take out another gown from the wardrobe. Her mother always insisted they dress up for dinner, and with James in residence this rule was strictly adhered to.

Carolina only nodded when Hannah presented the rose-colored satin. The gown was simple, yet elegant, and made Carolina look much older than her fifteen years. The snug bodice was trimmed with ivory lace and fitted with an overdress of powdery rose gauze that gathered at the waist with a wide ivory ribbon and flowed out to cover the skirt of the gown. Lifting her arms to accept the gown, Carolina continued to think of James' accident. This was the first time she had really given much thought to it and to the fact that a man had been killed. It seemed quite likely James had known that man; perhaps they had been friends. If so, it might answer a lot of questions about his reticence toward the railroad. But was it possible such a tragedy would have turned him against the railroad? Odd, but she had never thought of James Baldwin as a man of such deep sensitivities.

Hannah was hooking up the dress and suggesting what to do with her hair, but Carolina barely heard the woman. There seemed to be something more to James Baldwin, and she wanted to understand what that something was. Whatever it might be, it was complicating their relationship as student and teacher and clearly putting an end to any ideas related to the railroad.

———

A festive atmosphere reigned supreme in the Adams dining room.

Boughs of holly and pine greenery draped the mantel and sideboards. Huge red ribbon bows and candles made sharp contrast to the green, and gold-colored stars were tucked into the branches along the way to reflect the candlelight.

It was Sunday, one of those rare occasions when the entire family dined together. Usually the younger children ate in the nursery in order to allow the grown-ups an opportunity for civilized conversation and a peaceful meal. But on Sunday the regimen was relaxed, and Margaret and Joseph enjoyed the companionship of their youngest charges.

This time conversation around the table was light and merry with the little ones sharing ideas of what they hoped to find under the tree when Christmas finally came. Georgia wanted a music box with real mother-of-pearl inlays on cherrywood. She proclaimed to have seen just such a box in Washington when they'd last been there in August. Penny wanted a dollhouse with three floors of rooms and furniture to fill all of the spaces. And Maryland wanted baby dolls and candied orange slices, which came out sounding like, "Bebes and owang swices."

Carolina ate her meal in preoccupied silence while Virginia struck up a new subject devoted to the social season already in full swing.

"The Milfords are having a party next week, and the Montgomery party is the very next night. I thought our party would fit in nicely on the Saturday after next. That would make it almost a full week from Christmas and leave plenty of time to notify the guests."

"It sounds perfect, Virginia," Margaret said and turned to James. "Virginia arranges parties quite well. In fact, there isn't much she can't handle when it comes to the home."

James smiled. "I'm certain you speak the truth."

Carolina listened with halfhearted interest to this exchange. All the while she wondered how she could approach the subject of the accident with James. Perhaps if he talked to her about the circumstances surrounding the accident and whether he and Mr. Davis had been close, she could get him to change his mind about tutoring her on the locomotive.

"Carolina, you've been very quiet this evening," Joseph remarked. "I hope you aren't letting your studies overwhelm you."

Carolina glanced up. "Not at all. I'm very much enjoying my studies."

"Is she a dedicated student?" Joseph asked, turning to James.

The look that crossed James' face seemed to Carolina to be one of pride. "She is a far better student than most men. I believe she is capable of learning much."

"Still, whatever can she hope to do with that learning?" Margaret chimed in. "Better by far she know the workings of a home than any number of mathematical calculations. She can't hope to secure a decent marriage if she is unable to tend a home."

Carolina wanted to run from the table and found it strange when James came to her defense. "I agree the running of a home should be uppermost in any woman's mind; however, Carolina could find those number calculations assisting her in her duties. Women often use mathematics and never realize it."

"How so?" Margaret seemed intrigued.

"There are the calculations for the needs of your people. Food enough to feed the family as well as the slaves must be figured into the financial affairs of the plantation. Then, too, you must be able to determine how many bolts of cloth it will take to clothe your people or even to make a simple garment for one of your children. There are many applications you might not consider as a matter of mathematics, but they are there nevertheless."

"I had not imagined," Margaret replied.

Virginia, composed and sedate with her hair piled high on her head and her mother's pearls clasped around her neck, finally entered the subject. "I know very few women, however, who would find value in studying locomotives."

Carolina's head snapped up to meet her sister's smug expression. The statement had been made as an intended insult, but Carolina wasn't about to let it go without addressing the issue. "Locomotives are going to change the future of this nation. That, in and of itself, should interest everyone."

"I heartily agree with Carolina," Joseph replied.

Carolina noted that it was now James who grew sullen and silent, but his host seemed not to notice.

"The railroad will connect us to the Mississippi and beyond," Joseph continued. "I know the lands west of the Mississippi are planned for Indian homelands, but it will only be a matter of time before white settlers are stretching to overtake that land as well. Why, there are already a good number settled in Texas. Mark my words, one day the United States will own all the land from coast to coast."

"Gracious, Joseph," Margaret said. "What would we ever want with all that land? We could never hope to see it all settled. Why, there simply aren't enough people."

"Lay claim to the land, and the people will come. They're going there without it even belonging to America proper. There are great vast lands that, once cultivated, will produce food and livestock to provide for our nation and share the burden of our toil here in the East. And too, as the nation is settled and secured with transportation such as the railroad can offer, we will find ourselves a stronger country and capable of dealing with the nations of this world."

James seemed to draw even more within himself as Joseph continued. "There are possibilities we have not yet even imagined. I applaud Carolina's interest in the matter. I think she will find in her lifetime that the railroad will reshape this nation and the attitude of all Americans. Don't you agree, James?"

James looked up with a sorrow in his eyes that Carolina immediately wished she could ease. "I believe rail travel will grow quite rapidly," he said and offered nothing more.

"I think locomotives are smelly," Georgia added, not to be left out of any conversation. "And they set things on fire. At school we learned that the engines give off such sparks they ignite the grass."

"You are studying the railroad in school?" Joseph asked, putting down his fork.

"No, not actually," Georgia replied. "Our schoolmaster has his house near the tracks on the north side of Washington. He doesn't like the railroad because he's always having to put out the fires."

"That's one small problem," Joseph said, resuming his meal. "I'm certain they will find a way to combat it. What of you, James? Any ideas on how they might resolve the problem of sparks?"

James was clearly uncomfortable with the subject. "I've not given the matter much thought."

Carolina could bear it no longer. To speak in private with James and learn of his attitude toward the railroad was one thing. To make it a dinnertime conversation was something else. Seeking to change the subject, Carolina spoke. "Papa, will you be going into Washington City before Christmas?"

"I suppose I might. Why do you ask?"

"I haven't finished my Christmas shopping." She smiled sweetly at her father, and only when her sisters joined in to suggest they make a trip did Carolina cast a quick glance to where James sat.

His gaze met hers and seemed to reflect gratitude. Carolina gave only the hint of a nod before turning her attention back to the discussion. It was enough he knew she cared about his discomfort. Perhaps it would be enough to open the door to a conversation regarding the accident.

Twenty-Five

Truce Between Friends

*A*fter supper Carolina made her way outside for a brief walk. Her father and James had retired to the study for some male discussion while Virginia and Margaret began addressing the details of the upcoming party. For once, Carolina was grateful to be ignored. The biting cold of the wind stung her cheeks, but the air was invigorating and she ignored the discomfort and walked on.

The garden, now brown and dead, would no doubt soon be covered in snow. The thought saddened her. She'd never liked winter with its deathlike grip upon the land. Nor had she cared for its long dark nights and short gloomy days. In winter the light was subdued, and all of nature was subjected to the despair that the sun might never again shine in full. Of course there were splendid days when the sun reflected in brilliance against full fields of snow, but they were so few, and they never satisfied her like a field of green against warm brown dirt. No, she longed already for the flowering trees of spring and her mother's beloved daffodils and irises.

A lone lantern hanging along the path between the main house and the slave quarters rocked gently in the breeze and gave off strange shadowy patterns on the pathway. The ghostly apparitions played games with her mind, and Carolina shuddered. She thought of Granny, so old and feeble. So near death. It was not believed that Granny would live through another winter. Granny said it didn't matter a single bit to her. She was heaven bound, and the good Lord could fetch her home anytime He saw fit.

Thinking of this, Carolina stared up at the starry sky and wondered at the images there. Was heaven somewhere up beyond the pinpoints of starlight? Was anything truly up there? Sometimes the stars looked close enough to reach up and touch. And other times, like tonight, they seemed to be so far from reach that Carolina felt small and insignificant. Perhaps it was all just an illusion. Perhaps heaven was an illusion as well, and if it were, then where did you go when you died?

Making her way around the house, she passed the tiny family cemetery. Death made her think of the man who'd died in the derailment. She remembered the pain she'd seen in James' expression at supper. It wasn't just discomfort with the subject; it was a deep penetrating grief. If locomotives and railroad talk caused him that much sorrow, she reasoned, perhaps it would be better to just drop the subject.

I've been selfish, she concluded. I've not given a single thought to what he must be going through. If Mr. Davis was his friend, James must have been with him when he died. Carolina couldn't imagine for a single moment what it must be like to watch someone you care about die. She had not even been born when her brothers died. What if she happened to be there when Granny died? How could she ever bear such a thing? How could anyone?

Pulling her cloak tight, Carolina heard the moaning sound of the wind as it rushed through the stand of trees. The dogwood and redbud trees, now void of leaves, made a line of spectral figures along the path, causing Carolina to shudder. Suddenly she wanted to be back in the house, safe and warm. Thoughts of death were taking a greater toll on her than the icy blasts of wind. Crossing the yard at a run, she came up the steps of the side veranda and paused to catch her breath.

"You ran like the devil himself was chasing you." The voice was the rich baritone of James Baldwin.

Carolina nearly jumped a foot. She couldn't see his face clearly, for the only light was that which shone out through the window, but she heard him chuckle.

"Sorry, I didn't intend to startle you," he said.

The apology sounded sincere and Carolina decided to let it go. "I'm afraid," she said, hoping to put the matter to rest, "I got a little spooked."

"It's a good night for it." His tone immediately became sober.

Carolina stepped closer in order to make out the details of his face. Impulsively, she decided to apologize for her behavior regarding the railroad studies. "I'm glad to find you here," she began. She noted his puzzled expression and continued quickly before he could offer comment. "I have come to realize I was wrong in pressuring you about the railroad. I won't do it again. You must have endured a great deal, and I was insensitive to forget the accident."

He remained silent and his face seemed to take on a stern, almost harsh expression.

"I hope you can forgive me," she said quietly. When there was still no response, she added in as even a tone as she could, trying to hide her awkwardness, "Good evening, Mr. Baldwin." Carolina turned to leave.

"Wait, please don't go," James said, surprising her with his urgency. She turned back to face him. "Yes?"

"I . . ." His voice trailed away, and he turned his focus toward the dark shadowy yard.

"You have every right to be angry with me," she said, trying desperately to fill the intense silence. "I was only thinking of myself, but you must understand that I've developed an absolute passion for the railroad. I let that overwhelm my better judgment." She was rambling, saying anything and everything that came to mind. Suddenly it seemed very important that he understand. "I guess I didn't associate my ambitions with the toll it would extract on you. Especially given the accident and—" She stopped abruptly, afraid to mention what she had just learned from the magazine.

After several moments had passed in silence, James finally spoke. "I appreciate what you did for me at supper." He hesitated, glanced at her, then skittishly looked away. "I've been lost inside this problem for some time, and I can't say as I know how to deal with it properly. I know of your enthusiasm for the railroad. I once held the same feelings."

"But you don't now?" Carolina asked softly, her voice barely audible above the growing force of the wind, which made her toes tingle and whipped up under her skirt.

"No," James answered. "I want to run as far away from the railroad as is humanly possible."

Suddenly Carolina saw a vulnerability in James she had never noted before. She had been so wrapped up in perceiving him as the elder, the one to be in awe of, that she had failed to really see the person James was. There was very much a lost little boy in James, and that aspect was both endearing and confusing to Carolina.

"But why?" she asked, trying to be sensitive.

James walked away from her a few paces and stood up against the veranda rail, staring out into the darkness. "I knew a wonderful man . . . his name was Phineas Davis."

"The man who died in the train derailment?"

"Yes." James didn't bother to turn around. "He and I became acquainted. I didn't know him long, but we had many of the same goals, the same dreams for our lives—and we both loved the railroad. Phineas was responsible for creating the new engines used by the B&O Railroad, and he had just offered me a job working with him when the accident took place.

"I had already accepted the position, and for a few moments life seemed so good. Then, in a literal wink of an eye, everything fell apart. The train derailed and Phineas was killed instantly." He sighed and covered his face with his hands. "I can still see his face in death. The look of disbelief and confusion. I dream about it still."

"I'm so sorry." The words seemed inadequate. Carolina felt her youth and inexperience as never before.

"I never wanted to see another locomotive as long as I lived, and then I came here and you immediately began to besiege me about the railroad. . . ."

"You do believe that I am truly sorry about that?"

James turned to face her. "Yes . . . I know that."

Still, he sounded so miserable, and Carolina felt an urge to mother him—she who was but a child herself.

"It's not your fault, don't you see?" he went on. "I'm trying to keep from having to deal with this, and you, in your way, have forced me to see it straightforward. It's not just Phineas—although I will miss him. It's much more."

Carolina forgot the numbness in her feet and the bone-chilling wind. She forgot everything but the man standing before her. Only yesterday it seemed they were childhood adversaries. And literally yesterday they were adversaries in a different way. But suddenly this man emerged from that level to become a person of deep feeling.

Drawing a slow breath she spoke the words that had been on her heart all evening. "Perhaps in confronting it, Mr. Baldwin, you can finally be free of the pain."

"Pain?"

"It's plain to see. You didn't need to speak; your eyes said it all." She paused, wanting to make certain the words were just right. "I saw it in your expression tonight—the way it hurt you when we discussed the railroad."

He nodded. "Yes . . . pain. Can you even imagine it, Carolina?"

"No, not really. But I want to, Mr. Baldwin. I want to understand." She warmed at the intimate use of her first name.

"Why?"

"Isn't that what friends do?"

"Friends?" He smiled. "I'd like that . . . so much more than whatever we've been since I came." He paused, seeming to give careful consideration to his next words. "It's just that I thought I knew what I wanted from life. The railroad had become everything to me. When I woke up in the morning I thought instantly of locomotive designs. And every time I heard the bell or whistle blast I thought of how I would one day be an important part of linking the country together. I truly loved it."

"Then why abandon it?" she probed gently.

"I may not have known Phineas Davis as well as I would have liked, but he believed in me and wanted me to join him in working for the B&O."

"That's all very well and fine. Still, why turn your back on what you obviously love?"

James' expression turned cold. "Phineas died at the hand of the very thing he loved. How can I possibly go back to the railroad and work with the engine designs he began, knowing all the while that the railroad cost him his life?"

The wind picked up, and again the low moaning sound echoed through the buildings and trees. Carolina shivered, but not from the cold. "Your friend died doing what he wanted to do. You said yourself, it was the thing he loved most. How can you hold it against him to have lived and died the way he chose?"

"But he didn't choose to die out there in a train derailment," James insisted.

"No one ever really chooses their way of dying, but they do choose how to live. Your friend had a dream and a desire to see that dream fulfilled. He put his life into it. Why not his death? Would he have put the railroad aside if he'd known it would kill him?"

James shook his head. "Probably not. Knowing Phineas it would just give him cause to burn the midnight oil a little longer."

"I would be that way, too," Carolina replied. "I seriously doubt Mr. Davis would have done things one bit different. My mother once told me I should never let fear keep me from living my life and seeking my dreams. It's my desire to have an education. And with that education I'd like to know more about the railroad and how locomotives work. But I don't want to be responsible for causing you, or anyone else, pain. If I have to wait until I'm grown and capable of living on my own, I'll get that education." She swallowed hard, uncertain she could continue with what she had to say. "So, if you want to end this position as my tutor, I will understand. I'll even be the one to address the matter with Father." The very thought of him quitting caused Carolina's eyes to fill with tears. She prayed he wouldn't go, yet she felt so filled with remorse for her actions of the past weeks. "I won't be responsible for grieving you further," she added in a wavering voice.

James reached out and touched her hand. Carolina hadn't realized how cold she was until his warm fingers folded around hers. "Please don't feel badly about what happened. You had no idea how I felt."

"Yes, but I didn't have to pester you every day since your arrival, and . . ." She paused, wondering if she could think clearly with his thumb gently rubbing across the top of her hand. "I . . . uh . . . I haven't been very nice to you. I've been argumentative and I'm sorry." She struggled to keep her emotions in check.

James looked at her sternly for a moment. "I think maybe it's been that very nature that has kept me from feeling too sorry for myself." He paused and offered her a smile. "I've had to keep on my toes in order to deal with your attacks. Maybe God knew if I sat at home in Washington, I'd only grow more withdrawn and distant."

Carolina felt a surge of hope. Perhaps he would stay and continue the lessons. She had to prove her sincerity. "So shall we call a truce, Mr. Baldwin?" Her cloak hood fell back and the wind toyed with her curls.

"I'd like that, and I'd like it even more if you would call me James . . . that is, if we are truly to be friends."

She gently disengaged her hand. Her mind was a mass of confusing thoughts. "Very well, James." She went to the door and, with a hand on the brass handle, turned to add, "I promise not to bring up the subject of the railroad again."

Twenty-Six

A New Subject

The following morning Carolina had no sooner seated herself at the table when Virginia entered the room on the arm of James. Grimacing to herself, Carolina listened to Virginia's sickeningly sweet praise for James' healing progress. Does she never tire of such blithering? Carolina wondered.

"Christmas at Oakbridge is positively wonderful," Virginia said in a voice dripping honey. "You'll absolutely love it."

"Yes," Carolina said, pushing back her book and turning to frown at her sister. "Virginia puts on quite a display. Well, maybe I should say"—Carolina tapped the book as if trying to think of the right words—"Oakbridge puts on quite a display, and Virginia is merely a part of it."

While James closed the door, Virginia whirled around to stick out her tongue at Carolina. Carolina only smiled and noted that James was trying hard not to do the same.

"Well, if you're ready to begin our studies, Carolina," James said in an authoritative air, "I've a new subject to add to our schedule." Virginia, realizing she'd been dismissed, quietly took a seat by the window and drew out the doily she'd been crocheting.

James went to the secretary and brought back a two-foot-long scroll of papers, which he immediately began to unroll on the tabletop. Carolina's eyes widened at the sight of the locomotive schematics laid out before her. She looked up at James, questioning with her eyes the object at her fingertips.

"You wanted to know about such things," he offered by way of explanation. "I thought perhaps this would be a good way to start."

"But I thought . . . I mean I told you I . . ."

"I remember what you said," James replied, taking a seat beside his pupil. He lowered his voice and added, "I did a great deal of thinking after our talk last night, and I've decided you were right."

Carolina wondered only momentarily if Virginia found this conversation strange. Gingerly she reached out and touched the paper. "Are these your designs?"

James smiled. "Yes. They're the same ones I showed to Phineas Davis. He, of course, had his own designs, and shortly after his death a prototype was built using a horizontal boiler. My designs aren't intended to actually be put to use—they were mainly a training exercise for me. However, I've tried to include some of my own ideas, such as a shorter boiler to accommodate the crooked track. Would you like to know more about them?"

"Oh yes. Please!"

"See here?" His long slender fingers traced the edges of inked perimeters. "The largest component of the engine is the boiler. The earliest known steam engine was created by the Egyptians about 100 B.C. They noted that if water was boiled over a wood fire, steam could be directed through pipes into a hollow ball pierced with a couple of bent tubes. When the steam reached the ball it would hiss out through the tubes and make the ball spin. They had no idea what to do with the new creation, but no doubt they realized even then that it was something of value."

"But when did they start using railroads?" Carolina interrupted excitedly.

James smiled indulgently. "Actually the railroad has a much earlier origin than you might think. Eighteen hundred years ago the Greeks made wood rails on which to move heavy wagons by oxen and horses. This made it easier for the animals, and sometimes humans, to pull the loads because the rail made it smoother. Centuries later, it was realized that iron would last longer and be smoother yet, and the modern rail was born."

Carolina turned her attention back to the engine design. "So they took the Egyptians' idea and made a bigger boiling pot, and the hissing ball became cylinders that pressed the pistons and moved the drive wheels?"

James laughed. "It seems you know a great deal more than I had realized."

"Father told me about the transference of steam from the boiler to the drivers. I asked him about it after we saw the engine in Washington."

"This design differs from the engine you saw."

"Yes, I see that. The boiler is horizontal instead of vertical," Carolina said, rather proud of herself for recognizing the difference.

"That's right. Phineas designed vertical boilers for the B&O because the rail line is very curved with many twists and tight turns. A horizontal boiler would jump the tracks constantly because the length would never be able to keep up with the turns. Vertical boilers allow for the entire engine to be little more than fifteen feet long, whereas most of the horizontal boilers being designed are at least half that again."

"So why not keep with the vertical boilers?" Carolina was totally taken in by the drawings.

"You can't increase the boiler size on a vertical boiler. If you make them taller, most won't fit through the tunnels or pass under the existing bridges. Without increasing the size, you can't increase the power. Also small boilers keep the overall weight of the engine down."

"Why is that important?" Carolina eagerly turned to meet James' eyes. His face was only inches from hers, and it instantly made her nervous. Quickly lowering her face to the schematics, she asked again in a shaken voice, "Why . . . is that important?"

James seemed unaffected by the encounter. "The tracks on the B&O are weak. Most American track leaves a great deal to be desired. They've used strap rail on most of the B&O. This is thin strips of iron laid on top of wooden stringers. These stringers are fastened to wooden ties to hold it in place. The newest method of laying track is to use a T-rail."

"I've heard Father discuss it," Carolina stated, recalling to mind the time she'd eavesdropped.

"Well, one of its many advantages is that it's a lot stronger and can bear up under the heavier weight of the horizontal boilers. The Washington Branch of the B&O uses T-rail."

"So if the rails are being adjusted to take on greater weight, why not straighten out the curves while you're at it?"

"Exactly," James replied. "And so they are. Even now there are small portions of the B&O rail between Baltimore and Harper's Ferry that crews are working to remake. But because of cost, they are mostly just straightening the line a bit and reusing the strap."

"So eventually, when the money is available, they will rebuild the line?"

"That is the plan. Mr. Thomas would like to see the entire line west to the Ohio redone in T-rail. It will make it safer and more sturdy and better able to handle the larger engines."

"Then your ideas for a horizontal design shouldn't be rejected." Carolina's matter-of-fact tone was intended to encourage James. She wanted to keep him in whatever positive frame of mind would allow for his continued good nature toward this subject.

"James is giving up that nonsense with the railroad," Virginia announced from where she sat. "He told me so not two days ago. Isn't that so, James?"

James rolled the papers up and shrugged. "I might have been a bit hasty in my decision."

"I hardly think so," Virginia replied coolly. She eyed Carolina with calm disdain, as though knowing already that her sister had something to do with this change of heart. "Your father is offering you a stable job in banking. It isn't everyone who can simply waltz into a position of such social importance."

"Money isn't everything," Carolina interjected strongly. "If a man has to be about something, why not let it be something he enjoys?"

"Such childish notions," Virginia said with a stilted laugh. "I would expect that view from someone of your immature age, sister dear."

James interrupted the conversation here. "Ladies, I've been hired to tutor, not to argue. Let us return to our studies. I have yet another design to show you."

Virginia sullenly resumed her crocheting, but not before Carolina offered her a triumphant little smile. It was then and there that Carolina decided if she had anything to say about it, James would return to his dream of the railroad.

———

When Carolina and Virginia left the classroom to prepare themselves for the midday meal, James sat back on the sofa and ruminated over the morning's progress. It gave him great pleasure to recall Carolina's excitement when he had produced the locomotive designs. He had been a bit shaky at first when he had launched into the discussion, but she had not noticed at all. And before long, he too had practically forgotten his pounding heart and trembling hands.

It felt good to talk about the railroad again. Very good. Of course, talking was a far cry from riding a train again, but perhaps it was a start. And how odd that little Carolina had been the one to boost him in that positive direction. She was wise beyond her years. There were times when he thought he ought to be learning from her. He might know science and mathematics, but there was so much about life that eluded him.

The simplicity of her response, if not the wisdom, had made him think about his reaction to all that had happened. He remembered her simple words, *"Would he have put the railroad aside if he'd known it would kill him?"* The railroad might not be important enough to die for, but dreams, hopes . . . yes, he believed they were.

Maybe he would never be able to step on a train again, but that didn't mean he couldn't continue to produce his designs. And it certainly didn't mean he ought to give up after that one unfortunate incident. He had a talent for design, or so Phineas had told him, and he had a decided aversion to banking. After much thought and Carolina's sweet encouragement, he decided it was better to face the terrors of the rails than the horrible boredom of banking.

At least he wasn't ready to make any rash decisions. He feared Virginia might never let him live down his hasty words of two days ago, but he'd handle her somehow. In the meantime, he still had to recuperate fully. Who could say what might happen during that time? Why, Carolina might just get him aboard a train before his stint at Oakbridge was over.

Twenty-Seven

Something to Think About

A week before Christmas James entered the sitting room without Virginia's ever constant presence. Carolina was already hard at work, head bent over her book, pen in hand. He could hardly believe the progress she'd made. Already she commanded a good understanding of algebra, and the problems presented her were rationally examined and questioned when that understanding failed her. She was an avid student, and since their agreement to a truce, he found her company quite enjoyable as well.

He also found Virginia's company enjoyable, but for an entirely different reason. Virginia was . . . well, the kind of woman a man naturally found alluring. She was delicate and charming with her talk of the social season and of helping the children at church to put on a Christmas pageant. She always managed to speak of domestic affairs as though her heart beat for their very existence. And perhaps it did. Seldom did Virginia broach any subject other than that which might appeal to her feminine nature. James doubted seriously that Virginia even knew there was a political or industrial world, except that the people who participated in such things were often those at her parties.

Yes, he found Virginia to be a fine companion. Her beauty alone ought to be enough to keep any man interested and content. He was content at any rate. He'd already decided to propose to her after the New Year.

"Oh, bother!" Carolina exclaimed, rallying James from his thoughts.

"What's the problem?" he asked, closing the door behind him.

"Oh, I didn't know you were here," she said, seeming somewhat embarrassed. "It's really nothing. I just spilled ink." Getting up, she

176

went to the secretary where she'd purposefully tucked a few rags for just such occasions.

James watched her bite her lip as she concentrated on cleaning up the mess. She wore her hair down, with only a delicate pink ribbon to hold it back away from her face. The dark brown ringlets danced over her shoulder when she bent to her task, and without thought James reached out to keep them from merging with the inky mess.

Startled, Carolina immediately straightened, and James dropped the silky curls. "Sorry," he said, feeling his face redden a bit. "I feared your hair was about to change colors to indigo."

Carolina, still holding the inky rag, nodded briskly and returned to her task. "I should have paid better attention to what I was doing." Her voice sounded rather stiff and formal, and James worried that he'd offended her with his behavior. The few times he'd touched her hand or brushed her arm with his, she'd always reacted the same way. No doubt she was still harboring some anger against him for his original attitude toward her education. If that were the case, he could help rectify the situation here and now.

"You know, Carolina, I don't believe I've told you what I think of your progress."

"I beg your pardon?" She finished with the ink and discarded the rag in a bin by the fireplace. Briefly studying her hands to ensure that none of the ink would follow to her clothing, she nervously smoothed her skirt.

James motioned her to the more comfortable sofa. "Here, let's take a moment from the studies."

Carolina eyed him strangely but did as he suggested. She sat on the edge of the yellow-striped sofa, back stiffly straight, hands folded in her lap. James limped noticeably as he retrieved a chair and brought it to sit in front of her.

"I just wanted to take a few moments to tell you how well you're doing. I know I had my misgivings in the beginning, but I'm very impressed with your ability to comprehend the subjects we've taken on." He paused, trying to gauge her reaction, but Carolina's face remained fixed. "I suppose I have always looked at extended studies for women as a waste of time. But you have taken such joy in what you are learning that I think perhaps the purpose resolves itself in your pleasure, if nowhere else. It seems to me that should you never be allowed to do anything more with what you've learned here, you would find happiness in what you had."

Carolina frowned. "Are you telling me that you're finished tutoring me?"

James shook his head. "Not at all. I merely wanted you to know I recognize your keen intellect. You are unlike most women . . . perhaps due to your youth or your father's obvious indulgence . . ."

"Are you saying I'm spoiled?" Her brow arched slightly, the old ire returning to her tone.

James ran his hand back through his dark hair. This wasn't going the way he'd intended. "Not at all. I'm simply saying you're different from other women. Oh, bother. I'm not saying this well at all."

Carolina calmed. "I'm sorry. I suppose I'm a bit testy today. Virginia put me off at breakfast, and I've not had much patience since."

James offered what he hoped was a sympathetic smile. "What happened to put you two at odds?" It was always something—usually Virginia baiting her younger sister and Carolina losing her patience.

Carolina sighed. "She wants me to occupy her former suitors at the party so that she can save most of her dances for you."

The look on her face was one of such utter displeasure that James couldn't help but laugh.

"It's true!" Carolina exclaimed before he could say a word.

"I've no doubt it is," James replied. "Virginia must have forgotten I am in poor shape for much dancing."

"Oh, she'll find a way to monopolize your every moment. And I will still be left to do her bidding."

"It seems as though you were asked to tend the dying rather than enjoy an evening of flirtatious adventure."

"Is that what you call it? Flirtatious adventure?" Carolina relaxed a bit. "My, my, but I would have given it almost any other name."

"That bad, eh?"

"Utter misery," Carolina replied dejectedly. "After all, Virginia has discarded those men for one reason or another."

James chuckled at this and added, "Yes, but consider Virginia's intellectual standards and the things she considers important in life."

Carolina seemed to brighten at this. "I'd not thought on the matter in that light. I suppose you have something there. Those young men might be rather wonderful. Although perhaps it is not too complimentary of yourself."

He put one hand to his chest and the other to the air. Striking this melodramatic pose, he said, " 'But love is blind, and lovers cannot see the pretty follies that themselves commit.' "

"Shakespeare at a time like this?"

He dropped the stance. "Of course. When better? Then again, I suppose this discussion is most inappropriate. You cannot hope to be objective, and in fact, neither can I."

"Still, you won't have to dance with those men."

"I should say not," James said, breaking into a hearty laugh. "And strange this party would be if I did. Why can't you get Georgia to help you? She looks to be coming along in age. Isn't she old enough to be seeking suitors?"

"Not quite. She's only thirteen and not even out of common school. Her beaus might well have to court her while climbing trees and jumping fences. Although Mother would have us all married by sixteen if she had her way."

"So you're nearly out of time," he teased and watched her obvious discomfort played out in the nervous lacing and unlacing of her fingers.

She wasn't given a chance to reply because her father chose that moment to burst into the room.

"I hope I'm not interrupting anything critical." Joseph strode into the room, an animated expression on his face, a glint in his eye.

"Not at all," James said, getting to his feet. "We were actually discussing the party."

"Well, take a look at this," Joseph said, extending a recent copy of the *National Intelligencer*. "Charters have been granted for over ten proposed rail lines."

James gave a cursory glance at the article. "People are excited about the railroad. It's evident in things like this. Individual lines are bound to increase."

"I've long considered the benefits of supporting other lines and in fact have already made a few investments, but until now I've never considered the idea of starting one of my own."

"Oh, Papa!" Carolina exclaimed and jumped up. "Are you truly going to form your own railroad?"

"I don't know, but the thought is an intriguing one. Just imagine what people around here would say."

"Imagine what Mother would say."

Joseph chuckled and replied, "She would blame the wanderlust for sure. But seriously, James, do you think it a conceivable notion?"

"Certainly. All of the major railroads have been started by private citizens. Usually several men work together to bring such a thing about, however."

"Several men, but no women, eh?" Carolina piped up.

Joseph's eyes sparkled. "Perhaps there have been no women who were interested in owning a piece of a locomotive."

"Then here's the first one," Carolina announced. "Oh, Papa, if you start a railroad I want to be involved, too."

Joseph put an arm around her shoulder and offered her a squeeze. "I wouldn't dream of excluding you on such a venture. What do you think I should do first, James?"

"I'd suggest a long talk with Philip Thomas at the B&O. He was instrumental in the start of that railroad, and if anyone could give you advice it would be he."

"Wouldn't he see me as a rival?" Joseph asked seriously.

"Perhaps. But what of it? The positive promotion of the railroad can only benefit the Baltimore and Ohio. Choose a path that won't threaten the B&O, and Thomas will probably be quite supportive. Maybe he would even allow you to purchase locomotives from his shops at Mt. Clare."

"I'll post a letter immediately," Joseph replied. "It certainly can't hurt to get more information. In fact, James, what with your interest in the railroad, maybe you would consider coming in on this project with me."

"I have no capital to invest, sir." James could only think of his family's financial affairs and how imperative it was that he marry in order to boost those poor ledgers for the future.

"Bah, who's talking money? I'm talking about what's up here," Joseph said, pointing to his head. "You have a vision for the railroad in general. You have designs and ideas for engines, and you could easily guide me in decisions related to how we could approach this mission."

James was definitely taken aback by this idea. Working with the B&O had seemed as close to his dream as he could imagine. "It would take years to actually get the thing off of paper and into reality."

"And what of it? You could spend that time expanding your knowledge of the business. Go to work for the B&O and get experience building your engine designs. In the meantime, I could be raising the needed capital and deciding a course for our road."

"Don't forget me," Carolina said. "I could help in keeping your books and correspondences. Maybe even venture out with you to study the land."

"Exactly right! This is sounding more possible all the time. What say we include your father, as well?"

James remembered his father's negative attitude toward the railroad, but the idea of Leland Baldwin joining in simply to promote good relations between the two families seemed at least a remote possibility. "I'd be happy to ask him at the party."

"It's settled then. We'll discuss it at length after Christmas." Joseph left after giving Carolina a hearty pat on the back. He seemed quite happy with himself and even forgot to take the paper back when he exited the room.

"Do you think Father's proposal a possibility?" Carolina asked James when they were alone.

"I think that man can accomplish anything he sets his mind to," James replied in sincere admiration. "Now I see where you get your determination."

Twenty-Eight

A New Venture

Leland Baldwin rearranged himself uncomfortably on the blue brocade armchair in one of the Oakbridge drawing rooms. The highly ornate Gothic frame seemed hardly sturdy enough to hold his weight, and it made him increasingly more nervous by the minute. Light strains of music filtered in through the closed doors. This was followed by much laughter and singing as the gathering of guests joined the piano with a hearty chorus of "Deck The Halls."

He should be with the others, toasting the holiday and sampling the splendid fare laid out on long sideboards. Instead, he found himself spirited away by a very animated James, and now he awaited his son's return with some trepidation. While he was relieved to see James acting more his old self, Leland always became suspicious when his son singled him out for private discussions.

"We're here, Father," James said, entering the room with Joseph Adams.

"Leland, forgive me for taking you away from the party, and after you braved the inclement weather to come out," Joseph said, giving Leland a hearty handshake. "I won't keep you here long."

Leland awkwardly rose in greeting. "I am just honored to be your guest, Joseph. Now, what's all this about a private proposal?" Laughter sounded again when a sour note was struck on the piano, and the chorus was started again.

James went quickly to close the door, only marginally shutting out the party. "Perhaps another time would have lent itself to a more businesslike atmosphere," Joseph said, taking a seat across from Leland, "but I feared it would be past the New Year before I'd have a chance to speak with you again."

"Is there a matter of urgency?" Leland questioned anxiously.

James pulled up a chair. "Not really urgency, Father, but something that has taken the interest of Mr. Adams."

"Not only me, but of my daughter and your son as well," Joseph replied.

Leland smiled. Ah, he thought, so there is to be an engagement announced for Christmas. He'd not thought James would be so joyous about the situation, but relief flooded though him as he imagined what his son's union with Virginia Adams could mean for the Baldwin affairs.

"This is good news," Leland gave an enthusiastic nod of approval directed toward James. "Mrs. Baldwin will be delighted."

James frowned. "I don't see why Mother would find this of any interest."

"Good grief, son! You're her only child. Of course she will find this of interest. After all, it isn't every day you send your son off to be married."

"Married!" James exclaimed and Joseph laughed heartily.

"I'm afraid I gave you the wrong idea, Leland. This is an entirely different matter."

James reddened at this, and Leland tensed and drew in a tight breath.

"Then what is this all about?" Leland said rather testily. "You mentioned my son and your daughter."

Joseph rubbed his muttonchop whiskers. "And so I did. I spoke of Carolina, however, not Virginia. And the proposal I'm seeking to include you on is one based upon railroad interests."

"Railroad. . . ?"

"That's right. In the last few days your son and I have done some talking, and after searching through many of the newspapers and journals, I find that railroads are being created very nearly every day. James and I have discussed the possibility of starting our own rail line, and we wanted to include you in the project, if you were of a mind to join us."

Leland's disappointment was evident. "I've no time for such foolery. The railroad will see its day and fade away. It can't hope to last. Why, James is evidence enough of the serious problems to be considered. That accident cost the B&O a small fortune. Phineas Davis is dead and my James is left wounded, maybe for life. Even with the dangers aside, I've told you before it's a very risky business. You can't hope to see a decent return on your investment, at least not for a long, long while. Maybe not even in your lifetime."

"Don't be so pessimistic, Baldwin," Joseph replied. "The B&O is still doing quite well. There are a multitude of other rail lines as well, and all are showing some margin of profitable business. I propose a line that would run from Falls Church to Washington. It would link all the families in this area and be small enough that the price would be quite contained."

"If it's that small, what possible merit would there be?" Leland shifted his weight and silently wished the conversation could be concluded. He'd hoped with the accident that James' interest in the railroad would be at a standstill, if not an end.

"There's a great deal of cotton in this area that could be shipped on the rail, not to mention passenger traffic into the city. If a line were to be laid from Falls Church, I could actually ship my cotton to New York City and eventually even Boston, without it ever having to leave the rail cars."

"Shipping via the river and canals is cheaper," Leland suggested.

"Not necessarily, Father," James joined in. "The canal is having a great deal of trouble. There are constant battles for right-of-way, and the cost of usage is rising."

"And your railroad is not suffering the same effects?"

"Not to the degree of the canal. The railroad, once laid, won't cost as much in upkeep. It will still need to be maintained, but slave labor of the area plantation owners could assist in that and save the line a small fortune. Each plantation owner could pay a fee to use the line, and part of that fee might well be to offer up the use of slaves to improve or maintain the line."

"Not to mention that once the line is actually in place, the number of people simply riding in and out of Washington will help to support it," Joseph stated.

"That's right, Father. The Washington Branch charges two dollars and fifty cents per trip between Washington and Baltimore, and in the four months since that line opened, they've already carried more than ten thousand passengers."

"That's unheard of!" Leland exclaimed. No one had told him this before, and he found it hard to believe.

"It's true enough," Joseph announced. "Several months ago I invested in the B&O, and the figures James quotes are directly from Thomas. They are increasing their passenger loads each month, and the freight revenues are increasing as well. In one year the B&O grossed $260,000 in revenues."

"And you believe there would be enough interest from the folks of this area to support your short line into the city?" Leland was quickly starting to rethink his attitude toward the railroad.

"I believe in time and with the right laying of the line, it will pay for itself. It shouldn't take all that long, either." Joseph seemed more than confident in his beliefs. "James and I have even discussed the possibility of extending the line southwest to Fairfax and maybe eventually south, all the way to Richmond. Just imagine the possibilities there."

"But don't these things require a charter?"

"Indeed. And that, in all honesty, may well take the bigger portion of our patience. Still, while we are waiting, we can start putting together the funds. I have enough capital to put up in order to show our ability to see the project begun. You could help by soliciting some area investors and maybe even government officials to consider purchasing subscriptions in our line. That will speak volumes to the legislature."

"If we can get at least half of the projected funds lined up through pledged and actual subscriptions," James interjected, "other investors and plantation owners will soon follow suit and see the merit of investing."

"And you believe people would be willing to do this?" If this were indeed true, Leland was already seeing the possibilities for benefits to his own financial needs.

"Of course they will. There are many wealthy people out there who have a desire to see the railroad move forward. They will see the development of another line as a boon to the entire industry."

"Remarkable," Leland muttered. "But what of the fact that little visible progress will be evident at first. I mean, it will take time to obtain a charter, and monies will surely have to be laid out in order to have surveys performed and such. Then, too, what if the charter is never granted?"

"That's always a possibility," Joseph replied. "But this is where I come in. I have friends in the capital, and I can provide some of the initial funds to get things going. We purchase the needed surveys and set down our plans on paper. James will be able to establish good connections for us with the B&O shops, and when the time comes perhaps we can even count on one of his designs to grace our first tracks."

Leland pulled out a handkerchief and mopped his perspiring brow. The Christmas merriment outside the room was already forgotten. The singers, though just as rowdy and boisterous as earlier, were scarcely of concern to Leland in light of this new information.

"And investors, even government investors, will understand that these things take time and that the money needs to be in the bank ready to draw against, even when there is no evidence in the physical nature of the promoted rail line?"

185

"It's very common in these things," James assured. "It also allows us the ability to request pledges rather than actual funds. This way people can raise the money gradually, and we can show strength for the charter."

"But again, what if the charter is never granted?"

Joseph shrugged. "Then we return the money or rearrange our plans and try again. Of course, the funds already expended for the charter and surveys will simply be losses that the investors will risk."

Before Leland could say another word, a light knock sounded on the door. Joseph rose to open it, and Carolina entered the room, carrying a tray of drinks. "I've brought some Christmas cheer," she said brightly. Leland grunted and struggled to his feet, as did James.

"You're just in time, daughter." Joseph took the tray from her and held it out to serve first Leland and then James.

"In time for what?" Carolina took a cup as it was offered her and waited while her father claimed the remaining portion.

He held his cup up high. "I propose we toast the formation of a new rail line."

Carolina grinned, and Leland thought she looked every bit as delighted by the prospect as his son. What a queer young woman to find interest in the making of masculine corporations.

"Are you with us, Father?" James asked.

"Yes, Mr. Baldwin," Carolina chimed in, "are you going to join us in our venture?"

Leland held up his cup. "How could I resist such a lucrative proposition?"

"Then here's to the Potomac and Great Falls Railroad! The P&GF!" Joseph declared.

"To the P&GF," James and Carolina said in unison.

Leland smiled and touched his cup to theirs. "To the P&GF!"

"You're terribly quiet, my dear. Are you unwell?" Edith Baldwin asked her husband on their journey back to Washington. She snuggled close to gain warmth, and Leland absentmindedly put an arm around her shoulders.

"I'm quite fit," he answered, deep in thought. The prospects of what he'd learned this night had intrigued him. To imagine people would invest their money in a project that might take months—more likely years—to show some type of action, much less any type of return. He was beginning to realize the possibilities for what could eventually turn his financial woes around.

"It was a lovely party, and our James seems quite content to escort Virginia Adams. I don't think he left her side for more than a few moments all evening. That is, after you finally joined us."

"It couldn't be helped. There was some business to discuss, and it took a little longer than we'd intended."

"Well, no matter. I hear from Margaret Adams that her Virginia is quite taken with James, and confidentially, she believes we will hear something of an engagement announcement by spring."

"That would be wonderful," Leland murmured, but his mind was clearly not on the conversation. Already he was organizing his next move. He felt Edith shiver and move closer still, and he reached out to pull another blanket over their laps. "This should help."

"Did you see how well he looks?" she murmured.

Leland realized for the first time that she had been as preoccupied in her thoughts as he had. Only her thoughts were clearly on their son.

"Yes, a remarkable recovery."

"He no longer uses his crutches, and he even managed a few of the slower dances. I think in time that limp will completely disappear." Edith sighed contentedly. "Will he join you at the bank after he and Virginia are engaged?"

"I don't think so. At least not at this point. He's quite taken with the railroad again."

Edith stiffened and pulled away. "I forbid him to reinvolve himself with that misfortune. It nearly killed him."

Leland nodded. "Yes, it did. But James is a grown man, and he is independently minded. He has a strong conviction about the railroad, and he's even managed to sway my original misgivings regarding it for the future."

"No!" Edith exclaimed and moved a space away. "You can't tell me you've actually encouraged him to take it up again? Please tell me you at least tried to convince him to join you in banking."

"Now, Edith, this is a matter for men to discuss. You've a soft mother's heart but no mind for business. James himself pointed out the remote possibility of his ever being in another accident of those proportions. And he will be involved most likely in the business end of the venture. He'll have little cause to ride the thing. Besides, the railroad is becoming safer all the time. I think it is the way of our future." He felt as if he was practicing a speech for all of his potential investors.

Edith pondered this for a moment, then with another shiver she eased back against her husband. "I suppose you're right. But I still fear that hideous metal monster will take him away from us."

"Nonsense and bother," Leland reassured. "James will be quite safe.

He's a talented young man, our son."

Edith hugged him. "I'm so glad you think so. I wondered if you two would be at odds with each other forever."

"Not at all. In fact, this evening I joined him in a venture."

"You did? What was it?"

"The railroad, what else?" Leland laughed. "Joseph Adams has it in his mind to start a railroad."

Edith said no more, obviously uninterested in learning more of the business venture. Leland once again grew absorbed in his own thoughts. He had big plans to make and couldn't be bothered with his wife's prattle. He kept thinking of what James and Joseph had told him. It was still quite amazing—fabulous fodder for his devious mind. If people would give over their money to invest in a railroad that might never come to be, then why not create more than one of these ventures? Paper railroads would be an easy thing to promote. Low subscription prices would urge even the average man to involve himself in the future development, and Leland knew there was much he could do to promote the railroad to his friends and bank depositors. The possibilities were endless, but he knew innately that for his schemes to succeed, he must not take even James into his confidence regarding the matter.

PART III

Spring 1836

As I went down to Louisville,
some pleasure for to see,
I fell in love with a railroad man,
and he in love with me.

I wouldn't marry a farmer,
for he's always in the dirt;
I'd rather marry the railroader
that wears them pretty blue shirts.

I wouldn't marry a goldsmith,
for he's always weighing gold,
I'd rather marry the railroader
that has to shovel up coal.

—Welby Toomey

Twenty-Nine

Elections and Revolutions

$\mathscr{S}$pring came early to Washington City, and amid the cherry, dogwood, and redbud blossoms, a spirit of anxiety and festivity made for an awkward balance among the citizens. It was an election year, promoting a circuslike atmosphere among government entities. The White House sought to encourage the support of Vice President Martin Van Buren for the presidency, believing "Vannie" could carry Jacksonian democracy into the forties. Opposing parties were still arguing among themselves, but the Whig party had nominated William Henry Harrison of Ohio for their candidate. Hugh Lawson White had accepted an independent nomination, as had Daniel Webster. But the real and very frustrating focus of April 1836 for the President was neither the man who would succeed him nor the slander against his "reign." The most prominent issue General Jackson had to deal with was Texas.

"First they send me this," Jackson said in a rage, waving a letter, "stating that the Alamo is a slaughterhouse and all is lost. Jim Bowie and Davy Crockett are both dead at the hands of Santa Anna, and Sam Houston has barely managed to escape capture. If I know Houston, and I do, he'll probably regroup and make a stand. Nevermind he has less than four hundred men to fight against Santa Anna's seven thousand!" He tossed the letter down and picked up another, never giving York Adams a chance to even comment.

"This one is better yet. This is from Stephen Austin. It seems on March 2 the Republic of Texas declared independence, and he requests"—again Jackson consulted the letter—"that the United States 'openly' take up the cause of the rebellious province." With a toss, this letter quickly joined the other on his desk, and Jackson searched his desk for something else.

191

"Get me a map, Adams. Where's that map of the Texas territory?"

York quickly pulled the map out from beneath the littered mess. Jackson had already pored over the parchment at least twenty times. "Right here." Jackson stabbed his finger at a particular spot. "This is where Sam Houston will go down in history." York leaned over the aging President's shoulder to see the words "Buffalo Bayou."

Jackson sat down hard in the high-backed leather chair. York could see that the tirade had taken a great deal out of the President. His health was failing him, and depression seemed to come easy in the face of growing attacks from his enemies. Jackson blamed them for the death of his beloved wife, Rachel, who after hearing their slanderous attacks during her husband's first presidential campaign had taken ill to her bed—never to recover. Now the same people were taking their toll on Jackson himself.

"Texas is determined to break free of Mexico and enter the union, but that whole situation opens up yet another issue, and that is one of slavery. The North and South are already straining at the bit and itching for a fight. South Carolina threatens to secede every time the wind changes directions, and this would be just one more issue to fling in the face of the North. John Calhoun sees Texas as a promising expansion of slavery, and while I sympathize with the South and own slaves of my own, as the President of this country I cannot in good faith ignore the concerns of our northern brothers."

"Still, Texas need not be only an issue of slavery," York said sympathetically. "There are a great many Americans settled in that Mexican state. They do at least deserve our consideration."

Jackson nodded slowly and sadly. "Mr. Adams, this is going to be the death of me yet."

"My father would say that it isn't the hounds chasing the fox that kills him, it's the getting caught that does the old fellow in." York offered Jackson a lopsided grin. "The way I see it, they're just nipping your heels a bit."

Jackson laughed. "I'd say Calhoun and Clay have 'pert' near taken off a toe or two."

York relaxed and enjoyed the joke. This was the Jackson he enjoyed working for and with. Unfortunately, time and the strain of the position had taken a vengeful toll on Jackson, and where Henry Clay and other adversaries couldn't touch him, the heavy mantle of national responsibility had nearly drained him of life.

"The Mexican government should have realized the inevitability of this," Jackson said, sobering and rubbing his chin thoughtfully. "They allow over twenty thousand Americans to settle and own land, then decide to halt immigration because those settlers are showing up with slaves. They think to simply turn off the flow by passing a law. They have no means of enforcement, and now, as they try to assert their authority, I find myself in a very delicate situation. If I intercede on behalf of Texas, I will alienate the North. And if I take up the side of Texas independence and annexation into the Union, I will forever go down in history as the President who set aside foreign treaties in order to strengthen the slavery issue."

"And to do nothing?" York questioned.

"At this moment neutrality is my only recourse," Jackson said with a sigh. "I would take Texas under our wing quicker than the crack of a good rawhide whip, but as much as they stand out there caterwauling for it, I must ignore them."

He fell silent for a moment, then startled York by slamming his fist down on the desk. The room echoed with the sound. "Mr. Adams, I need you to pen a letter for me. This will be a draft, but it must start somewhere."

York nodded and went to his writing desk. The items he needed were already waiting, and with nothing more than a glance, York let Jackson know he was prepared to take down the words.

"To the honorable Stephen F. Austin . . ."

Thirty

Tea and Confusion

"*B*ut your coming out must be something special," Julia Cooper, Carolina's closest friend, was saying.

The other ladies in the room nodded and added their reassuring comments.

"Oh yes, Carolina, this is a once-in-a-lifetime privilege."

Virginia and her friend Kate Milford both answered in unison, "It's the party to bring you into adulthood."

"And secure you in marriage," Julia added. As the only married woman in the group, she was esteemed.

Carolina rolled her eyes. She'd heard all these things so many times she wanted to scream. "Marriage is not on my mind and neither are coming-out parties."

Virginia shook her head. "She's been like this ever since Father allowed her to be tutored by James Baldwin."

"Tutored for what?" another young lady asked with a giggle.

"Now, stop that, Sarah Armstrong. You know James and I are very close to an understanding."

Carolina listened to the animated discussion as it wove in and around her private life. Mother had promoted the tea, saying it would be an excellent time for the young ladies to gather and exchange ideas for Carolina's coming-out party. Virginia had been all for it; her reasons, no doubt, were merely to have another social event to flaunt her blossoming relationship with James. Carolina did not want to even think of that fast-approaching milestone in her life. It scared her and bored her all at once.

But none of these girls could understand her feelings. All of them had been raised to be lovely and loved. So had she, but she couldn't bear it if that were all there was to life. Staring silently at the group of young women, Carolina instantly realized how out of place she was. They were discussing how to entice men without being improper and whether it was better to accept a marriage proposal on the second or third asking, for no well-bred woman would make it simple for a man and affirm his first request. Carolina knew they thought her odd. Even Julia, her lifelong friend, rebuked Carolina before they sat down to tea for straining her mind to learn all manner of unnecessary subjects.

Lifting the china teacup to her lips, Carolina wondered if any of these women would ever know what it really meant to live life. They were molded into the ideal hostesses and, as wives, would serve any house proud. But did they desire nothing more?

I do want a husband and a family, Carolina thought. I want to know the feel of a man's arms around me and to hear him speak my name with longing.

And in a way, she did envy her sister a little. She was going to get what she wanted. She would have the love of a man. Of James Baldwin. But Carolina didn't want to think of that. James Baldwin had become a puzzling complication to her life. When he talked of politics or the railroad, Carolina found him exhilarating, and when the discussion lent itself to the study of Shakespeare or Keats, she knew a tender and sensitive side of James that no one else seemed to comprehend. She didn't know what to make of it, nor of the strange sensations that overcame her whenever he was near her. Her heart would race if he chanced to touch her; a thrill would course through her if she happened upon him unexpectedly. And to think, only months ago she had fiercely hated him. Well, maybe not fiercely—maybe not hated.

It couldn't mean anything. A schoolgirl infatuation no doubt. She remembered how Maine had fallen in love with their schoolteacher when he was eleven. That's all this was. Nothing more. It couldn't be anything else.

Sarah's high-pitched giggle brought Carolina back to the tea party. For a brief instant she feared they had read her thoughts, and she reddened. Then she realized they had been responding to some comment by Julia. She tried to relax and keep her thoughts focused on the present.

"The party is set for April 30," Virginia informed them. "Invitations will be posted Monday, and that will give you plenty of time to have a new gown made. I'm going to have a beautiful gown of pale pink silk, and with any luck at all, I'll announce my engagement within a fortnight of that party." More laughter followed and Carolina grew very uncomfortable.

"What is your gown to look like?" Julia asked, leaning closer to

Carolina. "Something daring and delightful, no doubt."

"My coming-out gown was sewn with seed pearls and diamonds," Sarah Armstrong offered. "Mother said you only came out once, and society should definitely remember you when you did."

"Your gown is hard not to remember!" Virginia exclaimed. "Whatever became of it?"

"I'm saving it for my wedding gown," Sarah said proudly. "The gown cost a fortune, and it would be an honest pity to wear it only once. Still, I've never had an occasion that merited wearing it again. I'll have it remade and wed in it."

"What a remarkable idea," Kate Milford said with a flush to her face.

"Well, my wedding gown is going to be quite stunning," Virginia began. "I've been making lace for nearly four years."

"No!" exclaimed Sarah. "You don't say! What a wonderful idea. The labors of your hands will grace the very gown that will take you into wedded bliss. How delightful."

"I wish I'd thought of that," Kate said enthusiastically. "I suppose I could start now, but . . . well . . . I'm hoping for my own proposal this summer, and if Jonathan Donnelley manages to work up his courage and ask, I believe I will accept on the first proposal." This brought laughter from all the girls, with the exception of Carolina.

No one noticed that she'd had no chance to speak up about her gown, even if she'd known what her gown was to be. Her mother had plagued her for weeks to make a final choice, but Carolina found that sitting at Granny's bedside reading was more preferable to standing for a gown fitting. Wordlessly, Carolina got to her feet and pretended to busy herself at the tea cart.

"Oh, enough of this. Do play us something on the piano, Virginia. Mother was so impressed with your abilities at Christmas." The other girls confirmed Kate's request and soon the group had gathered around the piano.

Carolina took the opportunity to slip unnoticed from the room. She made her way outside without benefit of bonnet or shawl, knowing full well she'd no doubt vex her mother by freckling. A stroll down the cobblestone walkway led her to the gardens and a quiet repose to collect her thoughts. Maybe she'd even visit Granny. Granny always seemed able to help her think through her problems.

My problem, Carolina thought, is that every time Virginia mentions her intentions toward James, I feel ill.

She couldn't understand her reaction and wondered silently how to deal with the situation. If Virginia was right, and most likely she was, James would one day be her sister's husband, and Carolina would have no other choice but to deal with it. But what was it exactly she was dealing with? Her memories brought to mind James' twinkling blue eyes and boyish smile whenever she understood a new concept. She did care a great deal about him, and his misery over the railroad and subsequent emergence from that crisis did bond them in a way, but was there more?

Pushing deeper amid the sweet scents of wisteria, Carolina had no sooner taken a seat to contemplate the matter than her mother and father appeared.

"Well, I thought you ladies would still be discussing the party," Joseph said good-naturedly.

Carolina squared her shoulders a bit. "I was on my way to visit Granny. But they're all still plotting and planning."

"Then why are you out here and without so much as a parasol or bonnet?" Margaret questioned. "You should be in there deciding things as well. It is, after all, your coming-out party they are discussing."

"I suppose the subject does not hold the same appeal to me as it does the others."

"Unheard of." Margaret paled. "I cannot believe a young lady of your upbringing would not find it a marvelous affair. This is your passage into adulthood. You will be received in your own right now, and gentlemen will come to call in earnest."

Carolina shrugged. Carolina wondered why her mother couldn't accept her as she was. "I doubt it will much change things if I have a big party or a little one. I'll still turn sixteen, and I'll still be more interested in my studies than my dance card."

"Carolina!" Margaret exclaimed and dropped her hold on Joseph. "I will not tolerate such an attitude from you. A great deal of work and cost is going into making this a memorable event. The least you could do is pretend you are honored by our efforts."

Joseph gave Carolina a sympathetic look but agreed with his wife. "Your mother is right. This is a fine old tradition and one of which you are entitled."

"Have you no interest in meeting and marrying a suitable man?" Margaret questioned.

"Of course," Carolina replied and thought she saw a shadow of relief in her mother's eyes. "I just didn't plan to do it all within the next month!"

Margaret was clearly perturbed, and even Joseph frowned at Carolina's outburst. "This isn't like you, Carolina," her father said sternly. "I can't allow you to speak so disrespectfully to your mother."

Carolina was a rush of emotions. Her stomach was churning from memories of the tea conversation and especially of her sister's claim to James. What could she say to her parents at this junction? That she suddenly realized James meant more to her than a tutor? That she was on the verge of considering whether she might actually have feelings for him? The thought sickened her. She couldn't care about James that way. Virginia was absolutely right. James belonged to her and no other.

"I'm sorry," she murmured contritely and felt a cloud of depression settle over her.

"You are to have a fitting this afternoon," Margaret said, putting the matter behind them. "Since you seemed incapable of choosing a gown, I made the choice for you."

Carolina thought to protest but instead nodded meekly. "Which one did you pick?"

Margaret smiled. "Well at least that seems to have sparked your interest. I chose the ivory silk with peach tulle. It will complement your dark hair, and the drape of the bodice will accent your figure. No man there will be able to keep his eyes off of you."

Joseph patted his wife's arm. "There now, Mrs. Adams, it will all work out."

Margaret smiled. "I need to make an appearance and bid the young ladies hello. If you'll excuse me, Mr. Adams. Carolina."

Carolina waited until her mother had disappeared from the garden. "Oh, Papa, this is so much bother, and I'd really rather it be happening to someone else." She twisted her hands nervously and wondered how to deal with her fears.

"My darling," Joseph said, taking a seat beside his daughter, "this party is an important occasion in your life and in your mother's life. You've been unduly harsh with her, and I would like for you to consider her feelings in this matter. She loves you a great deal, and it is of the utmost concern to her how others receive you."

"I know, but . . ."

"Hear me out." Joseph was stern but not harsh. "If you can find it in your heart to take an interest in this party, I will offer you a reward of sorts. It will be our little conspiracy to boost your mother's spirits."

"What do you have in mind?" Carolina cocked her head, curious. What was her father up to?

"Philip Thomas has invited me to come to Baltimore and observe various workings of the railroad."

Carolina felt her pulse quicken. What was he suggesting?

"I propose," her father continued, "to take you along with me as a birthday gift."

"Oh, Papa, truly?" Carolina dared not to even hope.

"Truly." Joseph smiled and patted her arm. "You must do your part, however. This party means a great deal to your mother, and I want her to be happy. Please find it in your heart to show interest in your party. Join in with the plans and show some enthusiasm, even if it's the enthusiasm you feel for the trip that will follow the party. Can you do this?"

Carolina put her hand atop her father's. "If it means so much to you, Papa, I will do it even without your promise of a trip. I've been selfish and didn't realize what it meant to Mother. I'll go right away and apologize."

Joseph stood and pulled her along with him. "That's a good girl." They walked a space before he added, "The trip still stands. I want to allow you this because I know what it means to you. The actual trip might not take place until late May or even June, but you'll have that to look forward to."

Carolina couldn't keep the excitement from her voice. "Will we be gone a very long time?"

"At least a week, maybe two."

"Oh, I'm positively speechless, Papa!"

Joseph laughed and wrapped her arm through his. "Now that is something I thought never to see."

"Granny?" Carolina called softly, taking a seat on the stool beside the bed. She gently touched the old woman's hand.

"That be yo, Miz Carolina?"

"It's me, Granny." The old woman never bothered to open her eyes, but the hint of a smile played on her lips. "What trouble yo' in now?"

"You always seem to know me so well," Carolina sighed. "But it's not just trouble, I have some wonderful news to tell you as well."

"Better de bad first."

Carolina nodded and stroked Granny's hand with her fingertips. "Well, you know that I'm to have a coming-out party." She didn't wait for Granny to reply. "I simply dread the very idea. I don't want to be bothered with the ordeal, yet everyone, including Father, feels I should enjoy this wonderful honor."

Granny's chuckle was a weak, barely audible croak. "If dats de bad, then what's de good?"

Carolina smiled. "The good is that Papa says if I am very good about the coming-out party, he'll take me on a train trip to Baltimore. Oh,

Granny, I want that more than anything. Even enough to pretend how happy I am about the party."

"And what of yor young mon?"

Carolina dropped her hold on Granny's hand. "What young man?"

"Yor Mr. James."

"He's hardly mine, Granny. He only tutors me and that's been divine." She paused, trying to figure out how to rationalize her fear into words. "I suppose I'm afraid it's all going to come to an end. Mother and Papa expect James to wed Virginia and then, no doubt, move far away and start their own family. I lose my tutor when that happens."

"And yor heart," Granny added.

Carolina looked at the old woman in complete amazement. When she said nothing, Granny continued.

"Yo think I need eyes to know dat yo love James Baldwin?"

"But, Granny, he's intended for my sister. Whatever gives you the idea . . ."

"Ders some things what need no explainin'. I hear how yo talk of him. Yo sound jes like Miz Mary when her papa brings her candy."

Carolina thought on this for a moment. "But, Granny, I can't love him. He belongs to Virginia."

"Bah. Yo don' know what mon yor heart will pick. Ain't gwanna stop lovin' him jes 'cause he's yor sister's mon, are yo?"

Carolina shook her head. "I don't know what I'm going to do. That's the problem. I'm supposed to come of age and choose a husband. I'm supposed to put childish notions of going to college behind me. I'm supposed to be somebody else, but inside, I'm not any of the things they want me to be."

Granny nodded. "And yo never will be."

Carolina sighed. "I suppose I have to find that truth inside, the one you told me only I would know."

"If yo want to be happy, yo will. If not, jes let them live yor life for yo."

"I can't," Carolina said softly. "I can't let them live it for me, and I'm afraid to strike out and live it for myself. Oh, Granny, why does growing up have to be so hard?"

Thirty-One

Nighttime Dispute

$\mathcal{J}$oseph Adams draped his waistcoat over the back of a chair and continued undressing. Margaret sat at her dressing table brushing out her long brown hair, chattering about the plans for Carolina's party. He loved and admired this woman in a way he felt inadequate to express. Their marriage had come about more through arrangement than overwhelming adoration, but love quickly blossomed, and Joseph could not imagine loving another.

He watched her for a moment after donning his nightshirt. She scarcely seemed to realize his interest. At thirty-eight she was still in her prime, and her figure did not betray her, despite the nine children she'd borne. His desire for her was as great as ever, and the thought of her in these quiet moments of intimacy only fanned the flames.

Putting aside the brush, Margaret turned and saw him looking at her in that old familiar way. "I suppose Carolina's party is not on your mind just now." Her voice was low and soft.

"Actually, I was remembering your coming out," Joseph said. And as she rose, he stepped toward her and took her into his arms. The cranberry velvet dressing gown she wore seemed to bring out the flush in her cheeks. "You were the most beautiful woman in the state. You still are, you know."

"Oh, goodness! And you are the best liar." She laid her head on his shoulder. "But I daresay our daughters alone have long since taken that honor."

He touched his lips to hers, heard her sigh, and knew he could never want for more than this. "You will always be my beauty," he whispered against her ear.

She brought her arms up around his neck. "You are kind to say so, Mr. Adams."

"I only speak the truth, madam. You have captured my heart for all time."

She broke away, smiled alluringly at him, and slipped off the robe. "Perhaps we should put out the lamp."

He nodded and quickly went to the task.

"You know," Margaret said, slipping beneath the covers, "I wouldn't be at all surprised if Carolina isn't married within the year. She's such a lovely thing in her new gown, the fellows will just naturally flock to her side."

Darkness permeated the room, and Joseph went to the window to draw back the drapes to let in the moonlight. "Carolina isn't like Virginia or even Georgia. Already at thirteen, Georgia is avidly seeking suitors, at least when she can stop long enough to come down from the trees. But Carolina is talking of going to college."

"College is out of the question," Margaret said harshly, breaking the mood of their earlier moment. "Carolina will marry properly and set up a household. It was barely tolerable to allow this tutelage, and were it not for the benefit to Virginia's marriage plans, I would never have agreed."

Joseph got into the bed and felt her immediately stiffen when he reached out for her. "There's no need to discuss this now, is there, my dear?" he cooed. "I thought we had a much more interesting topic to share."

"You can't just sweep this under the rug and hope it will go away, Joseph Adams. Carolina is spoiled and overindulged. She believes the world should change its rules simply because she finds them amiss. That is not something I will sit back and allow."

Joseph realized there was no putting this discussion off. "You have four other daughters to so guide; what will it harm to allow one to follow her own path? I had rather fancied the idea of sending her to a university or college. There are several schools of fine reputation that are now allowing women to attend. True, most do not allow for any degree to be attained, but nevertheless the education could be had for a price."

"That price would be your daughter's reputation! Is that what you want?"

"Shouldn't Carolina be allowed to make that choice?" Joseph asked hesitantly. "I mean . . . that is to say, is she not the one who will have to endure the consequences of her decision?"

"Carolina isn't the only one who would be affected by this decision. People would question our sensibility in allowing such a thing, and *you* still have three daughters and two sons who haven't yet chosen mates.

How can they hope to marry properly if the reputation of this family is sullied by a thing such as sending a woman to college?"

Joseph lay back against his pillow and sighed deeply. "Must what others think always influence our choices and decisions? Is not the path of least resistance often also the more boring and uneventful choice?"

"Proper behavior and solid moral conduct has little to do with boredom. Carolina is an accomplished young woman. Let her take that with her into a marriage of means and high repute."

"And put aside all that she dreams of?" Joseph's voice took on an edge of rising ire.

Margaret immediately picked up on her husband's mood. "You have done this," she said haughtily. "You have created this scandalous situation, and now you have no idea what to do with it. If you allow it to continue, she'll be fit for nothing but growing old with her books. I insist that after her coming out, you put an end to the tutoring." She turned to offer him her back, making clear that she was through discussing the matter.

Joseph's temper was held in check as he answered, "No, I will not. I cannot take away the one real pleasure in her life. I will try to understand your reluctance in regard to college, and I will say no more on that matter for now. But I have promised Carolina a trip to Baltimore, where she can better immerse herself in her love of the railroad, and I will not take back that promise."

Margaret turned on him in a single motion. "You can't be serious! You can't subject our daughter, a young genteel woman, to the type of lowlife hooligans who work for the railroad."

"What do you know of it, Margaret? You barely even saw the locomotive at the celebration, and you've been nowhere near the railroad since. Are you not harshly judging something you know nothing about? I hardly propose to drop our daughter into a sea of cutthroats and no-accounts. She won't be out of my sight, and the pleasure it will bring her is something I can give, even if I can't give her the world's acceptance of her dreams."

"I suppose your mind is made up."

"Yes, it is."

"And it matters little that I object to this trip and this continued education?"

"It matters, but I cannot change my mind on the subject."

"Very well," she said.

Margaret's voice quivered and Joseph feared she might cry. Reaching out to her, Joseph was stunned when she slapped his hands away and once again turned her back to him.

"You want no part of me on this subject," she stated in a sobbing voice, "therefore you get no part of me."

She sobbed inconsolably while Joseph wondered if he'd done the right thing. He had given Carolina his promise, and he couldn't take it back as though it meant nothing. But, on the other hand, he saw how grieved his dear wife was over the same issue and felt he had to be loyal to his love for her.

Putting his hand under his head and staring up at the ceiling, Joseph wondered if he'd made all the wrong decisions. Had he created a monster in Carolina by opening her mind to the world? Had it been cruel to give her a brief glimpse into the heart of her desires, only to put down a gate and forbid her to go any further?

Perhaps Margaret was right. Perhaps he should announce after the party that since she was of age, James Baldwin's tutelage would no longer be needed. That of course would not sit well with Virginia. There seemed to be no easy answer in the matter. All he had wanted was to give something special to Carolina.

He imagined his dark-eyed daughter's response to ending her education. She would be devastated, and the sorrow in her eyes would no doubt bring back memories of a time when he laid his own dreams to rest. Still, he could not allow this thing to stand between him and Margaret. He loved his wife and could hardly bear to hear her cry.

Reaching out, he pulled her, unwilling, into his arms. Stroking her hair he simply held her while she controlled her tears and lay rigid against him. "I cannot bear for this to be between us," he murmured. "I love you and my heart is ever yours. Don't hate me for poor choices. I've always struggled to make the right ones."

It seemed right to humble himself before Margaret. She relaxed against him but remained silent. Joseph didn't want to press the issue too hard, and after kissing her lightly on the forehead, he held her close and fell into a fitful sleep.

Sometime during the night, Joseph awoke with a start and realized the source of the anxiety that was keeping him from a peaceful night's rest. "Father God," he prayed, "I should have sought you out on this before, but it seemed a small matter, and I thought myself capable of dealing with it. Human wisdom fails me, and I fear I have caused more problems than would have been the case if I would have put the matter in your hands to begin with."

Margaret sighed against him but remained in a deep sleep.

"I have hurt her," he continued, "and it was not my desire to do so. Please forgive me and help her to forgive me as well. Guide me in the matter of Carolina's education. She has such desires and hopes for the future, and I fear quelling those, as mine were, by denying her the objects of her dreams. Show me the way. Teach me what I am to do." He faded off to sleep, the prayerful words still on his lips. "Show . . . me . . . the . . . way."

Thirty-Two

Indecision

*J*ames entered the family sitting room to find Virginia seated alone before the blazing hearth. She seemed so perfectly arranged there on the elegant velvet divan that it was as if she'd planned this time for them to be alone—and perhaps she had. James knew she was anxiously awaiting some word of commitment from him, but as of yet he'd found it difficult to give. To take on Virginia Adams as wife meant he would clearly be in for changes in his life. Changes he wasn't certain he was ready for.

Turning sparking blue eyes on him, Virginia smiled coyly. "I wondered if you would make your way here." Her voice was alluring, beckoning James forward.

"Your mother told me I would find you here," he said, knowing full well he'd been the object of a conspiracy between mother and daughter to bring him to this room. "And how could I resist the possibility of having you to myself for a few moments?"

Virginia blushed appropriately at his bold statement and motioned to the settee. "Please join me."

James accommodated her, feeling a strange confusion of emotions. She was beautiful and alluring, and he knew himself to be most fortunate that she was interested in him. He studied the delicate features of her face—the small upturned nose, dainty rose-colored lips, flushed high cheeks, and pale blue eyes.

"You look beautiful tonight," he said, before even realizing the words were out of his mouth.

"Thank you." Virginia lowered her eyes coquettishly. "I wore this gown especially for you."

James felt his face grow hot and didn't know if the cause was the fire in the hearth or the woman beside him. He looked at her intently, trying to find some real fault with her. True, she was shallow minded, hardly well-read, and able to converse intelligently on only a handful of the most unstimulating topics. But who could fault her for that? That was the kind of woman men were supposed to seek out. She knew nothing of the world around her, and if her father and mother weren't friends with the President, she'd probably not even give the matter consideration enough to know who was in office.

"You're looking at me as though I'd grown a second head," Virginia said, suddenly drawing him from his thoughts.

"Sorry, I was simply admiring your assets," he grinned. "You are charming and delightful, and I am glad to have the peace of this moment in order to tell you so." The words came so easily, yet part of James sensed he was only spouting what he knew to be the right thing to say. The words were true, of course, but—

"You've been living with us for nearly six months," Virginia said, jarring him once more from his thoughts. "Do you realize that?"

"I do. In fact, that very thought crossed my mind this evening. This place—Oakbridge and all that is here—has been a healing balm to me. Why, I've completely recovered from my accident." In more ways than one, he thought, but for some reason he couldn't admit the other things to Virginia.

"It's been wonderful having you here," she was saying. "I've learned so much more about you. Things I might never have known if we'd simply courted."

James smiled broadly, amazed at how readily the response came. Virginia wasn't bad at all . . . not at all.

"Such as?" he asked, warming to the flirtatious mood Virginia was spinning.

"Well, I know you don't care for eggs, and you detest it when your hair falls below your collar." Her face brightened. "And I know the cut of coat you prefer and your favorite color."

James narrowed his eyes slightly. "Which is what?"

"Green."

"Fair enough, you're correct on all accounts." James noted that nothing in her calculations of him went further than the surface observations.

Virginia surprised him by continuing. "I know, too, you don't hold much stock in slavery or in church."

He concealed his surprise. "Why do you say that?"

Virginia smiled. "I'm not blind. You scarcely allow any of the servants to wait on you. Even Jericho, whom Father put in your charge, stands about idle most of the time. And you left the room in a complete state of disgust when our overseer spoke of the Milfords' missing slaves and how there was to be a manhunt for them."

"I wouldn't have believed you to find those matters of importance."

"Everything about the plantation is a matter of importance, and everything regarding those I love is of special importance to me."

James was stunned nearly into silence. He did manage to ask, "Am I to understand. . . ?"

"That I love you?" Virginia finished the question. "Why act so surprised, James? Certainly you can't have been unaware of my feelings all these months?"

"I see . . ." James could still not recover from his shock at her bold declaration.

"No, I don't believe you do," Virginia stated evenly. "But I will endeavor to make myself clear. I'm eighteen—almost nineteen—years old. I'm the daughter of a prominent plantation owner and businessman. I'm not without my charms, and many have paid me court; however, I've been very reluctant to settle down and marry just anyone."

"And why is that?" James asked, genuinely interested.

Virginia folded her hands and looked into the flames. "So many of those who have been interested have been such *boys*. Their affection, even their love, has not stirred me. It is different with you, James. I feel such passion when I am around you."

"Miss Adams!"

"Do you think me positively brazen? But sometimes a woman must be when a man is a taciturn sort, when he appears to need a bit of a nudge to express his true feelings."

James knew this was his opportunity to express the passion he should feel for her. She was so beautiful, so desirable. He was stirred by her beauty. But passion? Perhaps that was too much to hope for.

"I could not be around you without having feelings," he said, trying to infuse his tone with the kind of passion she was looking for, while at the same time remaining as noncommittal as possible.

"I knew it!" she said, her eyes glowing. "It is sometimes such a burden being the daughter of a wealthy man. I have had one or two suitors who have turned out to be only after my father's money. I never believed that of you, James, but it is so heartening to be completely assured of that fact. You have shown me now that your intentions are pure."

Her words caused James to grow uncomfortable, but he said nothing, following Virginia's example of staring into the fire. He felt a terrible urge to reveal his father's deceit, to declare that he himself was no fortune hunter, but that he was merely trying to be an obedient son. But she would never understand that his predicament was no reflection on her charms.

She tittered softly. "Goodness! It is foolish of me to even wonder about such things. You are a Baldwin and the Baldwins have their own fortune and good name. You are secure in your position in Washington and needn't come to the Adamses for a step up into society. Your mother is highly esteemed and keeps company with the elite capital social circle. Your father is an important man, and you yourself have a sterling reputation. I can respect you and honor you as an equal in the realms of genteel folk and love you as a man."

She said nothing more, and James knew she was waiting for some similar statement or declaration of love. He had come to care about her, and perhaps he could tell her that, but it bothered him deeply that he was chasing her fortune. Still, how could he let his father down and admit the truth?

Suddenly, overcome by a gnawing sense of guilt, he found himself voicing words he had been avoiding all along. "I do care for you, Virginia. You are the only woman I wish to be with."

"Oh, James!"

"My only hesitation in making a deeper commitment is that I desire to have my future in order before I take on the responsibility of marriage. But I suppose one thing you ought to know, and I fear it may not please you." James' voice was barely audible. "I have come to believe my future will still be in the railroad business. I am not certain in what capacity, or if . . . I still have the . . . uh . . . aptitude for the work. But I've been in contact with Philip Thomas, the president of the Baltimore and Ohio."

"Yes, I know him. We've had him to dinner here," Virginia interjected.

"Yes, well, Mr. Thomas has offered me a job, whenever I'm ready to accept it. My accident has not dulled my fascination with the work of designing and planning railroads. I want to see the business go forward."

Virginia shifted as though uncomfortable, and James thought a brief expression of worry creased her brow.

"I don't pretend to be interested in things such as that," she said. "I only know the railroad very nearly took your life, and I can't imagine feeling loyalty to a thing when it has so deeply scarred you."

"But life is full of things that scar," James remarked. "No one escapes the pain and suffering of this earth."

"But neither does a wise person put himself in a position to be hurt again, *if*"—she stressed the last word—"they can avoid that position."

"I feel I must give it another try. As I said, I don't know how it will work out. But it is too deeply a part of me to let it go so easily."

"Maybe the accident was God's way of trying to redirect your life. Father says God sometimes works through the strangest of circumstances."

James thought of the six months he'd spent at Oakbridge and knew he could easily agree with this. If he hadn't come here, he'd no doubt still hate the railroad for the death of Phineas Davis. If he hadn't come here, he might easily have taken his own life in abject despair. But he had come here, and a young girl had wrapped him in her passion for life and her hunger for knowledge, and through it, James had found comfort and a reason to go on. Unfortunately that girl had been Carolina, not Virginia.

"Talk about God makes you uncomfortable, doesn't it?" Virginia seemed to conclude from his silence.

"Perhaps," James replied, glad that Virginia was unaware of his reflection on Carolina. Religion was as good a cover as anything. He'd never seen much use for religion in his life, and while he knew it to be the socially acceptable thing, church attendance was not among his favorite ways to pass a Sunday. He would much rather have watched the horses run, read a good book, or even thrown in a line and fished away the hours. Instead, he'd found himself forced to attend the very strict and pious Falls Church—for which the town was named—where none other than George Washington had once been an esteemed member. The stiff formal worship left him desiring nothing more than a hard fast ride atop his mount after escaping the highly ornate building and grimly proper congregation.

"I find it difficult to deal with the severity of God at times," James answered honestly. "But I believe in His omniscience, if that's what is worrying you." He tried to sound casual, but Virginia's frown only deepened.

"Father says that believing in God is all well and fine, but a person needs a daily walk with Him as well."

"And you have this daily walk?"

Virginia bit her lip. "I suppose I don't live up to the expectations my parents have for me regarding religious consideration. I have a sharp tongue, especially where Carolina and York are concerned. They both have been intolerable at times, and I've not taken it well."

"Intolerable?" James hoped to get off the subject of religion altogether.

"Well, Carolina is very stubborn, and though I've tried to help her become a lady, she's determined to disgrace this family by pushing into the realm of places where she is not wanted, nor welcomed. I've tried to speak with her as a sister and in sisterly love," she said, as though she were looking for James' approval or confirmation. He nodded and she continued. "I've tried to tell her how her attitudes have caused our mother great grief and positioned this family awkwardly when it comes to polite society. But Carolina thinks only of herself."

"I don't know that I agree with that. She is a very spirited young woman and holds her dreams and desires in the highest degree of importance. But then, so do you. You desire to marry well and keep a home and husband. You see yourself as a wife and mother, and those are admirable ambitions. But even so, why fault your sister for being unconventional?"

"She's mean tempered and cares nothing for me," Virginia said rather haughtily. "York and I used to be close, but now she's clearly his favorite, and he bows down to her every request."

"Not quite. As I understand it, York chose work in Washington over Carolina's desire for him to remain at Oakbridge."

"What are you talking about?" Virginia sounded rather indignant.

"York told me she was devastated when he decided to accept the job as aide to President Jackson. He had promised to tutor her a bit, but when the job opportunity presented itself, he could hardly resist. It meant disappointing Carolina, but his own path was as important as her dreams. So I don't know that I would think him as devoted to her as you believe."

Virginia got to her feet and seemed to struggle for words. "I don't want to talk about them. I want to talk about us."

James immediately got to his feet. "Us? What about us?"

"That's precisely what I'd like to know."

"I thought we'd already discussed that," James said rather lamely.

"And there was nothing more you wanted to say?"

"I thought you understood. My future is so uncertain right now. I am not even certain, now that I am recovered, how much longer I shall remain here at Oakbridge."

"So you won't be tutoring Carolina much longer? Is that what you're saying?"

"I suppose in a way, I am. Although I've not given your father any kind of notice to end our arrangement."

"And had you planned to tell me about it?"

James saw the pain in her eyes. "Of course I would have spoken with you of it." He wondered how he might comfort her without actually offering some type of promise.

Virginia swept the skirt of her gown to one side and edged her way around the settee. "I've made my feelings clear, perhaps foolishly so. I have no desire to be ill thought of by you, and I pray that is not so."

"I could never think ill of you, Virginia."

She nodded. "It is enough, then, that you know my heart. What happens from this point is, I suppose, out of my control."

———

But control was Virginia's specialty, and she wasn't about to lose her only real chance at a summer wedding. James Baldwin was going to marry her if it took every conniving, underhanded plan she could muster. First, however, she had to deal with Carolina. Perhaps it was her sister's fault that James had changed his attitude about his future. He hadn't even wanted to talk about the railroad when he'd first arrived. Now he was considering working for it once again.

Virginia had hoped, with Carolina seeming to be involved with her coming-out party, that James would be left more to her manipulations. She hadn't been disappointed when Carolina had cut her lessons short that afternoon to join their mother in planning the menus and decorations for the ball. What had been disappointing was that no matter how Virginia had tried to set the scene of romance, James Baldwin remained reticent beyond expressing his affection. Somehow, she had to draw out the passion she knew he must feel and put it into action.

"Carolina!" Virginia called softly and knocked lightly on her sister's bedroom door later that evening.

Carolina, already clad in her nightgown, opened the door. "Virginia? Whatever do you want?"

Virginia pushed her way into the room. "We need to discuss James."

"James?"

Virginia eyed her carefully. "Yes, James. Why? Does that subject not bode well for you?"

"I . . . it's just . . ." Carolina fell silent and snapped shut the book she had been holding. "What has this got to do with me?"

"That's exactly what I'd like to know," Virginia said stiffly. She looked Carolina over from head to foot and didn't like what she saw. It was suddenly clear that her sister was no longer a child; instead, she was every bit a rival.

Carolina flopped onto the goose-down mattress and yawned. "I haven't any idea what you're talking about."

She appeared for all intents and purposes to be completely bored with the topic of discussion, but Virginia was not convinced. "I intend to marry James, and I won't allow for any interference on your part. Whatever notions of glory you've been putting in his head regarding the railroad, you can just forget."

"What?" Carolina was genuinely stunned.

"James is thinking about returning to work for the railroad. This could happen in short course and will very likely involve him moving north to Baltimore."

"This is news to me," Carolina replied.

"I won't allow you to interfere." Virginia stood directly in front of her sister, a force to be reckoned with. "I mean it." She shook her finger to emphasize her mind on the matter. "I will marry James Baldwin, and if you know what's good for you, you will stay away from him and keep your notions about the railroad to yourself." Carolina appeared to cower at the hateful words, much to Virginia's delight.

Going to the door, Virginia turned. "I am completely sincere in this. I can make life most miserable for you if you cross me. It's too late for me to start another courtship all over again. I want James Baldwin. Mother and Father want me to marry James Baldwin, and I believe even James wants this arrangement. He's just afraid to take the extra step forward."

"But you'll give him the push he needs. Is that it?" Carolina snapped, suddenly finding her voice.

Virginia gave a calculated smile. "I'll do whatever it takes to ensure our nuptials. If that means putting you in your place, or manipulating him, so be it. Consider yourself amply warned, little sister."

Thirty-Three

Coming of Age

$\mathcal{F}$rom the moment Carolina opened her eyes in the morning, she felt a foreboding of the events to come. This was her sixteenth birthday, a day any young woman should look forward to with absolute delight. But Carolina wasn't just any young woman, and she dreaded this day as she had no other.

Sitting up to yawn and stretch, Carolina tore the mop cap from her head and let her brown curls tumble down her back. The house was uncommonly quiet, and so for a few minutes she did nothing but enjoy the peace of the morning. It was no doubt to be her last quiet moment for some time to come.

The room bore a slight chill, but it was refreshing, and Carolina pushed back her covers with great abandonment and went to the window. Clad only in her white cotton nightgown, she drew back the curtains and welcomed the day.

How she loved spring. The orchards were in full bloom, showering the ground with dainty-petaled flowers whenever a stiff wind blew up. Yellow-flowered sassafras and persimmon trees set their colors against the reddish purple of redbud and newly blooming lilac. Beyond these walls the world was alive with color, and Carolina longed only to embrace it all and hide herself away within it.

With a heavy sigh, she tied the curtain in place and plopped down dejectedly on the window seat. Why must I endure this day? she wondered silently. Coming of age was a highly celebrated tradition, she knew full well. From the time a girl was little, she was taught about this pinnacle of life. Once presented to society in a coming-out debut, people treated her differently, and the world expected certain things of her. But in some ways, coming of age was a bit like being caught stealing cookies. The mere existence of one's hand in the jar proved one's guilt,

214

and there were certain penalties to be faced. Despite the joy of the treat—the cookies or the newly given respect—there were definite disadvantages to the situation as well.

Hugging her knees to her chest, Carolina laid her head against the windowpane and tried to work up some enthusiasm. How can I look forward to this day? Virginia is angry at me, believing that somehow I've tried to interfere between her and James. My own feelings are such that I can scarcely address her in conversation without worrying I might betray my heart. And tonight I'll be expected to become a young woman who desires nothing more than to seek out a husband and settle down to a life of hostessing formal dinners and giving grand balls.

She thought about her little ruse over the last weeks in trying to show enthusiasm for the party in order to please her mother. Would she now have to go through life performing that same deception? Following the course set for her by society and never at liberty to seek her personal fulfillment in her own way? Finding her identity in that of her husband?

At the sound of her bedroom door opening, Carolina looked up and found the warm brown face of Hannah to be a welcome relief.

"I sees my little chicken be up and about," Hannah said, smiling wide. "Happy Birthday, Miz Carolina."

"Thank you, Hannah." Carolina got up from her place at the window and stretched her arms into the air. "I was just noticing how beautiful it is outside. All the trees are in bloom and the flowers are glorious."

"Yassum, I hear tell Miz Margaret say she gwanna have the best of 'em at de party."

Carolina frowned, but a quick glance indicated Hannah, who was busy laying out her clothes, had not noticed. No sense in having to answer to Hannah for her concerns about the party.

"Mother said that Miriam will be mostly helping me with my clothes and hair from now on. I'm going to miss you, Hannah." Carolina paused for a moment, realizing yet another change due to her coming of age. "I can't imagine life without you here in the morning first thing and tucking me in at night."

"Babies grow up, Miz Carolina. Old Mammy is for takin' care of babies, which you ain't rightly one any mo'."

"Oh, I know all that. I know, too, you'll just be down the hall in the nursery seeing to my sisters, but it won't be the same. Nothing will be the same." She bit her lip, which had suddenly started to quiver. There was no way Hannah wouldn't notice that. For a slave without education, Hannah was wise beyond her station.

"I 'spect you've been thinkin' on dat for some time. Growin' up ain't a thing to be put off. You got no choice but what you make it. So go have a bad time today. Won't change a thing. You is still gwanna be sixteen an' dey is still gwanna be things expected of you, child."

Carolina smiled and nodded. "I know. I know. Granny told me the same thing."

"Granny knows." Hannah came forward with a cotton morning dress. The white material was printed with tiny purple and pink flowers and seemed to complement Carolina's morning observations of the blossoming spring. The skirt was trimmed in wide-paneled lavender lace with a ribbon of the same color at the waist. The bodice, with its capelike bertha collar, was trimmed in a narrower version of the skirt lace and bore a tiny lavender ribbon bow at the center of the neckline.

Carolina anxiously accepted the white cotton undergarments and allowed Hannah to corset her in, although she didn't really need the supporting garment. Fitting her arms into the elbow-length flounced sleeves, Carolina tried to steady her nerves. In her mind she ran through the day's agenda. There was to be a lawn supper in the late afternoon with time to retire and rest before the ball. The ball itself would start after eight and last well into the night. There would be toasts to her at midnight, and a buffet of mouth-watering treats would be laid out for the visitors. Those who were to spend the night would dally another hour, maybe two if conversation stimulated them to do so. Others who would make journeys back home would leave as soon after the birthday cake as possible, offering congratulations and teasing questions about whether she'd picked a young man to marry.

She knew these things because her mother had told her it would be so, and now, waiting for Hannah to hook up the back of her dress, Carolina shuddered and wished it were the next day with the party well behind her.

There was little more time to worry about the day. York arrived soon after breakfast, bringing with him a birthday gift of two novels and much discussion on the happenings in Washington. Hannah gave Carolina a present of finely crocheted mitts, which Carolina assured her would be perfect with her coming-out gown.

Later in the morning Carolina made a brief visit to Granny, who spent most of her time in unconsciousness. Sleep seemed to be all the old woman could handle these days, and Carolina always hesitated to disturb her slumber. Feeling comforted that Granny had made it through yet another night, Carolina returned to the house, slipping through the kitchen entrance, where Naomi barked out orders to a bevy of dark-skinned staff.

Passing through the house, Carolina inhaled the sweet fragrance of multiple bouquets and garland trim. Some servants busied themselves setting out crystal, china, and silver, while others rolled up rugs and removed unneeded furniture to storage. No one seemed to take notice of her as she moved from room to room.

Fleetingly, she wondered where James was, but Carolina's mother had made it clear there would be no lessons today, so he was probably somewhere enjoying the respite. It was just as well he was gone. Her thoughts were confused enough.

She found Maryland running up and down the stairs, as usual. Brown curls bobbed as the child enjoyed her favorite game.

"Maryland Adams, how many times has Mother told you not to run on the stairs?" Carolina asked, with hands on hips. She tried to sound stern, but Mary looked so sweet and happy.

" 'Free times," Mary answered, and as she skipped down to where Carolina stood she held up her hand, her face contorted in severe concentration. She tried hard to isolate three fingers, but her hand didn't want to cooperate, much to the child's consternation.

"I'll bet it was more than three times," Carolina said, lifting the squirming Mary into her arms. She rubbed her nose against Mary's and laughed at her sister's giggles. "Now, Mistress Mary, how did you get out of the nursery?"

"I wun," Mary answered. "I wun fast."

"Yes, I'll just bet you did." Carolina started to climb the stairs. "Well, I'm taking you back. Hannah has probably worn herself out looking for you."

"Don't wanna go." She wriggled against Carolina's sturdy hold. "No! No! No! Don't wanna go!"

Mary's protest was ignored by Carolina. "I'm sure you don't. But look, today is my birthday, and they are planning a special party for me. I don't want the party, but it makes Mother happy. You want to make Mother happy, don't you?"

Mary stopped wriggling and nodded solemnly.

"Very well, then you must go back to the nursery, and I must prepare for my party."

After depositing Maryland in the nursery, Carolina went to her room. Hannah had already laid out her ball gown. It would be Hannah's last real duty for her, and the thought made Carolina sad. Lightly fingering the material, she remembered a time when gowns and finery were far from her mind. Why, it seemed like only yesterday she was climbing trees and running on the stairs herself. Looking up, Carolina caught sight of a package on her dressing table. Curious to see who had sent it, she quickly forgot the gown and went to the gift.

The package was quite large and nearly covered the surface of the table. There was no note on top of the box, so Carolina decided there was no other choice but to open it. Inside was a single piece of paper.

Darling Daughter,

On this, your birthday, I pass to you a tradition begun by my great-great-grandmother. For over five generations, mothers have gifted their daughters with a sterling tea service on their sixteenth birthday. This is to start you off well in a life of hostessing in your own right. I pray you enjoy this gift as I have enjoyed mine. One day you will make a fine wife and mother, and this tea service will forever remind you of your transformation into womanhood.

Love, Mother

Carolina picked through the cotton batting to pull out the silver creamer. She held it up to catch the fading light from the bedroom window. It was lovely and ornately designed with intricate curlicues and vines on the handle. She thought of her mother picking it out for her and the hopes that must have crossed her mind.

"She probably already sees me married and moved away," Carolina mused and returned the creamer to the box. She wanted to be happy about the gift; she truly did. But something inside rebelled at the very thought of its domesticating implications. Why couldn't her mother be happy with planning Virginia's life out? Why, she practically had Virginia and James engaged. But this thought only prompted more concern, because as soon as Virginia was safely married to James, Margaret Adams would no doubt turn her full attention to seeing Carolina married off as well.

Carolina wasn't sure which bothered her more—the idea of James married to her sister or her mother's manipulative plan to see her plunged into marital bliss.

Thankfully, she didn't have time to ponder that question further. The guests were arriving for the lawn dinner, and she must go greet them.

———

"Hold still, now, while I secure this necklace," Margaret said as Carolina nervously fidgeted. "There. I knew it would be perfect."

Carolina had to admit her mother was right. Creamy pearls were the crowning touch to the elegantly draped neckline. The necklace was an unusual design with three sweeping strands of graduated pearls, offset in the center with a peach and ivory cameo. The cameo, a carving of her mother at the age of eighteen, was one of Margaret Adams' prized possessions.

"It's truly beautiful, Mother. Thank you for all you've done." She leaned over to kiss her mother on the cheek.

So far, the day was progressing beautifully. Dinner had been enjoyable and the afternoon weather had been perfect for the outdoor event. Now it was time for the ball, and Carolina's knotted stomach hinted that this would not be the relaxing affair dinner was. She would truly be on display now. Through the closed door, Carolina could hear the orchestra warming up and the sound made her shudder a little.

"I just hope everything goes well." Carolina's tone was a bit shrill with nerves.

"It will," Margaret replied, giving her daughter a soothing pat. "I've seen to every detail. Which reminds me, I'd better go and see to it that the musicians are properly arranged. I'll send your father to present you. You wait here until he arrives."

Carolina nodded and waited until her mother was gone before motioning Miriam to help her.

"My hair seems loose on this side."

Miriam inclined her head in agreement and went to work to ensure the coiffure remained stable. When she'd finished, Carolina went to stand before the cheval mirror. The transformation from regular everyday life to the fairy-tale princess in the mirror startled Carolina. This was her first glimpse at the full effect, and it left her nearly breathless.

The silk gown was completely draped and veiled with the peach tulle. The bodice was just low enough to separate it from the more childish designs Carolina was used to wearing, while revealing nothing more than creamy white shoulders and neck. Still, the draping gave an alluring hint of womanly fullness before narrowing sharply to a petite basque waist. The skirt, rich and full, seemed to glitter in the soft light when Carolina twirled in front of the mirror. For the first time she noticed that the tulle had a modest weave of golden thread amid the peachy blush. It was this that caught the light and gave the dress an enchanting glow.

Moving around the room as though she were waltzing, Carolina suddenly felt her heart soar with anticipation for the evening before her. She was to be the belle of the ball, and even Virginia wouldn't dream of upstaging her little sister's coming-out party.

Giggling nervously, Carolina checked her hair again and nodded approvingly. Parted in the middle, the ringlets were pulled back and pinned high to cascade down her back. Added to this, a peach-colored ribbon daintily trimmed her hair and disappeared into the curls. The style was all the rage and suited Carolina well. Going to the dressing table, Carolina pulled on Hannah's mitts and smiled. Now, all she had to do was wait.

The waiting turned out to be more nerve-wracking than Carolina had imagined it would be. She couldn't sit down—it would wrinkle the dress and ruin her debut. She couldn't walk out in the halls because she hadn't yet been presented for the evening, which was the *formal* presentation and much more important than the earlier festivities. So, confined to her bedroom and now without even Miriam to talk with, Carolina silently wished for the time to pass more quickly.

Music drifted down from the third-floor ballroom, along with the animated sound of voices and laughter. Carolina knew that every family in the county would have turned out for this night, as well as many families from Washington City. It was to be a grand occasion, and it was even rumored that President Jackson himself would honor the family by attending. Carolina knew this would be to her mother's absolute delight.

The knock at her door interrupted her thoughts and put an end to Carolina's waiting. Opening it revealed her father's smiling face.

"My, my, but you do this family proud, Carolina," her father said and leaned down to kiss his daughter on the forehead.

"I'm very nervous, Papa," she admitted. "This whole ordeal is both terrifying and exciting."

He nodded with a knowing look. "Life is often that way. We push it away for fear of it overwhelming us and at the same time beckon it forward and hold it tight."

"That's exactly how I feel. How did you know?"

Joseph Adams shrugged. "I've been through much in the way of pomp and ceremony. Usually it was on someone else's behalf, but I too have had my moments. Just relax and realize you are among friends. I have the utmost confidence in you, my dear."

Carolina took her father's arm and held it tight. "You have given me so much, Papa," she whispered. "I've cherished it all. The books, the tutoring, and mostly your understanding. All of it has given me a new outlook on the future, and I pray I might always be this happy."

The music was much louder with the door open, and with a glance upward, Joseph gently tugged her along with him into the hall. "Come. They are waiting for you."

Thirty-Four

No Longer a Child

*C*arolina entered the ballroom on the arm of her father. In her family it was tradition, as it was with most, that she not be allowed to attend a formal evening ball until after being presented to society. Now, standing near the threshold with all eyes directed toward her, Carolina felt her heart nearly beat out of her chest.

The room fell silent, and Joseph cleared his throat with a couple of gravelly coughs. "I am delighted to have the privilege of your company this evening. I am even more delighted to present my daughter, Carolina, to you on this, her sixteenth birthday." Everyone clapped politely, and before another word was uttered the orchestra struck up a waltz, and father led daughter to the dance floor with great flourish.

"This is your dance, my dear," Joseph said, and taking her into his arms, he twirled her into the steps of Weber's *Invitation to the Dance*.

James leaned casually against the wall and watched Carolina with guarded eyes. She swayed to the music, a vision in the glittering gown, seeming not to even be aware of the crowd around her. She laughed at something her father had said, and the amusement of the moment found its way into her eyes, making them sparkle with delight.

"Where have they hidden her?" one young man asked his companion.

"Behind her sister, I'd say. Virginia is more to my liking; why, just look at the way that pink dress of hers shows off her shape."

"I still say that the younger Miss Adams is just as stunning. I only wish that gown were done up a little differently. You can't get a good look at her ... well ..." He laughed. "Shall we say, her womanly charms." Both men laughed at this.

James prickled at the continuing conversation regarding Carolina's obvious attributes. When he could tolerate no more, he turned to glare at the younger men until they fell silent. Oddly their crass comments about Virginia hadn't rankled him nearly as much as those concerning Carolina. It's only because she's so innocent and inexperienced, he thought. Virginia could hold her own among any crowd and, no doubt, with any suitor, but Carolina was different. She was clearly an unplucked blossom, just starting to bloom. He could not feel charitable toward the hooligans he'd overheard, trying to force their attention on one so naive and pure.

James was startled at his protective reflection. And he smiled slightly at what Carolina's response to that protectiveness would be. On this of all days she'd be furious at being treated like a child. But James wondered if that was entirely where his attitude had come from. He tried not to think about it.

The music ended and everyone clapped again for the young woman being presented to society. When the orchestra started up a lively reel, couples soon joined Carolina and her father on the floor, and the evening of dance was officially begun.

James realized he'd be expected to seek out Virginia for this dance, so leaving off with his brooding, he went in search of her. The rhythmic pulse of the dance was contagious, and he found himself walking to the beat. Little by little the atmosphere was getting into his blood.

He spied Virginia in the middle of several young men, all who seemed to be begging for her company. When he was within earshot he heard her exclaim, "I couldn't possibly dance with any of you just yet. I've promised the first dance to James Baldwin."

The statement, though accurate and completely acceptable, caused James to pause. The full implication of the message was that she belonged to him and all others were to keep hands off. At least that was the message he received.

"Gentlemen," he announced, trying not to feel hemmed in by the statement, "I believe this dance is mine."

Virginia smiled amicably at the others and extended her arm to James. "I'll see what I can do about the next dance," she flirted openly, not noticing the scowl on James' face.

"You shouldn't encourage them," he said, leading her to join the others.

"I'm not an engaged woman," she answered coyly and added with a smile, "at least not yet. I suppose we could rectify that."

Before James could answer she was swept into a chain of feminine dancers, while he went in the opposite direction in a circle of men. It would take several moments before they'd come back around to dance with each other again. He didn't mind the lapse at all, and even less so when the wreathing chain of men and women stopped and Carolina reached out to take him as her partner. But James hesitated slightly, fearing to allow himself to fully enjoy the moment.

"Step it up, Jimmy, we're being bested by the others," she laughed and twirled around him, moving first in front and then behind in cadence with the music.

James swallowed hard and tried to concentrate on the dance.

"You look like you've been sucking persimmons," Carolina whispered when the dance brought them cheek to cheek.

James laughed at this, and the shock seemed to wear off a bit. "I just wasn't expecting to get to dance with you this early on. You make a fetching picture tonight, and I feel very honored to—"

"Oh, be done with it, James," Carolina frowned. "I'm not a child anymore. I know you'd rather be dancing with Virginia. Don't worry. They'll circle you back around before you know it."

Before he could answer, Carolina was whirled to the next partner, and James received the thick-waisted Kate Milford. It went on like that until James had experienced eight such partners before Virginia was on his arm again.

"My, but this is fun," she said in complete delight.

"I was thinking it's rather like being the grain at a mill."

"Why, James Baldwin, what a thing to say!" She pretended to be offended with his observation, but he saw through her pretense.

"Well, if you'd had your feet ground into the floor as many times as I have, you'd feel the same way."

Virginia laughed and the sound rose up lyrically against his ear. The music ended, leaving the breathless couples clinging to each other's arms for only a heartbeat before sedately backing away.

"Mother has a wonderful recipe for party punch. Would you like to partake?"

"I think it might do me well at that," James replied, taking Virginia's arm. "You look very lovely. That shade of pink becomes you."

"This little old thing?" she drawled rather seductively.

James laughed as he was intended to do. He knew full well that Virginia had no doubt labored for weeks, maybe even months, to pick just the right shade of pink in the proper type of material for the most delightful style of gown.

"Mother insisted I wear something bright without upstaging Carolina. Of course, she's still such a child with her silly notions of books and locomotives. It will truly be a chore for Mother to tame her down."

"No doubt," James said, barely breathing the words.

Virginia guided them to the refreshments and motioned the servant to bring two cups of punch.

James downed his drink quickly, hardly tasting the contents. "It's good," he said and gestured for another.

"Oh, look," Virginia squealed in delight, "Naomi's cranberry tarts. She makes these with dried berries and fresh cream. You simply must try one."

"Maybe later," James answered, replacing yet another empty cup on the servant's tray. "Is there anything stronger than this to drink?"

"Well, of course," Virginia purred. "Papa has mint juleps with the finest French brandy and fresh pineapple."

"Not to cast dispersion on your mother's punch, but I believe I'll procure one with haste."

"Let me," Virginia said sweetly. "I'll only be a moment."

He watched her walk away and suddenly realized he was trembling. He looked past the pink swaying form to where Carolina laughed in the arms of the uniformed Daniel Armstrong. Glancing from one woman to the other, James suddenly wished he'd partaken of mint juleps earlier and left the lighter stuff to someone else.

Turning away from both women, James put his mind on the feast at hand. Most of the third floor was devoted to the ballroom, and with the west end taken in dancing, the east end was reserved for refreshments. James actually felt hungry as he noted the succulent delicacies laid out for their consumption. He had just signaled a servant to prepare a plate for him when he noticed his father motioning to him from the far end of the table. He was with Joseph Adams, and James wasn't surprised at the direction of his father's comment.

"James, my boy, Adams and I were just discussing what a fine couple you and Virginia make. We've been rather surprised you two haven't yet come forth with an announcement," Leland pressed the issue without shame.

Joseph Adams smiled conspiratorially at James, leaving him with the feeling of being the one left out of the joke. Leland nudged James in the ribs before continuing. "I think you'd find this evening a fine time for such a . . . uh, undertaking."

James shrugged, gave a noncommittal grin, and left their company as soon as he could. But as he considered his father's words, he thought perhaps he ought to propose to Virginia just to get it over with. He was going to do it. He had to do it. Why wait any longer?

Then, as if in answer to his question, he spied from the corner of his eye a blurred vision of peach tulle. He cursed silently and went in search of his julep.

Thirty-Five

Discord

*C*arolina had enjoyed a dozen dances without so much as a pause to rest. The party was much more to her liking than she'd ever imagined possible. Her "nerves" had left her after that first reel and she was now feeling positively gay. It was already eleven o'clock. At midnight, they would bring out a huge birthday cake, and she would cut the first piece and receive birthday greetings and gifts from her guests. It was all very well planned out, and for once, Carolina was glad her mother had seen to every detail.

But she was too famished now to wait till then, so she allowed Daniel Armstrong to lead her from the dance floor to sample the delicacies on the refreshment table.

As she sat waiting for her partner to bring her a plate of goodies, she glanced across the room, aglow with pride. Her girlhood friends who were of age were there to share in the festivities, and for the first time in her life, Carolina didn't feel outdone by them. Julia Cooper offered her a tiny wave from the arm of her husband but made no move to join Carolina. It didn't matter. Julia and her husband, William, were to spend the night at Oakbridge, so there would be plenty of time for conversation later on.

Noting that Daniel had gotten involved in a conversation with a few other young men, Carolina rose to her feet and headed toward the group with the intention of expediting matters. The orchestra began a Chopin mazurka, and several groups of eight couples separated to begin the elaborate dance.

"Oh, Carolina, you look positively all grown up," Mrs. Milford said, stopping her before she reached her destination. The woman lifted Carolina's chin with her fleshy hand. "And your face is as smooth as an angel's."

Carolina thanked her, even though she wondered how many angels Lenore Milford had actually seen. The woman chatted on about inconsequential matters, unaware of Carolina's growling stomach, until Margaret Adams appeared and questioned her daughter as to the whereabouts of Virginia.

"I haven't seen her in some time," Carolina admitted. Without realizing it, she scanned the room for James.

"If you see her, send her to me immediately," Margaret said. Then as an afterthought she asked, "Have you been enjoying your party?"

"Very much, Mother. You did a splendid job of arranging it. I've heard many people say so."

"Indeed!" Lenore Milford chimed in. "And you must bathe this girl in buttermilk to render a complexion such as this. What is your secret, Margaret?"

With this chance, Carolina quickly moved away from the two older women and continued on her mission, reaching the table just as Burgess Milford was speaking.

"I say it's a waste of time and money," Milford said in between nursing a mint julep. "I don't see the railroad as anything more than another newfangled contraption. Within another year or two, they'll see how unmanageable it is and move on to something else. Besides, with the economy showing signs of decline, no one will want to risk their money in something as worthless as an iron horse."

"I disagree, sir," York Adams replied. "The railroad is the key to America's future."

"Some future," Burgess said, answering the unspoken challenge in York's tone. "I happen to know that already the Baltimore and Ohio is having to remake their westward line. They had planned to be at the Ohio River by this time, but one thing or another keeps falling apart on them, and they've failed to reach their goal. Now, as I hear it, they are facing bankruptcy due to costly masonry bridges and small profit rates."

"That can't be!" Carolina exclaimed, causing all of the men to stop in their conversation.

"I beg your pardon," Burgess said indulgently. "This would not be a topic for a pretty little thing such as you to discuss. Especially on her birthday."

Carolina glared at the man. "I am perfectly content to discuss this topic on my birthday or any other day. I happen to believe in the strength of the B&O. I think your figures are probably derived from those who have never desired to see the line succeed."

"Now, Carolina," York began, but she'd have no part of it.

"I'm serious. The Baltimore and Ohio has experienced its problems like any other line. Maybe more. When they lost Phineas Davis, they lost a competent engineer who had innovative thoughts on the future of the company. They have struggled with strap iron rails and even now are involved in a campaign to raise private funding to replace stretches of these poorer tracks with iron T-rails. True, the profit margins are poor, but they will increase when the line is moved west to the Ohio and brings in freight from the National Road."

The men stared at her in complete surprise.

"My sister is quite an advocate of rail travel," York offered by way of explanation.

"It does seem a bit unnatural that she would be so well versed in the operations of such a business," said Daniel, not harshly but with obvious surprise.

"Why is that?" York questioned.

"She is a young woman, and it is inappropriate for her to partake in such a discussion," Burgess said, eyeing Carolina with disdain. "I should say my sister Katy has been taught to keep her place in polite society."

Carolina refused to relent. "I happen to have a father who believes a mind, whether it takes residence in the body of a male child or female, is worth utilizing to the maximum accountability. I enjoy discussions of the railroad. I am sorry if that is intimidating to . . ." she paused for emphasis, *"polite society."*

"Well, I've never been so insulted before," Burgess Milford said, sucking in his paunchy gut and throwing back the last of his drink. "You, young woman, should learn your place."

"I have," Carolina replied, so angry now she didn't care if her rudeness was uncalled for. "I believe it to be on the board of one of the future railroads of America."

"No board of directors would allow such a thing," Burgess said with a laugh.

"And why not? If I have the knowledge of how to better direct the company, or if my insight into problems and profit losses is more beneficial than the opinion of another, male or female, would I not be the logical one to sit on that board?"

"Ludicrous! No man would listen to female advice unless it came in the form of suggestions for the draperies in the house or discussions on hostessing teas."

Carolina ignored her brother's reproachful frown. "And I, sir, wouldn't listen to the advice of one such as yourself on the future of the railroad. The profit figures for passenger travel are up for this year, and while the freight figures are slightly reduced, they will pick up again in late summer when shipments of flour are moved to the East Coast. The railroad is not without its problems, the biggest, perhaps, being men such as yourself."

"You, Miss Adams, should be put across the knee and spanked!" Milford raged, his face turning dark red from his embarrassment and anger.

York interceded. "You cannot speak thus of my sister, sir. I will not have it."

"No one asked you, Adams. If your father and mother would have done a proper job by this child, there would be no need for me to speak of such things in the first place."

"I will not allow you to besmirch the good name of my father!" York's voice raised just as the orchestra reached the last note of the mazurka. All heads turned to see what the problem might be.

Carolina found herself in the middle of the two angry men. However, they were now hardly aware of her close proximity. York had already balled his hands into fists, and Burgess Milford had raised his hand to jab an accusing finger in the middle of York's chest.

"You are a perfect example of where your father failed. I understand you were turned out by your university for disruptive behavior and ungentlemanly conduct." He jabbed the finger again, only harder this time. "It seems to me *you* are the one besmirching your father's good name."

York swung at Milford, and in the next moment Carolina found herself pulled back by strong arms. Stumbling, she glanced upward to find James Baldwin holding her.

While Burgess Milford nursed his bruised jaw, two other men in the group were grabbing at York, who was poised for another blow. This encouraged two of York's friends to join in the ruckus on his behalf. Several more blows were exchanged, and the table was bumped and dishes clattered and a few broke. It appeared as if the fight might rage out of proportion.

"Oh, stop!" Carolina shouted, but no one was listening to her now.

"Come on," James whispered in her ear, pulling her with him through the crowd.

Tears poured from her eyes, blinding her as to where James led. She followed obediently, feeling terrible for what she had done.

"It's all my fault . . . I never should have opened my mouth," she choked out between sobs.

"No, you probably shouldn't have, but then, Milford should have kept his mouth shut as well."

Carolina allowed him to assist her down the back servant stairs. She had no idea what he had in mind, but at this point it didn't matter. She only wished to be as far from the ruckus as possible.

She heard James tell Naomi as they passed through the kitchen that he was taking Miss Adams for some air in the gardens. He advised her then of the fight and directed her to tell Mrs. Adams where she could find her daughter. Naomi stared with disbelief at this information. After all, this was to be a perfect night of youthful enchantment, not a free-for-all brawl more common to taverns and back alleyways.

Thirty-Six

The Proposal

The night's chilled air was mingled with the scent of lilacs and dwarf irises. A huge milky moon hung overhead in a star-filled sky, while lanterns stretched throughout the garden walkways to create an enchanting wonderland for courting lovers. Ignoring the two or three couples strolling about, James found an isolated bench where he and Carolina sat.

Crying softly into her hands, Carolina looked very young and very vulnerable. James reached out a hand to pat her shoulder but, thinking better of it, pulled back quickly. Instead, he took out a handkerchief from his waistcoat and offered it to her with the slightest brush on her arm.

"Oh, thank you," she replied, her voice shaky. Her hand touched his only briefly during the exchange, but it was enough to cause James to wince as if scalded. Much to his relief, Carolina was too busy dabbing her eyes to notice his reaction.

"I've totally ruined everything." Carolina looked up mournfully at James, her eyes glistening in the moonlight with tears. "I didn't mean to do it, but that man made me so angry." She fell silent for a moment, then began again. "I don't suppose you heard everything, but Mr. Milford was terribly negative about the railroad. I made mention of a few facts. . . ." She paused to look down at her hands. "Well, maybe more than a few facts. . . ." Her voice trailed off.

James watched her study her hands and the handkerchief she held. She looked so very forlorn. So very beautiful.

"You didn't ruin anything," James comforted. "Grown men argue and even draw guns on each other within the austere walls of Congress itself. A gentleman should know better than to take up offenses at a party, so rest assured it was not your fault."

For a moment she seemed to forget her own woes. "They draw weapons on each other in Congress? Oh!" she exclaimed, stomping her foot. "And they're chastising *me* for the unladylike things I do." Anger seemed to have replaced her contrition, and she stood to her feet. "I have never been what my mother or society expects me to be. When they want blue, I give them green. When they say walk, I run. I've never been able to make myself over into their picture of perfection, but I have tried. Believe me, James, I have tried."

"I believe you," he said softly, wishing he could say more to help.

"I read my mother's *Lady's Book* and learn about the latest fashions and how to properly arrange flowers, but I find the whole thing monotonous and stifling. I'd much rather be reading the *Niles Weekly Register* or the *American Railroad Journal*."

"I'm glad to hear it," James said without thought.

Carolina looked at him rather surprised. "Why would you care? Virginia tells me you plan to leave here soon anyway. She says our tutoring days are to come to a close in order that you might give her more proper time and attention."

James wanted to tell her that Virginia did not know his every move. Instead he offered Carolina a supportive smile. "I'm glad you enjoy the *American Railroad Journal*, because I purchased a subscription in your name for your birthday gift."

"James, you can't be serious. A subscription costs five dollars. I certainly can't accept a gift of that value from someone I'm not even related to."

James knew he sounded rather cynical when he replied, "But if your sister has her way, we'll soon be related."

"Yes, I know."

"Besides, I'm your tutor and your father instructed me to purchase whatever I need in order to train you properly. I simply believe this will allow you a better understanding of what's going on in the world regarding the railroad and other items. Now you'll have your very own subscription and no longer be dependent upon your father or myself for a copy."

"James, I am grateful, but be reasonable. Look what my education caused tonight. Do you think my mother will ever allow me to continue with my studies when she learns it was I who started the fight?"

"But you didn't. Milford's bad manners preceded your questionable actions. And your brother threw the first punch. Milford had no right to speak to you that way. He should have been put from the house in disgrace."

"Oh, Father would never hear of that," Carolina said with a slight smile tugging at the corners of her mouth. "He rather likes to argue with Burgess's father on occasion. Though I'm sure they never exchanged blows. Anyway, this certainly wouldn't be one of Father's choices."

James smiled. "See, it's not as bad as you figured. You can still make sport of the evening."

Carolina looked up at the house and James' gaze followed. The orchestra was playing a soft sedate number and in the lighted windows, he could see people gathered in whispering groups.

"I wish I could fall asleep for a score of years. Then I could wake up and find the world happy to accept me as I am," Carolina remarked drolly.

"You've been reading Irving's 'Rip Van Winkle,' I see."

"Yes, and I don't think I'd mind so very much waking up to have this nightmare well behind me."

"But what of the things you would miss?" James asked softly as he rose and went to her. Carolina raised her gaze to meet his.

"Things I would miss?" She murmured the words in a barely audible tone. Her eyes were wide.

"Your family. Friends . . ." He let the word linger in the air. The intensity of the moment was too much, and James reached out to run his finger along the fine soft curve of her jaw. "I would miss you."

"You would?" she asked in a voice that betrayed disbelief.

"Of course." He looked down at her with all the tenderness he felt. The moonlight on her face made her seem a thing of dreams. A spirited enchantress from the deepest recesses of his imagination. Without realizing it, he had taken hold of her arm and was gently drawing her close to him.

"Why," she whispered, "why would you miss me?"

James' heart raged within him. When he looked deep within her eyes, he saw an innocence there that frightened him but also thrilled him in a way he had never felt around Virginia. And he innately knew it wasn't Carolina's sweet beauty, nor the intoxication of the moonlight that had stirred him so. What filled his mind now was not a vision of creamy skin and peach tulle, but rather of a girl bent over a book, chewing the end of a pen, engrossed in the depths of her thoughts.

But this was the wrong place. She was the wrong woman. He forced himself to think of Virginia and the compelling duty before him. Quickly he moved away from Carolina.

"I'm sorry, I seem to have done it again," she murmured, pain clearly written in her expression.

"No, it's not that." James reached out, but now it was Carolina who backed away. "Wait, I need to explain—"

"No," she said, shaking her head and biting her lip. "No, you don't."

"Carolina! James!" It was the voice of Margaret Adams.

"Here, Mother," Carolina called out quickly.

Margaret appeared with Virginia close at her side. Virginia smiled brightly at James and didn't so much as acknowledge her sister's presence.

"Are you all right, child?" Margaret looked Carolina over from head to toe. "You look positively ill. I couldn't believe it when they told me you were nearly in the middle of that confrontation. Men can be so thoughtless." She glanced up and met James' worried look. "Thank you, James, for rescuing her. It would seem a small thing to ask men to contain their politics to other occasions, but apparently it isn't. We are in your debt."

"It was my pleasure," he assured her.

Margaret nodded and put an arm around Carolina's shoulders. "Come along, Carolina. Your father has calmed things down, and there's still the birthday cake to cut."

"Oh, I don't think I could. I never want to face any of them again," Carolina said, greatly ashamed that she was near tears again.

"And that is exactly why you must face them. A good hostess learns to deal with such inopportune moments as graciously as possible." Margaret pulled her in one direction while Carolina cast a panicked expression over her shoulder at James and Virginia.

James watched Carolina leave, wishing silently that he could do something to prevent her from having to return to the party. He knew how she hated being paraded before the onlookers. He'd felt that same sense of dread, and now she would have to deal with the embarrassment of facing those people and pretending nothing was amiss.

He was practically unaware of Virginia until she hiccuped and giggled. Turning in surprise, he met her saucy expression.

"We're alone," she said. She seemed different, not quite her usual reserved self. She twirled in the moonlight, causing her skirt to bloom out around her. "We should dance here under the stars."

"The dance is over, Virginia. It's time for the cake. Don't you want to go upstairs and celebrate with your sister?"

"No! Carolina is a ninny, and her party is no fun." She hiccuped again.

"Virginia, are you all right?"

She swayed a bit. "I'm dizzy, but that's to be expected." James reached out to take hold of her arm, but instead, she threw herself into a full embrace. "I'm in love and that makes me dizzy."

James caught the unmistakable odor of liquor on her breath. No wonder his mint julep had failed to appear. "Virginia, you are quite tipsy!"

She looked up at him with childlike innocence. "Just drunk on your love." She snuggled against him and swayed back and forth. "Dance with me and tell me how you love me. Tell me again how my eyes are like starlight and pledge your undying devotion."

James glanced around nervously for fear someone might have overheard. His mind was still on the pain-filled expression with which Carolina bid him farewell. He had hurt her feelings, clear and simple. It wasn't that he said anything out of line, but his actions were inexcusable. Tomorrow he would have to find a way to apologize without demeaning her.

Virginia whirled around in circle after circle, laughing like a child. She reminded him of Maryland in full display of antics. And like Maryland, Virginia was seeking attention.

"Virginia," he said softly, trying to get her to stop moving. "You mustn't do this. Settle down or someone will see you."

"Let them," she said, and boldly leaning up on tiptoes she planted a lopsided kiss half on his lips and half on his chin. "There, I hope they all saw that."

"Virginia!"

His pleas were ignored as she fell into his arms. When he looked down to speak, she wrapped her arms around his neck and kissed him again. Only this time, the kiss was long, deep, and perfectly placed. James couldn't help but respond.

Yet even as he returned her kiss, he thought about how he had felt moments ago with Carolina. What could it have meant? Surely nothing more than . . . he didn't know, and he was afraid to find out. Carolina was a child, but also a woman who stirred his heart. Virginia stirred him, too, but in another way altogether. He was a grown man, yet his emotions were as flighty as a boy's.

"Virginia," he said with a sigh, knowing he was lost to the emotion he felt inside. Vaguely he knew Virginia was merely a convenient receptacle for the passions burning inside him. But he was glad of her presence and her advances, for they forced him to remember who he was and what was expected of him. It was not that hard at all for him to return her ardor. To do anything else was stupid, and not a little silly, too.

"You do love me, don't you?" she asked in a little-girl whimper.

"Of course I do," he replied hoarsely.

She kissed him again, only this time more awkwardly. James took her face in his hands to better slant her mouth to his. The kiss stirred his blood, and his mind was a mass of confusing, conflicting thoughts.

"And you will marry me, won't you?" she whispered when his lips left hers for the third time.

"Of course," he murmured without the meaning of what he'd just said fully registering in his mind.

Virginia pulled back and James opened his eyes in a dreamlike state. Still his mind refused reasonable thought. There was nothing beyond this moment. There was no one else in the world but this one woman. There couldn't be.

Virginia smiled in a drunken smirk. She swayed a bit, steadied herself against the nearby bench and laughed. "You won't tell them, will you?"

"Tell them what?" James asked breathlessly. The effects of her womanly charms upon him had taken its toll.

"That I proposed and you accepted. You mustn't, you know. 'Tisn't proper," she slurred the words and swayed. Plopping down hard on the bench, her gown pouffed out around her, making a whooshing sound. "Get down on your knees and propose proper-like. Then you can speak with my father tomorrow."

James stared at her mutely for a moment. Propose? Had he really accepted her proposal of marriage? He ran through the words in his mind and realized suddenly that he had responded to her kiss by agreeing to become her husband.

"James?"

He shook his head as if he could shake away the scene. "What?"

"Please do it properly," she said, holding her arms out to him.

Without knowing what else to do, James went forward and, as if in a dream, knelt in front of her. She smiled with delight, and her face revealed all the happiness she felt. That and the intoxication of the mint julep. Perhaps, he thought, she won't even remember this tomorrow. Yet within his heart, James knew there was no way around this. He'd taken advantage of her drunken state, and now he was paying the price.

Still, he thought, it wasn't such an awful price. Virginia's beauty was enough to charm any man, and she had a genuine affection for him. Remembering her warmth and responsiveness in his arms, James felt his heart beat faster. Virginia leaned forward in anticipation, and James made up his mind. His father expected it. Joseph Adams expected it. And clearly, Virginia expected it.

And Carolina. . . ? Surely she could not expect otherwise herself.

235

Thus he easily convinced himself that he could learn to be happy married to a woman like Virginia. I'm certain of it, he reasoned. And without another thought to the future or the past, James opened his mouth and very properly asked Virginia to become his wife.

———

Upstairs in the Adams' ballroom, Carolina stared at her guests with a fixed expression of joyful tranquility. She felt neither emotion, but her mother said it was imperative she show her guests how congenial she could be. The Milfords, of course, were long since absent. Whether they left of their own accord or had been asked to go, Carolina didn't know and didn't care. From now on, the name Milford would be a painful reminder of her indiscretion.

She received her friends and neighbors with all the proper verbiage expected of southern women and opened their gifts to compliment and thank each person as though the article in hand was exactly what was missing in her life. Crystal decanters, silver and brass candlestick holders, and fine bone china quickly amassed and filled the gift table. It was quite an abundance of treasure, and Carolina knew, without the subtle and not quite so subtle comments of her guests, that this was to be her bridal dowry.

The only gift she could imagine being remotely useful to her right away was James' subscription to the *American Railroad Journal*.

James.

He hadn't even bothered to reappear for cake. How terribly ashamed of her he must be. How very childish she must have seemed in his eyes. First, causing the fight at her own coming-out party and then pressing him for feelings that he couldn't possibly pretend existed. Oh, she wanted to be swallowed up by the earth and die. Humiliation was a dreadful companion.

Yet through it all, she had to remain the perfect smiling hostess. The recipient of unwanted attention.

"Yes, Mrs. Winstead, I am quite certain I have never seen a lovelier set of gilded mirrors."

"No, Mrs. Barclay, I haven't any tablecloths as lovely as this."

She raved on and on about the gifts and the wonder of becoming an adult and even allowed her mother and friends to anticipate which of her male guests might make a perfect match for her. When finally the clock struck one and the party guests were ushered to their rooms or carriages, Carolina hurried to the solace of her room and slammed the door behind her.

Hot tears of misery coursed down her cheeks as she grabbed at her hair, pulling out pins and ribbon with a vengeance. "He didn't even come back!" she declared to the silence of her room and threw herself across the bed in order to have a long and proper cry. Coming of age was a grief she could have lived without.

Thirty-Seven

The Morning After

*I*t seemed to Carolina that scarcely had her head touched the pillow when light was suddenly flooding her room to announce the day. Miriam was humming a lively tune and seemed undisturbed by the fact Carolina was hesitant to stir.

"I've laid out yor gown, Miz Carolina. Yo best be up and around so's I can arrange yor hair a'fore breakfast."

Carolina opened her eyes a bit wider. With the thought of a full table of overnight guests, she moaned. "I don't want any breakfast." There was absolutely no way she could endure the stares and questions of those who'd stayed on at Oakbridge. They'd all been properly polite and void of questions the night before, but today would be quite another story.

"Ah, Missy, yo oughtn't worry bout dat party none. Folks know wasn't none of yor doin'," Miriam comforted, hands on hips. "I is gwanna help Miz Virginia with her hair whilst yo get yorself up and around."

Carolina sighed and resigned herself to the fact that the day would go no further until she acknowledged it in full. Scooting up against the wooden headboard, she stretched. This was a good enough sign for Miriam, and the slave took herself from the room in short order.

Thoughts of the party came immediately to Carolina's mind, causing her cheeks to grow hot. Mother had been right about one thing, she thought. Politics were a surefire way to ruin a social gathering. Still, upon reflection, it wasn't the ball's more subdued ending that caused Carolina to moan in misery. That right belonged clearly to her behavior toward James Baldwin.

"What a fool I was," she said aloud with a groan. "My head was full of moonlight, and my heart was full of stupid little-girl ideals."

She remembered the way James had looked positively grief stricken when she'd pushed him for an answer about missing her. "Of course, I couldn't recognize his attempts at polite conversation. It was only his desire to take my mind off of the fight and my own sorry state."

How could she face her family this morning? She couldn't bear the idea of sitting through breakfast with everyone discussing the events of her party. Nothing was working out the way she'd hoped. Nothing at all. To most, the party would go down in county history as the night a woman dared to interfere in a gentlemen's discussion. But to James it would always be the night that Carolina overstepped the bounds of propriety. She could well imagine appearing at church to find the genteel folk of society whispering her name with cold disdain, but that didn't bother her nearly as much as thoughts of James' disapproval.

He hadn't even bothered to return for the cake, she thought and fought to keep the tears from welling in her eyes. Neither he nor Virginia had reappeared in the ballroom, and even though the party had concluded amiably, their absence had signaled a kind of comeuppance in Carolina's mind.

Pulling the cover over her head, Carolina uttered another dejected moan. Surely she could just stay in her room until the gossip died down. But while Carolina realized that avoiding the public could be quite easily attained by hiding within the walls of Oakbridge, there was clearly no way she could hide from James Baldwin.

"He must know how I feel," she said and drew the covers around her tight. "I can't bear to face him. I just can't. Not after I put my heart on my sleeve like that."

"Miz Carolina! Am I gwanna have to git Hannah to help me?"

"I'm coming, Miriam." She threw back the cover and dragged out of bed as though headed for her execution. "Couldn't I just take my breakfast here in my room?"

"No, ma'am," Miriam said, shaking her head adamantly. "Not with a houseful of folks. 'Sides, there's sumptin 'portant yo Papa wants to be discussin'."

Carolina rolled her eyes, and her shoulders dropped dejectedly. "No doubt," was all she could manage to whisper.

———

Twenty minutes later, dressed and made socially presentable, Carolina purposefully had Miriam leave her hair in a simple gathering of curls at the back of her neck. She didn't desire to appear the grand lady today. There was no need to draw attention to herself in a manner that would only remind everyone of her immaturity and her inability to keep her mouth shut.

Gingerly, she peered into the dining room before entering. They were all gathered, apparently awaiting her appearance. Julia Cooper and her husband were engaged in conversation with James and Virginia, while Margaret was giving last-minute instructions to one of the servants. There were over half a dozen other families represented at the table. The Wilmingtons, Swans, Baldwins, Sinclairs, and Barrymores took up one side of the table, with Carolina's family, the Coopers—senior and junior—the Winsteads, and Barclays taking up the opposite side. With a determined breath, she stepped into the room.

"Ah, Carolina," Joseph said with a spirited smile, and all heads turned en masse to welcome her. "Come sit so we can have our devotions and prayer."

The despair and disapproval Carolina had anticipated meeting with at this gathering was nowhere to be found. Even her mother was smiling as though in on a wonderful secret. Virginia giggled into Julia's ear, while James seemed to stare, preoccupied, at the plate in front of him. Thankful his eyes were on the table and not on her, Carolina took her seat and waited in confused dread for what was to come. Only York appeared to be less than joyous with his black eye and swollen nose.

Joseph picked up the large worn Bible that had accompanied him to breakfast for as long as Carolina could remember. "Psalm sixty-seven is the place of our Bible reading. 'God be merciful unto us, and bless us; and cause his face to shine upon us; that thy way may be known upon earth, thy saving health among all nations. Let the people praise thee, O God; let all the people praise thee. O let the nations be glad and sing for joy: for thou shalt judge the people righteously, and govern the nations upon earth. Let the people praise thee, O God; let all the people praise thee. Then shall the earth yield her increase; and God, even our own God, shall bless us. God shall bless us; and all the ends of the earth shall fear him.' So ends the psalmist." Joseph closed the Bible and smiled upon his family. "We should always remember to praise God for His blessings. The earth is ripe to bear new crops, and our hearts should also bear witness of growth in His wisdom."

Carolina barely heard the words. She looked up to find James' gaze upon her, but when he quickly looked away, Carolina was more mortified than before. He hates me, she thought. He hates me for my childishness last night at the party and for my unladylike manners in the garden.

"God provides goodness in the wake of bad," Joseph was saying, and Carolina found herself wondering if he would mention the party.

Surely he wouldn't be so heartless as to make her an example before her family and friends.

"Let us bless the food and this day." They all bowed in prayer while Joseph continued. "Heavenly Father, we thank you for the bounty you have provided. We thank you for the food upon our table and that which grows now in our fields. Your mercy has blessed us without measure, and we are humbled before you for the love you have bestowed upon us. In the name of our Savior, Jesus, amen."

"Amen," the table chorused in unison.

Carolina looked up, expecting her father to take his seat as usual, but instead he directed his attention to Virginia. "I believe there is an announcement that needs to be made."

York and Carolina seemed the only ones surprised by these words. Questioning her brother with her eyes, Carolina received a shrug and could only wait for her father to speak again.

"I am very pleased to announce that James Baldwin has asked for Virginia's hand in marriage. I have given my consent, as has Mrs. Adams. James, I want to be the first to welcome you into the family." James stood and received a hearty handshake from Joseph, as well as a congratulatory slap on the back while Edith and Leland exchanged looks of conspiratorial satisfaction.

Carolina felt her mouth go dry. She couldn't look at James, and so she managed a weak smile at her sister. Virginia nodded with an air of smug satisfaction, while Georgia and Margaret, unable to contain their joy, hugged her simultaneously as the table erupted in hearty approval.

"Has a date been agreed upon?" York questioned.

"No, not yet. We've only just agreed to wed," Virginia answered before anyone else could.

"Well, no doubt you will want to do it before summer is out. No sense in letting a whole year pass by in planning and engagement parties," Margaret said authoritatively. If this declaration shocked her guests, no one said so.

Virginia nodded. "I think a summer wedding will be just what we both desire. Why, we might even use the gardens, where James proposed to me. But, of course, James and I should discuss this privately before making it a public issue."

"I couldn't agree more," Joseph remarked, taking his seat. James followed suit. "Now we should partake of this wonderful breakfast before it gets too cold."

"I, for one, am positively ravenous," James announced with a grin. It seemed to Carolina he'd broken out of his mold of shocked silence. He dug into the platter of sausages before another word was spoken.

Margaret regarded Carolina with an all-consuming look. "You are quite pale this morning, Carolina. Were you unable to sleep last night?"

"I slept quite well, thank you. It just seemed morning came a bit earlier than usual."

York laughed at this. "I'll say. It seemed to come a bit more painfully as well."

Joseph dismissed the remark with a disapproving look before turning to Carolina. "Daughter, I know I speak for all of us when I say we are deeply sorry for the disruption of your party. The Milfords had no right to say such things in your presence, and while I believe York to be a bit too quick to the fight, I suppose such a thing was taken completely out of his control. A coming-of-age party should be an occasion for joy and happiness, and I fully blame Burgess Milford for last night's conclusion. That aside, however"—he smiled warmly at Carolina—"I believe the party came off quite well." Approving murmurs came from around the table. "You were quite a vision, and you did your family proud."

Carolina almost felt the breath taken from her. No one seemed to think the party ruined after all.

"Oh, and the gifts were simply divine," her mother was saying. "So many priceless treasures. What a fine collection to add to your hope chest." Again murmurs of approval sounded, this time mostly by the women.

"Still, you look completely spent," her father said, picking up his fork. "If you wish to remain home from church, your mother and I will allow it this once."

"Thank you, Father, Mother," Carolina answered. "I would very much appreciate that." She had nearly forgotten it was Sunday.

"Maybe I should stay home as well," York announced. "I've no doubt Burgess Milford will be doing likewise."

At this several of the men laughed aloud, but Carolina noted James was not among their numbers. Instead, James was staring directly at her. What did he mean to convey with his stern expression? she wondered.

The words of a favorite poem suddenly came to mind and haunted her like nothing else could have:

Oh, not to me, oh, not to me!
That look of cold disdain—
From others I could calmly brook
The careless word—the chilling look
But oh! from thee—'tis pain.

And surely it was more pain than she'd ever known in her young life. It was all she could do to keep from bursting into tears and begging his forgiveness. And still, he stared at her with an unyielding look that seemed to question her without words. His eyes were searching hers as though looking for something he'd lost. The intensity was too much, and Carolina quickly looked away. She'd nearly made a fool of herself with her emotions bubbling over like a caldron aboil. There was no chance she would make that mistake again. Not if she had anything to say about it.

Thirty-Eight

The Ship

*E*ating leftover cake that afternoon, Carolina was finally beginning to laugh again. She listened to her father speak of the multiple blackened eyes in church that morning, including a most swollen-faced Burgess Milford, who eyed York throughout the service as if he would start the altercation all over again.

Margaret overlooked the sport her menfolk were making of the serious breach of protocol and instead focused on her eldest daughter.

"Well, Virginia, you are going to have a great deal to do in order to get ready for your wedding, especially if you and James still plan to have a summer wedding. There are many tasks ahead of you that will need your utmost attention. I, of course, will allow you freedom from helping me with the house. Carolina will take over your duties."

At this Carolina started and nearly dropped her fork. Margaret looked hesitantly to Joseph and then turned a stern gaze upon Carolina. "Your tutoring, of course, will no longer be a consideration. James will need time to seek employment as well as time to escort Virginia to the proper social events and so forth. Your new duties assisting me will keep you more than busy and will not allow you time to linger over books."

"But, Mother—" Carolina cast a desperate look at her father, who was conveniently looking in the other direction.

Margaret waved away any further protest. "It's already settled. Your father released James from his tutoring duties this morning."

Carolina knew the look she gave James was an accusatory one. His eyes seemed to plead with her for understanding, but he said nothing. It was Virginia who spoke.

"Carolina will find it much more difficult but far more satisfying to set about the business of housekeeping and such. And I heard Sarah

244

Armstrong mention her brother Daniel is already quite interested in my little sister. There may not be much time for Carolina to learn everything she needs to know before she finds herself engaged as well." The words were spoken lightly, but Carolina noted a trace of sarcasm in their delivery.

"How delightful!" Margaret exclaimed at this news. "Daniel Armstrong is a fine young man."

"Delightful for whom?" Carolina blurted without thinking. All faces turned to stare in surprise at this outburst.

"Carolina," her mother began in a tone that made clear her disapproval, "you have been given your freedom for too long. You show a clear lack of appreciation for what you've enjoyed. I will not have you spoil your sister's happy day with childish tantrums. Surely you do not wish for James to witness your disgruntled nature."

Carolina bit back an angry retort. She really didn't care at this point what James witnessed of her, but nonetheless she chose her next words carefully. "I have no argument in helping you run Oakbridge. This is my home, and I love it. However, I have not one whit of interest in becoming the wife of Daniel Armstrong. To encourage such a thing would be to live a lie."

Margaret chuckled. "No one said you had to marry Daniel Armstrong. There are many eligible young men in the area. Now, I am sure we don't want to bore our guests further with a *family* discussion."

"We can talk later if you like, Carolina," Joseph said rather helplessly.

Carolina shrugged as if she didn't care, but she had to keep her hands clenched into fists so she wouldn't cry. The rest of the time was torment, but she kept her mouth closed. When the guests finally departed and her father beckoned her into the parlor, she almost refused. She felt as though he had betrayed her, too. But, of course, she could not be so disrespectful of him and she followed. Her mother was already there.

"Carolina," Joseph said gently, "I am sorry for how your birthday has turned out. I know what high expectations a girl has for her sixteenth birthday—"

"I don't care about that, Papa!"

"Carolina! Don't interrupt your father," Margaret warned.

"I'm sorry. It's just that what really bothers me is losing my chance at getting an education. I enjoy my book learning," Carolina said, trying to ignore her mother's furrowing brow. "I'm not trying to act the part of spoiled child, but I fail to see why the one thing I love should be taken from me."

"There is no reason you can't have your books, child," Joseph broke in. "The library is still at your disposal, and I will bring home new volumes whenever possible."

"Now, now, Mr. Adams," Margaret chided. "You mustn't encourage the child to neglect her duties. This house does not run itself. There is a great deal to manage. Why the overseeing of the house slaves alone—"

"I understand," Joseph interrupted. "I simply see no reason to put an end to all of her studies. Granted, James will be about his own business, but she learns quite well on her own, and there is our joint interest in the railroad. Carolina is an important part of that." He looked tenderly at Carolina, and she could almost forgive how he seemed to have turned on her earlier. He continued. "I believe we can fit everything into a day. Besides, there is the trip north that I promised her."

Margaret said nothing more, but the look on her face told Carolina she was clearly disturbed by this turn of events. Carolina felt tears threatening to spill from her eyes. Her throat ached fiercely where a solid lump formed to mark her misery. She held her breath and bit her tongue to keep from focusing on her fate, but nothing could take the words from her brain. She was losing everything.

Asking as politely as possible to be excused, Carolina made her way to her room. She vaguely remembered the words of her father's morning Scripture reading. Something about God's blessings and praises being offered up to Him.

"I don't feel much like thanking you for these things," Carolina murmured in prayer. "I feel more like you have deserted me, and instead of making your face to shine upon me, it seems you have turned it away."

Spying her books on the dressing table, Carolina marched across the room and, with an angry swipe, scattered them from the table to the floor. They landed with a loud resounding crash upon the wood, heaped in hapless disorder, much like Carolina's dreams.

When the last of his things were loaded into his father's carriage, James excused himself to attend to what he termed unfinished business. Carolina had avoided him all week, and now that he was leaving, James was determined to make her face him and allow him to explain—though exactly what he had to explain he didn't quite know. He only knew *something* had to be said. He knew she blamed him for the demise of her schooling. He didn't want her to give up on her dreams because of him.

On top of all else, two days after the party the old slave Granny had died. He knew Carolina was grieved and deeply sorrowed by the announcement, for the slave woman had been a special person in her life.

He left his father and Joseph discussing cotton prices and new methods of shipping and bounded up the grand staircase in search of his elusive friend. The library, the one room he expected to find her in, revealed nothing but the silent rows of books on their shelves. These were her true friends, and even if they'd been capable of speech, they'd not betray their mistress, James was certain.

The music room was empty, as was the main sitting room and more intimate family parlor. Knowing it to be a bold move, James cautiously made his way to Carolina's bedroom. His knock caused the door to open, revealing the room in its feminine splendor but missing the object of his search. He didn't know what compelled him, but he found himself stepping into the room. Perhaps it was the lingering scent of lilacs and rose water that so reminded him of her. On the dressing table were stacks of books and beside these were several sheets of paper and a pen and inkwell. A closer look revealed the papers to be a copy of the *American Railroad Journal*, and on one page someone, presumably Carolina, had circled something of interest.

Picking up the journal, James saw it was a poem entitled "The Ship." No author was given, but the first stanza was circled, and James read it aloud: "Where art thou going? Far away. To seek a distant shore. . . . Gaze ye upon me while ye may; you will not see me more."

A breeze outside caused the curtains at the open window to flutter, and James returned the paper to the table and went to peer outside. There on the lawn near the flowering orchards, Carolina walked alone. He watched her for several moments, forgetting all about the impropriety of being in her bedroom. She looked so consumed with her emotions that James wondered if she even realized he was leaving on this day. Surely, if her mind had not been grieved with her losses, she would have at least made the proper appearances to bid him farewell.

He nearly called from the window, then stopped himself as the curtain again caught the wind. The touch of the material against his face brought into perspective his position. Glancing down he saw something white sticking out from beneath the window-seat cushion. Taking them in hand, James smiled. They were Carolina's smudged gloves. Once, when they had been alone studying the principles of steam, she had confided to him about her soiled gloves. He lifted them to his nose the way she'd described having done a thousand times. The faint scent of grease brought an ironic smile to his lips. It was almost more nostalgic of Carolina than rose water. Gently he ran his finger along the black stains. Looking from the gloves to the woman outside, an idea struck him. James tucked the gloves in his pocket. He determined to go to Carolina and offer her an encouraging word. He would hold the gloves up as a banner of hope and endurance. He would remind her of her dream and hold her accountable for the future of it.

"There you are!" Leland exclaimed as James descended the stairs. "I thought I might have to send out a search party. Come along, your mother was expecting us an hour ago."

James started to protest, but Leland was already moving him with huffing and gasping strides to the carriage. "We must hurry. Joseph, I will be in touch with you regarding that matter of shipping," Leland remarked.

"James, I'm certain we will soon be seeing you. You are always welcome, as you know."

James took Joseph's extended hand, but his gaze roamed to the fields beyond. Carolina was nowhere in sight, and for reasons beyond his understanding, James felt a hollow emptiness in her absence. He could just tell them to wait while he had a word with Carolina. Yet suddenly all the words he had thought of saying seemed so lame. He was letting her down. What good would it do to prattle on about her dreams but to ease his conscience? It might make her even more angry at him.

He touched the gloves in his pocket and wondered what he should do. He couldn't very well offer them to Carolina's father and explain how it was he came by them, yet to keep them would break Carolina's heart. Still, it would also force him to seek some future moment of privacy, when her anger and disappointment had dulled, in which he could return the gloves. Somehow that lifted his spirits a bit.

James climbed into the carriage, and as it moved down the drive, he was haunted by the words of the poem Carolina had circled in the magazine. "Gaze ye upon me while ye may; you will not see me more." Carolina was gone and there was no chance to ease her pain or resolve their circumstance.

"Did you say something?" Leland asked.

James started. "What? Oh no. Nothing . . . nothing at all."

PART IV

Late Spring 1836

We surely live in a very fast age;
We've traveled by ox-teams, and then by stage
But when such conveyance is all done away
We'll travel in steam cars upon the railway!

—James Crane

Thirty-Nine

A Waking Dream

"Carolina, I swear you're as nervous as a cat in the cream house," York declared and urged the driver of the carriage to pick up the speed. "My sister has a train to meet, and we wouldn't want her to miss it." Joseph and York both laughed at this.

"You'd think she'd never been on a train before," Joseph said with a wink at his daughter.

"Perhaps it's because she's never actually taken a seat on a train before."

Carolina pretended to be miffed with York's jocular teasing by giving her chin a little upward jerk, but in truth he was right. She was anxious and excited and probably fidgeting like a little child. But this trip was important to her. No, she thought silently, this trip is *everything* to me.

It had only been by focusing on the trip to Baltimore that Carolina was able to bear the many changes since her birthday. James had moved back home with his parents, and although he appeared from time to time to escort Virginia, his presence was clearly relegated to memories. Carolina found she missed his company more with each passing day. And each time Virginia spoke of her intended, there was an aching in Carolina's heart that she could not—and dare not—explain.

She didn't want to think of such things now. This day was too wonderful to tarnish. Carolina felt the nervous flutters in her stomach as the three-story brick depot came into view. "Are you sure I look all right?" she asked, reaching a hand up to feel her new hat. The pink beret, complete with dyed feathers and trailing ribbons, was the height of fashion, and her father had paid the outrageous sum of thirteen dollars to procure it for her. But he had told her with the glow of fatherly

251

love in his eyes that this was her special time, and she deserved for every aspect of it to be the best and finest his money could buy.

"You know, Carolina, you are in grand company," said Joseph. "The President's niece has a copy of that very same bonnet."

"Oh, don't try to make me feel better," Carolina replied drolly, nervously adjusting the beret.

"It's true!" York exclaimed. "Father wouldn't lie to you. But you look far better in the bonnet than she. Now just relax and mind your manners. You'll put all of Baltimore to shame."

"I'd rather not shame them," she said, then suddenly shrieked aloud when the unmistakable blast of a locomotive whistle sounded. "Oh, Father, we're too late!"

"Nonsense," Joseph answered and patted her arm soothingly. "We're here on time, and we have our tickets in hand."

"They wouldn't dare leave without you!" York stated quite seriously, then winked.

"Oh, bother with the both of you." She craned her neck to see all that she could. "I'm not ashamed of my anticipation."

The carryall came to a stop, and York quickly jumped down and reached back up to receive his sister. "You look quite perfect," he whispered against her ear and then kissed her lightly on the forehead. "Don't go breaking any hearts in Baltimore."

"Of course not," she said absently, her patience dwindling as her father settled the fare with the driver and instructed the porters where to take their bags.

Finally Joseph came to join them and couldn't resist saying, "You know, if you aren't up to this, we can put it off a few weeks. . . ."

Carolina answered him by gracefully maneuvering her flounced cotton skirt into hand, and in a swish of pink and white, she swept past her father and brother with ribbons sailing behind and feathers fluttering in the breeze.

———

When she first caught sight of the engine called the *J.Q. Adams*, Carolina thought how appropriate it was that she should make this important trip on a locomotive that bore her surname. The grasshopper engine had a vertical boiler like all the other B&O engines she'd seen either in person or on paper. James had told her there were plans among the designers at Mt. Clare to create horizontal boiler engines. It was all too wondrous to imagine.

The depot hummed with activity, and Carolina found herself engulfed in a swelling crowd of well-wishers and travelers.

"It's a good thing we secured tickets," Joseph told York.

"Now I'm glad I won't be making the trip with you. The afternoon heat will make that car seem like an oven."

"I'm sure your sister will never notice."

Carolina heard the words of her father and brother but gave them little consideration. She wanted to memorize every detail of the moment. To remember for the rest of her life what it felt like this first time boarding the train as a passenger bound for a destination.

She allowed her brother to hand her up into the car, then turned and smiled brightly. "I'll see you Friday."

"Happy travels," York replied, then assured Joseph he'd have the carryall there for them at the appointed time.

Joseph urged her forward, and Carolina felt her lips go dry. "I can't believe it's truly happening. It seems like a hundred other dreams I've had." She moved down the narrow aisle of wooden bench seats.

Joseph laughed. "Well, it most certainly is happening. In a matter of a couple of hours we'll be in Baltimore, guests of Philip Thomas and the B&O Railroad. You'll have your fill of locomotives before we return on Friday."

"That would be impossible," she murmured, but her father didn't seem to hear.

"Louis McLane!" Joseph declared to a stately gentleman not two feet ahead of them.

The tall gentleman turned a questioning eye to Carolina and her father, then recognition dawned. "Joseph Adams. Well, sir, it has been a long while since I've enjoyed the pleasure of your company." He gave a curt nod to Carolina.

"I should say so," Joseph replied. "Once you left the auspices of the White House, I thought to never hear from you again. What are you doing now that you no longer fill the seat of secretary of state?"

"I'm president of the Morris Canal and Banking Company. Have a seat with me, and I shall be more than happy to engage you on the entire two-year lapse."

Joseph turned to Carolina. "This is my daughter."

"Miss Adams." McLane gave a more formal bow of acknowledgment.

"Carolina, would you mind if we joined Mr. McLane?" Joseph asked.

Carolina was actually glad for the reprieve from small talk with her father. "By my leave, Father."

Joseph immediately resumed his conversation with McLane. "We have business in Baltimore."

"As do I," McLane said and motioned to the open seats.

Carolina took her place beside the window. From here she could watch their progress and note every tree and flowering plant along the rail line. From here she could imagine the rails outstretching to take her far beyond her Virginia home with the respectability of womanhood carefully put in its place. Her father and McLane were deep in conversation concerning the various banking institutes, and while normally she might have eavesdropped in order to learn more about the situation, today she was totally devoted to the railroad.

I'm truly here, she thought. I'm here and within a matter of hours I'll be in Baltimore. What might my grandfather have thought had he lived to see this day? She all but pressed her nose to the soot-smudged glass. *Am I the only one who sees the significance? Has everyone else already taken this mode of transportation for granted?* The colors and smells seemed to blend into a swirl of emotions and memories. A thousand times before, she had imagined this very moment. And every time, she had awoken from her thoughts to find them nothing more than dreams of imagination. The screech of the locomotive whistle brought it all back into perspective. This was real; it wasn't a dream this time.

She thought of the very first time she had seen the locomotive in Washington City. It seemed so long ago, but it had not even been a year. So much had changed for her since then, and deep within she felt that that locomotive had been the catalyst for all the changes. Thinking of that day brought to mind her smudged gloves. They seemed to have been misplaced. She hadn't seen them since shortly after her birthday party. She had looked everywhere and even questioned the slaves, fearing they might have mistaken them for trash and disposed of them. But the gloves had disappeared. Trying to be mature about the matter, she told herself that perhaps she would find a new memento of the railroad today.

Running her gloved hand along the wooden seat, Carolina waited in nervous anticipation for the first lurch of the car. Would it come smooth in a gliding motion or rough and uneven? She hadn't long to wait. The movement, jolting and hesitant, gave the first sign of forward motion. Jerking against each other in a metallic tug-of-war, the cars groaned against the pull, but the ever efficient grasshopper engine held fast and surged them ahead. Carolina suddenly realized she'd been holding her breath and let it out with a long sigh.

Joseph turned from his conversation to squeeze her hand. "And so our adventure begins, eh?"

Carolina nodded, near to tears from the emotions coursing through her. She looked back out the window to the world now slipping by at the steady rate of six miles an hour. Soon they would speed ahead to fifteen miles an hour, possibly more. Would the countryside simply be a blur of colors and indistinguishable structures? Her hands felt clammy inside her gloves and perspiration formed on the back of her neck, but she gave it no mind. It either came from her excitement or from the heat, but either way, it didn't matter. She was on her way to Baltimore. She was in a passenger car of the Baltimore and Ohio Railroad, and somehow her world seemed not so small and insignificant anymore.

Forty

Along the Way

*I*f someone would have described for Carolina the beauty that would pass by her window, she'd have doubted the integrity of the teller. She had known the states of Virginia and Maryland to be lovely, but the richness of color and the glorious contrast of vegetation and wildlife was far more than she'd ever anticipated.

Thick forests of oaks, poplars, elm, cottonwood, and hickory edged up to the clearing that had been set aside for the railroad. A right-of-way wide enough to discourage the smokestack sparks from setting fire to the countryside had been established, but to hear tales told, it did little in actuality to keep the deed from happening. Fire was perhaps the most protested, negative aspect of rail travel. Fire was so greatly feared in the city, in fact, that her father had already told her the passenger cars would be hooked up to horses at the Mt. Clare station in order for them to journey into Baltimore proper.

Someday, she thought, mesmerized by the way the ground sped by up close yet seemed to hardly move at a distance, they'll find a way to work through all these problems, and locomotives will travel everywhere. James had assured her it was only a matter of time, and Carolina believed him with all her heart. There was a great deal about James she'd hoped to forget on this trip, but at every turn or jostle of the car, she instantly remembered some spoken word or article he'd shared. He was to be her sister's husband, and there was no room for the thoughts she held inside her head. James would be her brother-in-law, nothing more, and the sooner she dealt with that issue, the better.

They'd made several stops for water, coal, and passengers, yet it seemed to Carolina they'd only ridden a short way when McLane leaned her direction and spoke.

"We're not far from Baltimore now. This is Relay, Maryland." The locomotive was slowing. "We'll take on water here, maybe a few passengers, and then cross the river on the Thomas Viaduct. It's a masterpiece of design and construction and one of the prouder portions of the B&O's ever growing line."

"How interesting," Carolina murmured, uncertain how to respond to this man she scarcely knew. If she showed too much interest, would it create an embarrassment for her father? She was determined to repay her father's generosity in taking her on this trip by being as well-mannered as possible.

"Mr. McLane was just telling me about this bridge. It's quite fascinating, my dear." Her father's words seemed to indicate to Carolina that any interest shown would be well received.

The sound of the wheels beneath them changed in pitch, and glancing out the window again, Carolina watched as the train rolled to a stop beside a three-story depot. "Will we have time to walk about? Perhaps view the bridge?"

"There'll be plenty of time for that," McLane assured. "In fact, I'd be happy to escort you and your father to a viewing platform the designer had built in order to view the progress of construction. We can be up and back before you know it. How about it, Adams? Are you interested?"

"Quite." Joseph got to his feet. "Lead on."

Carolina found the afternoon walk invigorating as she followed Louis McLane and her father up a rocky pathway. They left the road and climbed a grassy knoll resplendent in blossoms of pink lady's slipper and dogtooth violets. When they reached a small wooden platform, McLane offered his arm to help Carolina up the five short steps to view the bridge.

"How glorious!" exclaimed Carolina. The bridge stretched across a large chasm in a series of elliptical arches.

"That's the Patapsco River down there," McLane said for her benefit. "The bridge is some sixty feet above it in order for the freight boats to comfortably pass beneath. The entire span is over six hundred feet long, and this is the only stone-arch bridge in the world built on a curve. Of course, it's difficult to see just how much it curves from this vantage point, but the engineer told me it is a full four degrees."

"Indeed?" Carolina's interest was piqued. "The arches give it a stately look, but you're right—it doesn't look so very curved from where we stand."

"There must be at least a half dozen archways," Joseph remarked.

"There are eight to be exact," McLane replied. "Ben Latrobe, a gentleman who once worked as a surveyor for the B&O, created this design. Folks were certain it couldn't be done. In fact, they laughed at the design when it was first described. They were sure it would collapse under its own weight, but as you can see, it's quite reliable."

Carolina thought of the sixty-foot plummet to the bottom of the Patapsco and shuddered.

"Oh, I assure you, we are quite safe," McLane said, noting her reaction. "That Maryland granite won't be moved. I'd venture to say this bridge will stand for generations to come. The Romans couldn't have done a better job, and I speak quite knowledgeably from a recent trip abroad." He smiled warmly and Carolina returned his gesture. She was far too excited to be truly worried.

"I have the utmost confidence in the B&O Railroad, Mr. McLane," she said.

"As do I," he assured.

Joseph mopped his brow with a handkerchief and agreed. "I wouldn't have wanted to miss this sight. Say, you mentioned Ben Latrobe designed this bridge. I knew his father, God rest his soul. As an architect he laid a great many of the designs for the city of Washington."

McLane smiled. "It's a talented family. Ben has just returned from working with the Baltimore and Port Deposit Railroad to once again take charge of surveying for the B&O. His brother John is offering legal counsel to Philip Thomas."

"You know quite a bit about the B&O," Joseph remarked.

"Let's just say I have acquired a deep interest in the company."

Carolina remained quiet, simply taking in the sight and committing it to memory. A light breeze lifted the edges of her flounces, causing them to ruffle in the breeze like the flagging stems of the lady's slippers. Overhead, light wispy clouds hung like cobwebs against a pale blue sky. It was a moment forever hers.

A single long blast of the locomotive whistle was their cue to return promptly to the *J.Q. Adams*. Carolina descended the rickety wooden steps and took her father's offered arm for the return walk. Jagged rocks threatened to bruise her feet even through the protection of her sturdy traveling boots, but it was of little matter. The day was perfect, and the Thomas Viaduct held a silent challenge. They said it couldn't be done. The bridge couldn't possibly work. It would collapse beneath its own weight. Somehow, these thoughts seemed akin to the hundreds of statements she'd heard in regard to her education and her desire to be a part of the railroad. It was almost as if the bridge beckoned her to go forward. To defy them all. To prove them wrong. She was here, after all. That in and of itself said something very important.

And when they arrived in Baltimore and the conductor yelled, "Charles and Pratt Station—end of the line!" Carolina knew it was not the end, but only the beginning for her.

Forty-One

Philip Thomas

*C*ompared to Washington City, with its forty thousand residents, Baltimore, a town of more than sixty-five thousand, was a teeming metropolis. Carolina had never seen the like, and she gazed about with wonder as the carriage sent by Philip Thomas drove her and her father from the station. The claim that the city was the second commercial city in the world was far-fetched—even Carolina realized that. But it was the third largest city by population in America, and it certainly looked as though it could compete with London or Paris in commerce.

The Thomas home was a stately mansion on a broad tree-lined avenue. A couple of servants unloaded the baggage from the carriage while the butler led them into a finely appointed parlor where Mr. Thomas greeted them warmly.

"I have to apologize," he said, "for not meeting you myself at the station. I lately find myself embarrassingly disposed by an illness my physician is unable to diagnose. I hope you had a pleasant journey here."

Joseph nodded. "It was one well worth taking. But I'm sorry to hear about your illness. It would seem we came at an inconvenient time."

"Don't give it a thought. I only regret that I will be unable to show you around as I would have liked. However," he said, taking a seat and motioning for Joseph and Carolina to do the same, "I have made arrangements, and I don't believe you'll be disappointed."

"Mr. Thomas, we certainly don't wish to put you to any unnecessary discomfort." Joseph purposefully avoided his daughter's eyes. He knew how important this trip was to Carolina. She had suffered a great blow with her mother's intolerance toward continued education.

"I assure you it has been seen to. I have even arranged a special treat as you suggested I might. Tomorrow, you will board the main stem rails

260

and be taken to the place where they are making repairs to the line."

"Marvelous," Joseph said, then turned to Carolina. "I suggested to Mr. Thomas we might enjoy going out on the line where the men are working."

Carolina's eyes widened in surprise. "Mother would suffer a fit of apoplexy if she knew."

He smiled conspiratorially. "Well, she doesn't, so I suppose we will keep it to ourselves."

"Your rooms have been made ready. Would you like to see them now and perhaps freshen up before dinner?" Philip asked.

"I would imagine Carolina would like to rest a bit," Joseph said, hoping his daughter would remember her genteel manners enough to take the hint of his dismissal.

When she was accompanied upstairs by a servant, Joseph turned to Philip with concern. Thomas was breathing rather hard and looked decidedly piqued. "You look spent. Is there anything I can do?"

"No, but there is something I have decided to do." He paused, his face taking on a strained look of sorrow. "You will find out sooner or later, and I'd rather it be from me. I'm resigning from the B&O."

"What!"

Philip folded his hands across his lap. "I can't continue like this. My health is failing me daily, and there are other problems as well." He paused as if trying to decide whether to continue. "There are also those who say it's time for new leadership. We are only a quarter of the way to the Ohio River—our original goal—which we should have accomplished by now. A great many investors, including those in the government, are questioning my ability to get us there."

"Philip, I hope you know I am not one of those. I have complete faith in you. Your detractors can't possibly understand what you're up against," Joseph offered. "Giving in to them isn't the answer."

"Besides a faithful supporter of the B&O, you've become a good friend, Joseph." Philip looked resigned. "I've been at the helm since the company's inception. We've laid over one hundred and fourteen miles of track both west to Harper's Ferry and south to Washington. I've had a good presidency, and we've accomplished a great deal, but, Joseph, there are some big problems ahead of this company. Problems bigger than me and my ability to see the company through."

"Such as?" Joseph was still dumbfounded by Philip's announcement. When one thought of the B&O, Philip Thomas was just as naturally considered. In the minds of many, Thomas *was* the Baltimore and Ohio Railroad Company.

"There are problems getting west of Harper's for one. We aren't even certain that line will be built, and there is a great deal of arguing about the best route to take, when and if it is built. We'd hoped to be in Cumberland before now, and because of our shortcomings the line is missing out on a great deal of freight. If we could at least reach Cumberland, we could pick up cargo from the National Road."

"But you have a fine company. The *American Railroad Journal* called the B&O 'the Railroad University of the United States.' "

Philip attempted a smile. "I read that article too, but I doubt seriously they'd call us that now. Not if they took a close look at our financial ledgers."

"Surely it can't be all that bad."

"We're nearly bankrupt. The costs of stone masonry, replacing and building new equipment, and trying to renovate the deteriorating lines are all taking their toll. Why, west of Ellicotts Mills, the road has deteriorated so badly that I'm afraid it will have to be completely taken up and relaid with T-rails. So, you see the difficulty in laying new track when the old stretches are in great need of repair and upgrading."

Joseph frowned. "But I'd read that total receipts were up nearly ten thousand dollars over last year this time."

"True, but expenses are up nearly double that. Profits are way down, my friend, and that causes the board of directors, and the stockholders they represent, to give a serious look at the man in the president's chair."

Joseph said nothing for several moments. He had expected to hear how well the railroad was doing, and this news of bankruptcy hanging in the wings as well as Thomas's impending resignation was most discouraging. He thought about his high hopes for starting his own railroad—the Potomac and Great Falls. Was that to be just a fine name for another of his unrealized dreams?

"Are you determined to do this? Resign, I mean." Joseph watched the man carefully for any sign of hesitation, but there was none.

"I am. I've had a good run, and now it's time to turn matters over to another man. Perhaps a new, younger mind will put life back into the line."

"Do you have someone in mind?"

Philip nodded. "As a matter of fact, I do. Do you know Louis McLane?"

Joseph nodded. "I do indeed. In fact, we shared our ride up from Washington with him. He was very kind to my daughter and took much time explaining all about the viaduct named after you."

"McLane is a good man, and he's a visionary. He's succeeded with projects when everyone else thought them sure failures. His service as secretary of the treasury and as a representative of Delaware in both houses of Congress gives him a solid background for all the dealings we must have with the government. And as Jackson's minister to England and as secretary of state, his international credentials are impressive also."

"I know," Joseph said. "I met him in Washington when he served the President. Some say he's hard to work with, but he gets things done. He's a definite adversary of waste, whether it be in man hours or dollar figures."

"It's good to hear yet another positive opinion of the man." Philip rose to his feet and swayed a bit.

Joseph was immediately beside him offering a supportive arm.

"Ah, this confounded sickness!" Philip complained with great frustration. "It makes a man feel his age more than one wants. Would you care for a drink, Joseph?"

"No, nothing for me, but I'd happily pour for you."

"Yes, a drop of brandy ought to steady me." Philip returned to his seat and sat down heavily, then continued as Joseph poured the brandy from a decanter. "Most importantly, McLane knows the European financial market. He's got friends in England who will do most anything for him, and I'm afraid in order to see the Baltimore and Ohio truly add the Ohio to its list of destinations, we will need to seek foreign investors."

"And you believe McLane will do this?"

"If it does become necessary, I know he will. We've been corresponding regularly for the past few months, and I feel confident in his vision for this railroad. He won't let it die away like some might. Other men might give up at the first threat of the impossible. Cut their losses and run. McLane won't. Of this I am sure."

"From what I remember of his days in Washington, I believe that assessment to be a correct one," Joseph answered, handing Thomas a snifter of brandy.

"I hope so." Philip contemplated his drink for a moment as if trying to decide whether to share the next bit of information with Joseph. "I'm going to suggest he be offered four thousand dollars a year with regular increases," he finally said.

"Four thousand! Well now, that will be hard to ignore."

"If he can turn the company around, get them moving forward again, it will be a mere pittance of what he's truly worth."

The woman who'd led Carolina away to her room appeared in the arched doorway and frowned disapprovingly. "Mr. Thomas, the doctor instructed you to take a nap before dinner. You've barely time to do that now."

"I'm well aware of that, Aggie, and I'm just now coming." Philip struggled to his feet, taking the extended hand Joseph offered. "Thank you," he said, straightening. "We will eat at seven. Aggie, please show Mr. Adams to his room." The woman in black bombazine and a starched white apron gave a sour-faced nod and, without a word to Joseph, headed up the stairs.

"We will speak more of this later," Philip stated, "but for the time, I'd appreciate your confidence on the matter."

"Of course."

"Feel free to use the house as your own. My carriages are at your disposal, and with the rest of my family away visiting relatives up north, you needn't fear conflicting with anyone else's needs."

"You are a most gracious host, Philip. I believe I'll just take it easy this afternoon."

Thomas nodded and walked slowly from the room with Joseph at his side.

———

Joseph reflected on their conversation the remainder of the day. Even after their quiet meal and after-dinner interlude in the parlor where Carolina entertained them on the pianoforte, he still pondered the effects of Philip Thomas's planned resignation. It could well destroy the company. If the stockholders misunderstood Thomas's action and lost faith because of his move, it would bode ill for the operation.

Remembering the delight in which Carolina had shared her interest in the operations of the railroad, Joseph was glad Philip had sworn him to secrecy. Carolina would grieve over the possibility of the B&O's demise, and since the threat was premature, there was no sense in working her up over it. Then, too, his mind warned him against continuing with his own railroad schemes. If the B&O, with all of its prominent backing, was struggling to stay alive, how could a small private enterprise hope to make it? There was much to consider.

Crawling between the lightweight coverlet and crisp cool sheets, Joseph leaned over and blew out the bedside lamp. His mind was consumed with thoughts. There was also still the matter of strife with Margaret. She had scarcely spoken to him when he'd departed with Carolina for Washington and the depot. A noisy argument only last night had left them at odds, with Margaret choosing to sleep in the nursery with Mary and Penny.

His heart was heavy with the memory of it. Margaret felt he had hopelessly spoiled Carolina, and in truth, perhaps he had. But it was scarcely the child's fault, he thought. They had enjoyed a life of good fortune and blessings; why not allow the children to reap the benefits of such a life? Margaret plotted and planned for each of her daughters to marry well, stressing the importance for the family, as well as the child. He could understand her reasoning but not her way of bringing these things about. It relegated courtship to covert deceptions and managed circumstance, and while Joseph and Margaret's marriage had been arranged in such a fashion, he'd never understood the meaning of such until he'd had marriageable daughters. And now, to promote peace in his own marriage, he would have to appease Margaret's anger by finding a way to shift Carolina's focus from books and faraway places to domestic training and the artful selection of a husband. Perhaps his daughter would save him the trouble by falling in love of her own accord and turning her interests to more feminine pursuits.

Tossing to his right side and back again to the left, Joseph knew little peace. Philip's announcement to resign took a decided position in the background, however, as Joseph contemplated how to keep his family from pulling hopelessly apart.

Forty-Two

Unexpected Companion

"Ah, here he comes now," Philip said to Joseph and Carolina. "I told him to meet us here at seven."

Carolina looked up to find James Baldwin striding toward them as though he hadn't a care in the world. The shock must have registered on her face, because James laughed out loud.

"I suppose this must be a surprise to you both," he said as he tipped his top hat and bowed low over Carolina's gloved hand. "I had to be in Baltimore on business for my father. There was more than enough time to depart from the tedium of Uncle Samuel and join you two for a bit of fun."

Carolina was aghast. James Baldwin was the last person she'd thought to have to deal with. Why, it had been weeks since she'd even laid eyes on him, longer still since she'd had to speak with him face to face. Lowering her gaze, she frowned at the plain blue serge suit and white shirtwaist she'd chosen to wear. Mr. Thomas had warned her of the dirt and debris that accompanied all construction sites and suggested she dress quite simply. Then, too, the new summer warmth was making things a bit sticky and uncomfortable, so the outfit had seemed her best choice. Now it felt quite dowdy, and Carolina wondered why it should bother her so much.

"James, I'm delighted to have you come along with us," Joseph replied.

"I knew you all to be quite close," Philip said. "I met Mr. Baldwin some time ago, and his motivation to learn impressed me greatly. He called on me last week to say he was in town on business for his father, and naturally, I asked him to join us. It is especially fortuitous now that my health has been poor. I've asked Mr. Baldwin to tour you about the station yards and to take you on a ride west to the work camp. You'll be in good hands with young Baldwin, here." It was clear Thomas had the utmost confidence in James Baldwin.

James frowned slightly, then said rather hesitantly, "Excuse me, sir, but I didn't know this was to involve a journey by rail."

"Did I fail to mention that?" said Thomas. "No doubt since I only came up with the idea a day or so ago. You won't mind, will you?"

"Well . . ."

Why was he so hesitant? Carolina wondered. Could it be her? Had her display at the coming-out party so disgusted him? It hadn't appeared so at the time, but it was the only thing she could think of, and he *had* acted strangely that night. She was about to speak up, to somehow help him bow out gracefully, when he spoke.

"I'd be happy to," James said. "I merely have to rearrange a couple of small things, then I can be ready to go."

"Splendid!" Joseph said. "By the way, Mr. Thomas, has James bothered to tell you he's engaged to marry my oldest daughter, Virginia?"

"Why, no."

All eyes turned to James, who shrugged. "It's a rather new concept for me."

The men laughed, and Carolina thought James seemed uncomfortable with this sudden attention to his betrothal. She decided that might be the cause of his hesitancy. Just awkwardness about impressing his father-in-law-to-be.

While James spoke to one of the depot workers, Joseph joked with Philip about married life. Carolina couldn't focus on the words. She suddenly realized she would be spending the entire day with James. First in the close quarters of the private railcar Philip had lent them, and then throughout the day as they surveyed the work on the line. The thought of being out around the railroad rowdies was invigorating enough, but adding James Baldwin to the picture disturbed Carolina greatly. How would she ever manage to keep her feelings in check? She'd just have to. That was all there was to it.

Joseph was walking away with Philip, intent on discussing some last-minute matter, when Carolina looked up and noticed that James was staring at her with a strange expression on his face. If she didn't know better, she would have sworn it was regret.

"Have you been keeping up your studies?" he asked in a surprisingly gentle voice.

She nodded, realizing he was trying to put her at ease. "I just finished *The Last of the Mohicans* by James Fenimore Cooper."

"A great book. I've read it several times."

"I've read it twice myself," she admitted.

"What did you like best about it?"

"Are you two coming?" Joseph called from up ahead.

Carolina put a hand to her loose bonnet ribbons and gave them a tug. "We'd best hurry or Papa will grow impatient."

James took her elbow. It was only a polite gesture, but Carolina jumped as though he'd touched her with hot coals. "I can manage," she said and struck out ahead of him.

Rushing up beside her, James was undaunted. "Have I somehow offended you? You've hardly spoken to me since the night of your birthday party. You surely aren't still embarrassed about your outspokenness to Milford, are you?"

Carolina stopped dead. "Say nothing of it, I beg you. No one has risen up to accuse me, and I'd just as soon keep it that way. York has been kind enough to say nothing of my participation, and I'd appreciate the same courtesy from you."

"So it *is* the party," he said. "I wondered why you managed to make yourself conveniently absent whenever I was around. I assure you, Carolina, you have no reason to be embarrassed. Of course, I'll say nothing. Don't let it come between our friendship any longer."

Carolina pushed past him with an exasperated sigh. He couldn't possibly know how difficult this was for her or he'd not even broach the subject. She climbed into a passenger car that greatly resembled a stagecoach. If he wanted to believe her to be troubled over the party, then let him. At least she needn't explain her emotions and further embarrass herself.

Joseph received her with a questioning glance. "Are you all right? Is something wrong?"

"No, I'm just anxious to be off," she said, knowing it was only partially a lie. Plenty was wrong, but how could she explain it to her father?

James spoke briefly with one of the workmen, then joined them and closed the door of the railcar. He looked rather pale as he leaned out the window and called down to Philip Thomas. "We'll see you tomorrow."

Within moments the small engine strained and jerked forward in spasmodic little moves. *Clang. Clang. Clang.* The bell sounded and then a warning blast errupted from the whistle. Carolina moved next to James so she could get a better view out the window. James was gripping the handrail so tightly his knuckles were white.

"James, is everything all right?" she asked.

"Yes, of course."

"We are quite safe?"

He blinked at her, then let his lips relax into a smile. "Completely."

"You looked worried there for a moment."

"No . . . I was just thinking of another matter entirely. Now, you mustn't waste your time worrying about me. Enjoy your ride, Carolina. I know what it means to you."

And she did just that. In a few moments she had all but forgotten about James as she became caught up in the train's departure from Mt. Clare Station. But she did hear him chuckle as they left the station behind.

"That's more like it. Let's just hope you don't get a reputation for being unable to contain yourself," James teased.

Joseph laughed. "I doubt she'd mind so very much. You know her passion for these things."

"Indeed."

Carolina turned back around with a mock attempt at ire. She couldn't possibly be truly angry on a day like this. "I won't be made sport of. I simply wanted to view the Carrollton Viaduct when we pass over."

"Ah yes. The Carrollton. It's a fine bridge, but nothing compared to the Thomas," James said.

"Carolina was quite taken with the Thomas, weren't you, my dear?"

She smiled indulgently at her father. He had made this entire trip possible, and she loved him completely for his devotion to her dreams. Leaning over, she kissed his muttonchop whiskers and quickly returned her attention to the view. "I am quite taken with everything about the railroad. I can't believe we're actually going out on the line. It's so positively common, and I'm sure I've never experienced anything like it."

"You're not becoming a snob, are you, Carolina?" asked James. "I mean, in saying the railroad is common."

Carolina, momentarily forgetting her past concerns, shook her head firmly. "I only meant I've led a very sheltered life, and my mother has always sought to see me prim and proper in all manners and speech. She would have no part of a trip like this, and furthermore, would have no part of it for one of her daughters, either. I'm so looking forward to it."

"I can see that," James replied. He sat across from Joseph. Joseph chuckled and eased back against the leather upholstery. "This car is far more comfortable than the one we rode in on."

"This is Mr. Thomas's private car. He uses this to travel about. Other dignitaries have them as well. It's just a matter of how much you want to spend. I've even heard it told that many of these private cars are being expanded to include beds."

"How wonderful!" Carolina exclaimed before her father could respond. "Can you imagine it, Father? One day you could simply hitch up your private railcar and ride across the country without stopping for so much as a bed to sleep in overnight."

"You might get a bit hungry," Joseph said with a wink. "But I think you have the right idea. Maybe you could just expand the heat stove to fix meals on as well, and then you truly would be able to stay aboard."

The pitch of wheels beneath them changed, and returning her gaze to the window, Carolina gasped aloud and pulled back startled as the land fell away. Embarrassed by her actions, she had no choice but to laugh at herself and the surprised expression on James' face.

"Sorry," she said. "I do that every time. We come to those bridges, and for just a moment it seems as though we've gone right off the end of the world."

"Gives me a queer feeling right here," Joseph remarked and rubbed his stomach. "So I've stopped paying attention to the scenery and deemed myself content to simply enjoy the ride."

"There will always be bridges where there are rails. The railroad and the river must go hand in hand in order to provide water for the steam engine." Sitting opposite Carolina, James stretched his long legs out until they nearly touched her skirt. He was seemingly unaware of their closeness, however, and continued to speak. "Therein lies the concern of every railroad pioneer. In order to keep an engine running, one must have fuel and water. Fuel is being argued at every turn. Some feel that wood is by far and away the better of the choices. But wood creates terrible sparking problems, whereas coal is less a problem. However, coal doesn't seem to offer the same degree of fire, and most say it never burns fast enough. Anthracite, or stone coal as most call it, is a difficult, slow-burning fuel. A locomotive needs rapid combustion."

Carolina noted that as James discussed these things he not only relaxed, but there was also an enthusiastic glint in his eyes. He seemed quite content to speak on and on about it, as was she to listen. Perhaps it was the one true way she could avoid personal matters.

"They are making changes to the fireboxes," James continued, and Carolina eased back in her seat to enjoy his discussion. "They've experimented with the dimensions of the box and have come to realize that the larger boxes are the most successful."

"I read that coal was far more expensive than wood," Carolina offered. "Wouldn't it be more prudent, what with the abundance of forests and woodlands in this country, to resort to wood fuels alone?"

James nodded. "It will probably go that way. Coal isn't all that abundant. Pennsylvania has some good deposits, but industry questions whether coal will ever be a cost-efficient method of fuel."

"The B&O burns only coal," Joseph said, as though a thought had come suddenly to him. "What savings could they hope to attain if they were to switch to wood for their fuels?"

James shrugged. "It would be difficult to say. Wood is bulkier than coal, so you'd have to haul twice as much or stop more often. You're probably looking at, say, not quite two cords of wood to a ton of coal."

"How does that figure in dollars?" Joseph queried.

James sat thoughtfully silent for a moment. "Coal is costing between seven and ten dollars per ton. I know for a fact the B&O paid at least that much last year. Whereas wood runs maybe two dollars a cord. The pricing seems to be coming down as coal becomes more available in the area. Maryland is starting to mine its own, but not enough to make it truly cost efficient for the B&O."

"This seems to be an area worth checking into with regard to saving the company money."

"It could be," James agreed. "Trees are readily available, so they would provide an ample supply of fuel. If anthracite proves to be in short supply in this country, I've no doubt the B&O will adapt to wood."

The ride passed pleasantly in this manner for Carolina. She listened with avid interest as the discussion continued, but every now and then, her mind wandered and she allowed herself to imagine what it might be like to be in her sister's shoes, preparing to spend the rest of her life with this highly knowledgeable man. She pictured them sitting before a fire, congenially discussing the affairs of the B&O Railroad. She tried to conjure up visions of retiring with James at the end of the day while he entrusted to her some problem he was facing on the design of one of his engines. Without thinking of the consequence of this dangerous ground, Carolina took the scene even further and imagined herself nestled safely in James' arms, falling asleep to the rhythm of his breathing and the beat of his heart. She ached inside at the thought of it and turned away quickly to stare out the window, lest her two companions note something amiss.

I simply cannot be in love with my sister's fiancé, she thought and fought the tears that threatened to spill. I can't love James Baldwin.

Forty-Three

Change in Plans

The unexpected slowing of the train brought James to the window of their car. Peering out, he saw no reason for the unplanned stop, and when the locomotive was finally brought to a full stop, he jumped down from the car to investigate.

With hands shoved deep into his gray trouser pockets and his frock coat of navy blue open and flapping back from the light breeze, James knew he appeared the picture of relaxed consideration. But inside, in the depths of his soul, James Baldwin was anything but relaxed. He had made a concerted and, he thought, successful effort to hide his anxiety earlier. He never let on for an instant that this was his first journey by train since the accident. He had ridden up to Baltimore last week on horseback telling himself that he wanted the exertion and fresh air.

He had begun to relax after the train pulled out of the station. The company of Carolina and her father had helped considerably, in spite of the fact that Carolina's presence had produced other tensions within him. He had hoped that by sharing time with Carolina he would be able to put her at ease about the night of her party and his words and especially his actions. He had worried that her avoidance of him since then had been because she had felt insulted. And she had every right, considering that very evening he had become engaged to her sister. What a confused mess he had made of everything!

And if that wasn't enough, he was deeply concerned about their tutoring sessions being put to an end and what ill effects she had suffered because of it. At least she'd made no mention of her missing gloves, so she must not suspect him of being the thief. Often he'd taken them in hand and contemplated how he might return them to their mistress. But how could he ever explain why they'd come to be in his possession in the first place? So, they remained tucked away in Washington while he was here in Baltimore sharing the railroad with Carolina.

It was almost a relief to focus on the stoppage of the train—that is until he walked ahead of the still-hissing engine and immediately noted the problem on the rail up ahead.

"Snakehead!" the engineer called back, his face pale and sweat soaked. "I pert near didn't notice it."

James went forward to investigate the loose strap-iron rail. Perspiration beaded on his own forehead as he viewed the detached piece of rail. He stuffed his hands in his pockets once more, this time to hide their trembling. It wasn't a snakehead that had caused the wreck that injured him and killed Phineas. Rather, it was an iron chair, a deep-notched socket securing the rail to the sleeper, which had come loose, allowing the rail to pull out of alignment. But the similarities were too much the same for James to ignore.

He returned to the passenger car, which Joseph and Carolina were already about to exit. His voice was amazingly calm as he explained the problem to them. "Snakeheads are responsible for a great number of derailments, and if they should happen to break through the floor of a moving passenger train, they could cause severe injury and . . . even death. It's most fortunate the engineer spied it and was able to bring the locomotive to a halt before hitting it."

He was about to insist that Carolina remain on board, then thought better of it. No, better that Carolina get this taste of the line to balance her rather romanticized view of the railroad. He put his arms up to help Carolina from the car. She hesitated a moment, then obviously seeing no other recourse, allowed James' assistance. This caused James a moment of confusion.

She cannot bear to be near me, he thought and released her as soon as her boots touched the ground. Joseph followed his daughter to the ground. James watched Carolina as she drew closer to the damaged rail and studied the piece from first one view and then another. He was glad she didn't barrage him with questions. Nevertheless, Joseph had several.

"How frequently do these things occur?" Joseph asked.

"Often enough to cause a serious economic problem, not to mention the other obvious problems. A great deal of the expense in running a railroad is neither new equipment nor expanding the line. It's simple maintenance and upkeep of what we already have. This snakehead is typical of what strap iron will do if given enough time. The T-rails are much more reliable, but there's a tremendous expense in replacing the strap iron with it. The lines between Baltimore and Harper's Ferry are all strap iron. The company can't possibly afford to replace the rail and expand past Harper's Ferry at the same time."

"I suppose there's little to be gained in dragging the line westward to Cumberland if you can't get the goods shipped east of Harper's because of snakeheads."

"Exactly," James agreed, momentarily distracted from his more personal dilemma. "But the charters, stockholders' agreements, and stacks of paperwork enough to fuel this train point west and demand the expansion. We were to have reached the Ohio by now, but as you can see, that simply isn't going to happen—at least not soon enough to appease investors."

"But the matter is still one of good judgment. These sections of damaged track need to be maintained and repaired. The money spent in replacing damaged rail would surely be the most economical way to handle the matter."

"I would think so too, but Thomas and the board members' hands are tied. All they appear to see and hear is the constant harangue of government officials and private stockholders to create a return on their investment. So far, that isn't happening. In fact, there is still money due to be collected from the investors on that which they pledged in reserving subscriptions. But the financial affairs of this country are beginning to show a severe decline, and no one is much induced to part with what capital he has."

Joseph sighed. "Well, none of that helps us now, does it? What are we to do about our present predicament?" Joseph asked, nodding toward the snakehead.

"We'll have to go back," James replied.

"Can't it be repaired?" Carolina asked in a voice so hopeful James wished he could do anything to please her. Anything but what she really wanted.

"It would take too much time," he said.

The engineer came up beside them. "We've got some tools and such aboard and some crew members I was taking up to the work camp. If you're willing for a couple hours delay—"

"No!" said James sharply. "I won't risk our passengers."

"Risk—?"

"It's out of the question," said James flatly.

Walking back to their car, James tried to listen as Joseph struck up once more the conversation about railroad economics, but James' mind was far more aware of Carolina's stilted silence. As Joseph handed her up into the car, James watched her graceful movements and reserved manner. What a mature woman she sometimes appeared. Yet the slight pout on her face also resembled a petulant child. He knew she was terribly disappointed by the announcement that they would return to Baltimore, and feeling guilty, he hurried with a suggestion to ease her suffering.

"When we return, I would be very happy to tour you both around the Mt. Clare shops. There is a great deal happening there, and you would be very welcome to explore and learn about the operation." He noted the spark of interest in Carolina's eyes and continued. "There are designs in progress for new engines, and I can take you to the offices and show you drawings of those designs and maps of the various routes we are considering for the westward expansion of the line."

"That sounds good," Joseph answered for them both. "I believe Carolina would find it of great interest."

James turned to her. "I'm sorry this hasn't worked out as planned, but I promise you a most informative time."

"I suppose if that's all that can be done." Her tone was cool.

"Carolina," said Joseph with just a touch of rebuke in his voice, "we must make the most of the situation."

"Yes, Father." She paused, then added, "I'm sure I would find the shops and surveys of interest, and I'm certain I will continue to enjoy my stay in Baltimore." James knew her words were for her father's benefit, not his.

"That's the spirit!" Joseph declared. "Spoken like a true Adams."

Carolina smiled tentatively, then turned to look out the window. "How will they do it?"

"Do what, my dear?" Joseph questioned.

"How will we get back to Baltimore? Will they turn the train around?"

Joseph looked to James, who would have rather the entire matter just go away. "The engine will go in reverse. They'll simply push us back to Baltimore instead of pulling us. There's only a few cars attached, and it will be a much slower process with men both working from the engine and on the ground. No one wants to run into another snakehead without warning."

"How will they make it go backwards?" Carolina prodded, her gaze fixed firmly on James.

He shifted uncomfortably but tried to sound at ease. "There's a single-eccentric valve gear that allows for the steam to enter into the cylinder in the opposite way. The gear is reversed by moving the eccentrics along the axle so it can engage the reverse pin that is attached to a plate mounted on the axle. By doing this, steam enters the cylinder in the reverse manner from the way it had during the forward motion. Understand?"

Carolina's forehead was furrowed in concentration.

"It's all quite fascinating," she said, turning back to the window. "Maybe not near as fascinating as watching the crew repair the rail. . . ." Her words faded, leaving her attitude to become a wall between them.

Opening his mouth to make some statement that might vindicate his decision, James just as quickly decided against speaking. Easing back into his own corner, he too fell into a moody silence.

"Miss Adams, I am so very sorry that your trip west was prematurely canceled." Philip Thomas, dressed for business and looking better than he had the day before, greeted them upon their return to his home. "I would very much like to make it up to you both." He went to a mahogany rolltop desk and retrieved two tickets. "I have tickets to a concert at the First Presbyterian Church. It's to be a choral presentation and one in which I'm certain you would take pleasure."

Joseph smiled. "I'm certain Carolina would enjoy it. As for myself, I would more greatly appreciate a visit with you. There are some things that have come to mind regarding the westward line, and I would like to share them with you."

Philip nodded his consent, then turned to James. "Would it be too much of an imposition, Mr. Baldwin, to request you to attend with Miss Adams?"

James glanced at Carolina but received no indication from her as to her feelings on the matter. "I would be most happy to—if Miss Adams has no objections."

"I'm sure I shouldn't take up your time, Mr. Baldwin." Her words were forced. "You have already been too kind."

"My evening is completely free and at your disposal. What time is the concert?" he asked Thomas.

Philip handed him the tickets. "Six o'clock sharp." A rumbling sound came from outside, causing all heads to turn to the window. "You should allow yourself extra time in case the storm hasn't passed by then. It looks as though God intervened so that you would not have to be out in such harsh weather, Miss Adams."

Carolina only nodded soberly.

"I'll be back to escort you at five-thirty." James put the tickets in his vest pocket and took his leave.

Forty-Four

Uncomfortable Questions

Carolina knew it was childish to be angry at James for the cancellation of their trip. But it seemed to her he hadn't even tried to deal with the problem. The engineer had seemed quite positive about making repairs. Surely James must have known how much the trip meant to her. He could have at least attempted to do something about the snakehead. She didn't understand his insensitivity at all.

And now she was going to have to spend the evening with him. She had only accepted because she knew it would have upset her father if she had stayed at home sulking. But she dreaded the prospect of the awkward evening ahead, and she feared she would certainly vent her ire to James about the trip. But even more, she feared exposing other far more sensitive feelings. Of course, since he was engaged to Virginia, no one thought anything of permitting them to go out unchaperoned. Ironically, James *was* the chaperon!

But down deep Carolina wondered if she had so easily accepted the invitation to the concert because she longed to be with James. This one time she could pretend James was truly her escort and that his interest would be on her and not on her fairer sister. That thought almost made her forget her anger over the aborted trip.

The white muslin gown she'd chosen for its lightweight coolness was elegant yet simple. The neck was softly rounded and modest, with handmade Irish lace offering a dainty trim. The sleeves were soft and pouffed, and the skirt, not quite as full and heavy as most, was trimmed with a single ruffle of muslin along the bottom hem of the gown. A pale pink ribbon tied around the waist was the only color against the stark white. Carolina's dark hair was washed and shining to perfection. But after an hour of curling and struggling alone to pin it into a fashionable style, she wished she had heeded her mother's suggestion to take Miriam along on the trip. But Miriam answered to Margaret and would have brought back tales of all Carolina's activities, thus greatly limiting her freedom. In the end, however, she finally managed to make herself presentable. A capote-style bonnet of starched muslin completed her coiffure.

The housekeeper had just knocked on the door to announce Mr. Baldwin's arrival as Carolina took up her shawl and handbag. Nervously, she descended the stairs and wondered what the evening might bring. James met her at the bottom of the stairs, handsomely attired in a dark wine-colored tailcoat. His trousers were black and fastened *sous pieds* with the leg secured under the foot, a style that was quite popular.

"Good evening," he said, making a sweeping bow and taking her hand to his lips.

Carolina felt her face go flush. "Good evening."

"Might I say," James said quite formally, "you look radiantly lovely."

"Thank you," she murmured and uncomfortably took back her hand. "Is it still raining?"

"Not to speak of. The sky is quite overcast and very gloomy, but a parasol and closed carriage will suit us nicely. I refuse to have more plans ruined by such a small detail." His lips quirked into a hesitant smile, and she sensed how bad he felt about the trip.

"Ah, there you are. My, don't you look beautiful," Joseph said upon entering the room. "I do hope this evening proves entertaining. Philip and I will discuss business here, and I have instructed young James to accompany you to dinner after the concert. If that meets with your approval, Carolina."

James and Joseph both waited for her to assure them that it did meet with her approval, but Carolina found it difficult to speak. She realized how silly her illusions were about the evening. James was merely following her father's instructions. "I wouldn't . . . I mean," she stammered, "we shouldn't impose further upon James' free time. After all, he's already been good enough to escort me to the choral presentation."

"And I will happily escort you to dinner as well. I know of a place near my uncle's home, and the food is quite delectable."

"See there?" Joseph said, coming forward to give her a parting kiss on the cheek. "The matter is clearly settled, and you needn't have worried about interfering with James' evening. Besides, he no doubt pines for your sister, and at least you can offer him companionship."

Carolina felt her throat constrict at these words but pretended to be unaffected. She merely nodded and allowed James to lead her to the door. Once there, James accepted his top hat and umbrella from the butler and assisted Carolina with her shawl.

The skies were dreary and heavy in their low-hanging blanket of gray. The rain that had deluged the countryside earlier in the day had ceased, but the dark sky was threatening. Twilight was snuffing out what little light the day was offering, and the entire city was a system of shadows and darkened alleyways.

They made their way to the church in silence. Carolina was uncertain what could possibly be said that wouldn't bring her more pain and confusion. Her father's words, given in innocent suggestion, had wounded her deeply, and she desired nothing more than to forget them, though that was quite impossible.

As their carriage pulled up from the side of the church, Carolina could make out the cemetery. Shuddering at the haunting stones, lone sentinels standing vigil over their long-departed owners, Carolina felt her skin prickle. The haunted dreariness, however, suited her mood.

James paused at the foot of the carriage and offered his hand up to her, but Carolina hesitated to take it. Something in the dusky light moved, causing her to strain her eyes toward the shadows. She might have alighted and entered the church without ever seeing the man there, but James was at that moment hailed by a roly-poly man with a balding head and bulbous nose.

"Uncle Samuel," James said, turning to introduce Carolina as her foot touched the ground. "This is my uncle, Samuel Baldwin. Uncle, may I present Miss Carolina Adams, my fiancée's sister."

Carolina curtsied and acknowledged the man, grateful that his attention was on James and not on her.

"James, what good fortune it is to encounter you here. There is someone I'd like you to meet, if you have a moment."

"Carolina. . . ?"

"I'll be fine, James."

"Let me escort you to our seats, at least."

"I rather like the fresh air after the rain."

"All right. I'll only be a moment."

The words faded from her ears as Carolina took several steps away. Turning, she noticed the man was still there in the cemetery. He was tall, almost willowy, and clad completely in black. The latter made it difficult to distinguish him from the rapidly falling darkness. He stood beside a grave, head bowed, his face in his hands and shoulders heaving as though he was crying. Unmindful of James and his uncle, Carolina's curiosity drew her toward the churchyard.

Then she realized how unseemly her behavior was, intruding so thoughtlessly upon a man's grief. She stopped and was about to turn back when the snapping of a twig beneath her foot rang out as loudly as a church bell in that silent heavy air. The man dropped his hands and startled Carolina by lifting his face and staring accusingly toward her. She halted, so shocked at the fierce black eyes that seemed to pierce through her that she nearly forgot how deserving she was of his ire. The lighting of a nearby streetlamp offered eerie illumination in which to make out his features, but in a way it only worsened the severity of the man.

Carolina felt herself tremble. He scowled for a moment; then suddenly a part of his face seemed to soften. When he turned silently away it was almost as if he was absolving her of the violation.

Scurrying back to where James still conversed with his uncle, Carolina couldn't stop shaking. She pulled her shawl tight around her shoulders, but it did nothing to ward off the inner cold that the man's expression had left her feeling.

"Carolina, you should have told me you'd taken a chill. Come along," James said softly. He took hold of her arm, and for once she didn't jerk away to be free of his touch. At this moment she longed for the warmth of another human being more than anything else, and long after they were seated in the church, Carolina was still chilled by the memory of the stranger.

———

"Carolina, I don't believe I've held your attention at all this evening." James handed her into the carriage and waited while she quietly took her seat. "I hope the supper was to your liking."

Carolina nodded as James joined her in the carriage. The lamp had been turned up to allow them to see clearly, but James reached up to dim its glare. Carolina said nothing. Her emotions were raw, and her thoughts ran in all directions. The railroad impressed itself upon her as an indelible, and for once, unpleasant image. James was a constant reminder of those things a person might long for and desire but would forever find out of reach. And then the haunting memory of the cemetery mourner kept threading its way through her thoughts.

She looked intently at James for a moment, then lowered her eyes. A part of her wanted to speak her mind, to simply tell him how she felt and let him bear the burden instead of her. At least then he would share the load. Or would he? Perhaps he would be as insensitive to this as he had been to the canceled trip to the work camp. She twisted her hands in her lap, wishing she knew what to do. He said something and she only nodded absently in response.

"I don't believe you even heard me, Carolina."

She looked up with a quick shake of her head. "I'm sorry, no."

James' expression betrayed concern. "I'm quite worried about you. You've scarcely said two words this evening, and you took a considerable chill at the church. I'm afraid you may be ill."

"That's all you think, James?" she said harshly. "You have not a clue what is troubling me?"

"Yes, I suppose I do—"

She started to interrupt, but he held up his hand.

"You have every right to be angry over what happened today," he went on quickly. "I know I was hasty in canceling the trip. If only I could make you understand that I didn't do so lightly."

"Well, it was hard to take," she replied. Perhaps it was just as well he made no mention of her other anxieties.

"Who could know if we'd encounter more damage? I couldn't bear the thought of—" He stopped and looked away.

Carolina could scarcely fathom what could be the cause of the depth of emotion that had so suddenly come over him. She tried to be more sensitive as she spoke. "I understand your concern, James. But anyone who boards a train knows there is an element of risk. Perhaps that is even part of its allure."

He shook his head. "Carolina, you don't know . . ."

"Please, James, I want to understand."

He lifted his eyes to face her squarely. "Snakeheads cause derailments. Derailments just like the one that caused Phineas's death."

"Oh, James—"

"The last thing I want is to drag you into my personal battles."

"Battles—?"

"Carolina, I've ridden on a train only once since the accident." He blurted out the words in a rush, then turned away in apparent shame. "What a weak specimen you must think me now!"

She didn't know why what she thought should matter, but it apparently did, and she was quick to allay his fear. "James, you suffered a terrible tragedy. Anyone would have—"

"Even someone whose passion was the railroad? And the irony is that it's still my passion—at least it has become so again since you helped me face these things last Christmas."

"I helped you?"

"You didn't even realize it, really. But if it hadn't been for you, I would still be trying to convince myself I hated railroad work. Nevertheless, though my love for the work returned, I still could not step on a train without quaking."

"And yet you agreed to take me to the work camp?"

"I was in a position where I could hardly refuse without looking quite the fool."

"I would not have thought you a fool."

"No?"

She shook her head but could not speak, for his eyes searched hers with such hopefulness, such intensity. She'd never had a man look at her like that before. It made her feel weak and afraid and . . . ecstatic.

"Suddenly I feel so much better," he said breathlessly. "To voice my deepest, darkest secret and to be reassured by someone I trust that I am not as unhinged as I thought."

"I feel honored you trust me enough to confide in me."

"Yes, I do. I haven't even told this to—" He broke off, seemed to reconsider his words, then added rather lamely, "anyone."

Carolina spoke her next words without thought. "Have you told Virginia?"

"Not even her."

"Isn't that the kind of thing you'd want to tell the person to whom you are engaged?"

"I don't know. I've never been engaged before. I only know it is something I'd tell a friend, as I consider you to be, Carolina."

And Carolina knew then that *she* was the fool for thinking he would ever feel more toward her than friendship. Still, she pressed the issue as if she had lost all sensibility.

"I would hope the man I marry would also be my friend," she said.

"Oh, sweet naive Carolina!" He lifted his hand and lightly touched her chin with his trembling fingers. Then his hand dropped quickly.

She opened her mouth to protest his words, then found herself saying something entirely different. "James, how do you know Virginia is the one you should marry?" Her throat went dry, and she held her breath. What a thing to ask! How could she have such cheek? Yet she did not retract her impulsive words. Instead she only wondered what he would say. What could he say? Would he declare his undying love? No, of course not. He'd already made clear how he felt.

James was clearly taken aback. "How do I know she's the one? I suppose because when she asked, I agreed." He then gasped and put his gloved hand to his mouth. "I pray you will forget I said that."

"Why did you say that?"

James dropped his hands. He looked at her for a moment and then turned the lamp down once again, as if the lower light would hide some secret shame. "Carolina, as I said before, I look upon you as a trusted friend. I pray that trust is not misplaced."

"I assure you it isn't."

"Very well. Your sister did ask me first, although I in turn asked her to marry me. I didn't want it said that she had to pursue me in order to become engaged."

"That was most considerate of you," she replied evenly. "I suppose her reputation already leads people to conclude that she is somewhat desperate."

James nodded. "It would be unkind to force her to endure that shame. Besides, she wasn't quite herself. The party and all, you understand, don't you?"

Carolina sighed. "I understand a great many things people give me no credit for. It matters little what I understand." She knew she sounded bitter, but as James had said so eloquently, they were friends. Just friends.

They rode on without speaking for several moments. The clip-clop of the horses' hooves on the brick streets and the steady falling of rain upon the roof of the carriage lulled them into a temporary peace.

A part of Carolina wished to take back her words, while another part wanted a more personal answer. Why did Virginia meet his needs, when she did not? Why her sister, when she didn't share any of his interests? He had revealed things to her tonight he had never told Virginia, yet still it was Virginia he chose to marry. How could he look at her, Carolina, the way he sometimes did and still give his life to Virginia? She could not understand except to assume she was seriously misguided.

"You must be considering some very weighty subjects," he said after several minutes of silence. "I've only seen that look on your face during mathematics tests."

Carolina chuckled, trying to push away her growing melancholy. "I am considering calculations but not numerical ones. I suppose," she said sobering again, "I am a bit perplexed." She made the choice. She would ask him to explain why Virginia's beauty had won out over her ability to think and share in the dreams and ambitions of the railroad. She simply had to know.

"Perplexed? About what?"

"May I ask you a question?"

"Of course. You've been asking me questions for most of our relationship. Why stop now?" he teased.

"No, I'm serious," she said softly.

James sobered. "Yes, I can see that. Ask your question."

Carolina bit at her lip, then drew a deep breath. "Why are you marrying Virginia?"

It was James' turn to appear nervous and shaken. He pulled out a handkerchief and mopped his brow. Until that moment Carolina hadn't noticed him perspiring and wondered if her question had made him uncomfortable.

"You believe me unworthy of your sister? Is that it?" He replaced the cloth. "Don't you think it possible that I could love her?"

"I just want to know what it is about one woman that appeals to a man over another."

"This is rather an intimate topic for a man and woman such as ourselves to be discussing."

"James, you said it yourself. We are friends and you are my teacher. If I can't turn to you, who can I turn to?"

"I could be marrying into your family for your fortune."

"Be serious, James. Can't you give me a forthright answer? I simply wondered why you would choose my sister after all these years and with many other women available in Washington society."

James appeared to relax a bit. "My father said it was time to choose a wife. My mother provided me a list of suitable brides-to-be, and your sister's name was among those listed."

"I see."

"Your name was on that list as well," James added. "As were most of the available women in the city. Mother's welcome-home party for me was her way of throwing me together with the eligible young ladies of society. And, so as not to appear too eager, she included many of my childhood friends. Virginia's attributes simply outweighed the rest."

"What attributes?"

"This is getting rather embarrassing." He smiled weakly and loosened his collar a bit.

"Then I'll say no more."

After another brief silence, he asked, "Am I now entitled to ask a personal question of you?"

She swallowed. "Well, I . . . why, yes, of course."

"Why have you ignored me since the night of your coming-out party?"

Carolina shifted and looked out the window. Would this ride never end?

"You can't pretend I'll go away. I'll tell the driver to take the long way back if necessary, but I think I deserve an answer. After all, I've answered all your questions. You have been avoiding me for weeks."

"That isn't true."

"Oh, but it is, and you know it well." He fixed his gaze on her and refused to dismiss the matter. "Something happened between us the night of your party, and I think it is time we talked about it. I haven't much liked the feel of your cold shoulder. I thought perhaps it was your own embarrassment over the fight, but there's something more. Is it because I had to cease my tutoring?''

Carolina's breath quickened and she could hear her heart pounding in her ears. She bit her lower lip again, as if it might keep the words from being pulled out from the depths of her soul.

"Tell me, Carolina. Tell me now what it is that causes this distance between us.''

"No,'' she whispered, but it came out a whimper. "There's nothing.''

"You, my dear, are a poor liar." His words were stated flatly, without emotion. Leaning forward, he narrowed the distance between them. "Tell me.''

"You . . .'' She gasped for breath that seemed not to come.

"I what?''

His words were so low and husky. His eyes, so compelling in the dim carriage light. Carolina fought for control but knew she was losing the battle. She would tell him once and for all that she loved him.

He took her hand between his and held it fast. "What grievous sin did I commit that I could not help?''

Neither one noticed the carriage had come to a stop until the door was opened by the footman. Carolina quickly pulled back her hand.

James waved the footman away, then turned a hard serious look on Carolina. "You can't leave until you tell me what I did. Is it because I behaved inappropriately the night of your party?''

"My party. . . ?'' What was he saying? Perhaps it had not been entirely her imagination.

"That night was so confusing. I never meant to insult you. I only . . .'' His words trailed away unfinished. In his eyes appeared again that look that left Carolina both afraid and elated.

"What are you saying, James?''

His inner struggle was clearly evident in his expression as he answered. "The last thing I would ever want to do is hurt you. Yet it seems I have. But how, Carolina?''

She knew it was foolhardy and a great risk. She knew it would probably only deepen his confusion and perhaps even cause him to despise her. But her next words tumbled from her lips like a compulsion before good sense could stop them.

"You asked my sister to marry you—'' She lunged for the carriage door.

James was too quick for her and caught her wrist. "Why should that come between us?" he asked, genuinely puzzled.

Why indeed! So, it was her imagination after all. Swallowing her wounded pride in the clear evidence that James felt nothing more than friendship for her, Carolina finished her sentence with a weak smile. "It's nothing, truly." She tried to sound lighthearted. "It's just that you've put Mother into a mind to see us all married now. I'm put out with you for starting the whole thing. But don't worry, I forgive you." She then dashed for the door, leaving James in the carriage.

Hurrying into the house she blinked back the tears that streamed from her eyes, nearly blinding her way.

PART V

Summer—Fall 1836

. . . For see those smoldering embers
That lie along the ridge;
Oh, God, in pity save them;
It is the railroad bridge!
Too late to turn the lever,
Too late to stop the train,
Too late to soothe their sorrow,
Too late to soothe their pain!

—"The Chatsworth Wreck"

Forty-Five

Hampton Cabot

*O*akbridge in June was idyllic. The fluted marble pillars of the Greek revival mansion stood as support to a broad, ornate portico. The three-story mansion with its east and west wings sat as white magnolia against a valley of green. The house, over a hundred years old, had been home to several generations of Adamses. So named because of the ornately designed oak bridge that spanned a small tributary of the Potomac, Oakbridge Plantation represented southern hospitality at its finest.

It was this vision that rose up to greet Hampton Cabot. At age thirty he was pleased with the accomplishments he'd made. As a lad of eighteen he had been taken under the wing of Joseph Adams when both his parents were killed in a fire. Adams apprenticed him to his commission merchant in New York City so that he might learn the business. When the old fellow died, Cabot handily took over the post. Nevertheless, he considered himself for the most part a self-made man. His achievements had come through honest hard work and skillful trading—at least most of them. No one need ever know of the underhanded dealings that had destroyed men who were beneath his level of marketable cheating.

Cabot's bay gelding began to whinny nervously and pawed at the dirt. The spirited animal obviously did not like the idle pause. "Steady there, boy," Cabot admonished the horse. "We've a great deal of work set before us, and it is good to proceed with clear heads."

He urged the mount forward, all the while taking a mental inventory of what he saw. It had changed little since his last visit several years ago. There were vast fields of cotton stretching well behind the house and its manicured lawns. Orchards and cultivated gardens marked space southwest of the house, while to the east outbuildings of stone

289

and wood housed the necessary functions of laundering, sewing, and smithing. Slave quarters were lined in rows well behind the main house in order to keep the ninety-some servants listed on the Adams ledgers as valuable assets. It was impossible to take it all in from his vantage point, but Cabot intended to make himself very familiar with it before he journeyed north again. Ledgers were one thing, but a visual inventory of his own was something entirely different.

Reaching the broad portico steps, Hampton was greeted by a young slave who ran forward to take his reins. He relinquished these gladly and pulled his bags down from behind the saddle. The air was heavy with the scent of honeysuckle, but the sweetness failed to penetrate the focus of his thoughts. His senses were tuned into the dollar values and prestigious lifestyle of his employer's property and possessions. Brushing the dust from his traveling coat, Hampton took up the brass knocker and announced his arrival.

An aging Negro opened the door in greeting. The man stood slightly hunched but clearly at attention.

"Yassuh?" he questioned, extending a heavy silver card tray toward Cabot.

"Tell Mr. Adams that Hampton Cabot is here to see him. I am expected." He laid his card on the tray and waited in the foyer as directed while the man tottered off.

Cabot liked what he saw in the delicate crystal chandelier overhead. His eyes traveled around the room noting the marble-top entryway table and silver candlestick holders. On the walls were heavy gold-gilted frames surrounding tiresome portraits of one Adams or another. Cabot could care less about the stern-faced images staring down at him. He detested sentimentality.

Dropping his gaze to the floor, he noted the fine Italian marble. The shine was enough to see his reflection and to lend credibility to the costly price Adams must have paid to have it installed. Frowning only for a moment, Cabot tucked this new information into his brain and waited for the return of the servant.

"Come this way, Mr. Cabot, suh," Bartholomew said, returning the receiving tray to its place between the silver candlesticks.

Hampton was led to a first-floor study and directed to take a seat. He chose an antique throne chair, the only piece of furniture that looked capable of standing up under his two-hundred-pound frame. Stretching out long legs before him, Hampton was glad to be rid of his horse. He'd ridden the better part of two weeks, dealing with matters of business along the way and staying nights wherever it profited him most to do so. He'd won a fair size pot in Philadelphia, where he'd gambled for two days running, only breaking from the table to answer nature's call. Yawning now, tired of waiting for Adams, tired of playing games with other people's money, Cabot felt himself relax in the velvet-covered chair.

"Hampton?" Joseph said, questioning the man's sudden appearance at Oakbridge. "What causes you to leave New York?"

Hampton rose to his feet and studied his employer for a moment. It had been nearly two years since they'd dealt face to face with each other, and time had taken a definite toll on Adams. He was grayer, but not by much, and perhaps a bit thicker in the middle.

Extending his hand Hampton smiled. "I wrote you . . ."

Joseph thumped his head. "So much has been happening here lately, I completely forgot. But you are welcome nonetheless. Thanks to God there is always room for guests at Oakbridge."

"It won't be an imposition?"

"Never. I've told you many times you are always welcome here. But now that I am reminded of your letter, there was a rather mysterious tone to it. I hope all is well."

"There are problems afoot, Joseph," he said, never losing the catlike grin. "And since I wrote, they appear even more alarming. I thought we should plan a strategy."

"And so," Joseph told the family at dinner that evening, "Hampton felt compelled to come directly to us and offer forewarning of the waning economy. There are growing problems in the banking industry, and I'm afraid it will consume a great deal of my attention."

Margaret frowned. "We needn't discuss it at the dinner table, need we?"

Joseph wiped his mouth with his linen napkin and agreed. "I simply wanted to explain Mr. Cabot's arrival. I, for one, am grateful for his conscientious decision to come to Oakbridge." Then turning to his guest, Joseph added, "Hampton, you are welcome to stay on as long as you feel it is prudent."

"I can be spared from New York for a time," Hampton said, eyeing Virginia Adams with a smile. "I believe a short stay to discuss matters in complete detail would be advantageous to us both."

"It's settled then and we can discuss business at our leisure."

Hampton glanced around the table. "Your daughters have certainly grown up since I last saw them, and they are quite lovely." He spoke to Joseph, but all the while his eyes were on Virginia.

Georgia tried hard not to giggle, while Virginia blushed respectably, and Carolina seemed not to even notice the compliment. Joseph smiled at Margaret, whose eyes were alight with contemplation.

"Not to mention our two daughters in the nursery," said Margaret.

"And your sons. . . ?"

"Both are away from Oakbridge," answered Joseph. "Maine is studying in England, and York is under the employment of the President."

Hampton choked on his wine at this announcement. "I did not know you had an inside ear to the White House. Perhaps it will prove to your advantage once we more completely discuss the economic matters at hand."

"Perhaps. York does venture home as time permits, so you may well have a chance to speak with him directly. If not, it might avail us to journey into the city and see him privately. Until then, I hope you will make yourself at home and enjoy our hospitality."

Hampton again cast a gaze upon Virginia. "Perhaps Miss Adams would show me around the estate."

"This Miss Adams," Margaret interjected, "is engaged to be married. She has little time, what with planning her wedding, to escort anyone around the plantation. However"—Margaret turned her eyes upon Carolina, and Joseph well knew what that light in her eyes meant—"Carolina would make a most congenial companion. Carolina, you would be kind enough to show Mr. Cabot around the grounds, would you not?"

Carolina looked up startled. "I, uh . . ."

Joseph laughed. "I fear we've caught her daydreaming. Our Carolina is quite a progressive thinker and dreamer."

Hampton eyed her incisively, then smiled. "I like progressive thinking."

Carolina shifted uncomfortably and turned pleading eyes upon her father. Joseph wished he could dismiss her from this new duty, but there was no graceful way in which he could. Carolina would simply have to endure this new position and make the best of it.

"I'm sure she would love to," Joseph said, with a wink at his daughter. "Carolina can show you around in the morning."

Forty-Six

Advances

After a week of his company at Oakbridge, Carolina felt ready to run whenever the name of Hampton Cabot was mentioned. It wasn't so much his company Carolina resented, it was the condescending way in which the man treated her. He constantly asked if she needed to rest or if the light was too harsh or the temperature too warm. What does he think of the years I've spent living here without his watchful care? she wondered silently. Am I some mamma's babe to be left in the nursery for fear of overextending my delicate constitution?

She ranted inside and wished there was some way she could escape their morning horseback ride. She'd agreed to show Hampton the series of little falls upstream, only now she prayed there'd be some excuse to cancel or at least postpone their ride.

"The horses are ready," Hampton said, striding into the parlor with great abandonment. In his hand was a small brown paper package, which he tucked into his pocket without a word of explanation. "Miriam is also waiting, since your mother insisted we take an escort."

He grinned at her boldly, making Carolina wish either he, or she, could disappear from the face of the earth.

"Perhaps she feels the chemistry between us," he said.

The words were well out of line, and Carolina had little difficulty in putting him in his place. "I have studied chemistry, sir, and I recall nothing regarding human contact. Chemistry is not something I believe we have in common, Mr. Cabot."

"Please, I beg you, call me Hampton."

"I think not, *Mr.* Cabot." She rose to her feet, resigned to the task ahead.

Besides Cabot's demeaning attitude, Carolina could not quite explain what it was about him that she found objectionable. He was a handsome man with straight blond hair and pale chin whiskers. His skin was rather florid, no doubt from overexposure to the sun, and his eyes were narrow, also apparently sensitive to the light. His thin lips were given to frequent smiles that somehow never seemed to reach beyond his lips to his other features.

He was at least a foot taller than her five-foot-three frame, and she didn't care at all for the way he seemed to use his height as an assertion of superiority. It seemed inappropriate that whenever he was nearby, he would come to hover over her, as though offering her some human shelter. James was quite tall too, but he had never used his height in such a manner.

When Hampton moved toward her just now, Carolina could only pray that someone or something would distract his obvious infatuation with her.

"Please. I feel we are friends," he insisted. "We are friends, are we not?"

Carolina tried not to grimace. "We are barely acquaintances," she said stiffly. "Friendship is born over time. I feel, sir, that you are a bit too bold and presuming."

Hampton didn't appear affected in the least. "I suppose by more languorous southern standards, I am rather fast."

"That is to say the least."

"But Miss Adams . . . Carolina." He barely whispered her name. "You must know by now of my interest in you. Should I put off expressing that interest simply because etiquette says more time should pass between us? I thought to speak with your father and obtain permission, but perhaps you should be the one to break the news to him."

Carolina could only stare up at him in stunned silence. Was she misunderstanding the circumstance, or was Hampton Cabot announcing his intentions to court her? Surely it was only that and not that he'd lost his senses so much as to imagine her desirous of marriage!

"Here, sit down. You look as though you might swoon." He led her back to the settee, and Carolina did sit because the sensation of the blood rushing from her head was indeed making her dizzy.

"I know this is sudden, but look here—" He pulled the brown package from his pockets. "My intentions are quite honorable. I seek only to court you and give you time to know me better. Your father has encouraged me to stay on until such time as I feel business demands my return to New York. Until then, please give us a chance." He put the package in her hands. "This is a small token of my esteem. I was given to understand your enjoyment of books. I hope this volume of poetry meets with your approval."

Carolina still could not speak. She looked at the package in her hand, having no desire to unwrap it. But she had to do something—say something! She could not have this man pursue her when there was no hope of his feelings being reciprocated.

"I'm sorry, Mr. Cabot," she began through a tight throat. She held out the book. "I cannot accept this gift from you; neither can I accept your suggestion of courtship." There. She'd said the words and now he would give her a hurtful look, a polite bow, and leave her company forever.

It was not to be.

To Carolina's complete embarrassment, her mother entered the open door looking quite angry. "Carolina, you forget your manners."

Carolina said nothing of her mother's poor manners of eavesdropping, though the words were hovering close to utterance.

Hampton turned and gave Margaret a brief bow. "I'm afraid it is my fault, Mrs. Adams. The boldness of my ardor has offended your daughter. I suggested we speak to Mr. Adams regarding the possibility of our courtship."

Margaret smiled. "I assure you, Mr. Cabot, my husband and I would find it quite acceptable for you to pay court to our daughter. Carolina is an innocent young woman who is new to this realm of womanhood. It is merely a case of nerves that gives her cause to reject your suggestion. However, I will answer not only for my husband and myself, but for her as well."

Carolina turned an appalled look upon her mother, yet she well knew there would be no questioning the edict her mother was giving—not in Hampton's presence at any rate.

"Carolina will be happy to receive you as a caller," Margaret added, as if to punctuate her last pronouncement.

Hampton smiled generously at Margaret Adams, then turned to offer the same to Carolina. He bowed low over her still-extended hand and, ignoring the clutched book, turned it and placed a warm kiss upon her hand.

It was the first time a man had touched his lips to her skin, and Carolina nearly bolted from the settee to run from the room. Had Hampton lingered over her, or maintained his touch by holding her hand further, she would have done just that. Instead, he dismissed himself with a self-satisfied look of accomplishment and left mother and daughter to face each other.

"Mother, how could you?" Carolina demanded the moment they were alone. She was grateful Hampton had thoughtfully closed the door.

"I do this because you are too inexperienced to see the value for yourself. Hampton Cabot comes from a fine family, and while he was orphaned at eighteen and left nearly destitute after paying his father's expenses and such, he has amassed a small fortune of his own by working hard for your father. The Cabots were dear, dear friends, and I believe you could do far worse. Certainly they are acceptable to genteel society, and—"

"Stop!" Carolina sat back in complete exasperation. "I have no desire to court anyone."

"You are sixteen years old. I will not allow another daughter of mine to be overly choosy in her selection of a mate. You children these days think that the moon and the stars must shine between you and your choice of a spouse. It is far more important, I tell you, to make a financially secure choice and forget about this silly notion of love."

"So you will pack me off to the highest bidder as though I were one of the slaves?"

The sound of a slap against her cheek echoed in the room. Margaret stared at Carolina, stunned by her own actions. "I've never been so spoken to by a child of mine," she said in a shaky voice.

Carolina bit back another angry retort and jumped to her feet. "I'm not without feeling, though you might wish it so. A heart beats here," she said, slapping the book against her breast. "A mind, quite useful and capable, dwells here." She touched her head. "Would you have me ignore their bidding?"

"What of God's bidding?" Margaret questioned gravely. "What of His direction to be a keeper of the home? The Bible clearly instructs young women to be sober, to love their husbands, to love their children, to be discreet, chaste, keepers at home, obedient to their own husbands, that the word of God be not blasphemed."

Carolina wasn't surprised her mother had that verse memorized. "Father said that verse was directed to wives, of which I am not one. Nor do I desire to become one anytime soon."

"Perhaps your father will be able to talk sense to you. You obviously do not care about my heart on the matter. I've tried to raise you up properly. I've tried to be a good mother and offer sound counsel." She sat down wearily on the settee deserted by Carolina. "I do not seek to make you unhappy. It is my love for you that drives me to secure for you a good home. My worst nightmare is to imagine my children turned out on the streets without a penny to their name. Should something happen to your father or this place, where would any of us be?"

Carolina wanted to feel sorry for her mother, and in fact, a part of her sympathized with what the woman obviously saw as her parental duty. But this was her life they were talking about, and marriage to Hampton Cabot did not strike an appealing chord in any measure.

"I'm sorry for my outburst." Carolina wanted to say more but didn't know what would possibly offer comfort except her approval of the courtship, which she could never give.

"Simply give the man a try," Margaret said in a more moderate tone. "I don't ask you to marry a man you find abhorrent. Simply court him and consider his character. Your father thinks quite highly of him, and he doesn't offer such praise without it being fully merited."

Before she could answer, a knock on the door brought in Bartholomew. "The post, Miz Adams." He handed up several letters, newspapers, and periodicals.

"Thank you," Margaret said, dismissing the man. A quick examination revealed an item for Carolina. "This, I believe, is addressed to you. How very strange."

It was a new issue of the *American Railroad Journal*. For a moment Carolina wondered where it could have come from, and then she remembered that night in the garden and James Baldwin's announcement of this birthday gift. Reaching out to take the journal, Carolina realized she still held Hampton's unopened package in her hand.

An odd sensation of mingled regret and confused emotion coursed through her as she considered James' gift from the past and Hampton's promise for the future. The latter was of little or no interest to her, and the other *should* be of no interest but was. And the truth was hard to ignore, especially in light of the weekly reminder that would now come her way via the post.

The picture that graced the top of the journal momentarily distracted her mind from the two men and from the questioning gaze of her mother. It was a locomotive engine, sporting an engineer and full head of steam, pulling a car of wool and two more of passengers. Carolina was mesmerized for a moment. She could almost hear the whistle blow in that sad pining way.

Clutching the book and journal to her breast, she lifted tear-filled eyes to her mother. "I need to lie down," she said and walked from the room without further explanation.

Forty-Seven

Talk With a Friend

Julia Cooper had married William Cooper only the summer before. She and Carolina had grown up together, ridden together, were schooled together, and socialized as young women who'd not yet been presented into society. She was the closest and dearest friend Carolina had. Marriage had changed all of that. Now a very proper matron of society, albeit a very young matron, Julia was the type of daughter and wife that Carolina could not bring herself to be.

Carolina watched her friend with new eyes and yearned to express to Julia her deepest heartfelt secrets, yet something in her friend's reserved demeanor kept Carolina silent.

"They say Mother outdid herself in France," Julia commented, lifting a dainty china cup to her perfectly pouty lips. "There were over three hundred guests for Grandmere's birthday party, and the American ambassador was there as well. I wish Will and I could have joined in, but he said we needed to be practical. We were, after all, in Europe last year for our honeymoon."

"It sounds absolutely wonderful," Carolina remarked a bit more wistfully than she'd intended.

Julia smiled. "Don't worry, you'll find a husband and enjoy a delightful honeymoon of your own."

Carolina realized immediately that Julia presumed her desire was for the honeymoon rather than the travel. "Mother wishes I would marry immediately."

"Is there a prospect for marriage you've not shared with me?"

Carolina looked around the room nervously. "Let's walk in the garden, and I'll tell you all about it."

Julia nodded and put down her cup.

A light breeze blew, easing the summer heat. The Adams' gardens were well known for their beauty and variety of vegetation, and it was here that the two young women continued their conversation beneath the shade of parasols.

Julia Cooper, nearly the same height as Carolina, was by far the more petite of the two women. Her waist was barely sixteen inches when corseted, and her delicate bone structure led one to conclude that she was a fragile delicacy to be gently cared for. But to Carolina she was simply Julia. Julia, who had climbed over the wooden fence behind Bickerman's Mill in order to rescue a stray dog from certain death. Julia, who had agreed to and beaten out Carolina's brother Maine in a secret horseback race after school one day. Thinking of those carefree days of childhood, Carolina wondered if perhaps Julia would, after all, understand her dilemmas.

"My father's commission merchant Hampton Cabot has been staying on with us. He has taken an interest in me and has received my parents' permission to court me."

"How exciting!" Julia exclaimed. "Why didn't you say so sooner? Is he handsome and well-bred?"

"I suppose so," Carolina replied with a frown. Somehow this wasn't the direction she'd hoped to take.

"Tell me all about him," Julia insisted.

Carolina stopped against a backdrop of flowering wisteria. "I wouldn't know where to start. He's very tall, very big, and very bold. I don't care for him or his attitude. He pampers and coddles me and I detest it."

"Tsk, tsk. You could do much worse. Does your father think highly of him as a suitor and prospective son-in-law?"

"I suppose he must. My mother certainly does. Mr. Cabot was the son of good friends. When they died, my father took him under his care, and I suppose the rest is a matter of history. My father has benefited with Mr. Cabot as his commissioner. New York City is no place for amateurs, so I imagine Mr. Cabot to be very good at what he does. He wears fine clothes and seems to have an understanding and taste for the better things of life; therefore, I surmise he has done well for himself."

Julia appeared to consider this information behind knitted brows. "So what is it that you detest about him besides the fact that he treats you as a proper southern gentleman should?"

Carolina emitted a heavy sigh. "Julia, you seem so changed by married life. And perhaps that's fine for you, but the prospect scares me to death. I simply have no desire to rush into the institution."

Julia laughed and twirled her parasol. "Married life has its benefits, and don't be so naive as to suggest you don't know full well what I mean."

"Julia!" Carolina exclaimed. "You shouldn't talk of such things."

"Well, for all those old frumpy matrons who insist that marital duties are sheer drudgery and torture, I am here as proof that it is otherwise." Carolina's mouth dropped open, but before she could speak Julia continued. "Carolina, dear, you know I didn't marry Will for love. But I do love him now. I've grown to love him, just as Mother and everyone else said I would. There are far worse things than falling in love with a man and sharing his bed."

"Julia, you positively shock me!"

"Why? We used to suppose about such things and share our thoughts amidst childish giggles. Our imagination was nothing compared to the truth. I am simply being honest. And to tell the truth, it is you, Carolina, who appears to be changed."

Carolina took a hard look at her friend. "I suppose you are right. But I simply can't help it if I want things that are unusual for a young woman. I didn't set out to be . . . different." She sighed. "I know there is nothing I cannot talk to you about, but I feel so isolated. You are married and your entire world is now that of Mrs. William Cooper."

"Don't let me play you false," Julia said with a bit of a smirk, "there is still plenty of the old Julia to wreak havoc upon poor Will Cooper and his very proper world."

Carolina smiled. "I'm glad to hear it. I suppose one of my worst fears is that I'll marry a man and be forever remolded into whatever it is he expects me to be. There's so much I'm not ready to relinquish to marriage or a man. Then, too, perhaps I've not met the right man."

"Ah, but this Mr. Cabot just might be the right man, and you aren't giving him a chance. Has he given you any real reason to spurn his interest?"

"I suppose he hasn't. Although he is very bold and forward."

"There was a time when the Carolina Adams I knew would have cherished and respected that in a man. Wasn't it you who said you detested the games played in courtship?"

"Maybe it's because I don't know the way to play them," Carolina admitted.

The sound of feminine laughter caught their attention, and Julia put a finger quickly to her lips to silence Carolina. Then, just like two naughty children, they went in search of the laughter.

Carolina knew it was Virginia's laugh. She knew, too, that James was her companion that day. She knew these things because she'd gone out of her way to avoid them both. They were supposed to be out riding, and Carolina hadn't feared the possibility of running into them while entertaining Julia because they weren't expected back for some time. Yet here they were, laughing and teasing each other with such an air of genuine affection that Carolina wanted to bolt and run from the pain of it.

"James, you do make me blush," Virginia was saying in a sickly sweet drawl.

Carolina and Julia observed the couple unseen from behind a latticed archway. Miriam stood near, a silent chaperone, as Virginia hung on James' arm and peered up at him with all the adoration of a woman in love—either that or a woman who was about to drown and hoped the man would throw her a lifeline, Carolina thought sarcastically.

"Well, it wouldn't be right of me not to praise your loveliness," James said smoothly. "And this garden does pale in comparison to your beauty." James leaned down and plucked a rose to offer Virginia.

"My favorite," Virginia whispered, then touched the petals to her lips.

The couple walked on toward the house, leaving Carolina and Julia to stare after them. The display sickened Carolina. Julia had an entirely different take on the scene.

"See," Julia said in a hushed voice, "the game is not so difficult to play."

"I won't act like a lovesick cow when I'm only after a man's ring on my finger to avoid being an old maid!"

"Carolina Adams, you sound as though you are jealous."

"I am not!" Carolina's voice was raised in harsh denial. "What would I have to be jealous of? My sister believes her life's calling is to sit at home sewing pillowcases and producing miniatures of herself. I certainly have no intention of living that kind of life."

"Nor do I," Julia agreed. "Carolina, marriage is different for each person."

"How so?"

"Well . . ." Julia rubbed her chin in thought. "Suppose you married a man like your father? I'll wager he'd be happy to indulge your interest in the railroad, for instance."

"Maybe so," Carolina conceded. "If I found the right man . . ."

"But, Carolina, learn a lesson from your sister. She was far too particular in the type of man she desired for a husband. Many fine suitors sought her hand, as we both well know. My Will even ran after her for a time, but his patience wore thin. Virginia is a lovely woman, but because she's fickle and difficult to please, she risked never finding a suitable husband. It was pure luck she found a man like James still avail-

able. You may not be so lucky if you are too fickle in selecting a mate."
Julia reached out a hand to touch Carolina's arm affectionately. "Be
honest with yourself, Carolina. Few women can survive in this life
without being the wife of someone. The best thing to do is select the
one you think will benefit you the most—one who appeals to you as a
lifelong mate—and then make a decent life for yourself."

For once, Carolina heard a sensibility in the words her friend spoke.
Perhaps Julia was right. Perhaps it wasn't her place to avoid the inevitable but rather to manipulate it properly into what would be most
comfortable for her.

"I'll give it some thought, Julia."

"That's the spirit! I knew you'd come around. This Hampton Cabot
may just well be your perfect match. Give it a chance and test the waters."

"I said I'd give it some thought," Carolina replied. "Just don't expect miracles where my heart is concerned." Her mind was still on
James and the scene she'd witnessed with Virginia. He obviously loved
her sister, and for that Carolina was truly happy. Virginia might be a
bit obnoxious, but she was her flesh and blood, and Carolina desired
only the best for her. It wasn't Virginia's fault that Carolina had fallen
in love with James, and it certainly wasn't a love that was reciprocated.
No, better to accept things as they were and move ahead. Perhaps if
Hampton Cabot truly did admire progressive thinking in women, he
wouldn't mind so very much her desires to further her education. Perhaps he would even encourage her participation in the railroad and
help her to achieve her dreams.

There was a great deal to think about, and Carolina wasn't yet ready
to give up her freedom to anything or anyone. If she were like her father she would spend hours in prayer and meditation upon the Bible.
He seemed to find such comfort there, and Carolina truly wished she
could say the same for herself.

Walking back with Julia, nodding at the appropriate time to the
chattered small talk, Carolina began to wonder what it was that mo-
tivated her father to find comfort in Scripture and prayer. When I pray,
she thought, I'm never quite certain God hears me. I'm only a girl, after
all, and no one on earth believes me capable of saying anything worth
listening to, so why then should the King of the Universe?

Forty-Eight

Conversation on the Porch

The humid heat of July came upon the land with a vengeance, driving every living soul in search of cooler surroundings. Even Hampton Cabot escaped to the North, as did many families. Others went abroad as Leland and Edith Baldwin did, and only a few remained behind.

Carolina's family often went north to the New Jersey seaside home of Margaret's elderly cousin. Even when the management of Oakbridge and the duties of government kept Joseph near home, Margaret usually departed just with the children. This summer, however, they were all forced to struggle through the stifling muggy summer because of the demands of planning James and Virginia's wedding.

On the afternoon of July third, with anticipation running high and spirits lifted in preparation for the celebration of the Fourth, Carolina joined her father on the veranda. Joseph Adams was stretched out in his chair with his feet on a small ottoman and a straw hat pulled over his face. Carolina smiled at this casual picture of her father. It wasn't often she was able to catch him loafing. Fanning herself to stir even a slight breeze, Carolina accepted the offer of lemonade from one of the house slaves and took a seat opposite her father.

"Well, well," Joseph said, pulling down the hat and sitting up straight in the wicker chair. He straightened his waistcoat and suspiciously eyed his outer coat, which had been discarded in the chair to his right.

"Oh, forget it, Father," Carolina said, knowing that he was considering whether or not to put the coat on. "I'm not Mother and I won't scold you for sitting here in your shirtsleeves."

Joseph smiled. "I only did it because your mother is so preoccupied with Virginia and her wedding gown, she has scarcely taken notice of me."

Carolina nodded with only the slightest hint of a frown. "Yes, they will have to work hard to have everything ready by September." The twenty-eighth had already been announced to be the date of the wedding, and Carolina had endured two uncomfortable fittings for her bridesmaid gown. Putting aside her conflicting thoughts, which was nearly impossible, Carolina worked the fan back and forth.

"Your mother will no doubt have it all under control. I've yet to see her set her mind to a thing and not work it together."

"To be certain," Carolina replied. Movement on the horizon caught her attention. "Look, Father, riders."

Joseph stood for a better look and Carolina joined him. Two riders approached the oak bridge at a slow easy pace that denoted either the age of the travelers or their concern for their mounts in such weather. As they neared the house, Carolina and Joseph gasped in unison to find themselves about to entertain none other than Andrew Jackson himself. York rode at the aging President's side, clearly concerned for the health of his companion.

This time no protest was made when Joseph quickly reached for his coat. Carolina set down her drink and fan and helped her father adjust his collar. Grabbing up the straw hat, Joseph went out to greet his guests.

Carolina motioned the slave who lingered at the door to the house. "Quick, Missy, run and bring refreshments for our guests. That is the President of the United States with Mr. York." The girl's eyes widened in amazement before she hurried off to do as she was told.

"Mr. President," Joseph said, assisting Jackson from the horse. It was well known that Jackson's health had failed him, and just as well known that the demise had been helped along by multiple bloodlettings, continual battles with Congress, the banking situation, and the issue of Texas.

"Joseph," Jackson said, taking the offered hand and shaking it firmly.

"Come up out of the sun," Joseph said, leading the way. "York, good to see you, son. Is all well with you?"

"Very much so, Father." He tossed his reins to the waiting servant.

Carolina waited on the veranda steps, taking in the scene with some awe. She held her breath in anticipation of the introduction to come. This man, this very powerful man, was the overseer of an entire nation. By his authority treaties were made and broken. Under his direction the future of America could either benefit or be dashed upon the rocks of destruction. And here he was paying a call on her own father—and she supposed on herself as well!

"Mr. President, may I present my daughter, Carolina Adams," Joseph said as they approached the steps. Carolina curtseyed deeply.

Jackson slowly and arduously mounted the steps and made a gallant bow before her. Taking up her hand, he squeezed it lightly and smiled. "I'm very pleased to make your acquaintance, Miss Adams, and if you don't mind an old codger like me saying so, you are a very beautiful young woman." He didn't wait for her to reply but turned instead to York. "She reminds me of my Rachel."

York nodded. "Yes, indeed."

"Thank you," Carolina managed, feeling her face grow flushed. She had seen only one portrait of Rachel Jackson, and it had been painted when she was well into her years, but even Carolina had heard the stories behind the torrid love affair of the President and the unrivaled beauty of his once-divorced wife.

They took their seats, with Jackson sitting between Carolina and Joseph. There was no point made to dismiss Carolina, and so she eagerly took her place as hostess and sent Bartholomew to notify her mother of their visitor. She prayed her mother would linger over Virginia's gown, even though there was little chance of that, given the importance of the visitor. Carolina longed to listen to the men discuss the politics of the day and contemplate their views on the future.

Accepting a drink, Jackson raised it to Joseph. "To your health and well-being."

"And to yours," Joseph and York said in unison.

Carolina said nothing but tilted her glass slightly in acknowledgment and drank. It was just as well no one noticed the gesture. It would be pushing propriety to make too much of a spectacle of herself, and she didn't want to do anything that might bring about her father's disapproval and her dismissal.

"Whatever brings you all the way out here in this heat?" Joseph asked.

Jackson chuckled. "The stifling atmosphere in Washington has little to do with the weather. And in my mind it is far worse. What pleasure it is to breathe fresh air for a change and to feel the power of a good horse under my tired old bones. Thank God I only have a few months of my reign—oops, I mean, term—left."

Everyone joined with Jackson in a laugh over the intentional *faux pas*. Then Jackson continued, "I refuse to waste away to nothing in the capital. Many may figure, or hope, the old man is headed for pine—" This reference to his own demise caused the President to laugh even harder. "But I won't give Henry Clay the satisfaction of dying just yet. That is, not unless I can take him with me."

Joseph smiled. "No doubt Nicholas Biddle and John Calhoun would join Clay in mourning your passing."

"Certainly!" Jackson exclaimed and added, "They'd all join hands and weep over the dust on my grave for fear of its rising."

The morbidity of the conversation gave Carolina a chill, even in the midst of the breezeless afternoon heat. She thought of the man in the Baltimore cemetery and of the finality of death. Something in her expression must have noted her discomfort because the President turned to her with an apologetic expression.

"Forgive me for being rude, dear child. My enemies would say my mouth gets the better of me at times. And my friends would have to agree."

"That's quite all right." She smiled and immediately felt at ease.

"Ah, you do so remind me of my Rachel," he said in a faraway tone, as though forgetting he was not alone. "She had a most gracious smile, sweet and gentle, just like yours. No doubt the young men are standing in line to lay claim to your hand."

"I'm afraid you are mistaken, Mr. President," she answered with a lighthearted drawl. "My sister Virginia is the beauty of the family. It is she they stand in line for."

"Fools!" Jackson declared and immediately won Carolina's devoted friendship. He turned to Joseph but winked back at Carolina. "They'll come to their senses soon enough, and then I wouldn't want to be your father for all the bickering and feuding that'll take place over you."

"Carolina has always been more given to books and learning," Joseph said. His admiration shone in his eyes, and Carolina blushed again. "And don't let her fool you. She's just as pretty as any of her sisters."

"She's the one I told you used to sneak into Father's study and read the cabinet papers," York added.

Jackson's brow raised as if trying to decide whether he was being made the better part of a joke.

York continued, "Carolina loves the intrigue of business and government. Should she have been born a man instead of a woman, she'd no doubt give Henry Clay a run for his money."

"Probably would have given me one as well," Jackson replied, slapping his knee and guffawing with such energy that it startled Carolina. "Now, I know you're just like my Rachel. She was a quiet, considerate soul, God rest her, but she had a fire and a wit that could match mine any day. I admire that greatly in a woman."

Bartholomew quietly returned and after refreshing the drinks for everyone said, "Master Joseph, suh, Miz Margaret is napping. Do you wants me to wake her?"

The President answered, "Don't do so on my account. I shan't be able to stay long. I must attend a reception at the White House tonight."

"Leave her be, Bartholomew," said Joseph, then turned to the President. "She is quite exhausting herself with planning our daughter Virginia's wedding."

Carolina couldn't have been more pleased. In this instance she happily took on the role of hostess. She absolutely relished each moment as the President broke into a conversation regarding one subject and then another, his store of amusing anecdotes never seeming to run dry.

"Oh, do tell Carolina of the time you were in Boston with the Vice-President," Joseph suddenly requested. The story was well known and one of Jackson's most favorite to relate.

"We were in Boston by express invitation of the legislature," Jackson began. The old familiar sparkle was in his eye, and his expression was one of pure joy at the memory. "We were to be part of a military review scheduled to take place on the Common. I had been given a fine horse to ride—a real pleasure was that one. But several of my esteemed cabinet members, and of course Mr. Van Buren, were not quite as at ease with their mounts as was I. When we appeared in front of the troops, an artillery salvo was sounded. And as they will do," he chuckled, already amused by the memory, "the horses reared and became quite agitated. Having little difficulty with my own horse, I shouted to my attendant as to the condition of Mr. Van Buren. 'Where is the Vice President?' I asked, and the man lost little time in saying, 'About as nearly on the fence as a gentleman of his positive political convictions can get.' "

Joseph was suppressing a laugh because it was well known that Van Buren chose neither one side nor the other unless pushed to an absolute decision.

"And there was poor Vannie. His steed had brought up, tail first, against the fence and refused to move. I laughed so hard at the sight and exclaimed, 'And you've matched him with a horse even more non-committal than his rider.' "

Carolina smiled, trying to hold to her ladylike composure, but with her father and York and Mr. Jackson all given to fits of amusement over the picturesque story, she too gave in and laughed.

After another round of drinks, the conversation sobered and Joseph asked, "How is it with you and Congress these days?"

"I encouraged Congress to heed Senator Benton's proposed resolution that public land sales be transacted only with gold and silver as payment," Jackson told Joseph, "but the greed of land speculation is too powerful an influence."

"But the westward migration is something you yourself have encouraged," Joseph responded. Carolina was amazed that her father felt so free to speak his mind to the President.

"True enough and I continue to encourage it. As I told Congress, it cannot be doubted that the speedy settlement of these lands constitutes the true interest of the Republic. The very wealth and strength of a country are its population, and the best part of that population are the cultivators of the soil."

"I read that speech," Carolina chimed in without thinking. When all three men turned to stare at her, she quickly lowered her gaze in embarrassment.

"And did you think me accurate in the saying?" Jackson asked her seriously.

Carolina raised a questioning glance at her father.

"By all means answer the man, child," Joseph said with a smile.

"I found it quite valid," she replied. "I suppose that is why I am so supportive of the railroad."

"Ah yes," Jackson said, nodding his head. "The railroad is another issue that creates a great deal of strife these days. All articles of internal improvement create conflict for my office."

"Why is that?" she asked, genuinely interested.

Jackson shrugged. "It goes back to my adversary, Mr. Clay, as well as others. There are those who believe the federal government should provide the means for each and every operation of improvement, no matter the size, sensibility, or location. I, on the other hand, believe that internal improvements must be weighed on the basis of the effect they will have for the entire nation and not just an isolated part of it."

"But a railroad extending west would benefit a great many people. Add to that one extension many additional extensions, and eventually it will benefit the entire nation," Carolina stated confidently.

"Perhaps, but there is always the possibility that something will happen to meet one person's interest over that of another. Take, for instance, the problems with the Baltimore and Ohio Railroad. Your brother advises me that they must survey the land west of Harper's Ferry and decide the most economical route to develop. The state of Virginia believes that route should make its course through her beloved lands, with provisions that it not interfere with rail lines she desires to develop under her own direction in the future. However, she doesn't wish to lose the line and revenue in taxes and such that the B&O will pay for crossing her grounds. Pennsylvania would like to see the line move north and include a connecting route to Pittsburgh. Both situations would advance the line and make it possible to bring the railroad that much further west. The further west the railroad goes, the better it is for the advancement of westward expansion and settlements. Still, how can I favor one state over another by providing federal monies?"

"I believe I see the conflict," Carolina remarked thoughtfully.

"Then, too, Carolina," York chimed in, "how can you justify the B&O's line over that of another proposed line. Why, even your proposed line with Father and the Baldwins would have to be considered as a possible recipient of government funds."

"But our line wouldn't be designed to benefit all of the nation," objected Carolina. "Our line is only to benefit a few counties and possibly eventually expand to include several major cities and towns."

"Ah yes," York agreed, "but your line plans a direct route into the capital. That could be argued to be of benefit to the entire nation. Added to this, what about canals or federal roadways? There are hundreds of proposals for both, in addition to requests for railroad assistance."

"York is right," Jackson said. "I'm afraid these are exactly the kind of arguments I've been listening to for the last five years or more. There are many projects, some sound and justifiable, others pompous and without merit. Each state and local government sends their representatives to pursue my blessing and support. If I were to act as benefactor to all, the government would soon be in deep debt."

"But I read in the *Niles Register* that the government is financially in surplus," Carolina argued. "There has just been voted a Distribution Bill that you recently signed."

"With misgivings," Jackson replied, not at all offended by her outspokenness. "The best we can hope for is that by distributing the federal surplus to the states, we can force the deposit banks—those formerly keeping the surplus—to put an end to their business of making unsound loans for overvalued collateral. Having to produce large sums of federal deposits to turn over to the states will make those banks accountable and slow down their enthusiasm for making bad deals.

"The states must see their responsibility, even in this, Miss Adams." Jackson drew a deep breath and sighed, "But I don't expect them to. Not with the likes of Henry Clay spouting off his mouth at every turn. Rigging deals between northern industries and western settlers."

"Isn't that to the benefit of the entire nation?" Carolina questioned. She'd long desired to better understand Henry Clay's American System.

"Not unless you remove the South from the nation, which would suit John Calhoun just fine. I've fought South Carolina once already over the issue of seceding and I have no desire to do it again. Mr. Clay has no provision for the South and its improvement. He foresees great expansion west, but this leaves little attention to the South, of which you are considered a part by virtue of your residence here in the great state of Virginia."

"Mr. President," York interrupted, "I must advise you of the time." Only then did Carolina realize over an hour had passed.

Jackson nodded and it appeared to Carolina that a sadness crossed his expression. "Alas, my escape must be retraced?"

"I beg your pardon?" said Joseph.

"You asked me earlier what brought me out," Jackson said with a smile. "I had thought to escape the torments of Washington and the strife of political controversies." He got to his feet, bowing again to Carolina. "However, I find they follow me just like an old hound to its master. Miss Adams, you are like a cool spring breeze. Refreshing! I truly enjoyed our conversation. I hope you will come see me before I journey home to the Hermitage."

"I would very much like that."

She watched in silence as her father and York accompanied Jackson back to the horses. She heard her father offer a carriage for the President and Jackson's adamant refusal. She smiled at the President's tenacity and considered herself quite lucky to have shared his company on that sweltering day.

Forty-Nine

Leland's Schemes

*S*amuel, these are very convincing counterfeits," Leland praised his brother while studying the bank draft in his hand. He put one down and picked up another, noting each one to be a masterpiece. Just back from Europe and ready to get down to business, Leland had insisted that Samuel come to Washington for a very secretive meeting.

The pudgy, balding Samuel Baldwin grunted acknowledgment and struggled to pull down a waistcoat that was several sizes too small. Samuel, the younger of the brothers, looked several years older, probably due to his penchant for whiskey and tavern crawling every night. "I paid for the best and that's what we got. You'll find the same on the stock certificates."

Leland put down the bank note and reached inside the leather satchel on his desk. He pulled out a stack of quality paper and smiled. "Just to touch these would make one confident of their validity."

"Are you sure this thing will work? I understand the flooding of the market with counterfeit bank drafts, but why this sudden interest in the railroad?"

Leland sat down and motioned for his brother to do the same. "I've only recently come to understand the potential surrounding the railroad. While abroad I had a great deal of time to think this thing through. The economic state of this country can be likened to one of those newfangled circuses. You know, several things going on all at once.

"As you well know, Samuel, there's a huge excess in the federal reserve due to land sales. Another area, I might add, where we can benefit ourselves with these counterfeit notes. Speculation is making a fortune for many already wealthy investors. Joseph Adams has managed to

311

turn several very nice profits in land up north and to the west. I intend for us to be a part of that as well."

Samuel took out a handkerchief and wiped his face. "I only hope this bolstering can be done in time. That Distribution Bill just passed by Congress is a comedy of errors. It's going to pull federal monies from regular deposit banks and put them into the hands of the individual states. This will, I fear, squeeze the very life out of this bank unless we can somehow bolster the reserves of this institution before the first distribution payment in January comes due."

"I believe we are in time," Leland said, his eyes darting from Samuel to the closed office door, as though at any moment someone might intrude and learn his darkest secrets. "If I can manage to interest investors in railroad stock and get them to put up capital in exchange for these certificates, then I will have enough money to cover what will be taken from this bank. If not, I'll be hard-pressed to explain the insolvency."

"You are a convincing man, Leland, but I think even you might be strained to get investors without some formidable indication of its validity."

"How difficult would it be to get investors for a venture backed by Joseph Adams?"

"People would line up. He's both respected and trusted."

"He intends to start the Potomac and Great Falls Railroad and has invited me to become his partner."

"And he is privy to your idea of a 'paper railroad'?"

"Heavens no! He'd die of apoplexy if he knew. But there is no way he could ever know. Adams is a dreamer and is more interested in the *building* of the railroad than in its operation. I am certain he will readily agree for me, as the business mind of the partnership, to handle all the financial matters regarding the railroad."

"You may be able to get around Adams, but what happens when your investors have little or no return on their investment?"

"I offer to buy them out, of course. I can't very well have a scandal on my hands."

"What if Adams really starts to build?"

"I'm sure he will. But it is a lengthy and tedious process of obtaining charters and permissions from the state to build. Then, too, will be the chronic blunders related to shipping of supplies. We can blame the British for a great deal—there are enough alive today who well remember the burning of Washington at their hands. It should carry us far to place the responsibility of lost shipments and delays in receiving supplies on the shoulders of a country so many still despise. Without iron rail, we cannot lay track. And for those who very well might desire to see some physical progress, we will actually have requests for charters drawn up and perhaps an inexpensive survey, or better yet, a forgery of one already drawn up for another railroad. Can you check into that in Baltimore? I heard James say that they are working to decide what route will be surveyed west of Harper's Ferry. Now with the resignation of Philip Thomas in place and the board searching for another president, there will be mass chaos, and it might be easy to obtain records if the right man is put in charge of the mission. As I recall, the B&O once considered moving west of Washington. This might be exactly the survey we'd need. Do you know someone who might help us?"

Samuel smiled, making the jowls of his bloated face wobble. "I know just the man."

"Good, good. The key to this will be to solicit investors well known for their indifference to details. I can think already of a dozen or more Washington residents who will jump at the chance to be a part of the great railroad movement, but who will never look further than the stock certificates in their hands. If I can sell them on the possibilities of this great rail line, I could well see a million dollars pledged by fall."

"Yes, but how much of that money will be taken from you in January?"

"I'm not certain, but it doesn't matter. One way or another, we will still be in a good position to have whatever we want. Haven't we managed to purchase your new home with the counterfeit bank notes? It's only an added bonus that the banks on which those notes have been drawn have failed or will fail in time." Leland's smug expression made him more closely resemble his brother.

"So, did you do anything besides plot and plan while in Europe?" Samuel asked with a laugh.

"I spent a great deal of money," Leland retorted. "Which is exactly why we need to get right to work!"

"I don't believe it!" Leland slammed down the newspaper and jumped up from the breakfast table, nearly overturning it with his protruding stomach. "Jackson is insane!"

Edith calmly took her husband's tirade in stride while servants cowered in the background. "What has the President done to upset you this time, dear?"

Leland glowered at his wife, whose statement had made him feel as though he'd simply been overlooked in being invited for a social gathering. "It's beyond you to understand," he snapped, picking up the paper again. "I must get to the bank at once!"

The walk to his bank had done nothing to calm his temper. As far as Leland was concerned, July eleventh would forever be a black day. Unable to get backing for Senator Benton's bill to force the receipt of gold and silver only for public lands, Jackson had merely waited until Congress had adjourned, then declared an executive circular.

Leland spread the paper on his desk and again read the article, still unable to believe the deed had really been done. In the words of the paper, the President's intent had been ". . . to repress alleged frauds, and to withhold any countenance or facilities in the power of the government from the monopoly of the public lands in the hands of speculators and capitalists, to the injury of actual settlers . . ." To achieve this he had directed, the newspaper read further, "that only gold and silver should be received as payment for public lands, except in the case of *bona fide* resident settlers who were not buying over 320 acres of public land."

The conclusion of this was to further discredit banks, and Leland could well read the writing on the wall. There simply wasn't enough gold or silver to back the number of drafts already in circulation. Jackson thought that by discrediting the bank drafts, he would discourage land sales and bring a stop to speculation and inflated prices. This way, honest settlers would be purchasing the land instead of greedy speculators.

A knock at his door made Leland glance up sharply from his seething thoughts.

"Hello, Father," James said, striding into the bank office without waiting for an official welcome. "You were already gone from the house when I came down for breakfast, and Mother said you were quite enraged over something."

Leland glanced up from the paper. "Have you seen this?"

"The paper? No, not at all. Why, should I have?" He plopped down in the chair opposite his father's desk and waited for an answer.

"Jackson has gone behind the backs of Congress to inflict his will upon the people of this great nation. I'm enraged, all right. Read it for yourself!" He hurled the paper at a stun-faced James.

James read the words and shrugged. "Gold and silver is good, isn't it?"

Leland shook his head in complete exasperation. "This circular will devalue bank drafts and leave everyone scrambling to hoard gold and silver. The bank may well fold because of this."

"The article says he's done this in order to aid westward settlers and lower the prices of inflated property."

"That's what he *says*, but you know as well as I do that he detests the banks and wishes to see them put under."

"That's ridiculous," James replied. "The existence of your bank is an example of his encouragement, is it not? Did you not establish this institute upon the demise of the Bank of the United States?"

"This is different. Jackson fears the power of those who hold the wealth of the nation. He doesn't want anyone to benefit too greatly from this land rush west, unless it benefits him as well. First the Distribution Bill and now this!"

"But the Distribution Bill certainly isn't anything to cause you that much concern."

"If you were working at my side, as you should be, you'd know full well just how devastating that bill will be to us."

James shrugged and crossed his arms. "I would make a poor banker. My ignorance of your concern is proof of that."

Leland slammed down his fists. "The Distribution Bill will pull a large sum of money from this bank. Without that money to invest and earn interest on, the bank makes no money. Take enough of the assets from the bank, and before you know it, the bank will fail for lack of resources and earnings. Furthermore, if word gets out that I'm concerned in the least about this distribution, people will remove their money under the misguided notion that the bank is already in severe jeopardy."

"Is it?"

"Is it what?" By now Leland was red-faced and breathless.

"Is it a misguided notion that the bank is in jeopardy?" James' eyes never left his father's face.

Leland's attempt to regain control left him momentarily vulnerable to his son's scrutiny. "Banking," he finally said, sitting down hard, "is a troubling business."

"Yet you wish me to be a part of it?" James asked in disbelief. "How have I grieved you that you would wish this headache upon your only child?"

Leland nodded and said, "Perhaps you're right. Maybe you are better off with your railroads. As a matter of fact, I have seen the error of my thinking in regard to the future of those iron beasts. I have decided to join with Adams in the line he has proposed."

"What? Why, that's marvelous news, Father!"

Leland calmed a bit. "Yes, well, time will tell whether this venture is worthy of our praise or not."

"I must say, I'm impressed. You had once thought so little of the railroad. What changed your mind?"

"Perhaps you did, in part. Our discussion with Joseph Adams was an enlightening one for me. I had never truly understood the possibilities for the future in light of the slow return on one's investment."

"While it is true that initial costs keep stockholders from realizing much in the way of return on their money, the outcome in the long run will be tremendous. Mark my words!" James added.

Leland noted his son's enthusiasm. "I suppose I am glad you have pursued the Baltimore and Ohio. With the knowledge you gain there, perhaps you can one day come on board our company and offer the expertise we will need to see us through to completion."

"Why not start now?" James questioned. "I have never been adverse to working at your side, Father, only to working at your side in a bank. What son would not be proud to assist his father in such a futuristic adventure? Especially one that holds such promise."

Leland felt slightly panicked. He didn't like the idea at all of James' involvement in his shady scheme. "The B&O is a good experience for you and will allow you training that we will need. At this time, there is more in the way of bureaucracy and paperwork than what would keep your interest. However, when we actually find ourselves starting the venture in a physical sense, then yes, it would be my honor to have you at my side."

James smiled broadly. The pride in his expression made Leland want to look away, but instead he held his son's admiring gaze. Of course he would do nothing to see James ruined, but perhaps after enough time had passed with little action to the P&GF line, James would lose interest and stay with his beloved B&O.

Fifty

Wedding Plans

 $\mathcal{B}$ y August the heat and humidity had driven most of the area families north. People feared the sickness that always seemed to come in the damp unbearable weather of summer. Fevers, particularly yellow fever, ran rampant all along the Potomac.

Hampton Cabot wrote regularly, much to Carolina's dismay. He had requested permission of her father to correspond directly with her and had received the same without it ever being mentioned to her. Now, through these letters, he was constantly pledging his undying devotion. The latest missive told of his impending arrival, and Carolina sincerely prayed she would have cause to be elsewhere when he arrived.

James was a regular visitor to the plantation, and Carolina usually found reason to avoid him as well. At least she could enjoy York's visits as the family sat around the dining table with him. And amid talk of James and Virginia's upcoming wedding, York mentioned a certain young woman named Lucille Alexander.

"Her father is a congressman from Philadelphia, and they are renting a house in the city," York announced at the table one evening.

"How wonderful!" Margaret exclaimed. "I've heard of the Philadelphia Alexanders. A splendid family with a well-respected name."

York exchanged a smile with Carolina. Carolina was glad for York's company. She'd missed him greatly in his absences at school, but with his move to Washington she was reminded of just how fleeting their childhood was. Now Virginia was marrying, and York, with his interest in this Alexander woman, might well do the same. Maine was off to seminary in England and seldom came home for any reason, given the distance and expense of crossing the Atlantic.

"So the wedding is to be in six weeks?" York questioned, bringing the focus of the conversation to Virginia and James.

"There's still so much work to be done. I fear I'll never be ready in time," Virginia said in a way that let everyone know she expected sympathy.

"Poor dear," Margaret cooed. "You'll deserve a good rest when it's all finished."

"Yes, no doubt a long honeymoon abroad would do the trick," Joseph said with a sly glance at James. "I've been speaking with James about sponsoring such a trip."

"Oh, Papa!" Virginia exclaimed. "Truly? A trip to Europe!"

"My parents believe it to be overly praised." James seemed almost uninterested in the conversation. Or perhaps that was simply Carolina's imagination.

"Europe?" Virginia questioned in complete disbelief. "I can't believe it! Perhaps old people have not the capacity to properly appreciate it. I've always wanted to honeymoon abroad, and now my dream will come true. Oh, thank you, Papa."

Her pleasure was as evident as James' indifference. Carolina found herself studying him, wondering what secret it was that troubled his soul. It was so subtle, except to one who was a close observer. Later when they retired to the sitting room upstairs, Carolina momentarily relented of her determination to avoid him and tried to strike up a conversation with James, hoping to fathom the cause of his peculiar mood.

She started first with the trip abroad. "Exactly how long will you be abroad?" she asked casually, looking at Virginia but hoping James would speak.

"At least three months," Virginia replied. "You simply cannot go abroad for a shorter time."

"But, Virginia . . . dear, I don't have three months to give," James said.

Glad that only she and her sister were occupying the room with James, Carolina waited for the protest that Virginia was sure to make.

"Whatever do you mean?" Virginia was true to Carolina's expectations. "This is our honeymoon trip, and I expect for everything else to take second place. Three months would put us back home in time for the Christmas social season."

"I'm sorry, Virginia. I've just agreed to work full time with the B&O. After our marriage we'll move to Harper's Ferry, where I'll help work with the survey crew."

"Harper's Ferry!" Virginia exclaimed, losing all pretense of self-control. "I do not wish to live in Harper's Ferry. Why didn't you tell me of this earlier?"

"I only made my mind up yesterday," James explained. "This is the first opportunity I've had to discuss the matter. I thought it better to wait until we were alone"—he glanced at Carolina apologetically—"or nearly alone, to discuss it."

Virginia assumed an unbecoming pout. Carolina had never thought her sister anything but beautiful, but when she struck this pose it made her appear shrewish and harsh. Carolina felt a little guilty for starting the dispute. Had she done so on purpose? She couldn't admit to herself that she had, but she made an attempt to repair the damage by changing the subject.

"What will you do with the surveyors?"

James smiled weakly and shrugged. "I'm not sure. I voiced an interest in the expansion, and Ben Latrobe has been brought back on board by the B&O. He's in charge of surveying the line west from Harper's Ferry to Cumberland. Cumberland is the next goal, and that will extend the line another forty or so miles toward the Ohio."

"But I thought the company to be nearly bankrupt," Carolina commented. She noted Virginia's scornful look.

"They have suffered a great deal, but both Baltimore and the state have agreed to an additional stock subscription of three million dollars each. That's a total of six million dollars to be disbursed at one million a year over six years' time. The funds from Baltimore can only be used for expansion west of Harper's. They are desperate to connect to the West and pull in some of the freight business and passenger travel that thus far the Erie Canal has so greatly controlled."

"It sounds absolutely marvelous. Truly an adventure."

"Yes, but one which I had hoped my new wife would accompany me on." James offered a rather imploring glance to Virginia.

"Whatever do you mean?" Virginia asked.

"Simply that in order to live as man and wife, you will have to move west where I will be."

Virginia blushed and Carolina rolled her eyes when no one was looking.

"Keeping a home for you has always been important to me," Virginia said from behind a fan. She batted her eyes coyly and smiled. "Any decent young lady would seek to make a socially acceptable home. I sought to entertain and lift you up in the eyes of your peers."

"I do appreciate that, Virginia," said James.

"How do you expect that to happen buried somewhere in the wilderness?"

"Pleasing society is not as important to me as fulfillment in my work."

"But I want to live in a big city!" Virginia whined, suddenly losing all pretense at coyness. Her words caused even Carolina to raise her eyebrows. Virginia was undaunted. "I insist we live at least in Baltimore!" The whine turned into a demand.

James was quiet for several minutes, and when the clock chimed the hour he got to his feet. "You could always live in Washington with my parents. I believe that might well be the compromise we're looking for. As for Europe, I'm afraid I told your father it would have to wait until next spring at best. I have committed myself to the B&O, and a man is only as good as his word. For now, I must bid you good evening. If you would care to see me out, I would be happy for your company."

Virginia frowned. "See yourself out, James Baldwin! I'm quite miffed with you and cannot bear the thought of letting you see me cry."

Carolina wanted to laugh at this. If Virginia cried any tears, they'd be from rage, not from sorrow.

"Very well, I bid you good night."

With that James was gone, and Carolina felt it impossible to remain silent. "How can you treat him so rudely? Mother raised you better than that."

Virginia's searing look would have wilted a person of lesser strength, but Carolina was used to her sister's tirades. "You know nothing of men, little sister. And if you ever do snag a man who will overlook your eccentricities, you will better understand that certain liberties may be taken with your intended. I am simply being honest with James. He needs to know here and now that I should be consulted in all decisions."

"Will you go with him to Harper's Ferry?"

"I have no intention of living in Harper's," Virginia stated flatly. Then a strange look crossed her face, and she changed the subject. "What is this fascination you share with James regarding the railroad? I've never understood what drives him to give his life to this thing."

"What drives any man to give his life to his profession?" Carolina said. "James finds rewards in working for the railroad. I think you should be proud of him, instead of badgering him about his choices. And since when has any daughter of Margaret Adams been trained up to question her husband's choice of trade? Mother has always maintained that it is a man's prerogative to work at what he will, so long as he's a good provider for his family."

"Yes, I know that full well," Virginia agreed. "But why the railroad?"

For once Virginia seemed sincerely interested in Carolina's views, and Carolina tried to respond honestly. "From what I know," Carolina said, not wishing to share her intimate knowledge of James, "he sees the future in it. He knows the railroad will be responsible for opening the West. As the West is settled, the nation will grow stronger, and our position in the world will become more secure."

"Oh, bother our position in the world," Virginia said, getting to her feet. "Such matters are so unimportant to everyday life here. We needn't concern ourselves with what takes place across the ocean."

"Then why go there for your honeymoon?" Carolina felt a bit smug for her quick thinking.

Virginia's only answer was a huff before sweeping from the room as gracefully as her anger would allow her. Carolina shook her head and wondered at her sister. She could be so conniving and cunning, yet in matters beyond the plantation or society, Virginia was truly blind.

Carolina tried not to think how she would have responded to James had she been his intended. But of course the thoughts came anyway. And she knew she'd pack her bags so quickly to join him in Harper's Ferry that he'd hardly be able to catch his breath. How ironic life could be at times. Her papa talked so often about God's plan in the lives of His children, but Carolina saw no logic in such a mismatched pair as James and Virginia when the perfect match, in her mind, was so close at hand.

Fifty-One

Fever Strikes

Autumn rains finally came to break the heat of summer, but the dampness seemed to permeate everything, making it nearly as uncomfortable as the heat had. Carolina went about her duties as instructed, but at any given chance she could be found in the library, book in hand, intently seeking to escape the reality of her life.

One hot muggy afternoon she retreated to her room and perched on the window seat, which was rather cool as it was shaded by a tall magnolia tree. She had just opened *The Merchant of Venice* when her mother's voice penetrated the partially closed door of her room.

"Carolina! Carolina!"

Looking up from her book, Carolina dreaded the beckoning voice. Lately that voice seemed only to mean more work for Carolina, but she was involved in the intriguing story and had been allowed little time in the last few days to pursue it. Thus she resented the interruption. "I'm here, Mother!" she called, still hoping she wouldn't have to leave her reading.

"Carolina!"

Seeing there was no escaping her mother's call, Carolina rose, and taking her time, she straightened her skirt of green-and-white checkered muslin and retied the green sash.

"Come quickly!"

Now Carolina heard the urgency in her mother's voice, which held a clear tone of alarm.

Carolina hurried her steps a bit and checked the upstairs sitting room. No one was there. The music room was also vacant.

"Where are you, Mother?" Carolina cocked her head to listen for a reply.

"In the nursery. Hurry!"

322

Now Carolina was sure she detected panic in her mother's voice. Something was wrong! She burst through the door to Penny and Maryland's shared room and frowned. Her mother was bent over the flower-sprig coverlet of Penny's bed. "What is it?"

Margaret Adams straightened up, a fearful look overtaking her face. "Penny has a fever." Her voice strained to say the words. "Mary, too." Margaret nodded toward the cradle bed where Maryland lay fitfully sleeping.

Carolina held her breath. "A fever? How bad is it?"

"Bad enough!" her mother snapped. "Get Hannah and don't dally like you did getting here."

Carolina swallowed back an angry retort. I didn't dally, she thought. Not on purpose, anyhow. She went in search of Hannah and sighed. Perhaps she had dallied. "Hannah, Mama says come quick. Mary and Penny have a fever," Carolina announced, coming into the kitchen where Hannah was helping Naomi peel potatoes. The two women were enjoying a quiet afternoon together, but the moment of pleasure was clearly broken by Carolina's announcement.

Hannah pushed the unpeeled potatoes from her apron and struggled to her feet. "I be comin'. Ol' Hannah's bones be achin' sumptin fierce on account of de rain."

Carolina looked out the window. It had indeed started to rain again. But her mind was on her sisters. "What can I carry for you?" she asked, knowing the old mammy maintained regular supplies to be used in treating bouts of fever.

"Dat blue bag," Hannah pointed, then turned to instruct Naomi on having one of the boys bring up a caldron of water for the fireplace in the girls' room.

Carolina hurried back to the nursery with the bag under her arm. It was a fearsome thing to realize fever had come upon them. In the nineteen years since Hampshire's and Tennessee's deaths, the family had escaped the horrors of fever epidemics, and Joseph had always called them blessed. Carolina wondered if now they would find themselves cursed as so many other families had been in the past. It had only been two years since Kate Milford's younger brother had died from fever. Then there were the terrible slave losses suffered by the Williams and Cooper families. Was Oakbridge to be next? The very thought struck fear in her heart.

She entered the room and, noting her mother's harried expression, no longer felt angry for the harshness of her mother's words. The sight of Penny's pale face took away all thought of strife. "Hannah's coming, Mama," she said, feeling a tenderness toward her mother. Sometimes

Margaret Adams made it difficult for her children to draw close to her, but at times like these Carolina saw the facade of strength crumble, and her mother became human and fallible, just like everyone else. Placing the bag on a table, Carolina went to Maryland's cradle. "When did they get sick?"

"I don't know," her mother said wearily. "Penny seemed sluggish at breakfast, and Hannah suggested a dose of castor oil might work wonders. Mary refused to wake up from her nap, and when I checked on her I found her burning with fever."

"Is it Yellow Jack?"

Margaret looked at Carolina as if she'd spoken some intolerable word. "I pray it is not."

"But—"

"I do not know, Carolina," Margaret replied harshly. "I simply do not know. Perhaps Hannah will tell us. Where is she, anyway?"

"I's here, Miz Adams," Hannah panted, forcing her bulky body forward. "I'm a mite down and my bones are a-achin'." She mumbled on about the rain while checking first Maryland and then Penny. Carolina watched as Hannah put out a big brown hand to Mary's tiny forehead. Shaking her head, she waddled to Penny and did the same. "We bes' send fer de doctor. These chil'en be mighty sick."

"What is it? Flux?" Margaret demanded in a strained voice. She was still avoiding the dreaded mention of her worst fears. She'd lost two infant sons to the fever, and the very utterance of the word brought her grave sorrow. Carolina wondered if her mother, who still openly wept at the mention of the long-dead babies, could bear yet another loss. It was a seldom mentioned memory that Margaret Adams had suffered a tremendous breakdown after the deaths of her babies.

"Chil'," Hannah said, looking at Carolina with serious brown-black eyes, "go tell Jericho to fetch de doctor."

Carolina glanced at her mother and then back to Hannah. When there was no affirmation from her mother, who simply stared blankly at her daughters, Carolina went in search of the house slave.

A sudden crack of thunder made the skin on the back of her neck prickle. Trembling from the sudden noise, Carolina felt such trepidation within her soul that she could scarcely take a step forward. Halting at the stairs, she took a deep breath. Was it the fever? She ran a hand down her arm and shuddered. Would they die as so many others had? Would she, too, fall ill?

Her only other thought as she looked for Jericho was that Papa was away in Washington City. He had taken Virginia there to shop for her wedding. Carolina never felt the need for him more.

Dr. Granger from Falls Church arrived late that evening. The rain was falling in sheets now, and his carriage had gotten stuck in the mud several times. He told them the river was already overflowing its banks.

"The children are upstairs," Carolina said, holding the doctor's bag while Bartholomew took his rain-drenched overcoat and top hat. "My mother and Hannah are with them now."

The thin man was hardly any taller than Carolina, but his stern expression and air of authority gave him instant credibility. "Take me to them," he said, retrieving his bag from her hands.

After a cursory examination Dr. Granger turned to face Carolina and her mother. "It's yellow fever. I've seen nearly forty cases elsewhere in the county. I'll need to bleed them, then give a good strong dose of calomel to purge the system of poisons."

Margaret paled. "Bleed them? But they are so little and weak." Carolina put an arm around her mother for fear of her fainting.

"I assure you it's the only thing I can do for them at this point. If they are strong enough, it will cleanse them and aid in their recovery. If not, their skin will turn yellow with poison, and they will surely die. I wish I could be more gentle in the telling, but the truth is, I'm exhausted beyond my means and see no chance for rest in the near future. I've been treating cases such as these for over two weeks, and I see no end in sight."

Carolina felt her mother begin to tremble. "Come sit down, Mother," she said, leading her to the nearby rocker. Margaret seemed to be in a daze and said nothing more while the doctor went about his tasks.

"I'll need some bowls," he said, and Carolina instructed Hannah to send for them. "Also build up the fire and keep this room good and warm. The other family members should avoid the sickroom." Carolina nodded and turned to Margaret.

"Mother, should I send someone for Papa and Virginia?"

Margaret stared at her with vacant eyes. The news had been too much for her, and all her worst fears appeared to have been confirmed. Carolina went to her side and knelt down to take her mother's hand. "Mother?"

"No . . . they'll be better by morning, I just know it," Margaret finally replied.

"It is late and miserable out there," assured the doctor. "I doubt it is necessary for such urgency."

As Dr. Granger attached a tourniquet to Mary's arm, Margaret seemed suddenly to come to life. She jumped to her feet and threw herself between her child and the doctor. "No, you aren't going to bleed them. They're too little." She pulled the tourniquet off and tossed it across the room.

"Mrs. Adams," he protested, "bleeding is a common response to yellow fever."

"I do not care!" Margaret said, taking a firm stand. "You will not bleed my baby."

"Be reasonable, Mrs. Adams." He looked at Carolina. "How far away is Mr. Adams?"

"He is in the city," Margaret replied, taking up Maryland's lethargic body. She tucked a blanket around the moaning child and sat down in a rocker. "You will deal with me on the matter or no one at all."

"I cannot help these children if you will not follow instructions. A good dose of calomel to purge the bowels followed by tartar emetic to bring about vomiting will help cleanse the system. Bleeding will allow the impurities to pass out through the blood. You cannot hope to see these children survive without doing just as I say."

"Then leave us," Margaret said softly, yet firmly. "We will treat them as best we can, but you will not drain the very life out of them."

He shook his head and looked to Carolina as if expecting help.

"My mother feels quite strongly about this," Carolina said by way of explanation. "Perhaps there is another way?"

"If there is, it has not yet been told to the good physicians of this country," the doctor replied. He looked once more at Margaret Adams, gathered his things, then strode from the room still shaking his head.

Carolina lingered in the nursery a moment before following the doctor.

"Mother, why are you so against bleeding?"

"It's a hateful practice. No one will ever convince me it does any good." She paused and cast a haunted look at her babies. Then she added, "They bled your baby brothers when they were sick. They both died. . . ."

"Oh, Mother!"

"Carolina, where are your manners? Please see the doctor out."

Carolina left reluctantly and only because she had some further questions to ask the doctor.

"Dr. Granger," she said when she caught up to him on the stairs, "I read something in the *Niles Register* about a medicine called quinine."

Dismissing this idea with a brusque shrug, Dr. Granger spoke harshly. "Silly notions! Should your mother come to her senses, send someone to find me, and pray it is not too late. Should your father return, tell him of this conversation. Being a rational man, he will know what is best."

"I doubt my mother will change her mind," Carolina said, handing the man his hat and coat. She was angry at the implied message that because her father was a man he would not only be more rational about the matter but be more knowledgeable as well. For all her father's love of his children, she seriously doubted he'd spent more than a few hours in the nursery. Her mother was the one, along with Hannah, who best knew the children's needs.

Dr. Granger looked as though he might say something more, but instead, he hurried through the pouring rain to his carriage. Carolina found herself secretly wishing he might have argued with her. She wanted to tell him what she thought of his barbaric actions, and she wanted him to comment on the *Niles Register* article and the possibilities of using opium and quinine to treat cases of yellow fever.

"When Papa returns," she said aloud, though no one was there to hear, "I will assuredly tell him what was said."

Fifty-Two

LOSS

*B*ut her father didn't return, and neither could a rider make it through the rain into Washington. The torrential rains had turned all of the roads into impassable boggy messes, and two main bridges had been swept away in a rush of water. Unexpected flooding became a serious problem in many places, including Oakbridge, where some low-lying areas needed to be evacuated.

Margaret refused to leave the nursery, and because of this, Carolina found herself in charge of the plantation. Their overseer, Walt Durgason, came to inform her that the lower row of slave quarters was now mired under several inches of water from the rising creek. She instructed him to see the slaves moved to share quarters elsewhere and to keep her apprised of the situation.

The rain continued into the next day and the next, and so, too, did the fever. Penny and Mary seemed to grow weaker by the minute, and Carolina received word from Walt that over twenty slaves were sick as well. Among them was her beloved Hannah. It was clear now why Hannah had so quickly relinquished care of the children to a doctor. Carolina wanted desperately to go check on Hannah but found herself forced to address other matters instead. She was exhausted and had endured much beyond what she'd thought herself capable of. With each bleak and hopeless day that passed, Margaret would allow no one but Carolina to enter the nursery. She asked often for word of her husband, but Carolina had none to give. This only caused her mother to slip further into despair, and sometimes Carolina thought her mother had lost touch with reality altogether. Once she referred to Mary as Tennessee, thinking this was the same epidemic that had taken her two sons.

Another grave concern Carolina felt she must shoulder alone was the fear that the fever would strike other members of the family. Margaret had all but forgotten about her other children, so focused was she on the sick ones and the ones long dead. But Carolina lived daily with that gnawing fear. What if her mother caught it from her close contact with the sick ones? Or Georgia? Or herself? Will they die? she pondered. Will I?

Carolina tried to maintain some type of routine. She slept very little, taking only brief naps on a cot in the nursery. She had relegated Georgia to quarters on the third floor, much to her little sister's dismay. Georgia feared the fever, and the distance placed between her and her family members gave her reason to believe they were sending her off to die.

"Georgy," Carolina said, trying to soothe her sister's concerns, "I don't want to see you ill as well. Mother is so worried about Penny and Mary that it would kill her to have you come down with the fever as well."

"But why can't I stay in my room?"

Carolina gave her a hug. "Please just help me with this. I feel certain you should stay as far from the nursery as possible. Your room is only two doors down. I'll send Miriam to stay with you. Will that help?"

Georgia nodded, but the tears in her eyes made Carolina feel she had been a harsh taskmaster. Using the edge of her apron to wipe the perspiration from her forehead, Carolina struggled to clear her mind and decide what needed to be attended to next.

Going to the kitchen, she was met with an eerie silence. After four days the steady downpour of rain had stopped.

Carolina knew it would be days before the roads were passable, maybe even longer for the flooded areas. But if the rain stopped long enough, they might be able to get word through to Washington City, and her father would return home. She found herself praying for that with all of her heart. Her father held the strength and hope she had seen drained away from her mother's spirit. She hurried upstairs to impart the hopeful news.

"Mother," she said, entering the nursery with a smile. "The rain has stopped! We can send a rider out in the morning after Papa."

Margaret Adams said nothing as she moved from first one child to the next. Wondering if she'd even heard her announcement, Carolina want 1 to say something reassuring, and Margaret desperately needed to hear something hopeful, but still her mother worked without a word and never stopped to comment on Carolina's presence or the ceasing of the rain.

That night a shrouded silence held Oakbridge spellbound in its grip.

The ragged breathing of Mary and Penny wore on Carolina's nerves, and she prayed there would soon be an end to their suffering. Why didn't God act and heal the bodies of her sisters? I'm tired, God, she prayed. Can't this just be done with? Sweat soaked the back and neck of her dress. How she longed for a bath and a decent night's sleep, but there appeared to be no end in sight. Then she rebuked herself for her selfishness.

Dipping the cloth again into a pan of cool water and placing it upon her sister's forehead, Carolina said, "Penny's fever is still high, Mother." Not that it really needed to be announced, but the heavy silence in the room was too oppressive. She smoothed back dark brown ringlets from her sister's forehead and frowned. Even in the poor light of a single oil lamp it was easy to see how much Penny's skin had yellowed from the illness. Why wouldn't the fever break?

"I know," Margaret replied from where she rocked Maryland. They were the first words she had spoken in hours. "Perhaps I should have allowed the doctor to bleed them."

"I doubt bleeding would have cured them," Carolina spoke in a weary voice. "Father would say we are to trust God for our direction."

"Yes," her mother replied with a suddenly bitter voice. "He would. But your father is not here, and he doesn't have to watch them suffer."

"Papa has no way of knowing they've fallen ill." Carolina found her mother's tone alarming. "I'm certain he'd be here now if the roads were passable."

"Perhaps . . ." Margaret replied, but the word only betrayed more bitterness and doubt.

The night dragged on forever. Carolina heard the clock in the hall chime one and then two. It was difficult to stay awake, but whenever she dozed, hideous visions clouded her sleep. She imagined heavy blackness smothering her, and always she awoke panting for her very breath. Penny cried out and thrashed from side to side, bringing Carolina instantly awake. "Mother!" she exclaimed, pulling her hand back from her sister's forehead. "She's perspiring."

It was a good sign, and Margaret got to her feet, still holding Mary. "Keep wiping her body with the water," Margaret ordered. "I'm going to put Mary in bed."

Carolina nodded and started the procedure of care once again. Her arms ached from the work, but she continued faithfully in hopes it might save her sister's life. She thought about her father and wondered when he might return and if he were praying for them even now. *Trust God for direction . . . His will, not our own . . .*

Oh, Papa, I need you so!

She wondered if her father would claim those words now while two of his children lay so close to death. She put the cloth back in the water and got up to stretch. Her back was cramped from hours in the awkward position in which she'd held her vigil over Penny's bedside. She glanced across the room to where her mother had resumed rocking Maryland.

"Why don't you rest?" Carolina said. "I can watch them both while you sleep." Her heart filled with concern for her mother.

"No," Margaret said in a wavering voice. "I need to be here. Mary's so weak. I don't think she's going to live long."

Carolina masked the shock. As bad as she knew it was, she had not wanted to believe it was *that* bad. "No, Mother . . ."

"She's so frail and little. She's more angel than person now."

Carolina shuddered at the thought. Guilt racked her conscience. Perhaps she could have done more. She looked over helplessly at her baby sister. Her small body truly did seem lifeless in sleep, her tiny eyes closed behind long brown lashes. Reaching out, Carolina ran a finger along one flushed cheek. Her fever still raged.

"Can't we do something?" Carolina asked with tears in her eyes. Her desperation was a sharp contrast to her mother's seeming calm.

Margaret shook her head. "She's in God's hands now." Her voice was unemotional.

Carolina gained no peace from her mother's calm. It was in fact more frightening than inspiring. It was not real calm at all.

Carolina touched a hand to her mother's arm, but Margaret did not acknowledge the supportive gesture. Her eyes were vacant, and Carolina feared that should Mary die, her mother might well be incapable of dealing with it. I doubt I will be able to deal with it myself, Carolina thought.

"It's hard to watch your children die. . . ." Margaret said, but more to herself than to her daughter. "I'll always wonder if I did enough. Was I careful with them? Then there are the times I scolded them. The times I was too busy to stop and listen to their chatter. As I watch their lifeless bodies in sickness I know now there is no price I would not pay to see them laughing and chattering again."

"You've been a good mother. . . ."

"And yet, they linger. . . ." Margaret went on, oblivious of Carolina. "Death mocking me, haunting my memories with reminders of inadequacies. They hurt and suffer, and I'd gladly offer myself in their place." Suddenly Margaret broke into tears.

Carolina had never seen her mother cry, and it only confirmed her fears that things were terribly wrong. "Don't cry, Mama," Carolina whispered. "We only need to get through the night. Maybe Father will return in the morning."

"Curse your father for leaving me to bear this alone," Margaret spat out. Even her anger didn't cause Mary to stir. "At one time the rain would never have kept him from home. He would have moved heaven and earth to be at my side."

Before Carolina could say a word, Penny cried out, "Mama." She whimpered and thrashed at the coverlet that Carolina had placed over her.

Margaret put Mary on her bed and immediately went to Penny. "Pennsylvania Adams," she said, taking a seat beside the restless ten-year-old, "you must get well and wake up."

"Mama," Penny's tiny voice croaked. "I feel so bad."

"Hush, now," her mother soothed. "You're quite ill, but you will get better. Can you drink a little broth? It will help make you stronger." Penny barely nodded her head. "Good girl." Margaret turned to Carolina. "Please come feed your sister a bit of soup."

Carolina was quick to pick up the task and went to retrieve the bowl from where it warmed by the fireplace. She watched her mother pat Penny's hand reassuringly before going back to Mary. Carolina longed for the same reassurance for herself. Why did her mother react so coldly to her? She was, after all, offering her support and help. I'm here, Mama, she thought with a quick glance at her mother. I'm here, but you seem not to know it. Are you angry at me because I'm not Papa?

The aroma of the broth wafted up, and Carolina realized she'd not eaten a thing since lunchtime. Now, nearing dawn, she felt her stomach rumble in protest. Weakness from lack of food and exhaustion crept over her body. Carolina knew she would have to eat soon or risk becoming sick herself. Nevertheless, she spooned the thin broth into Penny's parched lips, but after only three spoonfuls, Penny turned her face away and fell back to sleep. Carolina tried to console herself with the fact that her sister had taken at least some of the liquid, but the shadow of death still hung heavy over the room, and there was no solace to be had. Carolina walked over to the window and gazed out to find the pink glow of dawn on the horizon. They'd made it through the night, she thought. The morning had come and the rain had stopped. The skies were clear with the promise of a new day.

"Look, Mama, it's morning."

"The Lord is my shepherd," Margaret whispered, hugging her baby to her breast. "I shall not want. . . ."

Carolina sighed. Papa would come today, she just knew it.

Margaret's murmured prayer had faded from Carolina's hearing, but suddenly her mother's voice rose in intensity. "Yea, though I walk through the valley of the shadow of death . . ."

Carolina's head snapped up.

Maryland! Her mother's face had turned pale. Carolina trembled at the sight.

"Mama?" she said fearfully.

But Carolina did not have to hear the words from her mother. She knew her sister was dead. Tears streaming down her face, she hurried to her mother's side. Margaret swayed on her feet, and giving her support, Carolina led her mother back to the rocking chair. Carolina averted her eyes from the bundle in her mother's arms. She didn't want to look, for she knew looking would make it real. Yet, in the end, she knew she must look or never truly believe her sister was gone.

She had never before witnessed death, and she now had to force herself to look death in the face. Oddly, it wasn't the awful vision she had conjured in her mind. The child indeed appeared only to sleep, a peaceful rest that she had not experienced in five days. Carolina sobbed and fell to her knees. It was of little comfort that her sister was out of pain's reach. The loss pierced through Carolina's heart like a white-hot knife. Her sister was dead and nothing could change that fact. Laying her head on her mother's knee, Carolina cried long and hard, though she had wanted so much to be strong for her mother.

"My baby is gone!" Margaret moaned.

Carolina tried to think of words of comfort. What were some of the things she'd heard people say at times like these?

"We must be glad for the time we've had," Carolina heard herself say. But even as she spoke the words she could hear how empty they were. Still, she rambled on, "We must remember our joy."

"What do I care for memories?" Margaret's voice was dry and brittle.

Carolina lifted her head and wiped at her tears with her lace-edged sleeve. She reached out to touch Maryland's soft brown curls. "It's as though she's only asleep." More platitudes. Was there no real comfort to be had?

"She'll never wake again."

"She's in heaven now, Mama. Maybe running up and down that grand stairway to heaven." Through tears Carolina added, "We don't have to worry about her falling anymore."

"Sometimes our fears keep us safe," Margaret spoke in a mere whisper. "And sometimes they keep us from ever doing the things God intends us to do. We mustn't hide ourselves away while life passes us by. When God calls we must listen and respond. Don't let fears keep you hidden from life, Carolina." Margaret continued to rock, gently touching Mary's cheek. "Were she back among us, I would gladly allow her to run on the stairs."

Fifty-Three

Broken Hearts

James listened patiently to Virginia's recitation of their guest list. In less than two weeks he was to become this woman's husband. He watched her while she chattered, her curls bobbing in ringlets from either side of her face as she carefully scanned the list. He looked away from her and toward the door, as if desperately searching for a way of escape.

"Have we missed anyone?" she inquired gravely.

"Not unless you meant to invite the entire state of Virginia," James said dryly. "I believe I know a couple of families in the southwest corner whom you left out."

Edith admonished him. "Now, James, these things must be tended to in proper order. It simply wouldn't do at all to overlook someone of importance."

James nodded and looked to his father for some kind of support. Leland merely shrugged. "I leave these things to the womenfolk," he said and went back to his game of checkers with Joseph Adams.

"They do these things so well," Joseph replied. "I should know, I have a whole houseful of them."

"Oh, Papa," Virginia laughed, and James thought it a grating sound rather than the charming attraction he'd once considered it. "Men know nothing of proper decorum," she continued. "Were it not for women, men might go about in shirtsleeves and knee breeches."

"I know a few old men who still wear knee breeches," Joseph told his daughter.

"True, but as you said they are old men, and they certainly do not care about their appearance. Still, such eccentricity can be overlooked in the very old."

"This is true enough, Virginia; however, age is no reason to be vulgar," Edith added.

James' mind wandered. The discussion of the past week since Virginia and her father had come to visit had been solely with regard to his and Virginia's wedding. Not only was it enormously boring, it made him most uncomfortable. Marriage had been only a game to him. A profitable, necessary game, invoked into being by his father's demands. But the reality of it all was now starting to grip him.

He watched Virginia at ease with his parents. He watched Joseph and Leland laughing about some matter, and he realized more than ever that he couldn't remain here in Washington. He couldn't continue the charade he'd been playing these past months. This was no game for childish amusement. This was real life and a very real matter of honor. Virginia expected a husband who could shower her in jewels and lavish her with attention. She would never find it entertaining to discuss locomotive boilers or the best route to Cumberland. She would never live in Harper's Ferry as he had proposed. And she would impose her will on him just as his parents had always done. He felt almost as frightened now as when he had first stepped on a railcar after the accident. Not just fear—but pure panic.

The conversation continued without anyone so much as inquiring about James' opinions. Not that he really cared. He never felt more strongly than now that this was Virginia's wedding, not his. He simply observed all that passed before his eyes, and with every moment he knew he had made a grave mistake. When supper was finally announced, James had lost his appetite.

The small gathering had barely taken their seats when a knock sounded from the kitchen door at the back of the house.

"Who could be delivering at this hour?" Edith questioned, then started to get up when Nellie appeared to announce a messenger from the Oakbridge plantation.

Joseph excused himself and followed the girl from the room, while James turned to hear Virginia describing the details of the bridesmaids' gowns to his mother. A queer feeling came over him as he watched and listened. He opened his mouth twice to comment, but words wouldn't form on his lips. He felt almost as though he were watching the scene of a play. It was as if he'd literally been taken from the room and placed at a distance. These people were like actors, each playing a part. The story was his life, and somehow he'd been removed from the action and decisions that were to guide its course.

"You might not know it," Virginia was saying, "but the lace on my gown is all handmade. I've worked on it for nearly four years."

"How marvelous!" Edith exclaimed and Leland nodded. "So industrious and cunning. Your daughters will no doubt cherish the gown."

"Even more so because it has been made over from my mother's wedding gown," Virginia replied.

Who were these people? James found himself wondering. The faces were familiar, as was the setting, but the characters and personalities seemed awkwardly alien. Or was he the alien one who did not belong?

I can't go through with this, he thought. I cannot marry this woman. Maybe later. When I have discovered if I can make my own way in life. Maybe after I complete my work with the B&O and join Father in his venture. Carolina's face appeared suddenly in his mind to haunt him. Something had happened between them in Baltimore when he'd escorted her to the concert. But he'd never been certain what it was. She had seemed on the verge of telling him something important, and yet all she would say when he asked for an explanation was that she was upset that his engagement to Virginia had made her mother intent on marrying Carolina off as well. But Carolina was not such a petty person. Could that truly have been all that was troubling her? Was she still angry at him for ending their tutoring sessions? Or was she angry because he'd not asked for her hand instead of her sister's?

He almost smiled at that notion. It was not only ridiculous, it was unthinkable. Carolina would never have such feelings for the man betrothed to her sister.

Women were strange creatures; that much he knew. He had tried his hand many times at conversing and socializing with them, and apart from Carolina Adams, whose interests went clearly beyond the realm of feminine interest, James had never felt truly drawn to any of them. Virginia Adams was beautiful, but even that seemed to have faded in his eyes during the course of their courtship. Virginia's appearance might be lovely on the outside, but inside she was harsh and calculating. He had seen her strike a slave girl across the face for dropping her favorite strand of pearls, and he had also witnessed her belittle Carolina when she thought no one was around. These memories left a bad taste in his mouth, and the more he thought about them, the more certain he was that he couldn't marry Virginia Adams.

Surprising the trio by suddenly getting to his feet, James decided to speak his mind. They were, after all, very privately assembled, and with both Virginia and her father here, it would work well to put the matter behind them. He searched in his mind for the right words. But before he could speak, Joseph Adams returned white-faced and shaking.

"Joseph?" Leland said, rising to his feet awkwardly. "Has there been bad news?"

"I scarcely can say the words," Joseph replied, looking first to his old friend and then to his daughter. "Yellow fever has taken several lives at Oakbridge, and we must return immediately."

"Is it mother?" Virginia cried out, throwing her napkin aside and getting to her feet. "Tell me, Papa!"

Joseph put his arm around her shoulder. "No, your mother is fine, at least in body. I'm afraid . . . it's Mary."

———

A stunned Joseph and Virginia returned to Oakbridge. Three days afterward Mary was laid to rest in the family graveyard beside the other Adams children, Hampshire and Tennessee.

Penny, still too weak to attend the services, remained in bed in a guest room where she had been moved immediately after her sister's death. Carolina stayed with her during the funeral and watched from the window. She felt relief from the reprieve, wondering if she could have ever made it through the painful ceremony. It wasn't her lack of faith that Mary had gone on to a better place. It wasn't the fear of breaking down in front of everyone. It was the isolation she felt. It was the overwhelming feeling that she had no one with whom to share this sorrow.

James was there. She knew this as well as she knew anything. The Baldwins had been one of the few families to make the journey. There were only a handful of friends from the community who attended. Most of the families were keeping safely away from the area of sickness and wouldn't return for several weeks. Others were burdened themselves by the fever and could scarcely be expected to come. But James and his parents had come yesterday, and each had done what they could to comfort their friends. Edith to Margaret. Leland to Joseph. And James to Virginia.

"What else could he do?" Carolina murmured against the windowpane. She couldn't see James from Penny's window, but she knew he was there among the black-clad group in the distance, taking his place beside Virginia.

Mary is dead, Carolina thought. She is dead and James will marry Virginia, and York will go back to Washington and life will go on around me, yet never really include me. What will become of me?

Perhaps everyone was right. Perhaps she should give up the foolish notions of railroads and universities. Maybe marriage to Hampton Cabot or someone else would at least free her from the misery she felt here and now. But that was a foolish reason to marry. Her father had always told her marriage was a sacred thing between man, woman, and God. It wasn't something to consider in jest, and it wasn't something you could rid yourself of later should you find it inconvenient.

"Did they put her in the ground?" Penny weakly called from the four-poster bed.

Carolina let the curtain fall back into place and turned to face her younger sister. "Yes," she replied. "They put her body in the ground."

"Won't she be a-scared?" Penny asked.

"Afraid," Carolina corrected. "No, because it's just her body that is there. Mary is in heaven where the angels are."

"Is Mary going to fly in the sky?" Penny's weak voice questioned.

Carolina smiled. "I don't know, Penny. If you were in heaven is that what you would do?"

Penny smiled. "I think it would be fun to fly around. I'd go really fast. Like when the boys ride their horses in the races. I'd go faster and faster and pretty soon I'd just fly up into the sky."

"That sounds nice," Carolina remarked. She sat down hard on the chair beside the bed. For all her youth she felt so old and tired. Even in the face of Penny's recovery, it was hard to feel any different. Life was a most difficult adversary.

Eyes still red from crying, Miriam appeared in Penny's room an hour later. Carolina knew that in addition to little Mary's death, several of the slaves had lost family members as well. Dear Hannah had died also, and services had been held the night before in the Negro church. Carolina had been the only family member to attend, though she could barely contain her own misery.

"Miz Carolina," Miriam said, coming to the girl's side, "you gwanna need some rest. You go on now. I's gwanna sit with Miz Pennsylvania."

Carolina nodded in agreement and left the room. The solitude would be refreshing.

"Carolina?"

She looked up as she closed Penny's door, and her breath caught. "James . . ." He looked as weary and sorrowful as she felt. His eyes, usually sparkling with boyish amusement, were somber and filled with concern.

"I've not had a chance to speak with you since our arrival," he said softly.

Carolina crushed great handfuls of black bombazine as she nervously twisted the skirt of her gown. "I know," was all she could manage to say.

"I'm so very sorry about Mary. How is Penny?"

"Better but very weak. The doctor fears she will always be fragile."

"Your mother seems to be taking this very hard," James continued. "She collapsed at the service."

"I should go to her," Carolina said but made no move to leave.

James put his hand on her arm. "No, they've already put her to bed with some herbal remedy of Naomi's. My mother is with her, as is Virginia and Georgia. I'd rather you stay and talk to me."

Carolina felt tears form anew, and she lowered her face. "Why? Why would you rather I do that? You should be with Virginia. That's where you belong, James."

He frowned. "It's only that . . . when I saw you this morning you looked so very alone. I thought perhaps you needed someone to talk to. And, maybe I'm wrong, but we have always been able to talk about such things to each other before."

She continued walking down the corridor, and he stayed at her side. Yes, of all the people at Oakbridge just then, he was the one person she felt would truly understand her grief. But with him so close, too many other sensations were converging inside her for her to feel safe in unburdening her heart to him. Carolina stopped and couldn't help but glance down the hall toward the nursery. Shuddering, she felt as if death's hand were upon her.

"You were with her when she died, weren't you, Carolina?" James said.

A full-fledged rush of tears spilled down her cheeks as she nodded. She'd thought her grief had played itself out, but all at once the pain hit her again and was almost too much to bear. Her memories of Mary and her desire for someone to comfort her rushed upon her.

"That must have been terribly difficult for you," James said.

"It was more difficult for Mother." She tried to keep her voice steady.

"You don't have to be brave . . . not for me, anyway." He reached up and cupped her trembling chin in his hand.

For the last three days she had been holding back, trying hard to be strong for everyone else—especially her mother. She didn't want anyone to worry over her. It was her mother who needed the family most. But except a few moments of private tears, she had kept it all bottled up within. It wasn't hard now to respond to James' gentle entreaty.

"I . . . I've never seen anyone die before . . . but for it to be Mary . . . so little, so helpless . . . so—" Her voice broke in a muffled cry.

"You once helped me over the death of a friend. I'd like to return that favor if there is any way that I could."

His voice began to penetrate the fog of her grief. His touch reached something lost and forlorn inside her.

"Oh, James! She can't be gone! She just can't be! Mary . . . sweet, dear Mary!" Carolina's whole body shook with grief.

James caught her trembling frame in his arms. "Just cry, dear . . ." he consoled, holding her tight, caressing her hair with his hand. "Let it all out. I'll be here for you."

Carolina could find no words to speak. She poured out her heart in tears of sorrow, wishing from the depths of her soul that she could change the past and bring Mary back to life. Why should little children die? Why would God turn away His face from their needs and leave them to suffer? Oh, Mary, my sweet baby sister, Carolina silently mourned. How can I bear your loss?

As if reading her mind, James whispered against her ear, "I would give anything to bring her back to you. I would give my life to ease your pain."

The words shook her almost as much as her grief. She sobered instantly. "Don't say such a thing!"

"But it's true," he insisted. With one arm still around her, he reached up with the other and wiped her tears with his fingers. "I would dry your eyes and give you back your joy, at any price. Any price."

"Nothing can change the past." Carolina held his gaze, wondering what it was she read in his intense blue eyes.

"Perhaps not." Was that sorrow she noted in his eyes? Was he sharing her grief? That must be it.

"James . . . Carolina. . . ?"

Carolina jerked quickly away from James' embrace to find Virginia coming down the hall.

"What are you doing!" The confusion in Virginia's voice was mingled with accusation.

"Carolina broke down over Mary," James said. "Thank God I was here. The poor dear has been keeping back all her grief."

Virginia gave each an incisive look. Carolina felt guilty, as if there really had been more going on between her and James, as if James had been returning the feelings she had toward him. But that wasn't so and never would be. He was but a dear friend comforting her in her sorrow.

"Well . . ." Virginia looked afraid for a minute. Then she seemed to shake off the mood, adding, "That was very kind of you, James. I am quite spent myself with grieving. I need your steadying arm as well."

James appeared to hesitate. He looked long and hard at Carolina, still not moving.

"I'll be fine," Carolina managed to speak at last.

"But . . . I . . ." he stammered and looked at her helplessly.

"Thank you for caring," she said, then pushed past him, desperate to retreat to the privacy of her room. Pausing only a moment, she looked back and saw him turn toward Virginia as she linked her arm firmly through his. They walked away together. As it should be. Without another word Carolina went into her room and closed the door.

Fifty-Four

The Letter

$\mathcal{I}$t was properly assumed that James and Virginia's wedding would be postponed until a suitable period of mourning could pass. This was a saving grace as far as James was concerned. He'd struggled at Oakbridge to confront Virginia with just the right words, but with everyone so stricken over Mary, he simply had not the heart to bring further pain to the family.

Back in Washington and secluded in his childhood room, James knew he had to do something. He felt himself a coward for being unable to confront her in person, but he was not so much a coward to follow through with this loveless marriage of financial convenience. He was at least enough of a man to finally stand up for himself, to pursue the life he wanted. But this decision wasn't entirely for him. He was thinking of Virginia, too, by saving her from a loveless marriage.

Still, it was highly improper for a proper gentleman to so shame a lady by breaking an engagement. Thus, it was nothing to approach lightly. If he committed such an act, it would no doubt ruin his reputation forever. No decent family would have him. Worse still, it could reflect upon his parents as well. They might be shunned from society. Perhaps his father's business would suffer. Yet what was that to the prospect of spending the rest of his life living a monumental lie? True, it wouldn't be the first marriage of convenience; in fact, many marriages were launched in that manner.

It was more than that. It wasn't merely that he did not love Virginia—he actually had no feelings at all for her. And that was probably worse by far. He did not even like to be around her anymore. The thrill he had once felt at her physical charms had long since dimmed under the glaring reality of her demanding nature. He would simply have to sacrifice too much of himself to form a union with her.

342

And then there was Carolina . . .

The very thought of her set his entire being into such an excited yet confused state that—well, it was practically sinful to even consider marrying Carolina's sister. But the idea of actually telling Carolina how he felt was just as appalling, though he had been on the verge of doing so many times. If he did so, Carolina would be scandalized and think far less of him than she did already. What a vicious circle!

There seemed only one course of action for him to take to break from that circle. Pen in hand, he drew a blank sheet of paper before him. He wondered how to properly word it without making matters worse. Dipping the pen in ink he began:

"My dearest Virginia, this is a most difficult letter to write—"

He stopped suddenly and shook his head dismally. He comforted himself with the fact that the time was really quite good. If ever such a tragedy as the death of a child could work for good it was now. Society would believe the marriage postponed because of the death, not canceled altogether. By the time folks began asking questions, Virginia could make it clear that she'd changed her mind. In fact, James reasoned, there would be any number of excuses she could give. Let her tell people her mother needed her, or that her own grief was too great to consider such a celebration. Let her tell them whatever she would, so long as he was no longer expected to marry her.

Still, he struggled even over the salutation. No longer desirous of deceit, he couldn't call her dearest or regard her with anything but the formality he felt. He balled up the sheet and tossed it to the floor, finally writing nothing more than her name, and then he turned to the heart of the matter.

"I cannot make a mockery of an institution so sacred as marriage," he wrote. "You deserve a man who can give you the life you desire—a home in the city, a sterling reputation, and an active social life. I have known for some time that I am not that man." He read over the words. They were formal, harsh . . . but he had never been a man for flowery speeches, even on paper.

"I realize my work at this time is more important to me than anything else. I should have been more clear about this when we became engaged. My heart and interests are bound elsewhere, and therefore I feel I have wronged and misled you. Forgive me, if you can, but I must ask that you release me from our engagement. I will, of course, allow you the privilege of making this your decision so that there need not be any public shame. And I will abide by your choosing a time more appropriate to make your announcement."

He sat back for a moment and tried to imagine Virginia's reaction to this missive. She'd not take it well. But her social standing was important to her, and she'd do nothing to jeopardize what other people thought of her. Should she make a scene and declare it to be James who had broken the engagement instead of herself, it would only reflect badly upon her and make her the center of ugly gossip. No, Virginia would do the proper thing, of this he was certain. Nevertheless, he knew she was an unforgiving woman and might risk all that in order to take every possible opportunity to publicly degrade his faithlessness. Either way, people were going to draw their own conclusions. He would be ruined. No secret ever remained hidden forever, and even if Virginia pretended that she had broken the engagement, she, too, would suffer socially. Her own family would be completely appalled that she was rejecting yet another suitor. How long would it be before she denounced him in anger to salve her own conscience and avoid any further personal retribution?

"And so," he concluded, "in return for your compassion and mercy, I will ease your burden by going west with the railroad. I will be gone for an undetermined time, and hopefully, when I return you will have put this entire matter far behind you and perhaps have married someone more worthy of your love. Sincerely, James."

He knew he had no choice but to leave. Perhaps his absence would help quiet the gossips. At least that's what he wanted to think. In reality he knew he was leaving because he simply could not face the consequences of his actions. As far as returning went . . . maybe he would stay away forever. There seemed only one reason for him to return at all, and that was in the hope that he might win Carolina's love. But it was a vain hope. Once Virginia confessed the truth, Carolina would hate him, as would her entire family. Even if he had the nerve to ask her, she would never agree to marry a man of his reputation, and neither would her father allow a man who'd slighted one daughter to marry another. Such a relationship would destroy Carolina's social standing. And that he could not do. He thought about what he had said to her after Mary's funeral—that he would die for her. He felt almost as if he were doing that very thing in leaving.

Sealing the letter, he called up a servant whose discretion could be trusted. "I'd like you to post this letter for me first thing in the morning—better yet, take it to Oakbridge in person tomorrow."

He then wrote one final letter, this to his parents. When it was finished, he packed up two carpetbags and quietly carried them outside, pausing only to place his parents' letter in a place where they would easily find it. It was late and his parents were asleep, but still he did not want to take any risks of waking them. He saddled his horse and walked it some distance before mounting and riding away at a brisk trot.

Virginia was very properly outraged. It was possible she shed more tears over James' letter than she had over the death of her sister. But the worst of it was that everyone was still so upset over Mary's death that no one had much sympathy for her.

"I won't stand for it!" she cried, knowing full well there was little she could do about it.

Her father tried to soothe her. "No one need ever know it was he who broke off the engagement, Virginia. Unless, of course, you cause such a scene the servants begin to gossip. This is a terrible thing, but you are an Adams, and I have every faith you will meet it with poise and grace."

"Father, make him marry me! You can do it. There are ways—"

"Is that what you truly want, daughter? A man forced into a union? I don't think so. You are worthy of better."

"I'll be an old maid, Papa! No one will marry me now!"

She wouldn't be comforted. She stormed from her father's presence, bemoaning her hapless lot in life. First Mary had to die and force the postponement of her wedding. She was almost certain if that hadn't happened James would have never had time to back out. She considered going to Washington City herself to make an appeal. He must simply have been struck with pre-wedding jitters. If that didn't work she concocted another desperate plan. "I'll pretend to have been compromised," she schemed to herself. "That would force him to deal with me publicly." But then word reached Oakbridge that James had packed up his belongings and left town.

There seemed nothing to be done now but to assume the attitude her father had suggested. She would be the refined lady. She would tell everyone that Mary's death had simply made it impossible for her to leave home in the near future. She felt the only honorable thing to do was to release James of his obligations, seeing that she had no idea when she would be ready for marriage.

Oh, but it galled her to be so graceful when all she really wanted was to tear James' heart out.

Fifty-Five

Carolina's Hope

The fifteenth of October dawned as a cold blustery day. Carolina slipped into a woolen petticoat and relished the warmth. The heavy black wool gown, now her daily companion, came on easily but hung rather limply on the frame that had lost so much weight over the last month.

No one had seemed to notice her wasting away. No one, not even her father, had come to her and spoken on the matters of Mary's death or Margaret's dark depression. Joseph spent most of every day with his wife, seeking for some way to help her through the mire of confusion that her mind had become. Penny, recovering as well as could be expected, was doted upon by Virginia and Georgia with little need for Carolina's presence.

James was gone, too. And Carolina found little pleasure in Virginia breaking their engagement. It was rumored that James had been quite devastated by Virginia's decision and because of this, he'd taken himself away from Washington. She knew James well enough to know he had not done this thing lightly. He was a man of honor and she admired his strength and spirit. It was painful to lose the love of your life. She'd learned that lesson the day James had become engaged to her sister. Yes, James was an honorable man who'd no doubt suffered greatly.

Of course Virginia would never agree with that, and for some reason, her fury was directed somewhat at Carolina.

"That blasted railroad took him from me!" she had yelled at Carolina. "And you encouraged it. What could I do, but break the engagement?"

If only Virginia knew that the railroad had taken James away from Carolina as well. But in that Carolina would have to carry her broken heart in silence. No one would ever know how deeply James' departure had hurt her.

The days passed in clouded routines that meant nothing and held no hope of ever meaning anything. The time became a kind of madness. The house had fallen again into Virginia's capable hands without so much as a word between the sisters to announce the occasion. Carolina found the situation frustrating and difficult to bear, but no one else seemed at all affected by the never ending silence.

Taking herself to the library, Carolina looked around her, trying to find some meaning, some comfort. Always before, this was the place where she could feel at peace. But this time was different. These books meant nothing, a startling revelation to be sure. Even now, seeking their solace, Carolina could only stare at the dusty shelves of idle volumes. They were words on paper. Nothing more unless a person chose to give them life. And she had no life to give them. No passion. No heart. No soul.

And they would always remind her of James and the dreams that would always remain far from her reach. So very distant.

Her father's Bible, an institution all its own, lay unopened on his desk. Carolina knew it never to be far from his side these days and wondered silently what solace he found there. She reached out and traced the leather cover with her forefinger. Maybe she would read it. This was the Word of God—His message to the children He'd put upon the earth. Her father said it was a message of hope and love.

But how could there be hope and love?

Knowing that the emptiness was destroying her inside, Carolina took up the Bible and held it tightly. "I know of God and this book," she murmured to the silent shelves of books. "On my father's knee I remember hearing stories of the coming of our Savior Jesus Christ and learning that He gave His life for my sins. There is hope in that and love. But my sister is dead, and there is no comfort to be found."

"You are wrong, Carolina. There is comfort." She turned to find her father, exhaustion clearly etched in the lines of his face. He smiled sadly. "He is our comfort."

Carolina looked down at the book in her hand. "I want very much to know that is true."

Joseph crossed the room and opened the window to let in some fresh air. "As do I. Sometimes I feel as though I'm smothering under a load of sorrow. Everything seems closed up and hidden away." He looked at Carolina as though seeing her for the first time. "You have nearly wasted away, daughter. Look at you. You're thin as a rail. Even your cheeks are hollow."

Carolina gripped the Bible even tighter. "There seems little reason to what has happened, Papa. There is no comfort in knowing I'll never again hear Mary's laugh. There is no comfort in a broken heart." She said the words before considering them. Hopefully her father would perceive her reference to a broken heart because of Mary's passing.

Joseph came to her and embraced her for the first time since Mary's funeral. It broke her will as nothing else could. She slumped against her father's chest and wept softly.

"It will pass," he said softly. "You will see. There is comfort and I will prove it," Joseph said, leading her to the settee. "Here, hand me the Bible."

Carolina did as she was instructed, wishing she could remain as a little girl in her father's arms. She watched her father leaf through the pages and finally settle on a passage of Scripture.

" 'I will not leave you comfortless: I will come to you. Yet a little while, and the world seeth me no more; but ye see me: because I live, ye shall live also.' " Joseph hardly looked at the book as he read the passage from the book of John. He knew it from memory. "And further on in the chapter, Christ tells us, 'But the Comforter, which is the Holy Ghost, whom the Father will send in my name, he shall teach you all things, and bring all things to your remembrance, whatsoever I have said unto you. Peace I leave with you,' " Joseph quoted the words as his voice cracked and tears came to his eyes. " 'My peace I give unto you.' "

Carolina reached up to take hold of her father's hand. Gently she gave a tug and he willingly sat down beside her. Lovingly she took the Bible in hand and found the place where he'd left off and started to read. " '. . . not as the world giveth, give I unto you. Let not your heart be troubled, neither let it be afraid.' " She looked up at her father. "I want these to be more than words. I want to know they are true and to take courage in them for the future."

Joseph put his hand over hers. "You can put your hope in these words," he said.

"How do you know this? How can you be so confident?"

Joseph pointed again to the Scripture. "There, back before those latter verses. See here."

She read where he indicated: " 'At that day ye shall know that I am in my Father, and ye in me, and I in you. He that hath my commandments, and keepeth them, he it is that loveth me: and he that loveth me shall be loved of my Father, and I will love him, and will manifest myself to him.' " She paused, feeling the first real spark of understanding. "I have but to love Him?"

"And," Joseph said, taking up the Word, " 'If a man love me, he will keep my words: and my Father will love him, and we will come unto him, and make our abode with him.' " Joseph closed the Bible and drew Carolina into his arms. "You have always heard me say that to believe in God is not enough. To know He exists is not to know His salvation and love. To know Him is to love and obey Him. It is to trust Him even when the way is unclear and all hope is gone."

"To trust Him even when your heart is broken?" Carolina asked, lifting up her eyes. James was gone, probably having done the only honorable thing he could. It might be the right thing, but it still hurt.

"Especially when it is broken." Joseph placed a kiss on her forehead. "For where else may you take your broken heart, if not to Him who made it in the first place?"

The way seemed much clearer to Carolina, and peace—something she'd not known in weeks, maybe months if the truth be told—settled upon her. "God does love me," she whispered.

"Of course He does," Joseph replied.

"And I love Him. Oh, Papa, I do love God, and I will seek to be an obedient daughter," she said, as though a sudden revelation had taken place. She hugged her father tightly and smiled. "I will trust Him and I will find my comfort in Him. I will see Mary again in heaven, and my heart will mend."

They sat quietly for several minutes, then Joseph said, "Come here, Carolina. I want to show you something. It arrived yesterday. I had no heart for it then. But now, perhaps it was sent by God himself to give you and me a new purpose to ease our grief."

He took her hand and together they rose and went to the desk. He picked up a thick envelope. It had been lying next to the Bible, but Carolina had not noticed it before.

"This a preliminary survey of a proposed route for the Potomac and Great Falls Railroad."

"Papa! I had forgotten all about that. Is it really going to happen?"

"It's but a step, Carolina. But the only way we can ever reach our dreams is to take that first step."

Carolina stared with wonder at the papers as her father withdrew them from the envelope. And she saw not a sheaf of maps and charts, but rather a promise for the future and hope amidst the dreams.

Carolina nodded. "Yes, Papa. I think you are right." She hugged him close. Perhaps the dreams were not so distant after all.

Books by Judith Pella

Blind Faith

Lone Star Legacy
> *Frontier Lady*
> *Stoner's Crossing*
> *Warrior's Song*

Ribbons of Steel‡
> *Distant Dreams*

The Russians
> *The Crown and the Crucible**
> *A House Divided**
> *Travail and Triumph**
> *Heirs of the Motherland*
> *Dawning of Deliverance*
> *White Nights, Red Morning*

The Stonewycke Trilogy*
> *The Heather Hills of Stonewycke*
> *Flight from Stonewycke*
> *Lady of Stonewycke*

The Stonewycke Legacy*
> *Stranger at Stonewycke*
> *Shadows over Stonewycke*
> *Treasure of Stonewycke*

The Highland Collection*
> *Jamie MacLeod: Highland Lass*
> *Robbie Taggart: Highland Sailor*

The Journals of Corrie Belle Hollister
> *My Father's World**
> *Daughter of Grace**
> *On the Trail of the Truth†*
> *A Place in the Sun†*
> *Sea to Shining Sea†*
> *Into the Long Dark Night†*
> *Land of the Brave and the Free†*

---

*with Michael Phillips †by Michael Phillips ‡with Tracie Peterson 9612